D0418859

On the Edge

Jenny Pitman

On the Edge

MACMILLAN

First published 2002 by Macmillan
an imprint of Pan Macmillan Ltd
Pan Macmillan, 20 New Wharf Road, London N1 9RR
Basingstoke and Oxford
Associated companies throughout the world
www.panmacmillan.com

ISBN 0 333 90807 4 (hardback)
ISBN 0 333 98953 8 (trade paperback)

1 3 5 7 9 8 6 4 2

A CIP catalogue record for this book is available from the British Library.

Typeset by SetSystems Ltd, Saffron Walden, Essex
Printed and bound in Great Britain by
Mackays of Chatham plc, Chatham, Kent

for

THE FAMILY

Acknowledgements

My husband David Stait,

Peter Burden,

Jonathan Lloyd at Curtis Brown Group Ltd,

David North, Maria Rejt and Peter Straus
at Pan Macmillan Ltd

and others for their support

1

The snow that had covered the Brecon Beacons for a week after Christmas was nearly all gone, leaving behind it no more than a faint tingle in the air.

Jan Hardy looked down on St Barnabas's church, where it lay in a fold of the bare hills surrounding it, circled by stout yews that gave added protection from the ravages of the Welsh weather. The squat building, with no spire or tower, had been constructed from stone and lime-washed more than seven hundred years before.

From the south, where the road snaked up from Painscastle over the brown bracken curves of the small mountains, the peaceful churchyard looked a suitable place for a man like John Hardy to be laid to rest.

'God knows, he needs a rest!' Jan murmured as she let the Land Rover coast down the hill towards the tiny hamlet where the church stood.

'Mumma?'

Jan wondered if the little girl in the child's seat behind her had recognized the bitter sorrow in her voice intuitively.

John's mother had told Jan not to bring the children to the funeral. They were too young to deal with it, she'd said. 'I'm not taking them for their sake,' Jan had replied. 'I'm taking them for mine. I need them beside me; I need to feel them there, to remind me that John's still alive in them.'

She tilted the driving mirror, caught a reflection of her own young, round face and glanced behind her, thrilled as ever at the big, beaming smile her daughter gave her. She smiled back as best she could. 'It's all right, Meg. There's nothing to worry about, I promise,' she said brightly, to back up the lie, while she wondered how much Megan would miss her father.

She looked at the old carrycot strapped into the passenger seat, where Matthew, just six months old, slept fitfully, as alert as his elder sister to the grief in their house, but unaware of its connection to the absence of the quiet, gruff-voiced person he sometimes used to see lying in bed. Jan couldn't tell yet how much he missed his father, or whether he missed him at all. For the last two months of his life, when he'd been at home, John had barely spoken – neither to the children, nor to Jan or his own mother.

Physically, he could have talked; he just didn't want to, as if he was ashamed of himself for letting them down – by promising to house them, feed them and keep them, then dying on them.

The hearse looked glossy and incongruous among the unruly gathering of farmers' vehicles, muddy Land Rovers and ancient saloons, all parked up the banks and in any slot off the narrow, sunken lane.

'They'll never all fit in that little church,' John's mother had said.

'It's too bad,' Jan had replied. 'There's nothing I can do about it; it's where John wanted to be buried.'

Olwen Hardy had crunched her old face into the frustrated expression she'd worn consistently since her only son had brought this independent-minded English girl back from the Three Counties Show at Malvern seven summers before.

It was hard to persuade sons to stay on the farms up here. They wanted so many things that farming would never buy them, especially not now, with twelve million ewes on the Welsh hills where once there had been four. It would take a full-scale disaster to restore the price of lambs, while the hill subsidies had quietly been whittled away.

Some farmers had tried to pretend it wasn't happening; they just put their hands over their ears when they found it cost more to produce a lamb for market than they'd get for it, especially with fuel prices soaring.

More and more of them were giving up. But John Hardy had always said he would stay. He loved the hills and the ewes. He understood the cattle, too, and had a real talent for growing corn in the few lower fields on the farm.

Even when he had faced a future that promised no more than permanent poverty, he'd shown no sign of wanting to give up. And by the time he'd reached thirty-five without marrying, Olwen had begun to hope that she would never lose him, that he'd be there to look after her, as he should, now her husband had passed on.

Jan thought about her mother-in-law's view of life as she reached the bottom of the valley and turned into the narrow cul-de-sac leading to the church. The only blessing she could see in the death of the man she loved was that she would no longer have to pretend that she liked his mother.

She found a space for the Land Rover just inside a farmyard beside the church. She stretched awkwardly over to the back seat and unstrapped Megan. She climbed down herself and went round to the passenger door to put Matthew on her shoulder while she waited for Megan to scramble out.

She was about to walk up to the church when another car pulled up and parked beneath a curtain of frosty lambs' tails on a hazel rooted in the stone wall. An old man and his wife, strangers to Jan, climbed out and looked at her with mournful sympathy. She wondered who they were. They would have needed only a tenuous connection with John Hardy to feel they had a right to attend his funeral. Jan had noticed since she'd arrived in the Welsh hills that funeral-going was a popular activity among the older people; there were so few other social activities to compete for their time, besides hunting in the winter, trotting races and village fêtes in the summer. She wondered if, like her mother-in-law, they would disapprove of her unfunereal outfit.

Jan had woken that morning and decided to wear her only good clothes – a well-cut green suit with a matching coat she'd found the year before at a shop in Hay. She had bought them with her own hard-earned cash from the hunters and point-to-pointers she kept in livery. She'd done it on the spur of the moment, which was totally out of character, because she'd had a dream that Rear Gunner, the best horse in her yard, had won the Foxhunters' at Cheltenham and she hadn't had anything to wear when she went up to receive her prize.

She remembered worrying how John would react, but he'd only admired her for her boldness and the way the suit flattered her rather less than willowy frame.

She didn't see why she should wear black to his funeral. It wouldn't mean that she missed him or respected his memory any more than she did already. Besides, he would have said it was a total waste of money to buy a new outfit just for a funeral.

The lane up to the church was lined with cars. The undertaker's men, in drab black suits, leaned against the crumbling wall of the churchyard and smoked surreptitiously, hiding their cigarettes in cupped hands.

Jan led Megan through the lychgate into the dark circle of ancient yews. By the wall at the east end of the church, she saw a mound of earth that had been dug out to make room for her husband's coffin. Instinctively she clutched Matthew more tightly and walked a little faster to reach the church before Megan saw the hole and asked why it was there.

A dozen people were clustered outside the small porch and a few more were standing in the porch itself. They moved aside to let Jan pass. Some nodded and murmured words of condolence. One or two stretched out a hand to touch her arm or her back.

Inside, the tiny church was full and warm from a hundred well-wrapped bodies which had dispersed its normal, musty smell. The people outside were there because there was nowhere else for them to go. Jan thanked God – with whom she felt she was not on the best of terms at the moment – that, although there was a slight frost in the air, at least it wasn't raining for once.

There were two small windows in each side of the church, and a smaller one at the east end. These provided the only light apart from two naked bulbs dangling from the roof and the two candles which burned on the altar in the tiny, rounded apse. In front of the altar, John's coffin rested on two trestles. Ash with silver-plate handles, it had been paid for by some clause in an old, almost forgotten insurance policy John had kept up with the NFU. Two wreaths, *From your loving mother* and *With all our love for ever, Jan, Megan and Matthew,* rested on top of the box.

The front right-hand pew had been reserved for the family. John's mother was already there, in the seat beside the aisle. Jan thought Olwen should move along, to let her sit there, but knew she wouldn't and so carefully squeezed between Olwen's knees and the front of the pew.

It needed only one flash from the older woman's eyes to convey her views on Jan's green suit and Megan's floral, smocked dress. Jan settled Matthew more cosily against her shoulder and beckoned Megan to sit quietly on the pew beside her. But the little girl was craning her neck to look at the coffin.

Megan stretched up to put her mouth near her mother's ear. 'Dad's in there, isn't he?' she whispered.

Jan looked at her and nodded. 'Yes, he is.'

'Will he be all right?'

Jan took a deep breath and wished she knew the answer. 'I'm sure he will.'

Soon after Jan had sat down, the vicar emerged from the vestry at the back of the church. He walked slowly up the aisle to the altar, where he turned and stood, gazing around at the tightly packed congregation.

He was a tall man of sixty, lean as a vulture, with a haunted air, as if at some time in his life he'd been severely tested and found wanting. He looked at Jan with a thin smile of encouragement.

He's not a bad bloke, Jan thought. She had met him a few times before John had become ill, and then more often when he'd started to call regularly as John's illness progressed.

John had seemed pleased by these visits, although he had never actually said so. Jan thought he probably appreciated the vicar taking the trouble when he had such a large area to look after for the Church in Wales – eight churches, ten villages and a hundred farms.

After John had died, the vicar had come to see Jan. Without becoming all intense, he'd been kind and practical. 'Make sure you don't forget to look after yourself, now,' he'd said. 'To God you're just as important as the children, you know.'

As the vicar started intoning the funeral prayers, Jan looked at the coffin and imagined John lying inside it. But she saw him as he had been before the organo-phosphates in the sheep dip had, as she believed, introduced the cancer which had destroyed his inner organs.

She remembered him as she'd first seen him, showing a Welsh black cow and calf in the special section at the Three Counties Show. She didn't have a particular interest in cattle, but her eye had been caught by the small, pretty animals and then by the man leading them. John's good looks weren't obvious; they were somehow obscured by his own introverted nature. But there was an unmistakable strength and dependability about him. He looked as if he was always sure about what he was doing – in sharp contrast to her current boyfriend, who told everyone he knew everything, but was too lazy to do anything worthwhile.

The vicar was used to giving funeral addresses about people he'd never seen in any of his churches, but he had known John Hardy quite well, inasmuch as John allowed anyone to know him. Jan was pleased that the vicar talked about the special qualities in John which might not have been known to many of the congregation. She glanced at her mother-in-law, sitting rigidly a few feet to her left. The old woman was looking straight ahead, with her lower jaw firmly clamped to stop it quivering. Jan felt sorry for her despite the antagonism there had always been between them. Olwen had lost her husband, now her son, and she was probably well aware that her grandchildren might not grow up within easy reach.

Outside, in the crisp January morning, the crowd clustered around the grave. In the silence, two crows barked harshly from a tall ash outside the magic ring of yews, and a magpie cackled as it fled across the pasture beyond.

As the men from the undertaker's lowered the coffin on two broad straps, deep into the peaty earth, Jan gave in to tears. She clenched her eyes and clutched Megan's hand, while she squeezed Matthew to her chest. When she opened her eyes, she gazed through a hazy film at the vicar, who stood with his purple stole moving in the breeze, praying for the last time as the men in black suits solemnly withdrew their straps from the grave.

A small man in a long black coat held out a wooden box to Jan, with some earth to scatter on the coffin below. She didn't want to let go of Megan's hand. She shook her head and glanced down at the little girl, who stared curiously as a few other people dropped soil onto the box in which her father lay. Megan glanced up and gave her mother a little smile which seemed to say that she understood.

Jan walked out of a small stone building in the middle of Hay-on-Wye and closed the dark green door behind her. She shut her eyes, took a long, deep breath and exhaled with relief.

She glanced up and down the narrow, sloping street to see if anyone was looking at her, although she didn't really care. The solicitor she had seen was new to Humphries & Co; the partner John always dealt with had retired earlier that year. This young man knew nothing about the history of the Hardys; he had no idea of the implications of the will John had left. One of the older partners, he told Jan, had warned him not to ask Olwen in as well, but it all seemed straightforward enough to him.

The late John Hardy had left everything – Stonewall Farm, the house, the bungalow, the buildings, the stock, the tackle, and twenty thousand pounds, which were the proceeds of a life policy he had never been able to increase – to his wife, Janine Susan Hardy, with the proviso that his mother should occupy the bungalow, where she currently lived, free of rent until her death.

When he was alive, John had never told them what he planned to do and Jan hadn't dreamed of asking – not because she was frightened to, but because she knew he wouldn't have told her. She had always assumed, though, that he would leave his mother with a significant degree of control over Stonewall Farm and she was sure that Olwen herself had been certain of it.

Jan had not told Olwen where she was going that morning; the solicitor hadn't asked her to, and she'd needed somewhere to leave the children.

Now she wanted someone to talk to, someone to share her relief, who would understand that she was not celebrating her acquisition of the farm, but the freedom to do what she wanted, to take the children and bring them up where and how she chose.

But Jan had never had the chance to make friends, either in the narrow, introspective valley where they lived, or here in the town, where she and John came only once or twice a month. She could think of only one person who might be glad to see her. Harold Powell, she was sure, would welcome any excuse to talk about his horses.

She walked down the hill towards the big stone clock tower which stood in the centre of the town and stopped when she reached the door of a small office with a plain, gilt sign on the window – *Harris & Powell. Auctioneers, Valuers and Estate Agents.*

The woman behind the reception desk looked up. She evidently recognized Jan. With a barely perceptible pursing of the lips, she stood up briskly. 'I'll tell Mr Powell you're here.'

Jan felt a sudden panic. Although she had trained point-to-pointers for Harold Powell for four years now, she had never been to his office. She shouldn't have come here. Not now, not just after John had died.

But Harold, forty-eight and six feet tall, came out of his office at the back, straightening a tie decorated with flying pheasants. 'Hello, Jan,' he said, an eyebrow raised in a faint question mark.

'Hello, Harold,' Jan said quickly, 'I was just passing, but I expect you're busy; I must get back home anyway. I've still got one of the horses to do.' She turned and started to open the door.

'Hang on, Jan,' Harold laughed. He'd had plenty of experience with coy women. 'I'm sure you've got time for a quick drink up at the Bull Ring.' He stepped quickly round the reception desk. 'You know – to cheer you up after everything?' His voice was deep, with a rattle of whisky in it. He was beside her now, smelling of tweed steeped in pipe smoke, and fresh shaving soap. His dark hair was thick and gleaming and he wasn't bad looking, even close to. His hand was on the small of her back. 'I never got the chance to talk to you at the funeral – there were that many people there.'

Harold spoke with a Herefordshire accent, unlike the people in her valley. He was the third son of a big farmer on the rich broad plain of the Wye valley east of Hay. She wanted to run back to her Land Rover, but that would have looked absurd and Harold confidently opened the door and ushered her back up the narrow street to a hotel on one side of a small square.

Half a dozen men, obviously with time on their hands, were already drinking in a gloomy bar. They nodded respectfully at Harold in his well-cut jacket and gleaming nut-brown shoes; they looked speculatively at Jan.

'Do you know Mrs Hardy?' Harold asked the oldest of them.

The man nodded. 'I was sorry to hear about your bereavement,' he said neutrally.

'Life must go on, eh, Jan? With all those horses to get ready for point-to-points. Jan's got four of mine,' he told the room in general. 'All good 'uns, too, aren't they, Jan?'

'They could win a few races,' Jan agreed.

Harold ordered drinks. 'Make that a large one,' he said to the woman behind the bar when Jan asked for a gin and tonic. He carried her glass and his tankard of beer to a table in the corner, between a lively log fire and the window. They could talk here without being too easily overheard.

'Thanks,' Jan said and took a sip, glad of the drink, if she was truthful, after the drama of the morning.

'What brings you into town, then?'

Jan thought he had probably guessed and that it would be easier to talk about it than to let him sit there speculating for as long as it took to finish her drink. 'I had to come and see the solicitor, to sort things out.'

'John had made a will, all right, had he?'

'Oh yes.'

'And everything's OK?' Harold prodded.

Jan looked back at him steadily, wondering why he should be particularly interested in her affairs, beyond professional curiosity, though that was more than enough of a reason round here. 'Yes. Fine, thanks.' She took a deeper breath. 'I'll be putting the farm on the market.'

He stared at her. 'What? Did he leave it all to you?'

Jan nodded. 'Yes, he did.'

'Didn't he make provision for his mother?' Harold sounded quite shocked.

'Yes, of course. She's to live in the bungalow, rent-free until she dies, but that's all right; it's well away from the farm.'

'Why do you want to sell up?'

Jan shrugged. 'What's the point of staying? I don't come from round here and they never let me forget it. And John had to work his guts out to barely make a living. I don't know how some of these people stick it.'

'But where will you go?'

'I'm not sure – nearer my mum and dad, maybe.'

'That's over Gloucestershire way, isn't it?'

Jan nodded. 'Dad's still got a bit of ground up on the hill.'

'What would you do there?'

'I'll get my own yard,' she said simply.

'You won't buy much of a place in Gloucestershire with what you get for Stonewall.'

'I don't need much of place – just stables and twenty or thirty acres would do me.'

Harold was looking at her with consternation. 'Look, Jan, you shouldn't do this without thinking about it a bit first, you know. You're probably just reacting to what's happened now, but I think you should stop around here. There's a lot of people who would be sorry to see you go.'

'Who?' Jan couldn't resist asking.

'Me, for one. You've done really well with those horses of mine.'

'I can still train them.'

'I don't want my horses in Gloucestershire. And as far as Stonewall's concerned, if you didn't want to farm it all yourself, I'm sure I'll find someone to rent the ground off you; that'd bring in a bit.'

'I just don't want to live in that valley any more; or that house.' She stopped for a moment and thought of all the lonely nights filled with bad dreams since her husband had died. 'It was all right when John was alive and well, but I can't live there on my own.'

Harold's face showed he was taking a calculated gamble. 'I doubt a woman like you'll be on your own for long.'

Jan stared back at him, deliberately looking more shocked than she felt. 'Harold, John's only been dead a fortnight! Have some respect.'

'I'm sorry, but I was only telling the truth. You're a young, healthy woman – ' he dropped his chin and looked up at her from below thick black brows ' – and very attractive.'

Looking at his big, shifty eyes, Jan wanted to laugh. Instead, she picked up her glass and tipped the rest of the drink down her throat. She stood up a little unsteadily. 'Thank you for the drink, Harold. I've really got to go now.'

Harold got up too. 'I'm sorry, Jan. I didn't mean to upset you.'

'You didn't.' She tried to smile. 'I've just got to go.'

She turned before he could try to talk her out of it, while the other men watched in silence as she walked out.

Jan felt as if she were floating over the brown hills as she drove back to Stonewall under a clear blue sky. It wasn't the grief still underlying every thought that made her feel detached, or even the gin: it was the prospect of freedom, triggered by her effectively public announcement that she would be selling the farm.

She wished now that she hadn't told anyone yet. Harold Powell's appalled reaction hadn't surprised her, but she knew it would be repeated across the local farming community, spiced with the view that they might have known someone like her from away would betray an old family by selling the farm.

I don't give a monkey's, she thought. They could whinge and bicker as much as they liked; the sooner she was gone the better. She would offer to take Olwen with her and if her mother-in-law declined the offer – which Jan was sure she would – that was just too bloody bad!

She knew that she would have to tell Olwen right away. A rumour starting from the bar in the Bull Ring Hotel might easily take wings and reach her own valley before she did. And Olwen would have accumulated a strong advantage if she knew before Jan admitted it.

Jan went straight to the bungalow, where she had left Megan and Matthew.

Olwen opened the door to her dressed in a pinafore that looked as if it had been made from a pair of pre-war chintz curtains. With her snow-white, thick curly hair and steel-rimmed glasses, she looked deceptively like everyone's idea of a cartoon granny. She led Jan into a cramped and neatly cluttered sitting room. Matty was sound asleep in his carrycot. Megan leaped up from an ancient, dog-eared jigsaw on the parquet floor. The old woman eyed Jan suspiciously. 'Ain't you got more horses to do yet?'

'Yes,' Jan nodded. 'I'm sorry, I got caught up in town. It took longer than I thought.'

'What was you doing?' the old woman asked brazenly.

'Seeing Humphries's about John's will.'

Olwen stiffened visibly; she blinked rapidly a few times. 'Why . . . why did you go on your own?'

'Because they asked me to.'

'But I should have been with you . . . at the reading of my own son's will.'

'They said it would be better if I told you about it.' *The bloody cowards,* she thought to herself. She went on quickly. 'John wanted you to live here in this cottage for the rest of your life.'

The implication of what Jan was saying wasn't lost on Olwen. She looked behind her, groping for the high, moquette armchair she normally occupied, and lowered herself into it with quivering arms. She looked at the floor for a few moments while the idea sank in. When she looked up, Jan could see she was already defeated. 'He didn't leave me this bungalow, then?' Olwen said.

Jan couldn't bring herself to utter a straight 'No'.

'He said you've the right to live in it for the rest of your life.'

Olwen sighed with a noisy breath and looked down at her bony hands. She suddenly seemed a lot older than sixty-nine.

Jan went on, 'I'll be selling the rest of the farm – the house, the buildings and the land. But you'll still have your garden.'

There was a flicker of defiance in the silver blue eyes that glanced up. 'I'll be here a long time, I promise you that.'

'I hope so,' Jan said, though she knew she was fooling no one. 'Would you mind if I left the kids here until three? I've still got one of the horses to do.'

Olwen grunted. 'Yes, you carry on. What's a grandma for if she can't look after her son's children?'

Jan drove another four hundred yards up the track beside the bungalow until she reached the big stone courtyard of buildings that was Stonewall Farm. On one side of the yard was a run of five stables, with another five timber boxes backing onto it. Five heads were gazing at her by the time she had parked the Land Rover outside the front door and climbed out. Three dogs, a lurcher, a Border terrier and the farm sheepdog, emerged from the hay store and rushed over to greet their mistress.

For a few moments Jan stroked the old sheepdog and listened

to a silence broken by a lone buzzard, keening as it circled high above to survey the land for unwary rabbits. Soon, she reflected, the air would be filled with the sound of lambs bleating and their mothers' answering grunts. And she realized she owed it to John to stay here at least until the lambing was done.

She glanced around. Philip and Annabel, who helped her in the yard, had both gone home, but Jan could see that they had done all that she had asked and left the yard as spotless as the old cobbles allowed – Annabel's doing, she guessed.

'Hello, boys,' she murmured to the horses as she walked over to the big grey head stretched over the first stable door. The horse gave a faint whinny and kicked the bottom of the door. 'Don't get so excited, Mister. I'm not going to feed you now, am I? You've got to do some work first. I'm sorry,' she added when the horse's head retreated, as if he'd understood and didn't like what he'd heard.

Jan took a head-collar off a hook beside the door and let herself in. The eight-year-old gelding had arrived from Ireland the previous spring, frightened and confused. He stood at nearly seventeen hands and Jan had to stretch her legs to the tips of her toes to fix his collar. She led him out and across the yard to the tack room, where she tied him with a piece of binder twine to an iron ring in the wall.

As always, she talked quietly to the horse all the time she was dealing with him. It was natural to her and she knew how much it reassured him. She fetched his bridle and an exercise saddle from the tack room and put them on. She left the girth loose, so he'd get used to having it there for a few minutes while she strode briskly up the steps and let herself into the house. Without a glance at the unwashed plates in the kitchen sink, she ran up to the bedroom and swapped her skirt and top for a pair of stretch jeans and a thick, scarlet fleece. On the way back down, she grabbed her well-worn chaps from a peg on the back of the kitchen door and walked out of the house still buckling them.

Within a few minutes, she had tightened the gelding's girth and scrambled onto his high back with the help of three well-worn stone steps. She headed up the bank behind the house, along a narrow cart track that led to the common grazing land on the top of the hill. Fred, her brindled lurcher, loped along beside her, weaving in and out of the scrubby thorns and gorse bushes like a snake.

With each long stride the horse took, the tensions of the day – the uncertainty, at first, of what the solicitor was saying, the obscure attentions of Harold Powell – released their grip on her shoulders. With her crop, she hooked open the gate at the top of the track, which let them out onto the open spaces where broad swathes of turf permanently cropped by a millennium of grazing sheep swept up between a thick growth of bilberry, bracken and heather.

She turned left and gee'd the big horse into a steady trot along a faintly rutted green track that followed the contour of the hill. The sun had appeared, gleaming through pink and silver streaks above the softly wrinkled face of the Black Mountains' grey-green bluff. She could feel the chilly wind rippling through the short blonde hair below her helmet, as if cleansing her of any wrong or selfish thoughts she might have had that day.

She would miss John, of course; she would miss him unbelievably. He had been completely dependable. Although, when fit, he'd been as strong as any man in the valley, he had been gentle and thoughtful and never pretended to know more than he did. John Hardy was as good a man as Jan had ever met and, while she might once have thought goodness in a man a guarantee of tedious wedlock, she'd never been bored by him. There had been nothing wrong in bed, either. All her memories of their love-making were happy – though there hadn't been much of that in the last few months.

But in his crass, man's way, Harold Powell hadn't got it so wrong. Life would go on for her. Although it seemed absurd at the moment, she didn't doubt that she would marry again and be able to live without being tormented every few minutes by a massive wrenching sensation in her chest.

Besides, John had left her two beautiful and infinitely precious children. From now on, their needs would come before any of her own. She owed that much, at least, to John's memory.

And that was why she was leaving Stonewall. Not simply because she felt alien and uncomfortable in the valley, but because, if she was going to see her children fed, clothed and nurtured in the way she wanted, she would have to make more than just a decent living. And she was never going to do that up here in the Brecon hills, where even the best farmers had drawn their belts in so tightly their stomachs were screaming.

But all Jan knew about was horses. They were all she had learned about as a child around her parents' small rented farm. She also knew that, while the Cotswolds didn't offer the best soil in the land for growing corn, the cosy, picturesque hills could produce a healthy crop of rich, potential horse owners.

The Brecon men also liked their point-to-pointing, along with their flappers and trotters, but few of them had much money to spare on good thoroughbred stock or training fees.

Jan was sure that John would have approved of her decision to move. That was why he hadn't tied her to the farm by leaving it to his mother. He had never said a word against Olwen in Jan's hearing, but she had no doubt that he was well aware of the relentless barrage of verbal and mental abuse the old woman had dealt out to her over the past seven years.

Jan wheeled the big grey gelding to the right and turned him up a long, turf-clad slope. She sat forward out of the saddle and squeezed his sides with her calves. Within a few strides he was reaching out into a strong canter and Jan couldn't help smiling. Mister Mack was the sweetest-paced horse she'd ever ridden; when he'd arrived at her yard, no one, but no one, had been able to get on his back. It was bringing him round last summer, from rogue to gentleman, that had shown her that maybe she knew more than most about caring for animals who had been emotionally scarred at some point in their lives.

As the ground levelled at the top of the ridge and she asked him for more, the horse stretched his legs until she felt like a flyer in one of the gliders that often came soaring over the hills from Shropshire. As she reached the end of the ridge, before it dropped down on the dark, north side, she came up fast on a cluster of gorse bushes – serious obstacles, four feet high. She kept the horse straight at the first, shortened her rein and felt him find a stride. He stood way back and flew it with a foot to spare. Jan shrieked and whooped, intoxicated for a moment. It had been the first time the horse had really seen his own stride and it was by far the best jump he had ever made.

As she pulled him up to a trot, she steered him back the way they had come. She leaned forward to pat the horse vigorously on the side of his neck. 'Oh, well done, boy! If you keep jumping like that, you're really going to win a few races, aren't you.' Not for the first time, Jan wished she hadn't had to sell him to Harold Powell. Of the eight horses in her yard, this was the one she would have liked most to keep in her own name.

2

A week after John Hardy's funeral, Jan could still hardly sleep. The day after hearing his will, she tossed and turned and woke long before the first light glowed from the east, chilled by the perspiration on her pyjamas.

There was no shower in the old farmhouse and she had to wash herself in the one unheated bathroom. To keep warm, she towelled herself down vigorously and dressed as fast as she could.

In the dark corridor she listened, but heard no sounds from her children. Downstairs in the kitchen she put a kettle on the hob and pulled up a chair to sit as close as she could to the oil-fired Rayburn – the one improvement she had managed to make to the house and the only warm spot in it for six months of the year.

She'd lain awake half the night, thinking about what she had told Harold Powell, and in the morning she was sure she was right. Whatever the farm fetched, she had to sell; this house and its bleak, ungenerous land would have to go.

She must rear her children, made even more precious now by their father's death, and she didn't want to spend the rest of her life battling against wind, rain and thin soil before she could even think about making a profit. She had lived on a farm all her life and she was well aware that she had neither the knowledge nor the commitment to earn a good living from farming, wherever she was. As far as she could see, horses in Gloucestershire were the only option. It was a daunting prospect for a thirty-year-old, widowed mother of two, but she'd never been afraid of a challenge.

Her mother had begged her to be practical when Jan had first told her she was marrying a farmer from the Welsh hills. She understood, of course, when Jan insisted that, however tough it was going to be, she and John Hardy loved each other. They were both fit and resourceful and, one way or another, they'd make a living and raise children on his unproductive two hundred acres.

It had been tough all right, but for the first few years Jan had thrived, despite the lack of comfort or encouragement from John's mother, and had thrown herself into being a farmer's wife. When she had been there a year, though, and no child had yet appeared, she'd decided to make her own contribution by doing the one thing for which she knew she had some talent.

She told everyone she met that she was going to make use of her experience by taking in hunter liveries and training racehorses to run in point-to-points. People had come to talk to her and look at the yard she had made from John's old stone barns and, eventually, some had sent her horses.

In her first year she'd had three wins from six horses and her name had echoed over the loudspeakers at the local courses. Over the next five years there had been steady success – eight or nine wins for each of the last couple of seasons. It didn't sound a lot compared to the big-time trainers under Jockey Club rules, but it was enough to make Jan the top point-to-point trainer in her area.

But, for all the work it took, and the difficulties of dealing with one, then two, tiny children, the stables had never brought in enough money to make up for the falling price of lambs and life in the hills had become seriously hard, until John had found himself working every hour of daylight and beyond to save the cost of an extra hand.

Maybe he'd been tired or careless with the dipping, but somehow, she believed, the regular contact with organo-phosphates had got to him and he hadn't quite reached his forty-second birthday when the cancer, undetected by their rural doctor, had finally claimed him. But, through it all, he had always praised Jan for her determination to add to their dwindling income. Now, though, she would have to more than double what she made from it – which gave her another good reason for moving on.

Revived by tea after her long night, Jan pulled herself together and went up to deal with her quietly burbling baby son.

Matthew was one of those children who had been granted the priceless gift of permanent cheerfulness. Jan didn't know how he'd done it. While he was still in her womb, until six or seven weeks before he saw the light of day, he'd regularly been galloped over the hill tops, leaping banks and gorse bushes on the way. But this seemed to have caused no pre-natal trauma and from the day he was born he had been an easy and contented baby. It was almost as if he had been determined to prove his grandmother wrong with his tireless good humour.

Jan picked him up and nuzzled him and his baby smells, kissing his chubby cheeks. The pleasure of being with him was like an elixir after her miserable night.

Megan seemed happier and bounced up and down on her bed to greet her mother. Downstairs, giving them breakfast in the now fuggy warmth of the kitchen with Terry Wogan on the radio, Jan felt much better. And at eight o'clock, as the first rays of a frosty sun beamed through the high kitchen window, Annabel came in.

Jan looked up at her and smiled. She couldn't help it. Annabel, with fine, pale chestnut hair that fell to her shoulders, was a willowy and quietly beautiful twenty-three-year-old, one of those serene people who never seemed upset or angered by anyone or anything. She had turned up at Stonewall out of the blue at the start of the last season and asked if she could help Jan out.

She had worked without a single day off until the last race in June, when she'd left as abruptly as she had come. Jan guessed that was the last she would see of her, but at the end of August, when the horses started to return from their summer holidays, Annabel had turned up at the house and asked if she could come back. By that time John was so weak he could barely work, and

Jan hadn't disguised her gratitude, for, though she had two other part-time lads, Annabel was in a class of her own.

Jan had been really glad to see Annabel anyway; she loved having her around the yard because she was always good company and in some ways, Jan realized, her calmness was a perfect foil to her own excitable vitality.

Their backgrounds, both rural, were otherwise very different.

According to Annabel, her father, Henry Halstead, an ex-cavalry officer, had come out of the army with nothing but his pension, only to find that he had inherited a three-thousand-acre estate from his aunt. Now he lived as far as he could in the way he imagined his grandfather might have done, just over the border in Herefordshire in a rambling, early Georgian mansion, which he never left unless he had to.

Annabel was his only daughter; she had one brother, Charles, who was five years older. She'd told Jan that Charles didn't get on with his father and had gone to live in the States as soon as he'd left university. She had said no more about it, but Jan had the impression that there was an uneasy, love–hate relationship between Annabel and her father and it was mainly for her mother's sake that she was still living at home.

She had been sent away to boarding school until she was seventeen, then after a brief period at college in London she'd gone on to Bristol University, which she'd left during her first year.

Annabel had revealed this edited account of her life to Jan sparingly when she'd first come to work for her. She'd told her how she hated London and couldn't bear the hustling and the hordes of people who all seemed so superficial. Reading between the lines, Jan gathered that something had happened there which had left her with unhappy memories and that things had also gone wrong at university. But, despite Jan's inquisitiveness, Annabel wouldn't tell her any more.

'Do you want some breakfast?' Jan asked brightly as she always did, knowing what the answer would be.

'No thanks; just a little water and lemon.'

'For God's sake, girl!' Jan chided her, as she always did. 'There's no flesh on you. Do you want to fade away completely?'

'I ate before I left the house,' Annabel said.

Jan never knew if she was telling the truth when she said this, so shrugged. 'Help yourself,' she said.

Annabel took a lemon from the basket of fruit that Jan kept for her and cut a slice. She helped herself to a mug hanging from the large Welsh dresser, put the lemon in and poured boiling water over it. She sat down and smiled at Matthew, who was propped up in a wooden high chair being fed by Jan.

'Hello, Matty,' she cooed, and the boy gurgled back with a fat, dribbly bubble.

'Hello, Annabel,' Megan squeaked, anxious for her share of Annabel's attention.

Seeing the children with Annabel, Jan said, 'If we go from here, they'll miss you,' she said.

Annabel glanced at her, with a hint of worry in her soft grey eyes. 'Go? Why should you go?'

'You know I went to see the solicitor yesterday?'

Annabel nodded and, fearing the worst, her eyes clouded more.

Jan saw. 'No, it's not bad news. John left everything to me, except his mum's to live in the bungalow as long as she likes. So I'm going to sell this place.' She gave the house around her an unaffectionate nod.

'Where will you move to?'

'Back where I came from. I'm going to see if I can buy a small place in Gloucestershire – a yard and a bit of decent grazing.'

Annabel's face fell. 'Oh, Jan! I'll miss you – and these two.'

'Will you, really? Miss me with all my shouting and swearing and riding out every day, even when it's blizzarding?'

'Specially that,' Annabel nodded with a grin.

'Then you'd better come with us.'

Annabel gave her a look so enigmatic that Jan didn't have any idea what was going through her mind. 'I'll think about it,' she said.

Later Jan took Matthew and Megan to the bungalow for the morning, as she always did when there were horses to do. Her mother-in-law was as tight-lipped as always, but Jan refused to be cowed by her accusing eye.

'What are you going to do when you haven't got me to look after these children?' Olwen asked. 'You can't just leave them with anyone while you go gallivantin' around the races.'

'I've thought of that. I'll get my mum and dad in,' Jan retorted and immediately regretted the provocation. To be fair to Olwen, she thought, she'd looked after the kids a hell of a lot since they'd been born. But, then again, Jan knew she adored having them. 'No, I'm joking,' she said quickly. 'If I do move, I'll make sure I've got a good girl to come in every day.'

But as she drove back up the track to the farm, she found herself wondering if she really was right to be selling up so soon after she'd been widowed, and leaving her mother-in-law behind. However annoying and interfering Olwen Hardy was, she was always there to have the children, and in Jan's life just then, that was a vital support.

Annabel was already tacking up the first three horses to go out, and Philip, as lackadaisical as Annabel was reliable, had shot up the track behind Jan in the battered pick-up his father had given him for his eighteenth birthday.

Philip, stringy, shaggy-haired and already minus his right incisor, was the third son of a farmer from further up the valley. He had no intention of following his father into farming, even if the option had been there, but he liked his country sports too much to leave. While working for Jan didn't bring in a lot of money, it gave him the chance to kid himself and his friends that he was going to be a jockey. Jan knew he never would be, but she gave him the odd ride to satisfy his urges. Once, by default, in a members' race, he had won, and now thought of himself in the same league as the Herefordshire farmer's son who had just become the champion National Hunt jockey.

Out of respect for John's memory, Jan had cancelled her entries in the last three accessible point-to-point meetings. Harold Powell, the owner most affected, had said he quite understood, but now she intended to start again on the following Saturday; she was sure John would have approved.

Soon Jan, Annabel and Philip were up on the horses they were exercising first, two of whom were due to run in four days' time. Five minutes later they were jogging out onto the firmly matted turf of the hill behind the farm.

Jan watched Annabel on Mister Mack, and prayed that if she and the children moved Annabel would choose to come with them. She didn't underrate the value of a familiar trusted face in new surroundings. Besides, where else would she find someone with hands so gentle and yet so confident, for whom almost any horse would behave?

She sent Philip on ahead for a while and walked beside Annabel. 'Would you like to ride Mister Mack when he races?'

Annabel turned to her and a broad smile spread across her face. 'You know perfectly well I wouldn't.'

'Yes, I suppose I do, but I still wonder why not. You're easily good enough.'

'No I'm not. I've no killer instinct. Nothing would induce me to hit a horse with a stick; I'd feel guilty trying to make it give more than it chose. I hate telling anyone what to do.'

Jan chuckled. 'What are you going to do when you get a man, then? You can't just let them do whatever they want – they'll walk all over you.'

After a moment's silence, Annabel said, 'Not all of them, surely?' After another pause, she asked, 'Did you have a lot of boyfriends before you married John?'

'A few.' Jan laughed again and thought of the groping boys at Pony Club camps and the inept, hasty love-making of one of the lads in the Cotswold racing yard where she'd worked between leaving school and meeting John. 'I found most of them too childish; I think that's why I went for John. He was totally solid. Anyway, I was too keen on the horses to take much notice before that.'

'Don't you miss riding races yourself now?'

'A little. No – a lot. I can honestly say the biggest thrill of my life so far was winning my first point-to-point at the Heythrop when I was seventeen. But now sending out winners I've trained comes close. It's certainly more nerve-racking.'

'Which horse did you ride for your first win?'

Jan smiled at the memory. 'God, he was a lovely horse – at least I thought so at the time. I don't think he ever won another race after that though. He was called River Rocket – a big grey, a bit like Mister Mack.' She nodded at Annabel's mount. 'He belonged to my dad's landlord, Colonel Gilbert. His daughter was supposed to ride him, but she'd fallen off the week before and cracked her elbow or something. She was really pissed off when I won on him!' Jan laughed. 'Of course, she rode him after that, which is why he probably never won again.'

'Is that the Gilberts of Riscombe Manor?'

'You would know them,' Jan snorted. 'All part of the old boys' Mafia, I suppose.'

'I only knew their son, George. He used to be a friend of my brother, Charley.'

Jan sensed that Annabel knew George Gilbert quite well, and stopped herself from saying what an arrogant, spoiled little brat he'd been when she'd known him. 'Winning on Rocket was the best, but now I'm a mother riding myself wouldn't really be an option, would it? Anyway, I've got a feeling that training the winner of a good hunter chase on a real race course would give me just as much of a buzz, maybe more.'

'They still go well for you, though, don't they?'

'They seem to. That's why I ride 'em as much as I can.' She decided to confide in Annabel a piece of news she had been keeping to herself up until now. 'I'm thinking of entering Rear Gunner in a hunter chase at Ludlow at the beginning of March.'

Annabel turned to her with sparkling eyes. 'Are you? How

brilliant – your first hunter chase! You must let me look after him there.'

'I'm glad you're so excited about it,' Jan said. 'Of course you can take him.'

'I'd love that.' Then Annabel's tone changed. 'I'm really sorry you're going to move, though. I can't tell you how much it's helped to keep me sane, coming over here every day.'

'I always thought working with me drove people insane,' Jan teased. 'And we won't be going just yet. I've decided not to be too hasty. We'll get near the end of this pointing season before I ask Harold to sell the place for me. It'll be a good four months before we finally move – plenty of time for you to think about coming with us!'

By the middle of February the point-to-point season was well under way and Jan was taking horses to at least one meeting every week. In order to qualify them to run, she'd hunted them all regularly with her local foxhounds, except Mister Mack who wasn't ready, and she was pleased to see how well they'd come through their winter training.

Annabel and Philip, despite his shortcomings, were good exercise riders, but Jan liked to do most of the fast work herself. She had no formal gallops on the farm, but was blessed with totally free access to the open hill tops, where the going on the sheep-grazed turf on its thin bed of peaty soil was nearly always good. It made her laugh to think how much it would have cost to make and keep a set of gallops like that down at one of the big racing centres. As it was, there were so many tracks over the hills they could vary the horses' work all the time, which stopped them from becoming bored.

She and her 'lads' took the horses out for regular road work, too, to keep their legs hard, and her little string was a familiar sight in the valley, when people passing would stop to ask which horse was which and how they were getting on, and, most importantly, when were they going to win.

At times like this Jan felt perhaps she was being unfair to the locals, until she reminded herself that the previous season, when things were beginning to go well, she'd had the chastening experience of hearing two people from her valley discussing her shortcomings as a trainer, when they didn't know she was on the other side of a display shelf in the supermarket in Kington.

As far as owners were concerned, point-to-pointing was only about sport, fun and honour. The prize money was negligible. As a result, the business was run on a shoestring, and relied heavily on the good will and enthusiasm of most of the people involved. Jan found it frustrating sometimes that she couldn't run her yard on a strictly business footing, and yet the need to keep everyone on her side had been a useful training in human management.

But one of the toughest aspects of trying to win point-to-points was finding the right jockey. Billy Hanks came from Riscombe, the village where Jan had lived until she was married. Six years younger than Jan, his elder sister had been her closest friend, and Billy had grown up in awe of the bouncy, green-eyed laughing blonde who could make any pony jump anything. Like the girls, he was horse mad and showed an exceptional natural talent from an early age. By the time he was eighteen he was one of the top dozen point-to-point riders in the Midlands. But he never forgot his earliest inspiration and now he would drive a hundred miles to ride for Jan if she asked him.

By the time March arrived, ushered into the Welsh hills with more than the usual amount of rain and bluster from the west, Jan had sent out nine runners, scored four wins, two seconds and a third, all ridden by Billy. *Horse & Hound* had already noted her success and a photograph of her had appeared in the *Brecon & Radnor Express*. But, as she'd told Annabel, running Rear Gunner in a hunter chase was going to be a completely new experience for her.

3

On the morning of 3 March, Jan woke at six-thirty. She'd only slept for an hour or two: the excitement of sending a horse to race on a real National Hunt track had kept her awake most of the night. But she sat up with the energizing tingle she always felt at the start of a race day.

She threw off the covers and swung her legs over the side of the bed. The air in her room was freezing and there was no sign of daylight through the curtains. She shivered, told herself to forget the discomfort and switched on her bedside light to dress.

Downstairs in the kitchen, she was making some toast and a mug of coffee to calm her nerves when Annabel arrived.

'Hi, Jan,' she said with her usual brightness. 'How are you feeling?'

'Bloody terrified, if you want to know the truth.' Jan wouldn't have admitted it to anyone else. 'Here, have some coffee.'

Annabel shook her head, and propped her slender backside on the corner of the table. 'Did you sleep all right?' she asked.

Jan was trying to eat her toast and Marmite. 'I hardly slept a wink, and when I did, I kept dreaming that when I unloaded Gunner at the race course he was covered in mud and all the other trainers were laughing at me. Then, when he started to race, he was either falling over, or passing the post with no one else in sight – until I saw that was because he was so far behind the others.' She laughed. 'We've got to turn that horse out looking a million dollars. Everyone will be wanting to see what he looks like and what sort of condition he's in after all the point-to-points he's won. And they'll be looking at us – new kids on the block and all that.'

'I can't wait! What does Billy think?'

'He phoned last night to ask how the horse was,' Jan said. 'I told him he looks ready to win the National and he definitely wouldn't be wasting his time.'

'How does *he* feel about Gunner's chances?'

'He's been doing the job too long to say, but I should think he's pretty confident. He had that lovely win on him ten days ago at Garnons, when he beat two of today's field by six or seven lengths. Right,' she said, getting up to swill her crockery, 'we'd better get on with it.'

'Sure,' Annabel agreed. 'What are we doing first?'

'Barneby Boy wants some fast work. He'll be running next week. And I'd like to give Gunner a quick canter before he goes racing, as he can be a bit thick in his wind. We'll take out three more when Phil arrives, probably about half-eight, knowing him.'

'What time do you want to load Gunner?'

'His race is at two-forty so I want to get to there by eleven-thirty to leave plenty of time to walk the course. It'll take us an hour to drive there, so we have to leave at ten to be on the safe side.'

Annabel nodded. 'We should be able to get everything done by then.'

'I've just got to go and get the kids dressed,' Jan said. 'Do you think you could take them down to Olwen's then? She's giving them breakfast and having them for the rest of the day.'

When Annabel got back from the bungalow, she and Jan walked down to the tack room and Jan pulled out her keys to undo the padlock which secured it. Even in a remote place like Stonewall, she thought horse tack was a popular target for opportunist thieves, despite John's old sheepdog, Fly, still standing guard, with Fred and Tigger the terrier, barking like mad every time anyone they didn't recognize walked into the yard.

They sorted out what they were going to need for exercise and what they would be taking to the race course. 'I want his bridle gleaming', Jan said, 'and his leather head-collar. I'll show you how to rub them down with glycerine when we get there, to make them really shine.' Jan knew that there would be people at Ludlow today who would notice her for the first time. She didn't intend this to be her last visit to a real race course with a hunter chaser and she was going to start as she meant to carry on.

She and Annabel took the exercise tack out into the yard. Barneby Boy was in the back row of stables and as Annabel disappeared round the end of the stone block Jan let herself into Rear Gunner's box and talked to him quietly for a few minutes to calm him.

Standing at 16.3 hands high, with a big handsome head and long ears, Rear Gunner had developed into a classic steeplechaser, bred by a local farmer using a popular stallion from over the border in Herefordshire. Harold Powell had bought the gelding from the farmer as an unbroken four-year-old and had sent him to Jan soon after she'd started up in business. She'd slowly brought the horse on through his sixth and seventh years without asking too much of him, watching him win his member's, maiden and intermediate races with ease, until he'd won his first open at the end of the last season. He'd won three more from four starts this season and was heading for a good placing in the regional championships.

Jan was very proud of what she'd done with him and though she didn't have the same affection for him as she had for Mister Mack, he was undoubtedly the most important horse in her yard. Having seen the overnight declarations, she didn't think he would win today. There were at least three better horses running, but there were quite a few worse ones, too, and if he showed some form it could be a boost to her new start in Gloucestershire.

After she had tacked him up and led him out of his box, she brought him over to her mounting block to help get her short legs over his high back. The tension of the day ahead had turned her knees to rubber, but she managed to heave herself up onto the saddle and walked him down the yard to join Annabel.

The horse Annabel was riding, Barneby Boy, was a half-brother to Rear Gunner, but a year younger and a slow developer. The same farmer had bred him, but he'd come to see Jan and told her he was sick of hearing how Harold Powell was boasting what a good deal he'd done with Rear Gunner and this time he'd decided to hang onto the horse, if she thought he was worth training. Barney, as they called him, didn't have the eye-catching good looks of his half-brother, but he had much the same temperament and a good turn of speed. He'd won a maiden race, which was for horses who had never won, and Jan had him entered in a restricted race the following week, with a pretty good chance, she thought.

But today she only had eyes and ears for Gunner.

She and Annabel walked their horses side by side up the green lane beside the farm and out onto the open hill. It hadn't rained since the previous evening, but the gusting westerly hit them hard from behind and got up the horses' tails.

'I don't want either of them to do much,' Jan shouted over the wind. 'Just follow me up to the wide track along the ridge, then come alongside me and we'll give them a quick three furlongs to wake them up. Stay with me if you can.'

Annabel nodded, her eyes shining. Despite not wanting to ride in races, she loved giving the horses fast work. Jan guessed it was the high-speed jumping that daunted her, though she'd often seen her take schooling fences at full racing pace.

Jan trotted up the hill between the banks of gorse and last year's bracken, excited by Gunner's big bouncy stride. Once they had reached the beginning of a broad, gently climbing strip of fine turf, which the wind had already returned to its normal firm springiness, she turned round in her saddle to beckon Annabel up to her. When she could hear Barney's breathing she kicked her horse into a canter, until she reached the level ground at the top of the ridge and eased him into a steady gallop, all the time feeling for anything in his movement that might be cause for worry or optimism.

She was pleased with the way he was going and when she glanced back at the small thorn tree they used as a two-furlong marker, she wasn't surprised to find that Barney, though going strongly enough, was slowly losing ground to his half-brother. She knew she'd done enough and gently began to pull Rear Gunner up as Barney caught up, with Annabel grinning broadly.

'God, he went well!' she shouted, nodding her head at Rear Gunner. 'This chap couldn't get near him and I was flat to the boards.'

'I wasn't,' Jan laughed. 'I didn't want to knacker him. But he feels great.'

When they got back to the yard, Philip had arrived on time – a measure of his excitement at their first race under rules – and had done all the feeds. They took out the next three horses, and turned out the last three to get some air and exercise themselves in the paddock.

They mucked out, cleaned tack and cleared up the yard together, as they did every normal day. Jan wasn't going to make any concessions just because it was their first run on a regular race course. When everything had been done the way Jan liked it, Annabel spent the last half-hour before they left grooming Rear Gunner until he gleamed like the polished leather of his bridle, with a beautiful geometric pattern of diamonds on his quarters.

'They'll all rub off in the lorry under his rug,' Jan laughed when she saw them.

'So I'll do them again when we get there,' Annabel grinned back.

Jan tried not to let her arms shake as she crunched the engine of her old, grey lorry into first gear and turned down the farm drive. She felt an extraordinary mixture of elation and trepidation at what the day might hold. She thought it a good sign that the sun was beginning to show itself through small blue patches in the sky for the first time after several days of heavy rain.

'With this wind and a bit of sun, the going should be just about perfect for Gunner today. The course at Ludlow's on gravel, so it always drains well.'

'What does it ride like?' Philip asked, hunched on the seat of the cab between Annabel and the passenger window.

'Pretty good, I think; Billy says he likes it, anyway.'

'Has he won a hunter chase before?'

'Yes, three or four last season. He's a bloody good little pilot and we're lucky to have him.'

'What weight does he have to do today?' Annabel asked.

'Eleven ten.' Jan nodded at the paperwork in front of Annabel on the dashboard. 'You'll find all the conditions in there – the Shropshire Gold Cup.' Jan raised her eyebrows with a grin. 'Not quite the Cheltenham Gold Cup, but that's what it feels like to me.'

Annabel picked up the entry form. '"The Shropshire Gold Cup",' she read. '"Three thousand, five hundred pounds added to stakes; for horses aged six years old and upwards which before February 25th have been placed first, second, third or fourth in a steeplechase, or have won two open point-to-point steeplechases. Run over three miles, about seven furlongs." That's lucky,' she went on. 'I see he gets no additional penalties for point-to-points won since January the first last year. And he'd have got a five-pound allowance if he was a mare.'

'That's his bad luck,' Philip laughed.

Jan, Philip and Annabel continued to chat for the eighty minutes it took to wind their way along quiet country roads, through Knighton, until they emerged opposite Ludlow race course on the main road a few miles north of the medieval town.

Two hours before the first race was due to start traffic was already being sucked onto the course. Jan felt her bowels tighten as she turned into the lorry park and saw the gathering of large, expensive horseboxes with some of the great names of National Hunt racing emblazoned across their sides. One of the big trainers from Lambourn had a runner in Rear Gunner's race. Jan had known she was up against this level of opposition, but suddenly it didn't seem very fair.

'Where's Billy?' Philip asked. 'He's usually waiting for us.'

'It's a bit different here from a point-to-point,' Jan said. 'He'll be in the jockey's changing room. I'll have to take his colours there.'

'What do we do first?' Philip asked.

'Find a place where I can park this and drop the ramp easily,' Jan muttered through gritted teeth, knowing that the tension was beginning to get to her.

'Don't worry,' Annabel said calmly. 'Look, there's plenty of space over there.'

Nobody spoke while Jan manoeuvred her unwieldy lorry into the place Annabel had pointed out.

'At least we got here,' Philip said when the engine was turned off.

'Is that supposed to make me feel better or something?' Jan tried to laugh.

'Do you know what we have to do now?' Annabel asked.

'First we've got to get this horse off and into the stables. Then, while you two are giving him a serious grooming and shining his tack with that bar of glycerine I gave you, I've got to go and declare. I think I have to sign the form up in the weighing room.'

'We'll get him off while you're doing that, Jan. I can ask where everything is.'

Jan thought Annabel with her willowy, innocent look might get more co-operation from the racing pros than she would. Besides, she had enough on her plate without having to worry about people looking down their noses at her for not knowing where to go.

'Thanks, Bel. I'll come and find you at the stables as soon as I'm done, then we can walk the course.'

As Jan went about the business of delivering Harold's newly made colours – scarlet with yellow chevrons, white sleeves and a black cap – and declaring her entry among all the bustle of a busy weighing room, she found it hard not to let her nervousness show. She couldn't help it – it was all much more brisk and businesslike than she was used to. At the point-to-points the officials in their temporary canvas billets were smiling, familiar faces with a healthy respect for her proven record of producing winners between the flags.

Here, she thought, she was right at the bottom of the pecking order and didn't they let her know it!

But she got through it all without making a fool of herself and was glad to be one stage nearer her debut under rules. She walked round to the race-course stables, where the usual stringent security arrangements were in force, to find she wasn't allowed in because she couldn't find her security pass. She was very relieved when Annabel appeared at the stable-block gate and told her everything was fine.

'He's travelled really well,' she said. 'That little bit of work you gave him must have done the trick. And he looks brilliant now,' Annabel laughed. 'And I mean brilliant – really shiny. And the tack's gleaming.'

'Hmm,' Jan grunted, annoyed at not being able to get in to see her own horse without going through the rigmarole of getting a pass from the clerk of the course. 'I'll take your word for it for now. I'll have to get another pass after we've walked the course. Where's Phil?'

'Back at the lorry, I think, or in the lads' canteen. He bumped into a bunch of rather dodgy-looking friends.'

'Dodgy?' Jan asked sharply.

'I don't mean dodgy like that,' Annabel reassured her quickly. 'Just all spotty with horrible spiky haircuts.'

'Let's hope so,' Jan said, still trying to sit on her anxiety. 'We'll have to walk the course without him, though, God knows, it might have taught him something if he really wanted to be a jockey.' Jan made a face. 'Which, let's face it, he's never going to be.'

'You can let him dream, though.'

'I do. I must be mad to encourage him, but I do.'

As Jan and Annabel walked towards the course, Jan pulled a race card from the pocket of her sheepskin coat. 'I'd better check where this bloody race starts from. I meant to look before we left, but I've been here enough times as a punter, so I should know, shouldn't I,' she chided herself.

'I don't suppose you thought you'd ever be sending a runner here yourself, not until last month when we realized how good Gunner was.'

Jan chuckled. 'Don't you believe it. I've been dreaming of sending out hunter chasers for years. You have no idea what a watershed in my life this is.'

'Yes, I have,' Annabel said quietly. 'And I really, really hope it goes well.'

They walked on in silence as Jan studied the map of the steeplechase course to identify the start of the race.

It took the two friends three-quarters of an hour to complete a circuit of the right-handed track, which the horses running in the hunter chase would do two and half times in under ten minutes. For the most part they walked in silence, while Jan studied the approach and the ground on either side of each fence. Between the fences she checked the firmness of the turf across the width of the track and made mental notes to pass on to Billy.

The strong wind of the early morning had dropped and there was a serenity about the round, wooded hills surrounding the course. Now only a mild breeze blew in from Wales and rippled the long grass between the fairways of the golf course in the middle.

As they walked the quarter-mile run in, they had a good look at the open ditch and then the water jump directly in front of the wrought-iron Victorian grandstand, which the horses would take in the earlier circuits.

'What do you think?' Annabel asked.

'He won't have any problems with these fences and the going will really suit him.' Jan shrugged. 'But who am I to make predictions?' Inside she was a lot more apprehensive than she was prepared to let on. She was beginning to realize that she'd had no idea how nervous she would be and she was beginning to feel queasy; she wondered how long she could hold it in. 'Right, let's get back and have a look at Gunner.'

Once she'd sorted out a stable pass, she went through the security gate with Annabel to find Philip hanging over the bottom door of Rear Gunner's temporary home. 'Everything all right, Phil?'

'Yeah, fine.' He swayed back from the door and Jan realized that he was already quite drunk.

'For God's sake, pull yourself together. I'm not having some drunken moron anywhere near my horses. Go back to the lorry and sober up.'

Philip looked shocked by her outburst. Jan was too, but she didn't feel like retracting anything as she watched him wander off towards the lorries.

In his stable Rear Gunner looked every bit as good as Annabel had said. 'Thanks, Bel, you've done a lovely job. You might even win twenty quid for the best turned out.' Out of habit, Jan felt the horse's four legs and his back, under his rug. He seemed pleased at the attention and aware that it was a big day for him. 'You show 'em today, Gunner,' she murmured into his big ears. 'You show all these big posh trainers what little hillbilly Jan Hardy can do.'

In the canteen Annabel ate nothing, as usual, and even Jan found it hard to swallow the thick ham sandwich she had bought herself. 'God, this running under rules malarkey is bad for my nervous system,' she murmured. 'It's much more regimented than I'm used to. Everything seems to be designed to make you feel inferior, when your only crime is never having done it before.'

'Stop getting a persecution complex,' Annabel said. 'I don't suppose anyone else has noticed that you're not sure of everything.'

'Don't you believe it. I bet this lot are past masters at reading body language.'

Jan didn't feel any better when, later, they tacked up their runner and Annabel led him to the parade ring twenty-five minutes before he was due to race. Jan had wanted the horse well loosened up and used to all the crowds and noise before he was asked to run. Once she was satisfied that he was settled, she started to look around for his owner.

Harold Powell had said he would get to the race course at least half an hour before the off and, sure enough, a few moments later Jan saw him, in a green tweed suit and a brown trilby, shepherding his reluctant wife through the crowd towards the nether regions of the race-course buildings.

Jan knew that Sheila Powell had always been a little wary of her, and on the one occasion she'd talked to her since John had died, she'd made it clear that she didn't approve of her husband's preoccupation with keeping horses with a trainer who was a woman and now was alone. Jan guessed this, as much as anything, was the reason for Harold's objections to keeping horses in Gloucestershire when she moved.

As he leaned down to kiss her on the cheek, from the corner of her eye Jan saw Sheila purse her lips. She stepped back automatically. The last thing she wanted was to make owners' wives jealous, especially when there were absolutely no grounds for it as far as she was concerned.

Harold took it in his stride. 'How's my horse?' he asked, a little louder than necessary, Jan guessed because he wanted anyone who could hear to know that he was an owner.

'He's looking fine,' she said, without too much emphasis. She'd learned early in her training career that it served no useful purpose to build an owner's hopes too high. 'I did a little work on him this morning and he's travelled well. Annabel's in the parade ring with him now to get him used to all the noise. Shall we go and have a look?'

'Let's get a drink first,' Harold said. 'I'll have a proper look at him when we go into the ring.'

Jan really didn't want one, but she realized that a lot of people thought it was one of a trainer's duties to drink with their owners.

The light, spacious bar, recently built to replace the old wooden clubhouse which had been burned down, was packed now with a jovial midweek gathering of sporting farmers and local businessmen. Jan sensed they were a friendlier crowd than she might have encountered at one of the great National Hunt courses and she relaxed enough to accept Harold's offer of a gin and tonic.

She felt quite green after the first sip, but she was damned if she was going to let Harold see what she was going through, so she told him what she thought of the course.

Harold nodded sagely and Jan suddenly realized that he was also trying to hide his nervousness at his first experience as an owner under rules. He kept looking around the room, nodding every so often with a knowing smile at various acquaintances.

'What are you going to tell Billy?' he asked.

'I want him to keep his powder dry until the last six or seven furlongs. There are twelve runners declared and most of these amateur riders will go off like scalded cats – they usually want to impress their mums or their girlfriends by being in front for a bit. Billy's been at it long enough not to bother. So I'll tell him not to be in too much of a hurry and tuck in ten lengths or so off the pace, in eighth or ninth slot. Then he can move up the far side on the final circuit, and get himself in a handy position to track the leader over the last two before that long run in.' Jan paused. 'Then I'll tell him to kick on a bit.' She laughed.

Harold grinned back tensely. 'And do you think he'll do it?'

Jan finished her drink. 'I'll tell you later.'

'When?' Harold asked anxiously.

'When it's all over.' Jan grinned. 'Now it's time I went and checked your horse. Coming?'

Harold glanced at his wife. 'We'll see you in the parade ring.'

Jan watched proudly as Annabel led Gunner around the parade ring. He had been the first in and, seeing him, the public had begun to drift over to lean on the rails. He looked magnificent, gleaming with condition, and, as she'd promised, Annabel had redone the diamonds on his quarters, which seemed to accentuate their quality. As the other runners appeared, in varying standards of turnout, Jan thought her horse stood out, even beside the three runners from big yards who were more fancied.

Unknown at Ludlow, Jan was able to stop for a few moments outside the ring, as if she were another punter, and listen to the comments. It was very gratifying to hear a total stranger say, 'That Rear Gunner looks well, don't he? I'll have a few quid on him.'

When she saw Harold and his wife coming, she joined them and they walked in together. A few moments later the jockeys trooped in, a riot of colour among the browns and khakis of the owners and trainers.

Billy Hanks strolled up to them, unwilling to appear impressed by the prospect of riding in a hunter chase. He tipped his cap and gave Jan and her owners a broad grin, displaying the wide gap where his two incisors had once been, before he'd left them embedded in a timber fence three years before.

Jan had spoken to Billy briefly in the morning, on her way from the lorry to the weighing room, but once he was in the dressing room she'd seen him only for a few moments when he was being weighed out and she'd taken the saddle from him. Now she gave him the instructions she'd outlined to Harold, with the added information that the good ground on the back straight was on the outside. 'Remember, most of these other jockeys won't be able to hold their horses early on, but just let them go, OK?'

Billy nodded. He knew the form in hunter chases. 'How did the horse travel?'

'Fine. Doesn't he look good?'

Billy chuckled. 'If it was a beauty competition, he'd win hands down.'

'He should be fine and, for God's sake, if you're in contention at the last, give it plenty of welly and he'll go on.'

'He did last time,' Billy nodded.

The instruction for jockeys to mount echoed around the ring. Jan and Billy walked over to where Annabel was turning Rear

Gunner in. Annabel held the horse steady while Jan checked the girth, pulled down the stirrup leathers and gave her jockey a leg-up. Billy dropped into the saddle with a grin and took the horse off to do a few more turns around the ring before they left for the race track. As she followed, Jan heard the course commentator announce that Rear Gunner's groom had won twenty pounds for the best-turned-out horse. She turned to Annabel. 'Well, at least we won't be going home completely empty-handed,' she grinned.

Jan didn't want to watch the race with anyone except Annabel, but she felt she had to be with the Powells for Gunner's first run under rules. However, she made sure that Annabel was with them as they crossed back over the course and climbed up into the stands to find a good viewing spot.

The course was laid out so that every fence was visible from where they were, and they all trained their binoculars on the start in the top left-hand corner of the track. The runners had already cantered the short distance from the parade ring and were gathering in front of the starter.

When she saw him raise his hand to the starting-gate handle, Jan took a deep breath; she wasn't conscious of taking another until the race was over.

As the runners set off on their trip over twenty-two fences in just under four miles, Jan didn't need any help from Harold's striking new colours to identify Gunner. She could tell him simply from the way he galloped.

The horse had taken a strong hold right away, but Billy wasn't panicking. Before they'd reached the first of the three plain fences on the back straight, he had Gunner under control and took it lying fifth, several lengths behind the leader, who looked as if he was running away with his jockey.

Rear Gunner's jumping was one of his strengths, and Billy knew exactly how to place him at a fence. Jan watched with satisfaction as they sailed over the next two comfortably and without any apparent strain. Before they started the long right-hand turn, the horse stood right off the open ditch and flew it, gaining a length and a half on the two inside him.

'Pull him back!' Jan muttered, concerned that her horse was seeing too much daylight already.

But Billy hadn't forgotten his instructions and allowed the two he had passed to cruise by him again. By the time they reached the water jump in front of the stand for the first time he was lying seventh in a closely bunched field. There were no fallers and the pack swung away towards the far side of the course.

When they reached the first fence for the second time, the early leaders were showing their tiredness. The third horse barely left the ground and didn't even get his front feet over the birch. In a terrifying cartwheel, he catapulted his jockey into the air and crashed to the ground in front of the favourite, who stumbled, depositing his own rider, and carried on without him.

Billy, on the outside, avoided the melee. He took the fence confidently and found himself lying fifth. Jan noted with satisfaction that her horse was going easily, on the bit but not fighting it, while his jockey sat motionless.

When they swung into the turn on the right-hand side of the course for the second time, they had already covered two miles. The two early leaders, never fancied, were weakening quickly and going backwards. By the time they reached the water again, one had pulled up and the field was much more strung out. Rear Gunner was now lying third of the nine still in the race.

Jan winced. There was a complete circuit left to run. She was sure Gunner didn't perform his best when he was near the front. But other than taking a hefty pull, there was no way Billy could ease their position. Nevertheless, although he looked as if he could easily have passed the horse directly ahead, he managed to steady Gunner in third place all the way down the back straight for the final time. Then, swinging wide after the open ditch, he moved up to lie second, five lengths behind the horse from the big Lambourn yard, who was still going strongly.

Beside Jan, Harold was bellowing so loudly she thought Billy could probably hear him. 'Come on, Gunner boy! You can do it!'

As they turned into the straight with the last two fences ahead, the leader was beginning to tire. Suddenly, Jan found herself hot and sweating: reading his form in the morning, she'd thought that three miles seven furlongs might be beyond his distance.

Gunner, by contrast, was still going strong. He'd gained a length at the third last. But the Lambourn horse was fighting back. As he came up to the second last fence, the jockey pulled his stick through and delivered a full, forehand crack on his rump.

The horse read the signal wrongly.

He took off a stride too soon. His front feet got over, but his back end was never going to make it and he ended up straddling the fence with his rider hanging round his neck.

Jan thought she was going to explode. Rear Gunner came up calmly with plenty of room outside the flailing horse. He popped the fence five lengths clear of the next horse and galloped on strongly to the last. Jan closed her eyes as he came to jump it. Nothing but this fence could stop him winning now.

Harold was yelling himself hoarse; even Annabel was screaming. The whole crowd roared their approval. Jan opened her eyes to see her horse cantering the last four hundred yards to the winning post. For a moment, as he passed it, she thought she was going to faint, until self-preservation kicked in and kept her on her feet.

Harold was hugging her; even Sheila didn't seem to mind, and when he let her go Annabel's arms were around her.

'Jan, that was absolutely brilliant! You've done a fantastic job on him! You must be so proud. Can I go down and bring him in?'

Jan couldn't speak for a moment. She just nodded. She could hardly think. Only in her wildest dreams had she dared to imagine that Gunner might win. She would have been ecstatic if he'd been placed, or just completed the course. And even though there was a bitter-sweetness to the win because one favourite had dumped its rider and the other had fallen, hers had done neither and had run on strongly to the end of the testing race.

Annabel had already hurried away. Jan stood for a moment and watched her go out on the course with a lead rein to meet the victorious Gunner. All around her people on the stands realized her connection with the winner and, checking in their race cards to see who she was, offered their congratulations. As she and the Powells made their way down the stand to cross the course to the winners' enclosure, more people seemed to have learned who she was and called out to her.

'Gosh,' Jan thought, 'if it's this good winning the Shropshire Gold Cup, what must it be like to win the Cheltenham Foxhunters'?' And suddenly that looked an intoxicating prospect.

Annabel, conscious that all eyes were on the horse, beamed shyly as she led Rear Gunner into the winners' enclosure, where his owners would receive their prize. Billy's gappy grin seemed to cover his whole face as he rode to the winner's slot and jumped down. Jan hugged him and Harold, still almost puce with excitement, shook his hand vigorously.

Jan felt she was still in a dream as she helped Billy to unsaddle their horse, and watched him go off to be weighed in, praying that nothing could happen now to upset the result. She hugged Gunner's big head and fondled his ears as she started to rub his sweaty neck. 'You big, beautiful boy,' she murmured, and his top lip twitched in recognition.

The wife of one of the local Jockey Club stewards had been asked to present the battered old cup, which, after a century of handling, had lost most of its gilt. Harold accepted it with unusual humility and Jan's hands were quivering as she took the small salver for the winning trainer.

Annabel had thrown a string rug over the horse and was wiping away the sweat on his neck. 'Shall I take him to the lorry or the stables?'

'Take him back to the stables first,' Jan said. 'Wash him down and I'll come and put his bandages on. It'll give him more of a chance to cool off before we load him.'

Annabel led Rear Gunner away from the enclosure and, now that the formalities were over, Harold was anxious to get to the bar and celebrate their win in the traditional manner. 'Come on, Jan. Champagne, and plenty of it – on me!'

Sheila Powell's eyebrow lifted, but tolerantly this time when she recalled that Harold would pick up a cheque for nearly four thousand pounds for his horse's win.

With some embarrassment, Jan felt a sudden surge of tears, but she had to hold them back. Before she could leave the enclosure a handful of racing journalists homed in on her with their notebooks at the ready and their pens poised. It hadn't even occurred to Jan that the press would want to speak to her, and suddenly all the tales she'd heard about misrepresentation and the tricks they played to get a story crowded into her head, and she found herself wanting to run.

'Well done, Jan,' said a man she'd never seen before in her life. 'Did you think you had a chance when you were on your way here this morning?'

'Of course I did,' Jan managed to blurt out. 'I don't even take a horse to a point-to-point unless I think I've got a good chance.'

'But you were very lucky today, weren't you?'

Jan suddenly saw red. 'Lucky? What do you mean lucky? I trained that horse to go the distance; he did; the others didn't. And jumping's the name of the game.'

'The favourite was obstructed when he lost his rider, though.'

Jan wished she could be less angry with them, but why the hell were they trying to undermine her win – her first under National Hunt rules? 'That doesn't mean he'd have won. Our time was pretty good, too, if you'd bothered to check. I'm proud of Gunner. He's run a super race and you know it. If you don't believe me, come and see him next time he runs.'

Ashamed of herself for rising to the bait, Jan turned and strode out of the enclosure, trying not to look back, before she said any more.

In the members' bar the last thing Jan wanted to do at that moment was drink champagne; she thought it might make her sick, but she felt she should at least take a sip, for Harold's sake.

'I tell you one thing, Jan, now you've really shown what you can do,' Harold took a sidelong glance at his wife, 'there's no way I'm going to take those horses away from you when you move.'

Sheila's lips tightened.

Jan wasn't going to be put off. 'That's great, Harold. I'm really going to need Gunner if I want to make any kind of impression and Lazy Dove's looking as if he might live up to his breeding before long.'

'You take them with you,' Harold said expansively, taking another massive swig of champagne. 'I wouldn't do better in any other yard in the country, not at this game.'

After a few more minutes of mutual congratulation, Jan had had enough. 'OK, Harold. I'm really pleased you're letting me take your horses with me, but don't forget I need to sell Stonewall for as much as you can get if I'm going to find anywhere half-decent to live.'

'I won't forget and we'll do our very best for you.'

'Thanks. Now I'll have to love you and leave you. I've got to bandage your horse's legs before I put him in the lorry.'

'Can't one of your staff do that? The lovely Annabel?'

'I'm sure they could, but I want to do it myself.'

By ten o'clock that night Jan had driven the lorry home, helped Annabel and the useless Philip to feed the horses, and picked up, fed and bathed her children. When she had put them to bed, she said goodbye to Annabel and made herself a mug of cocoa. She carried it up to her room and lay on her bed, fully clothed.

She felt absolutely drained by the exertion and emotion of the day. She knew, of course, that she'd been helped by Billy and by Annabel, but in the end she was the captain of her own small ship and whether it sank or swam was her responsibility and no one else's. She had guessed it would be exciting to win a race on a real course against serious competition from big professional trainers, but she'd had no idea just how big a buzz it would give her. And although a couple of reporters might have tried to imply that her win was the result of luck, rather than skill, she knew differently and that she was right to be very happy indeed with the way her horse had performed. She couldn't have asked him for more, although, perhaps, he had even more to offer.

Most of all, she felt that she had proved to herself that she really did know what she was doing; that she wasn't mad to think she could go on and make a living by doing this job well enough to bring up the children John had left her.

And above all, she was certain that, if John had been there today, he would have been very, very proud of her.

Two weeks after Rear Gunner's glorious win, Jan sat with Harold Powell in the Bull Ring Hotel in Hay.

Harold was shaking his head sadly. 'To get a fair price for Stonewall you've got to be patient. It might take a year or two for the right buyer to come along. That's the way it is with these hill farms. There may be some family sitting at home right now, thinking it over, working out if they can make it pay and prepared to take their time.'

He sat opposite Jan at the table by the window which they'd occupied when they had last had a drink in the bar.

She leaned towards him across the table. 'But I could sell it quickly if I wanted?'

'Yes; we could auction it for you, but if there weren't at least two real bidders, you wouldn't get any kind of a price.'

'I could put a reserve on it.'

'If it didn't sell, you'd still have all the expenses of the sale.' Harold gazed at her like a benign uncle. 'I'd strongly advise you to stay put until a real buyer appears.'

Jan shook her head. 'It'd be too easy to sit around and do nothing about it, always waiting for the next better offer. If I'm going to do it, I've got to move straight away at the end of the season so I've got the whole summer to get ready for next year. I must make a living, Harold, and this is the only way I can do it.'

'I can't argue that you're not up to the job – not after what Gunner did at Ludlow. But I still don't see why you can't do it from where you are.'

'There just aren't enough owners here. I'll have a much better chance of finding them over there. That's the main reason for moving – that and being nearer Mum and Dad.'

'And further from your mother-in-law,' Harold murmured.

'Well, you know what she's like. Do you blame me?'

'No, I don't blame you. I just don't want to see you lose money by doing things in too much of a hurry.'

'How long would it take to get an auction sale organized then?'

'No less than five or six weeks, really, if we want to get it properly advertised.'

'That would take us to the end of April, just after Easter,' Jan mused. 'OK, I'm giving you my formal instruction to get on with it.'

'But, Jan, why the hurry for God's sake? You're doing all right where you are; nobody's forcing you to go.'

'That's why I'm forcing myself. I know what I'm like; if I don't do it now I've made up my mind, I'll end up stuck in a rut and the whole idea will run out of steam; that's just the way I am. I've talked to a couple of agents in Tewkesbury; I've already had details of a place that might do very well. I reckon I could get it pretty cheap, which will help to get the new yard going a lot more easily. Now, what do you think I could expect for Stonewall?'

Harold was sitting gazing at her with dismay but, putting on his professional hat, he straightened his back and gave Jan a warning look.

'I don't think I'll jeopardize your chances of a good sale by discussing that with you here, but I will let you know in writing what our guide price would be.'

'And I'll want to hold a farm sale as soon as possible. There's the rest of the ewes, a load of tackle and feed and a whole lot of furniture I don't want to take with me.'

'That should realize quite a bit,' Harold sighed, making a note in the diary he'd pulled from his inner pocket. 'It's surprising what rubbish you can shift at a busy farm sale, and for the widow of a man like John Hardy I'd say it would be very well attended. Do you mind my asking – were there many debts to clear?'

'Only the bank, really,' Jan said with a quick grimace, 'but they know what the story is.'

'You know, I did read about a shepherd who worked for Lancashire County Council and sued them for damages for getting ill from organo-phosphate dips. He won eighty grand. There's a woman lawyer in this town who's been working on cases a long time; maybe you should look and see if there's anyone you can take to court over John's death.'

Jan leaned back in her chair and screwed up her face. 'No,' she said, shaking her head. 'I just don't want to go down that road.'

'But if you have some entitlement—'

'John wouldn't have wanted that. He hated causing anyone trouble.'

'But they caused him a bit of trouble – he *died* from it, for God's sake!'

'I'll think about it, Harold, I promise,' Jan sighed, although the idea of taking up arms legally over John's death appalled her.

By eleven forty-five on 21 April more than seventy people were gathered in the old assembly room on the first floor of the Bull Ring Hotel for the sale of Stonewall Farm, which was due to start at midday. Most were men for whom attending sales was an essential part of their lives, part of the mechanism by which judgements were made and decisions taken. They also liked to be present at critical moments in the macro-history of their land; changes of farm ownership in the area could have far-reaching effects.

The sale of stock and farm equipment on the ground two weeks before had gone well; a large, inquisitive crowd had come and everything had sold for reasonable prices. But the sale of the land was a different matter. It was still early in the year, too early to attract the leisure buyers who would sometimes turn up to pay a premium and create a stir. But generally it was a farm of only average potential, and as vulnerable at the moment as any other in the hills of mid-Wales.

Jan had set a reserve price on the sale of the whole which was twenty thousand pounds more than the minimum she thought she would need to spend on a Cotswold smallholding, to give her at least some buffer for the first few years in Gloucestershire.

Harold Powell, who was going to sell the property himself, looked well groomed and ill at ease.

'The trade's not good,' he had said to Jan when she arrived at his office earlier that morning. 'I just hope you haven't got yourself caught between the devil and the deep blue sea.'

'From what I can tell, at the reserve I've set, it should find a buyer all right,' she said. 'I'm not being greedy.'

'We'll do our very best for you, Jan, I can promise you that,' Harold said earnestly.

Jan recognized the words for the meaningless flannel they were. She didn't particularly mind; it was part of his job. She certainly wasn't under any illusion that she would be getting special treatment.

Jan had left Megan and Matthew with their grandmother. Olwen had made it clear that she didn't want to witness the disposal of the farm she had entered as a bride forty-five years before, when they still used a horse to plough the bottom fields, but Jan had refused to be moved by her sour tearfulness.

She was standing now in the sale room, behind and to the left of the rostrum from which Harold would run the auction. She felt detached, not at all nervous, as Harold stepped up onto his small dais and cleared his throat. The murmured conversation that earlier had filled the room subsided and a sea of faces turned towards him.

'Good morning, gentlemen . . . ladies,' he added, to a little laughter, as he acknowledged the handful of women scattered among the crowd. 'I'll not waste too much time with preamble; I don't doubt you've all already had a good look at the details of Stonewall and are aware that we are offering freehold vacant possession of the house, ground and buildings, all in one lot.'

There was a palpable tension in the air now, as there always was at the start of a sale. Jan thought that for a lot of people an auction held the same fascination as the spectacle of a group of men playing poker.

'So let's get the bidding under way,' Harold said in a business-like manner. 'Who'll get me started at two hundred thousand . . .?'

There was a grunt from the back, which Jan didn't understand, but Harold pounced. 'Fifty thousand?' he said disparagingly. 'Oh well, I'll let you have your fun.' After that, with the help of a young man of twenty or so gazing around eagerly beside him, Harold started to spot bids from around the room and the bid price mounted in steps of five thousand pounds.

Jan had been to enough sales to know that these were mostly from men who wanted more than just the spectacle but enjoyed being part of the drama, at no real risk to themselves as long as the price was obviously way below value. She could imagine them standing around later in the pub at lunchtime, boasting. 'I put a bid in, nearly got it, too.'

But as the price crept up, closer and closer to Jan's reserve, the bids came more slowly. Harold Powell's gaze swept the room from side to side as he cajoled the remaining bidders. 'Come on, now. There's still two of you who want it, but only one of you's going to get it – whichever's got the nerve,' he teased until, at last, the bidding reached Jan's reserve. Now that Harold had definitely sold the property, Jan saw a slight relaxation of tension in his neck, but no amount of eloquence from him could raise the bidding by another increment. 'Is that it?' he finally asked a man invisible to Jan in the far corner of the room. He picked up his shiny, mahogany gavel from the shelf of the rostrum, raised it and knocked down Stonewall Farm at the reserve price.

'Davies!' he said, to identify the buyer.

Jan had no idea which Davies; there were twenty farming families called Davies in the vicinity. She found that she didn't care; she felt no emotion, no resentment that the farm to which her husband had dedicated his life had now moved irrevocably beyond her control. John was dead. It was John she had loved, John she missed, not the farm that had taken him from her.

Ten days after the sale, Jan left the children with Annabel and drove to Gloucestershire. Her first stop was at her parents' house on the edge of the honey-gold hamlet of Riscombe.

Reg Pritchard, in his seventy-fifth year, could not and never would abandon the habit of farming. Although his wife Mary pleaded with him regularly to give up before he did any serious damage to himself, he still insisted on shuffling forty ewes from field to field on his remaining thirty acres and into the tired old buildings to lamb each January. His state pension brought in more than his farming activities, but, for him, to stop farming would be to stop living.

Soon after Jan had married John and gone to live in Wales, Colonel Gilbert, her parents' landlord, had suggested that Reg might like to give up a hundred of the acres he farmed. Reg had seen the sense of it and Colonel Gilbert had said that he and Mary could stay in the house, with the thirty acres, for the rest of their days. From Reg's point of view, as the land was there, it would have been a crime not to farm it. The overproduction of lamb across the United Kingdom and the ecological arguments against farming the less fertile margins of the nation's land didn't affect his view one jot.

Jan always loved coming back to Riscombe, where she had been born and brought up. Although the farm had been bigger then, it had scarcely been more profitable, and little in the house had changed for as long as she could remember. The big beech tree which she and her younger brother, Ben, used to climb as children still stood, spreading its grey, green-clad limbs skyward, like a giant bodyguard beside the house.

She felt the usual aching sadness when she thought about Ben, seeing his sun-browned face, creased with laughter, beneath a stack of thick blond hair as he swung from the branches with strong, supple arms. She still couldn't begin to understand what had made him walk out of the house, the day after his twenty-first birthday three years before. He'd sent cards, three or four from different parts of the world since he'd gone, to tell their parents not to worry, but he had given no address and he had never phoned or come back to Riscombe. Once he had sent a postcard to Jan from Disneyland in Los Angeles. She'd gazed at his familiar writing with wonderment, scarcely able to imagine how her brother, who'd grown up with ponies, ferrets and fishing, could be happy anywhere as exotic as California.

At the same time, she'd always known that there was a side to his character that yearned, almost lusted after adventure; that his guitar and music had replaced catapults and rabbiting. The small sum of money left him by Mary's mother had been just enough to enable him to go. Jan only hoped that he wasn't aware of the deep, unremitting sadness it had caused their parents. Reg was so disappointed that his son had turned his back on farming, after more generations than anyone knew, that he hadn't mentioned Ben's name in Jan's hearing in the past twelve months.

Reg was waiting for her at the front door as she parked the Land Rover. Putting aside thoughts of Ben, Jan got down and gave her father a long hug, feeling that he had shrunk a little since the last time she'd seen him. She noticed with concern that he had missed a few swathes of bristle in his shave that morning, when once he had been so particular. His hair, though, was thick, white and wavy, and had been carefully combed, not, Jan suspected, without a little vanity.

'How are you, Dad?'

'Oh, pretty much the same. Can't do so much now.' He shook his head at the frustration of it. 'Them ram lambs are gettin' too strong for me.'

'If you can't physically manage it,' Jan said, 'you should give up the ewes.'

Reg was shuffling back into the house now. 'What would I do then?'

Jan sighed. It wasn't the first time they'd had this conversation. 'You're a stubborn old bugger,' she laughed.

Mary had been watching out for Jan's Land Rover from the kitchen window. She had already made a pot of tea and was cutting thick slices from a dark, gooey chocolate cake as they walked in. Although she was fifteen years younger than her husband, she shuffled across the kitchen on short, arthritic legs to hug her only daughter, before standing back to gaze at her proudly, as she always did. 'Dad says you're thinking of moving back over here!' she said with a breathlessness that was beginning to worry Jan.

'Yes, I hope so. If I can find something I can afford, where I can keep enough horses.'

'What's this place like you're going to look at with Dad?'

Jan took a sheaf of estate agents' brochures from the bag slung over her shoulder, and sat down with her parents at the old pine table she'd known all her life to look at the details of Edge Farm, Stanfield.

'There's not much to the place,' her father said, 'and all the ground's on a bank, if I remember right.'

'That'll help get the horses fit,' Jan justified.

'S'long as you never has to plough it. These buildings ain't much either and there's no house.'

Jan had already absorbed these obvious defects, but she knew from the research she'd done that this was about all she could expect for the money she'd got from the sale of Stonewall. 'Dad, I told you on the phone, the agents said I'll have no trouble getting planning permission for a house, then I can build it as I want when I've got the money. I won't mind living in a mobile home for a few years, so long as I know what I'll be getting at the end of it.'

'But will that be all right, with the kids?' Mary asked anxiously.

'They won't mind. Mobile homes are very civilized theses days.'

Mary pondered this for a moment, but didn't voice any more doubts.

'How many horses do you think you can keep there?'

'Up to twenty, I should think.'

'There's not the grazing for twenty.' Reg shook his head. 'Not on those banks. The pasture ain't much there.'

'Reggie,' Mary chided him. 'Stop trying to put her off. It'll be lovely to have her close, now I can't get out much.'

'It's OK, Mum. Dad's just thinking like a farmer and he's right to. But it's OK about the grazing – most people take their pointers home for the summer. They wouldn't want to pay me for grass keep anyway.'

'What'll you do for money in the summer months, then?'

Jan had already been asking herself that, but she didn't want to worry her father. She screwed up her small round face and shrugged. 'I'll be schooling and bringing on young ones; maybe trading a few.'

'With them two kids, you'll need something steady coming in. I can tell you, though me and your mum would have liked a few more of you, I did sometimes thank our lucky stars we only had the two extra mouths to feed.'

'I never thanked my lucky stars,' Mary protested.

'Well, Dad, I'll just have to do what I can do. I know I can train pointers. I've already won eleven this season, as well as Gunner's hunter chase – that's why Harold's letting me bring his horses with me. It shouldn't be too hard to find a few new owners for next season with that track record. I'm sure I'll get more wins from Gunner and Lenny's Lad next year, and Lazy Dove, so long as we can keep his mind on the job, and that should bring in more owners.'

'*If* they win.' Reg grunted. 'There's no certainty in your game and you know it. But if they do, you're right; there's plenty of money round here these days, though God knows where it all comes from or what'll happen when it stops.'

'It's all townies, Dad, you know that. All wanting to be the country squire. Anyway, are you going to come and look at this place with me or not?'

A big stone barn was perched on a ledge on the steep, western face of the Cotswolds that had given its name to Edge Farm at least two hundred years before. The farmhouse that had once stood beside it existed now only as a partially buried, two-dimensional floor plan of its former self. With the stone building stood a black iron Dutch barn and a cluster of Scots pines of about the same age, which increased the farm's air of bleakness, wind-whipped as it was just below the top of the ridge.

The land for sale stretched in a thin slice from the bottom of the hill to the top, comprising six fields of permanent pasture, although the lowest and most level of them still showed the ridges and furrows of medieval cultivation. A rough track of limestone chips climbed two hundred yards from the lane up to the buildings. It was clear that the track often doubled as a stream in winter, to cope with the rain which fell when the clouds blown from the west were forced to rise after their passage across the broad Severn valley.

Jan parked the Land Rover in a yard that hadn't been swept for years. The big stone barn, picturesque from a distance, looked a serious liability close to, with a roof of rotting asbestos sheeting. The Dutch barn was fit for nothing but scrap. Jan turned to her father with a rueful face. 'I'm sorry, Dad. I shouldn't have dragged you out here.'

But she was surprised to see an eager light in her father's eye. 'We may as well look at the place now we're here,' he said and opened the passenger door to climb down.

Jan got out too and stood gazing at the dereliction all around them. 'I don't think I can handle this,' she said.

'Let's have a look at the ground,' Reg urged.

They spent half an hour walking the fields, assessing the grass, checking the fences and gates. Jan guessed the barn was two or three hundred years old as she stood in it and gazed glumly at the holes in the roof and the puddles on the floor.

'I tell you what,' Reg said out in the yard. 'This place'll be cheap. No farmer would give much for it and it's too windy for any of them townies. It looks like it's been on the market for years. If they want to sell it, they'll take a lot less than they're asking.'

'But, Dad, look at the barn! I need somewhere to stable my horses right away.'

'They'll be out mostly, this time of year, but anyway you could tarpaulin the roof and there's room to knock up ten stables in there with three-quarter-inch ply. It wouldn't look pretty, but it'd do the job.'

'Dad, what are you talking about? This place is rubbish and you know it.'

Reg shook his head impatiently. 'Not with a few ideas. It's a lousy bit of ground, really, but I reckon it'd just about do the job you want. And I smell a hell of a bargain.'

'I just don't think I can handle it.' Jan shook her head.

'Yes, you can,' her father said with fierce conviction. 'If anybody can, you can.'

After lunch the next day Jan picked up the telephone from the time-blackened oak dresser that had stood against the back wall in the big, gloomy hall at Stonewall for the past two hundred years.

She dialled the estate agents in Evesham and offered half the asking price for Edge Farm, provided there was completion by the end of the month.

The man she was talking to smoothly declined her offer at once.

'Well, let me know how close they can get to that, if they want to get shot of the place in double-quick time.'

'I will, Mrs Hardy.'

Jan cleared the line and dialled her father.

'Hello, Dad. I just did what you said and offered half the asking price on the farm. I'd hardly taken a breath when he'd already turned it down.'

'They'll be back with a good price – just you wait. I've been asking around. That's the fifth agent the land's been with in the last three years and they wants to get shot of it.'

Jan was nothing like so confident as her father, but she was as aware as him that getting the place cheaply was the only option; that to buy it at anything above a bargain price would be no achievement at all. But she was determined that she wasn't going to let herself get wound up and irrational about Edge Farm. Yes, she wanted it – but only if it really was cheap and would allow her to start this new stage of her life with some kind of advantage. She knew that to do the deal she had to keep her cool. She was grateful for her father's support and guessed that Reg, who had never owned a freehold in his life, was determined to enjoy the buzz of the chase with her.

The next day was Saturday and Jan was going to the races, so she didn't have time to think about Edge Farm.

She woke at half-past five, just before her alarm clock started buzzing. The usual adrenalin rush she felt at the thought of running her horses was no less intense, despite her successes of the last few months.

She walked across a worn rug on the bedroom floor and opened the thick curtains covering the window. She was met with a glorious view to the south, lit by the silky glow of a gold and pink dawn. The larks were already trilling as they spiralled high over the heather on the hill behind the farm and Jan sighed at this strange, fickle country, so bleak all winter, but suddenly seductively beautiful when the weather allowed.

Dismissively, Jan turned her eyes away.

Too bad, she thought, no amount of summer beauty could make up for the misery of winter. Besides, she told herself, to run a profitable point-to-point yard she needed owners and even her dad had agreed there was a lot more potential in the Cotswolds than there ever would be here in mid-Wales.

She washed and dressed in stretch jeans, a T-shirt and a tan cord blouson she'd had since she'd started her first job. She tiptoed from her room and along the corridor to check on the children. They were both sound asleep and she went downstairs with a clear conscience. Her neighbours' fifteen-year-old daughter would be up soon to give them breakfast and take them down to their grandmother's.

As she opened the front door, she heard Annabel's Golf turn off the lane at the bottom of the drive. She smiled and wondered why Annabel, with all the things that should have tempted her away, was so committed to this little yard of hers and all the horses in it.

She walked down and stroked Mister Mack's big pink nose while she waited for the Golf to appear round the end of the buildings. When it did, Annabel parked neatly and swung her long legs out of the driver's door.

'Hi, Jan!' she called, not too loudly, knowing the children would still be asleep. 'What a heavenly day! Isn't it unbelievable here when it's like this? I had the most beautiful drive over the hills. It was worth getting up at six just for that.'

Jan grinned. 'I can see how lovely it is, but I'm still moving to Gloucestershire.'

'I know.' Annabel laughed. 'I was just trying to remind you of what you'd be missing, but I'm sure you're right really; this place must have pretty awful memories for you.'

They sorted the tack they needed and talked about their runners' chances at the Llandeilo Farmers' Hunt point-to-point. The races were being held on a broad meadow in the valley of the River Teifi, in a beautiful, distant corner of Carmarthenshire. It was a long way to go but, as Jan saw it, its very remoteness improved her chances of winning. And she'd been in racing long enough to know that most people judged a racing yard solely by its strike rate – the number of winners it produced in proportion to the number of horses it ran.

They were taking three horses that day – Barneby Boy, Lazy Dove and Gale Bird, which belonged to Jan and was the only mare in the yard. From their previous runs and the way they'd worked that week, all three had a chance. Lazy Dove was another of Harold Powell's horses. Jan had entered him in the men's Open, the principal race of the meeting. The small gelding came from a long line of winning mares who had blazoned their family name across National Hunt courses all over the country. Lazy had the same grit and stamina as his female forebears, but a quirk in his nature matched his name and had made him difficult to train and ride. Jan was only running him today because she had persuaded Billy Hanks to come all the way to west Wales to pilot him. She was flagrantly cashing in on their longstanding friendship and his gratitude for Gunner's win at Ludlow.

'It's a three-hour drive for him, mind,' Jan said to Annabel, making a guilty face, 'but he's got the ride on the other two; both of them could win and he says he's picked up another good one from a trainer in Pembrokeshire.'

'He won on Gale Bird in the North Cotswold, didn't he?' Annabel said, as they carried saddles and bridles across the yard to the horses they were going to exercise before they left.

'Yes, but he was lucky, remember? The leader pecked after the last and went arse over head. Of course her five-pound mare's allowance will help.'

By seven o'clock they were on the top of the hill under a cloudless morning sky and the scene around them was breath-taking. The sun was already warm, but hadn't yet dispersed the pools of mist that lingered in the valleys below. There was scarcely any wind and the distant bleat of a late hill lamb drifted up the heather-clad ridge.

After the work, they stopped and dismounted to let the horses pick a little grass that the sheep had left. Annabel took off her helmet and shook out her long chestnut hair. She sucked in a deep breath of scented air and her eyes sparkled. She looked, Jan thought, as good as any girl in a glossy magazine.

'You really ought to go into fashion or films,' Jan said. 'You're wasted up here in the hills.'

Annabel turned to her. She seemed suddenly insecure and embarrassed. 'I thought you wanted me to come and help you set up the new place when you move.'

Jan laughed at her reaction. 'Of course I do, very much. But sometimes I just can't understand why you don't take advantage of what you've got.'

'You mean go to London and try to make money out of modelling or something? That's what my father's always saying. But I don't particularly need any more money. I've got all I want.'

'But what about boyfriends – men? You'd meet a lot more if you got into that world.'

'And the last kind of men I'm interested in.'

'What is it with you and men? You don't seem that keen.'

'It's not that I'm not interested, the trouble is all the men I meet only seem to want one thing and they just never stop banging on about it. I'm sure there's more to life and relationships than just that.'

Jan nodded. 'Even I came across that when I was your age, though I dare say I didn't have quite so many flinging themselves at me. And of course there's more to life, but you're right – it seems S-E-X is all everyone talks about these days.'

'That's why I love coming here, and talking about the horses and doing this.' Annabel waved a hand across the spectacular vista of hills stretching away to the distant shadow of Snowdonia in the north. 'Being in a place like this, at a time like this. This is what I call really special. And how many people are there up on these hill tops enjoying it? Maybe a dozen. It makes me feel really privileged.'

Jan nodded and gazed around her. 'Yes, I suppose you're right; in fact, you *are* right, but running my yard, even though it's so small, I always seem to have so much on my mind. Perhaps I just don't have time to appreciate it the way I should. Which reminds me,' she went on, changing her tone briskly, 'we'd better get back if we're going to get a couple more done before we load up. It'll take three hours to get there in the lorry and I've got to walk the course. They usually have this meeting a month earlier, but it was postponed because the course was waterlogged. I don't know what it'll be like at this time of year.'

No clouds blew in to change the outlook. Jan and her two 'lads' arrived at the small cluster of tents in good time to inspect the course, which lay in a pretty meadow among broad, parkland trees and set between steep wooded banks. It was obvious from the range of ages and types strolling in from the car park that the point-to-point was an important social event in this sparsely peopled corner of Wales. Jan couldn't help responding to the carnival atmosphere and she realized how much she enjoyed the meeting's informality and friendliness, compared to the serious, businesslike discipline of National Hunt racing. She was also quite relieved that Harold Powell had rung the evening before to say he couldn't come and see Lazy Dove run.

Gwillam Evans, the farmer who owned Barneby Boy, had already arrived, but he was a very unobtrusive owner. His horse was the first of Jan's three to go, due to run at one-thirty in the second race, which was the restricted hunts, open to horses qualified only with certain hunts in the area, the Radnor and West Hereford among them. He sidled up to Jan as she came out of the secretary's tent, looking around for her jockey. 'I've got the colours here,' he said proudly because his wife had made them. 'Has he come yet?'

'I hope so,' Jan said. 'He'll be bloody angry if he's driven a hundred and twenty miles then misses his first ride.'

Gwillam looked alarmed at the prospect of having no jockey.

'Oh, don't worry,' Jan said. 'He always gets here in the nick of time. I think it adds to the excitement for him.'

Billy did arrive – within an ace of the deadline to declare jockeys.

He reappeared from the tented changing room in a matter of minutes in Gwillam's colours and walked into the raw-timber-railed paddock, where Annabel was already leading Barney around with the other runners.

Jan stood in the middle and watched the opposition. There were several horses she had never seen before on which the form guide was able to shed little light; there were four or five with respectable form. Not one of them looked as fit as Barney. She caught Billy's eye and he sauntered over, watched eagerly by those in the crowd round the rail who knew that he was the leading point-to-point rider in the region.

'There's a bit of sticky ground by the rails in the bottom left-hand corner,' Jan said quietly, 'just before the fourth, so go a bit wide and take it on the outside. Otherwise, I should think it'll ride pretty well. It should suit him, but don't forget he's a bit like Rear Gunner. Don't show him too much daylight until you have to.'

Billy nodded absently and, as always, Jan had the impression he hadn't been listening to a word she said. But since he always followed her instructions as closely as he could, she had to assume he heard something.

'They don't look much,' he replied, still studying the other horses circling round them.

'Don't forget,' Jan said. 'There's always some potty farmer round here who thinks he can pull off a coup and once in while it happens.'

But Barneby Boy's performance, with Billy obeying his instructions to the letter, was almost an anticlimax. In a copybook piece of race-riding, Billy brought him alongside the leader coming to the last. They jumped it together as if they'd been synchronized, and it was only when they had taken another stride or two that Billy crouched down, leaned forward and urged his horse to get on with the job.

Barney stretched his neck and earned an extra yard with every stride right up to the winning post.

He passed it running on so strongly that it took Billy a hundred yards to pull him up. He turned and met Annabel running out onto the track to lead them in with his usual broad grin.

Gale Bird, in the maidens' race, didn't give Billy such a comfortable ride. Two from home she hit the top of the fence so hard that Jan had to shut her eyes, and found herself clutching her binoculars so tightly that her fingers hurt. But when she looked again the mare had recovered and seemed to have found fresh energy coming to the last. Billy was the first to take off and Gale Bird put down neatly with the fluid grace that had so impressed Jan when she'd first seen the mare.

To a roar from the crowd that had backed her, Gale Bird galloped home to give Jan and her team two wins in a row.

Back in the makeshift winners' enclosure, Billy rode in to a great reception. He looked almost as happy at his double as he'd been after winning on Rear Gunner. He jumped off, grinning and sweating. Jan threw her arms around him and once again felt a surge of feeling and tears welling up, just as she had at Ludlow. This time, she didn't succeed in holding them back and, shaking her head with a hopeless, apologetic grin, she helped Billy to unsaddle the horse and led the mare back to the lorry herself.

Annabel and an ecstatic Phil followed her and helped her to put the horse away before they took Lazy Dove from the box, with an hour to prepare him for his race, which was the last on the card.

The eight runners in the men's Open had completed one and a half circuits of the three they were set to run. They were approaching a big plain fence halfway along the back straight on the left-handed course. Lazy Dove had taken a strong hold as he always did. Jan had told Billy to not to fight him. He always seemed less troubled when he was in front and it was sensible to leave him there, provided, of course, it wasn't taking too much out of him.

Jan had watched the horse in trepidation as he approached each fence. So far, though, he'd done nothing wrong. Lazy Dove was a naturally athletic horse who, once he'd decided he was going to jump, did it with stylish poise.

She could tell even from the distance of three hundred yards that Billy was beginning to enjoy his ride until completely without warning, as they came up to the next fence, the horse veered sharply to one side, went up on his hocks for a moment before dropping down and careering off the course outside the wing.

A split second later Jan, gazing in horror through her binoculars, saw the reason for the horse's fright. A hare, which must have been quivering in the long grass and scrub inside the track since before racing had started, had flashed off across the meadow and disappeared into a hedge at the far end. Despite everything else going through her mind, Jan was deeply relieved that the problem had been caused by another animal, rather than some crazy fantasy in the horse's head.

Turning her glasses back to Lazy Dove, she saw that he hadn't decided to give up and was carting his jockey at a relentless gallop straight towards a large spreading sycamore tree. A second later he was under the lower branches, which swept over his head and took the jockey clean off his back.

The St John's ambulance was already in motion, bouncing its way across the ancient pasture while Jan ran as fast as she could across the middle of the course, worried equally about her jockey and horse.

As she ran, she saw Lazy Dove at the far end of the field being flapped into a corner by the few spectators who had chosen to watch from that part of the course, while one of the hunt whips, in his pink coat for the occasion, cantered with a determined air along the edge of the meadow to take charge.

Jan carried on towards the sycamore and the small group of people now clustered under it beside the ambulance. She arrived out of breath to find Billy sitting up, at least, while a black-uniformed woman with a very large chest held a slab of bloody lint to his forehead beneath his floppy blond hair.

He looked up, saw Jan and grinned. 'It's all right, I'm not dead. I was only out for a few seconds. I reckon the tree came off worse than me!' He nodded up at the smaller splintered branches above him. 'What's the horse doing?'

Jan glanced across the meadow. 'They've just caught him. He looks OK – thank God!'

'Did you see what happened?' Billy asked eagerly, earning a frown from the stocky St John's Ambulance woman.

'That bloody hare?' Jan nodded. 'Yeah, I saw it. I only hope it hasn't set Lazy back. It's just the sort of thing he takes to heart.'

'And it knackered our treble.' The jockey grinned ruefully.

'Was he going that well?'

'Didn't you see? He was going ever so sweetly and jumping like a gazelle.'

'Ah well,' Jan said sounding more philosophical than she felt. 'He's not dead, you're not dead and you can't win them all.'

Billy, bandaged and banned from driving his car by the doctor on the race course, was driven back to Stonewall by Jan, while Philip drove the lorry with Annabel for company. On the journey home Jan experienced a mix of emotions – elation at their double, frustration at Billy's injury and relief that Lazy Dove was still in one piece. She was reminded of what her father had said a few days before – racing was an unpredictable business and, on the whole, they'd been very lucky that day.

When they got back to the farm, Jan stopped off at Olwen's bungalow to pick up the children. Olwen, ambivalent though she was about keeping the kids for any length of time, was looking explosive.

'A firm of estate agents in Evesham phoned this morning, after you'd gone; they thought they was talking to you, not me, and they said if you was to increase your offer for Edge Farm by ten thousand, their clients would accept it.'

Jan, in the process of picking up Matthew and checking his nappy, stopped, frozen. She hadn't said a word about Edge Farm to Olwen, aware that it would achieve nothing but conflict. She closed her eyes. 'What did you say?' she asked quietly.

'I said they'd got the wrong Mrs Hardy, but I'd pass on the

message. If the firm's in Evesham,' she went on with more grit in her voice, 'where's Edge Farm?'

Jan accepted the inevitable. 'If you come up later, once we've got the horses done and the kids in bed, I'll show you.'

Up in the farmhouse Jan tried the agents' number as soon as she got through the door, but it was already after six. She hadn't expected a reply so soon and she didn't know how she would contain herself until the office reopened the following week. At the price they were asking, she knew she had the deal she needed.

Unable to keep the news to herself, she phoned her father, who chuckled gleefully and urged her to go ahead. She put the phone down, sharply aware that a whole new chapter in her life was about to begin.

By ten past nine on Monday morning the deal was done and the process of transferring ownership of Edge Farm, Stanfield, Gloucestershire to Mrs Jan Hardy had been set in motion.

5

Jan was standing in the grass parade ring at Doncaster Spring Sales. She leaned forward slightly and rested her hands on her knees while she focused all her attention on the dark bay gelding being trotted down the centre of the ring towards her.

From his breeding, the way he was built and his brief career on the flat, she reckoned the horse could have a bright future; but any weakness in his action or conformation could mean all the difference between a successful career as a hunter-chaser, or a few miserable years of disappointment and a lot of vets' bills.

Harold Powell had found the excitement of winning a hunter chase on a National Hunt course so superior to winning a point-to-point that he had now set his sights even higher. He had asked Jan to look for another horse and insisted that she find him something capable of running with a good chance in the Christie's Foxhunters' at the Cheltenham Festival.

If Jan bought this horse for Harold, he would be easily the most expensive she'd ever had in her yard. In the next few minutes she'd have to decide if she was going to bid up to the ten thousand guineas Harold had given her to spend or sit on her hands. She was completely oblivious to anyone or anything else in the grass arena and quite unaware of the copper-coloured gelding being led in behind her.

The horse's lad was about to bring him in through the entrance when he stopped dead, straightened his forelegs and dug in his toes. Throwing his head in the air with ears lying flat down an arched neck, the gelding stared wildly over flared nostrils at the people lining the rails around the edge of the ring.

The groom swore and viciously jerked the lead rein down to tug the leery animal into the ring. He turned left to lead him clockwise along the tarmac path that ran just inside the perimeter rail, where most of the lookers leaned.

One of them waved his catalogue to a friend on the far side as the big chestnut trotted nervously by.

The horse reacted at once.

He reared and yanked the rope with burning speed through his minder's fist to the knot at the end. Howling with pain, the groom hung on, but the horse, still back on his hocks, now had space to veer sharply towards the middle of the ring. As his front feet came down, his quarters swivelled in again, with muscles bunched to buck and lash out in fear and anger at being dragged into a place where he didn't want to be.

Right in the line of fire of the animal's rear hooves a small girl stood, rigid with terror as she saw what was about to happen to her.

A man standing near Jan saw her. With lightning instinctive reactions, he dived at the child, wrapped her in his arms and rolled away a split second before the iron-capped hooves whistled through the air onto where she had been standing.

The lad trotting the horse down the grass in the ring towards Jan pulled up short just as she became aware of the commotion behind her and heard hooves crashing to the ground.

Jan whipped round. Where Megan should have been standing, she saw only two long scars of brown earth gouged in the turf. Beyond it, everyone had scattered from the careering horse, with its groom still hanging on, grimly determined to bring it under control.

Jan searched around in panic. She couldn't focus through the mist that was suddenly clouding her eyes. 'Megan! Megan!' she shrieked.

'It's OK.'

Subconsciously Jan registered the deep, confident voice behind her. She didn't realize the man was talking to her until he spoke again, louder and more urgently.

'It's OK! She's here!'

Jan spun round. At the sight of her daughter safe, although in the arms of a complete stranger, she collapsed with relief. 'Megan, thank God!' She tried not to weep, but she was overcome by a surge of guilt at bringing her child here, then neglecting her.

By now the lad trotting the horse she'd been appraising had reached her side.

'Jaysus! That was so lucky.' He nodded at the man holding Megan. 'He grabbed the little lass in the nick of time! Right from under that animal's feet!'

Jan glanced at her child's saviour. 'Thank you! Thank you so much!' She saw the grass stains on his pale-lemon cord trousers where he'd dived across the turf to save her daughter and she thought how inadequate the words sounded.

'No problem,' he said with a smile.

'God, I feel terrible. It's my fault, I was so busy . . . I took my eye off her.'

'Well, don't worry. She's absolutely fine – aren't you?' he asked the little girl.

Megan, somehow diminished by the terror of what had happened and still utterly drained of her normal high colour, nodded uncertainly.

The man cocked a thick black brow at her. 'You'd be even finer if I got you an ice cream, wouldn't you?'

Now Megan's hazel-green eyes – just like her mother's – lit up and colour began to seep back into her cheeks.

The man glanced at Jan. 'If you want to carry on looking at that horse, I'll get her an ice cream and bring her back when he's been through the sales ring.'

He didn't seem surprised by her relief.

'That would be such a big help,' she said. 'I'm here on my own, I'm afraid.' She shrugged her regret at not coming to the sales with an entourage, like real trainers. 'But haven't you got a horse to buy?'

'I *was* going to have a closer look at that one.' He nodded at the frenzied chestnut, now being led round by two anxious lads, and laughed wryly. 'But I've decided he's not really for me.'

Jan looked at him for a moment. She hoped she could judge people as well as she could horses. 'Well, if you wouldn't mind looking after Megan for a few minutes, that would be a real help.'

'I'll see you in front of the agents' boxes afterwards,' he grinned. 'Best of luck.'

The bidding rose above ten thousand guineas, then fifteen thousand, until finally the horse Jan wanted was knocked down for nearly twenty thousand guineas to a name which meant nothing to her.

She tried to be philosophical; she'd had plenty of practice over the last few months, but she clattered down the steps of the sales arena with a despondent look on her normally vivacious face.

'It's OK. There'll be others,' a voice behind her shoulder said lightly.

She wheeled round ready to deliver a pithy retort, until she saw it was the man who had saved Megan. The little girl was still clinging onto his large tanned fist.

'I know.' She managed to grin. 'But it's not often I get the chance to spend that kind of money and I went way beyond my limit before I lost him.'

'Was the horse that good, then?'

'He'll win races', she said confidently, 'unless he goes to some plonker who couldn't train his own granny.'

'I should think some grannies take a bit of training,' he teased.

Jan laughed. 'Not so much as kids – they're much harder than horses.'

They'd reached the metal rail around the parade ring and leaned against it to watch the continuous stream of horses being shown off and presented in the best possible light by their vendors.

'This kid's not so bad.' The man nodded down at Megan, who was standing between them, finishing her ice cream. 'I saw her carrying your catalogue for you earlier this morning, when you were round at the stables looking at that big black horse from Wexford.'

Jan nodded guardedly. For the first time, she looked properly at the man to whom she had entrusted her daughter. Still in his twenties, she thought, nice lips, lazy chocolate brown eyes under a big flat cap of mustard checks. She didn't know him, but he looked familiar – one of those faces you saw around the races; better looking than most. As far she knew, he wasn't a trainer or an agent. Besides, he had the voice, the clothes and easy self-confidence of a typical horse-owning toff. But there was none of that snotty, aren't-I-close-to-God-Almighty arrogance about him.

'Who are you then?' she asked.

'I suppose it's time I introduced myself.' He held out a hand. 'Eddie Sullivan.'

'I'm Jan . . .'

'I know who you are,' he interrupted her with another gleaming smile while he took her hand for a second. 'I saw you leading in Rear Gunner after he won at Ludlow.' Eddie laughed. 'Actually, I thought you were the owner's wife, until I asked around.' He nodded at a light chestnut gelding on the far side of the ring, now prancing diagonally along the perimeter path. 'So, as a winning hunter-chase trainer, I wonder if you'd mind telling me what you think of him?'

As it happened, she thought quite a lot.

She'd spotted the horse as soon as he was led into the ring and noticed he was thin, with a rough coat which obscured some of his finer qualities. She'd already decided that if he went cheaply enough, she'd buy him. 'That wouldn't be an easy horse to handle.'

As if to confirm her opinion, the horse suddenly got up on his toes and performed a lively, uncontrolled pirouette around his lad, before tossing his head in the air and trying to snatch the rope from his hands.

'Do you think you could teach him some manners?'

'I haven't found a horse yet that didn't respond to a bit of TLC.'

'Is that your secret?'

'It works better than bullying them.'

'Mm.' Eddie nodded thoughtfully. 'I don't know if he'd be right for the job I have in mind.'

'What job's that, then?'

'I'm looking for something to ride in the Foxhunters' at Aintree next year.'

She didn't miss the sudden glimmer of determination in Eddie's strong features. She took in the furrowed chin, tanned cheeks and crooked nose, acquired, she guessed, in some schoolboy skirmish on the rugby field. 'What, with you on board?' she asked, slightly amused.

He heard the hint of disbelief, but didn't resent it.

'I can do twelve stone,' he said, shaking his head to deny her implication.

'Have you ridden many hunter chases?'

'No, but I've ridden a few point-to-points.'

'Well,' she said, and looked at him. She wondered if he was flirting with her, or just probing her for whatever information she could give him. The knowledge she'd gathered from years of loving and handling horses didn't come easily, and she wouldn't normally have dished it out free, just for the sake of a pair of dark, sexy eyes. 'That horse definitely isn't the one for you,' she said, glad to be telling the truth, 'but I hope you find what you're looking for. And thanks a lot for what you did for Megan.' She flashed Eddie a sudden smile. 'I expect I'll see you later.'

Jan walked away, towing Megan. She tried to look as if she wasn't in a hurry, but the horse she and Eddie had been discussing was already being led towards the sale ring. She wanted to get there in time to put in a bid, and she didn't think there'd be many for such a scatty-looking animal.

Fifteen minutes later and fifteen hundred guineas poorer, Jan was telling her local horse transport company where to deliver her purchase.

She walked away from the stables feeling pleased with herself. After another look at the animal, she was sure that she was right, that his unpromising demeanour was a superficial problem, due to lack of confidence, and if there was one talent in which Jan was willing to take pride, it was her ability to restore a horse's self-esteem. This horse was definitely an improver, she thought.

In the seven tough but happy years she'd spent with John Hardy on the thin-soiled hills beyond Offa's Dyke, nearly all the horses she'd been asked to train and run in the local point-to-points had come to the job after blowing their earlier chances under rules; all of them had one dodge or another. If it was physical, she'd learned from her father as much as any vet about repairing horses; if it was a psychological problem, she was prepared to lavish as much time, understanding and patience as it took. Where others wouldn't have seen the problem, or invested the time, she'd found it was an investment that nearly always paid off.

Giving Megan her catalogue to carry, and clutching her hand very tightly this time, she walked back to the parade ring. She wanted a second look at another horse she'd already seen in the stable yard earlier in the day. It was due to be sold in about half an hour and she knew that its vendor liked to give his lots a good long show before they went through the sale ring.

She'd been standing on the rail in her usual spot, with her back to the agents' boxes, when she felt another body ease into the small gap beside her. She turned from her inspection of the half-dozen horses in the ring and found Eddie beside her again, thumbing through his catalogue. 'Hello, you back, then?'

Eddie didn't answer for a moment. He was looking at the black horse from Wexford he'd been considering when he'd first seen Jan that morning.

He glanced at her and saw that she was assessing it too. They both knew that they were small players in this market, having automatically filtered out any entries with heavy swathes of black type which indicated large numbers of illustrious forebears or proven form. They could only afford to get interested in animals that came with nothing to recommend them but their physique. 'He's rather handsome, isn't he?'

'Huh,' Jan grunted. 'That's a typical mug's eyeful.'

'But you like the look of him.'

'Yes, he's pretty all right, but not enough bone – especially not for the job you want him for.'

'How do you mean?'

'If you want something that'll carry twelve stone for three or four miles, there's no point looking at anything that's got the slightest question mark in that department. You need a rugby player not a ballet dancer.'

'All right. What sort of horse would you recommend for me rather than that one, which I must say', he added pointedly, 'I like very much?'

Jan couldn't help a grin. He'd neatly offered to back off the horse they both liked if she dispensed her advice for nothing.

'As it happens, when you told me what you were after, there was one which caught my eye, and he's just coming in the ring now.' She nodded at the opening. 'That dark bay, looks like a sort of Ploughman's Pickle horse. He's no oil painting,' she admitted, 'but he looks as honest as the day is long and he's bred to stay.'

Eddie looked doubtfully at the big-boned horse. 'He's got an arse the size of a barn door. Maybe he'd keep going, but would he be fast enough to win?'

Jan nodded. 'He'll win all right. I'd say by next spring that horse'll be well ready to run in a hunter chase. He's the right sort and he'd look after you.'

'What makes you think I need looking after?'

'Because I've never heard of you winning a race and at your age you should have done by now if you were any good.'

'I'm a late starter,' Eddie retorted.

'Then you'll certainly need looking after.'

Eddie thumbed through the catalogue resting on the rail in front of him.

'"Russian Eagle"', he read, '"won his first point-to-point in Ireland last year. He has been given time to mature." What the hell's that supposed to mean?'

Jan looked at him, and allowed the side of her mouth to turn up. 'If you don't already know and you're a serious buyer, you should get yourself a good agent.' She nodded over her shoulders at the row of small blue and white boxes that the bloodstock agents used as offices.

'Oh, come on,' Eddie cajoled her.

Jan relented. 'He's probably genuine enough. Looking at his breeding and his conformation; he'd be a bit slow maturing, that's all. His sire usually gets late developers so he's never been really fashionable. I wouldn't think he'd make a lot of money,' she went on, dropping any pretence that she wouldn't help Eddie. 'And if you do get him, I'd say he'd give a bloke like you as a good a chance of winning the Foxhunters' as any horse in this sale. In fact, you seem made for each other.'

Eddie was beginning to get caught up in her enthusiasm, when they both heard a soft, deep-throated chuckle behind them. They turned round together, and found themselves staring into the intense blue eyes of a racing legend.

A.D. O'Hagan, builder's mate from Killarney turned global currency speculator, owned at least fifty horses in training in Ireland and England. Now he was surrounded by a gaggle of hangers on. He had no need to attend the sales himself, but although A.D. – as he was universally known – could have bought every lot on offer without making much of a hole in his bank balance, Jan guessed he still liked the smell of a horse and a bargain, and had come just to relax.

Eddie's jaw dropped at the sudden ghastly thought that A.D. might like the same big horse that he was beginning to fancy himself.

Jan didn't seem to share that worry; but she found she couldn't help grinning under the powerful but benign gaze of this fabled owner.

'D'you like the look of him, then?' the Irishman asked Jan, nodding at Russian Eagle.

'Yes,' she nodded emphatically, not prepared to have her view swayed by an owner, even of A.D.'s magnificent scale. 'He'd take a bit of training, mind.'

'I tell you what, if anyone ever trained that great yoke to get round and win a half-decent race, I'd send 'em half a dozen horses of my own.'

The big Irishman gave her a patronizing but not unfriendly pat on the shoulder, and continued his promenade around the ring, trailing his entourage of agents, minders, aspiring young trainers, members of his racing staff and drinking partners from his humbler days.

'He's talking bollocks,' Eddie said. 'I bet he just fancies the animal for himself.'

'No, he doesn't,' Jan said, 'but don't let that put you off.'

'No.' Eddie laughed. 'What does he know, anyway? He only had a hundred and twenty winners last season.'

'So would you if you owned as many horses as he does.'

'You're right,' Eddie said, with his mind made up. 'When's this Ploughman's Pickle horse being sold, then?'

'Don't you want to see him have a trot first?'

'You have, haven't you?'

'Yes.'

'Then that's good enough for me.'

The auctioneer, sleek as a well-fed black cat, gazed around his audience with a hurt and slightly puzzled expression on his face. 'You don't buy good horses like this sitting on your hands, you know,' he admonished. 'Come on now, if you want to buy it you've got to bid for it. This would be a proper trainer's horse. Masses of potential in him. He's already got off the mark at a quality point-to-point in Ireland. Come on, somebody put me in at five thousand.'

He swept the sea of faces with his eyes, in unison with the spotters behind him. 'All right, three, then. Who'll give me three to get us started?'

Jan found herself thinking about the auction in Hay-on-Wye a month ago when Stonewall Farm had been sold for not a penny more than her reserve price. Without warning, out of nowhere, a disturbing new thought began to creep into her mind. But she was distracted when, across the ring, she spotted to her horror that Eddie was about to raise his hand. She concentrated on him and, when she had caught his eye, shook her head very faintly. Relieved, she saw him allow his hand, already level with his waist, to drop back, while they watched the auctioneer still struggle for his opening bid.

'Come on now, ladies and gentlemen. He may not be Twiggy; at least he's got plenty of bone . . . Two thousand? All right, thank you, sir, a thousand guineas I'm bid.' And now that he was off, his voice cranked up a gear and his whole bearing became optimistic once again as he took another bid for twelve hundred.

Eddie gave Jan a big smile. He looked very grateful that she had nodded at him to stay his hand earlier. The auctioneer was already stuck at seventeen hundred, looking for the next bid of eighteen hundred. His gavel was in the air, hovering reluctantly above the top of his pulpit, when Eddie gave a slight nod. The auctioneer's eye, sharp as a buzzard's, picked it up at once and he pounced.

'New bidder,' he crowed. 'It's with you, sir, at the back.' He turned to the last bidder. 'Don't lose him now. You don't often get a chance to buy a horse this size.' He ignored the ripple of titters that ran through the crowd.

A moment later his hardwood hammer hit the top of the desk and Russian Eagle was knocked down to Edward Sullivan for one thousand, eight hundred guineas.

Outside, Jan saw Eddie following his new possession back to the stable, where the horse had spent two nights since he had arrived from Ireland to be sold. Jan didn't think the people who'd brought him all that way would be at all happy with the price they'd got, especially after the auctioneers took their five per cent. But the groom smiled affably enough. 'You'll have a lot of fun with him; sure he's a great horse, wonderful nature and a real Christian. Where's he to go?'

'Back to my place in Gloucestershire for now,' Eddie said.

'Do you have transport?'

'I haven't organized it yet.'

'We'll drop him off for you, on our way back to Fishguard. What's the address?'

'Hang on,' Jan interrupted. 'Now you've got him, who's going to train him for you?'

Eddie grinned. 'I don't know. I haven't decided yet.'

'You're not very good at making decisions, are you?'

'I'm all right at decisions,' Eddie protested. 'It's the choosing that's the hard part.'

'Well, I chose the horse for you, so I may as well choose the trainer – no extra charge.'

'Fine,' Eddie laughed. 'Where shall I send him?'

With a smile, Jan turned to the Irish lad who was waiting to be told. 'Stonewall Farm, Painscastle, near Hay-on-Wye.'

Jan drove home with Megan. For the first half-hour of the journey, the little girl chatted away about everything she'd seen and heard. To Jan's relief, she seemed fully recovered from her scare in the parade ring.

'Mum, why didn't you buy a horse?'

'I did, that skinny one,' Jan said, thinking of her fifteen hundred guinea purchase. 'A man with a lorry's bringing him back for us. I was supposed to find a good one for Mr Powell as well, but they were all too expensive.' She wondered what Harold would say when she told him she hadn't found him a horse. 'But the kind man who saved you from being kicked has bought a nice big horse and he's sending it to us, then we'll take it with us to the new farm.'

Megan's eyes lit up at the thought of the new farm. 'I can't wait to live in a caravan!' she said.

Jan smiled as Megan's eyelids fluttered down and a few moments later she was fast asleep.

In the evening, as Jan was putting Megan to bed, Eddie Sullivan's horse arrived at Stonewall. Through the window she saw a lorry creeping up the farm drive.

Outside the sun was still above the purple ridges in the west and the old stone buildings glowed in its oblique rays. Jan hurried downstairs and out of the house as the lorry pulled up just inside the gate. The young driver jumped down: it was the man who had handled the horse at the sale. He seemed happy to be on his way home as he dropped the ramp and led out the horse. Jan continued down the steps, towards the big bay, wondering, for a moment, if her judgement had been right. The man saw her and grinned.

'Hello there! Here's your new tenant.' He looked around at Jan's tidy yard and nodded with approval. He glanced up at the horse's head and gave its lower lip an affectionate tug. 'You'll be happy here, Eagle,' he said. 'A lovely yard and a beautiful lady to make a fuss of you. I'm quite envious, actually.'

Jan couldn't help grinning. She thought she didn't mind whether the man was fond of the horse, or just using him for some unsubtle flirting.

'Do you work in the yard that sold him?' she asked.

'Oh yes. I'm what you might call the general dogsbody.'

'Do you know this horse?'

'I do.'

'And—?'

'He's as good as gold. I told yer man, he's real Christian. And he'll gallop faster than you'd think, though he can take a bit of a hold.'

Jan nodded as she stroked the horse's broad snout. She wondered how strong a rider Eddie Sullivan was. He was certainly a well-built, athletic sort, she thought, and not carrying any surplus weight. 'I think young Mr Sullivan could have some fun with him.'

The Irishman shrugged. 'He seemed a touch green to me, but he must know something about the job; he's Ron Sullivan's boy. Right,' he went on with unexpected decisiveness, 'I've got a ferry to catch.' He handed the head-collar rope to Jan. 'Best of luck with him. And if ever you're over in Killarney lookin' at horses, be sure to call by and see us.'

Jan led Russian Eagle into a box on the front that she'd had vacated for him.

The stocky Irishman whistled as he raised the tail ramp on his now empty lorry and shot the bolts home. 'Goodbye to you, Mrs Hardy,' he called while she was still unbuckling the horse's head-collar in his box. 'And don't forget, a woman with a good eye like yours will always be welcome at Castlefort Stables.'

The horse headed for the rack full of fresh hay at the back of the box and Jan let herself out as the driver was already swinging up into his cab.

'Don't we owe you something for transport?' she called.

'No. It was on my way. Light a little candle for me if you want. God bless.'

He banged the door shut, fired up a noisy engine and manoeuvred the lorry out of the yard and down the drive.

As he went, Jan watched him. She was beginning to learn that people in the horse world were no more subject to stereotyping or prejudiced reputation than those in any other human activity. She'd already met with real kindness, and blunt ruthlessness, when she'd been least expecting them. These anomalies didn't surprise her so much now, but it hadn't even remotely occurred to her that Eddie Sullivan might be Ron Sullivan's son.

Now she realized why Eddie had seemed vaguely familiar. She was barely ten when she'd heard people talking about Ron Sullivan, who had come to the Cotswolds and bought one of the biggest houses in the area. Now Jan guessed she must have come across Eddie since then, perhaps around the local point-to-points, though it must have been when he was still a teenager.

But she had never met Ron in Gloucestershire or at the races. She'd seen him once or twice a few years before, when he'd been on a high and owned a lot of good horses in one of the big Lambourn yards, though not so much had been seen of him recently. She'd never had a conversation with him, but she'd read about him in the racing papers, she'd seen him interviewed on the television and she couldn't begin to match him to a son like Eddie.

As she watched the Irish lorry rumble out of sight down the

lane, her thoughts were interrupted as another one appeared and turned up towards the house. A few minutes later, she was leading her fifteen hundred guineas' worth of scatty chestnut gelding into his new home beside Russian Eagle.

'He's lovely,' Annabel laughed. 'But he's so big!'

She and Jan were in Russian Eagle's stable next morning. It was nine o'clock and the children were already down at their grandmother's bungalow. When Annabel arrived, Jan had been about to take Lazy Dove out for a little work on his own. He was one of only two horses in her yard still entered to run before the end of the season in two weeks' time.

With the rest of the horses turned out or at home for the summer, Jan had laid off her lads a fortnight before, to keep costs down during the lean time. But Annabel hadn't come to work that morning; she simply wanted to see what new horses Jan had bought.

'He is big, but I still like the look of him,' Jan said. 'And the little bloke who dropped him off said he could certainly gallop. Mind you, he said he took a bit of holding as well, and I don't think this chap who's bought him knows what he's doing.'

'Who is he?'

Jan laughed. 'It's funny really. I met him in the most extraordinary way.' She told Annabel about the manic horse that had gone on the rampage and lashed out at Megan. 'I was terrified when I turned round and couldn't see her, but this man had just dived in and lifted her out of the way. I was so relieved, I even let him take her off to get an ice cream before I knew who he was.'

'Well, who was he, for God's sake?' Annabel laughed impatiently as she stroked Russian Eagle's nose.

'Oh, nobody you'd know.' Jan stopped. 'Though, come to think of it, you might. Have you ever heard of Ron Sullivan?'

'What?' Annabel sounded shocked. 'A big, flashy property tycoon covered in gold rings and bracelets? *He* dived and saved Meg?' she asked with disbelief.

'No, no! Not him. His son, Eddie.'

'Eddie?' Annabel gasped and suddenly took her hand off the horse's nose as if it were red hot.

'A-ha! I thought you'd know him.' Jan started to laugh, but stopped when she saw Annabel's face. 'Do you really know him?'

Annabel nodded. 'You could say so. He was at school with Charley, my brother. They were in the same year and the same house, and Eddie Sullivan was always a bit of a hero – you know, a rugger star, played in a rock band.' Annabel gave a rueful laugh. 'It was a rotten band, looking back on it, but at the time I thought it was just the best and Eddie was very popular. I must have been about thirteen when I first met him. I suppose I built him up into a sort of fantasy figure and I was absolutely besotted with him for a long time after that.'

'So, how well did you know him?' Jan asked, intrigued, as well as amused by the coincidence.

Annabel sighed. 'He was my first boyfriend.'

'Good Lord! Was he your first lover too?'

Annabel walked to the stable door and leaned over the bottom half with her back to Jan. 'Yes,' she nodded.

'Oh dear,' Jan murmured. 'What went wrong? Was he a bastard?'

'No, not really. It wasn't his fault, but it caused some massive rows in my family, I can tell you. My father didn't like him at all – he particularly didn't like the fact that Ron Sullivan is his father. It was awful. I'll tell you about it some time, but not now. And I'd rather you didn't mention what I've said to Eddie. I mean, he was only twenty-three at the time, though I think he'd already had a lot of girlfriends.'

'None of the men I went out with were ever that popular – in fact I don't think John had really been serious about anybody before me,' Jan said. 'Still, I think I know why you're worried, but if you decide to come with me to Edge Farm I should warn you that I think Eddie'll be around quite a bit. He wants to ride his horse in the Foxhunters' at Aintree.'

'I was going to tell you today. I *do* want to come! It's just the excuse I need to get away from home without being too far from Mum, and I'm bloody well not going to let something that happened five years ago spoil it for me!'

'That's great! You can live in the caravan with me and the kids.'

'No, don't worry. You'll need some space for yourself. I'll rent somewhere in the village, but I'll come and help you with the move and sort things out over the summer – as a friend, I mean. You won't have to pay me or anything, not till you get the horses back in.'

Jan looked at her friend in amazement. It seemed almost incredible that someone should offer to be so helpful without any obvious benefit to herself. 'Bel, if you come, that would be great, but I'd have to pay you, especially if you're going to look after the kids and everything. I was going to see if I could get an au pair anyway.'

'All right,' Annabel said, understanding Jan's embarrassment at the offer of free help. 'Pay me what you would have had to pay the au pair.'

'It'll be so nice to have a familiar face around, especially when I first move.'

'Have you got a date yet?'

'I've got to be out of here by June the twelfth. That's three weeks tomorrow. The removal people are coming next week and Philip's dad is helping me with all the hay and other horse stuff.'

'What are you doing now?'

'I was just about to take Lazy Dove out.'

'Can I come with you?'

'There's only Gale Bird left who needs exercise. You could ride her and save me doing it later.'

'Great! I'll go and tack her up.'

They took their time, hacking the horses across the hills. With the larks trilling upwards in a soft breeze under a sky of patchy blue and white, Jan began to think for the first time about what it would be like to move away.

'You're right,' she admitted to Annabel. 'I will miss the summer mornings up here. I don't really know where I'm going to ride out from Edge Farm for long exercise, but there won't be anything like the freedom I have here.'

'It's too late to change your mind now.' Annabel laughed.

'I haven't. I'm just admitting that I'll miss the hills a little.'

They chatted about Jan's plans for Edge Farm and how she hoped to attract a few ailing or problem horses into the yard to keep her busy during the summer. 'When you think about it, I only have the pointers from September through to May, if I'm lucky, and I'll still need some income from June to August.'

'Then you'll definitely need help. Phil's not coming over is he?'

'No. I'm fond of Phil, but in this new yard I don't intend to carry any passengers. Anyone I employ is going to have to do their job when they're supposed to and in the way I tell them. With horses, you can't keep taking your eye off the ball because you're looking over your shoulder at your staff all the time.'

'Does that include me, then?' Annabel asked with a grin.

'For God's sake, I'd never have to worry about you!'

As they reached the brow of the hill above Stonewall Farm, they could see right the way to the bottom of the valley, where the lane joined the Kington road. A car had just turned off the main road and was speeding between the hedges faster than any local car would have done.

'I wonder who that is,' Jan murmured.

'It's some kind of flashy convertible; must be a lost tourist.'

As they dropped down the track from the common land to the farm, they glimpsed the car again.

'It's coming to see you, Jan!' Annabel laughed as the car stopped at the bottom of the drive for a few seconds, before turning in and making its way much more slowly up the deeply rutted track towards Jan's yard. 'Do you know who it is?'

'I haven't a clue.'

'It's one of those new drop-head Mercedes,' Annabel said with a hint of disapproval. 'What on earth's it doing up here?'

They lost sight of the car behind the buildings, but they heard it stop, and the engine turn off. Jan and Annabel almost held their breaths as they clattered down the last few yards of the track, round the back of the barn and into the yard.

A man in a dark-brown leather flying jacket was sitting on the stone mounting block with his back to them. A thin plume of smoke drifted above his head.

Both feeling a little fazed by this unlikely looking visitor, Jan and Annabel slid off their horses. Annabel hung back as he turned to greet them.

It was Eddie Sullivan.

'Good morning,' he said with a big, lazy smile at Jan.

Jan nodded and smiled back.

Annabel stepped forward and drew in a quick breath. 'Hi, Eddie.'

He looked at her more sharply and took a moment to recognize her under her helmet. 'Bel! What on earth are you doing here?'

'Bel's my head groom,' Jan said, 'the backbone of my yard.'

'How extraordinary! I picked the right yard, then,' Eddie said, betraying nothing of what Annabel had told Jan earlier that morning. He stood up, brushing dust and moss from his jeans, and stubbed out a small cigar on the cobbles. 'I hope you don't mind me turning up like this, but I'm on my way to Brecon and I couldn't wait to see my new horse. I wanted to make sure I hadn't just got carried away bidding for him yesterday. He is here, isn't he?'

'Yes. The groom who was looking after him at the sales dropped him off last night. He's in the end box.' Jan nodded at Russian Eagle's stable and Eddie walked over to it.

'Go on in, if you want,' Jan called. 'We're just going to put these horses away, then we'll have a look at yours.'

'God, the world's a small place sometimes,' Annabel muttered.

'I'm not complaining,' Jan answered under her breath. 'He's not my type, but he seems a nice guy. Now he's one of my clients you'll just have to try and get on with him.'

'I will, once I've got used to the idea. But you go and deal with him, Jan. I'll put these two in their stables.' She took Lazy Dove's head and walked both horses round to the back yard.

Jan looked over Eagle's door and found Eddie with his arm around the horse's neck.

He glanced at her with a grin. 'He may be as fat as Billy Bunter, but he's sure as hell got a placid temperament.'

'I haven't had a chance to look at him properly since he got here. I'll pull him out so we can get a better look at him.'

Eddie stepped aside while Jan buckled on a head-collar and led the horse out.

'He doesn't look quite so vast outside the stable,' he said.

'Don't worry about his size. I've seen bigger horses win races and he's carrying plenty of condition. He must have been on some really good grass over in Ireland before they sent him to the sales. He's obviously a good doer. He'd finished every bit of hay when I went in earlier this morning.'

'When do you think I could ride him?' Eddie asked.

Jan looked at him and couldn't help smiling. There was an unexpected, engaging naivety about him. She still found it hard to see how he could be the son of the notorious Ron, about whom rumours of commercial wizardry and anecdotes of skulduggery circulated in equal quantities. She was well aware, though, that among thoroughbred horses, for example, stallions often didn't stamp their stock, while the mare's qualities were more likely to be passed on.

'I'd leave him for a bit. Let him settle and get used to us. Then in two weeks' time, we're all moving to my new yard in Gloucestershire.'

'Are you? Where exactly?'

'Edge Farm, Stanfield.'

'Great! That's much nearer me.'

'Where do you live then?' Jan asked innocently.

'In Nether Swell, near Stow.'

'I thought you might. That's near my mum and dad, at Riscombe.'

'I heard you came from there.'

'Been doing your homework, then?' Jan asked, pleased that he had.

Eddie nodded. 'So, why are you moving back?'

'My husband died in January. This was his farm and I didn't want to stay here without him. Besides, I've got to make a living. I've got two young kids.'

'I've already met one of them,' Eddie reminded her.

'I never thanked you properly for that,' Jan said. 'It all happened in such a rush. It was being at the sales, I suppose. It always gets me wound up.'

'It's meant to, that's part of the whole thing – to give the auction as much sense of drama as possible; it makes people excited and clouds their judgement. It happens to me all the time at picture sales.'

'Is that what you do?' Jan didn't hide her surprise. 'I thought people who dealt in art were usually—'. Her voice petered out in embarrassment.

'Gay?' Eddie grinned. 'How do you know I'm not? Would you mind if I were?'

'No. It wouldn't matter one iota to me. My dad used to call a horse "gay" if he was a playful and lively character, but with all this political correctness you can't say it now. And – you might have gathered – I'm not very good at being PC. But anyway, you're not gay,' she added with a laugh. 'I know that.'

'How do you know?'

'From the way you look at women.'

Eddie looked at her and raised an eyebrow. 'Is that so?'

Neither of them spoke for a moment and Jan suddenly felt she'd gone too far. She'd been determined, since she'd suggested he sent his horse to her, that she would treat Eddie in a thoroughly professional manner, and now here she was, as soon as she saw him again, flirting with him, as good as telling him that she fancied him – which she did, but only in an arms' length, academic sort of way. The memory of John was still too fresh for her to contemplate any kind of physical relationship.

'Anyway,' she hurried on, 'I think you should leave riding Russian Eagle for a bit. Once he's settled in at Edge Farm, we could bring him in early and I'll take him out and exercise him a little to see how he behaves, then I could start schooling you both.'

She looked up and saw Eddie smiling at her slightly flustered delivery, and, perhaps, at the idea of her schooling him.

'Whatever you say. I'll allow you to be the boss in our relationship in all matters equine. I won't attempt to ride the horse until you say so, and I promise to obey all your commands. In the meantime, I wouldn't mind taking another look at him.'

'It's a bit late for that, isn't it? He's already here, but I'll trot him up, just for you, so you haven't had a wasted journey.'

Jan tugged the horse's rope and, setting off at a brisk jog, she gee'd him into a surprisingly elegant trot. Going a little faster, she extended it until she got to the gate, where she turned and jogged back.

'He does look lighter when he's moving,' Eddie said.

Jan nodded. 'That's what I thought yesterday. Let's hope he can jump and gallop, too. Now, have you seen enough?'

'Yes thanks.'

'Then I'll put him away. Would you like a cup of coffee up at the house?'

Eddie looked a his watch. 'No, thanks. I've got a date to look at some pictures in a house the other side of Brecon and I'm late already.' He took his car keys from the pocket of his leather jacket. 'Would you send me details of your charges? Here's my address.' He handed her a card with 'The Sullivan Gallery' and an address in Stow-on-the-Wold printed on it. 'And say goodbye to Annabel for me. Tell her I'm looking forward to seeing her again when you move to Gloucestershire. Is she coming with you, by the way?'

Jan, still holding Russian Eagle, tilted her head to one side. 'To tell you the truth, I'm not sure now.'

'I hope she does,' Eddie said. He walked to his car, opened the door and dropped into the driver's seat.

By the time Annabel came round the corner from the back yard, he was already passing the bungalow at the bottom of the drive.

In the weeks following the Doncaster Sales, Jan had to put most of her energy into moving. Olwen Hardy seemed to have accepted at last that her daughter-in-law and grandchildren were leaving Stonewall – at least, she was co-operative about having the children while Jan was busy.

Jan had not foreseen how harrowing the process of dismantling a household could be. Stonewall had been first occupied by John's parents in 1948, and in a large house with a lot of storage space very little had been thrown out since then. There were piles of musty books and linen, old domestic appliances, crockery, cutlery, kitchen utensils, farm accounts and records, innumerable household knick-knacks, lamps, ornaments – a seemingly endless catalogue of modest, serviceable objects.

Sorting it all and trying to decide what to keep, what to sell, what to give away and what to take to the tip involved some difficult decisions, but Jan was determined to be methodical and logical about the job. She had been given a lot of tea chests and cardboard boxes by the firm in Hereford who were going to do the main move for her. Besides these, she had found a pile of empty trunks and suitcases in one of the attics. Everything she thought she shouldn't discard until she'd had a proper look at it she packed into them and then labelled them to be stored in the Dutch barn at Edge Farm. For the time being all these items, and the furniture she wanted to keep for the house which she hoped one day would appear at Edge Farm, were to be kept in the barn, raised off the ground and covered by tarpaulins.

Dealing with John's personal possessions upset her far more than she could have imagined. Going through his chests of drawers and his cupboards, seeing the selection of clothes passed on from his father and in some instances, she suspected, from his grandfather, and his own practical purchases, as well as a few more colourful items she had bought for him, was like having him back in the room with her.

She picked up a Fair Isle sweater he'd always liked, buried her face in it and was instantly transported back by the evocative odours trapped in its fibres. When she found the shirt he had worn on the day they were married, which he had never worn again, she couldn't hold back the tears any longer.

Surrounded by a heap of unassuming, well-worn workaday clothing, she sat on the floor and cried helplessly.

Matthew, she thought, *is never going to want any of this, not even in twenty years' time*.

She went downstairs and brought up a roll of black plastic bags she had bought for the purpose and stuffed all the clothes into them, until she had ten full sacks which she labelled 'Oxfam'. One by one she carried them all down to the back hall, ready to take with her next time she went to Hay. She felt better after that. She was sure that was what John would have wanted her to do.

That night, to her surprise, she slept a little better.

When she woke, she lay in bed thinking about John and his mother.

She tried to imagine how she would feel if she lost one of her children before she died and realized she could think of nothing worse. Whatever Olwen might think of her, she had have loved her son very much.

With a sudden rush of guilt, she went down and carried all the plastic bags back up, emptied them and arranged the contents in neat piles around the room.

For the rest of the morning she carried on sorting and tidying John's possessions. When she came across a beautifully crafted eighteenth-century gold fob watch, engraved with the initials of some former Hardy, complete with its chain and crude letter seal, she picked it out to give to Olwen.

Later, after she'd checked the horses, she walked down to the bungalow with Tigger and knocked on the door.

Olwen opened it and stared at her as if she were a total stranger.

'Good morning, Olwen,' she said, fishing in a carrier bag she'd brought with her. 'I've brought down something of John's that I thought you might like to have.'

She took out the watch, which she had polished and wrapped in tissue paper, and passed it to the old woman.

Olwen took the package suspiciously and unwrapped it. She looked at the watch, turned it over and handed it back to Jan. 'I can't have this,' she said. 'It should go to his son. It's always been passed down from father to son.'

'Oh,' Jan said, feeling foolish. 'I'm sorry. Is there something else more personal you'd like instead? Maybe some of his clothes . . .?'

Olwen looked at her disdainfully. 'What would I want with any of his clothes?'

'I meant, as a sort of memento.'

'I'll come up, later, before tea, and select some items,' Olwen said firmly.

'Oh,' Jan said, taken by surprise. Olwen had declined every invitation to come up to the house since she had moved out of it. 'Fine. I'll try and have everything out for you to look at.'

Jan went back to prepare for Olwen's visit and wondered what she would choose. She decided that before she came she had better go through John's bureau, which stood against one wall of the sitting room and had always been locked except when John had been working at it.

Jan hadn't wanted to open it since he had gone, although she'd had to a few times to find bank statements and correspondence with MAFF, which John kept in there. Now she emptied all the drawers and pigeon-holes and spread out the contents.

Sitting on the floor in the middle of the room, she found several packets of photographs, for the most part grainy, monochrome shots taken with a rudimentary camera, but clear enough. One showed John when he was a boy of eight or nine, standing with his father, who was shearing a sheep in what was just recognizable as the yard outside. There was another of John when he was even younger, perhaps five, with a huge smile, sitting in front of his father on the pony old Mr Hardy had used to shepherd his flock out on the mountain.

In a small folder of its own, she found a more recent, good-quality colour photograph, taken six years before. She stared at it for a few moments, took it from its folder and turned it over. When she read the inscription, she sat back on her haunches and cried again.

'Jan? Are you all right?'

Jan looked up and saw Annabel, standing in the doorway with a sympathetic expression on her face.

Jan sniffed and nodded. 'I just found this,' she said. 'I've never seen it before and I never even knew he had it.' She held out the photograph for Annabel to see. It was a shot of a horse, obviously soon after winning a race, with Billy Hanks up, and grinning all over his face. On either side of the horse stood John, tall, dark, healthy and smiling shyly, and Jan, twenty-three years old, fresh, vital and beaming as if she would burst.

On the reverse, in John's old-fashioned writing were the words: *Jan's first winner – a Proud Moment!*

Jan saw a few tears glisten in Annabel's eyes, too, and she felt better for having shared a little of her grief.

Annabel handed back the photo. 'Isn't it wonderful that he never told you he had it?'

Jan nodded. 'I can just about remember someone taking a picture. But John wasn't much of a one for photographs and I would never have expected him to get a copy.'

'Look, Jan, as I was coming up the drive I saw Olwen on her way here. I thought you might want to be ready for her.'

Jan got to her feet. 'Yes, thanks. I wonder if she's expecting tea. Probably not, but I'll get it all ready anyway, just to give her the satisfaction of saying she doesn't want it.'

As it turned out, Jan was wrong. Olwen spent half an hour wandering around the house and rummaging through all the things that Jan had sorted out.

Jan left her to it and sat in the kitchen with the children, giving them their tea, until the white-haired old woman walked in.

'I'll have some tea', she said, 'in the parlour.'

Jan took a tray of the best cups and saucers through into the sitting room, where she found Olwen sitting upright on one of the old sofas, looking intently at the picture over the mantelpiece.

She said nothing. Jan poured some tea and waited.

'I'll have the clock in the hall', Olwen said eventually, without preamble, 'and that picture.' She nodded in the direction of the mantelpiece.

The painting, though probably not of great quality, was, Jan thought, the most interesting thing in the house. In a crude version of Herring's style, it depicted a sporting horse being held by a scruffy groom against a background of an unmistakably Welsh hill, which John had identified. He had always said the picture had almost certainly been painted for one of the big land-owning families of the Usk valley, who had historically kept horses to race in harness. He had had no idea how the family had acquired it.

Jan winced. She knew Olwen had asked for it precisely because she herself liked it. And more particularly because it depicted a horse.

Jan bit her lip and nodded. 'That'll be nice for you, Olwen, but I'm worried about the clock. Do you have a room high enough to put it in?'

'Yes,' Olwen said, prepared for the objection. 'It can go in the hall, where the ceiling goes into the gable.'

'Fine,' Jan said. 'I'll ask the removal men to drop it in to you when they go past.'

'Can you bring the picture down before?'

Jan sighed. 'Yes, Olwen, of course.'

Olwen's visit did a lot to bring Jan back to earth. Once she had taken the picture down to the bungalow, she found she could throw herself into finishing the packing with all her usual energy, until, on the second Saturday after Doncaster, between finally clearing up and organizing the removal firm, she went to the races for the last point-to-point of the season in the area.

She took Gale Bird and Lazy Dove with Philip, who had volunteered to come for the day and help.

It was the first time Lazy Dove had run since he'd been chased off the course by a hare at Llandeilo, but Jan was confident from the work he'd been doing at home that he'd recovered from the experience.

She was right. The tough little gelding battled hard to finish third, within two lengths of the winner.

But the highlight of the day and, as far as Jan was concerned, a fitting finale to her fourth year's training at Stonewall was seeing her own mare, Gale Bird, romp home in the adjacent hunts' race, despite Billy Hanks being unable to take advantage of her five-pound mare's allowance. This was the mare's second consecutive win, giving Jan a final score for the season of fourteen wins between the flags, and the hunter chase at Ludlow – enough to make her champion trainer for the region.

But she had failed to keep a check on Phil's celebrations after the race and, tired as she was, she had to drive the lorry home herself while he slumped across the bench seat beside her and snored. She was glad this was the last time she would have to worry about him, but even so she was going to miss him.

Jan's mind wandered and she found herself thinking of other things she would miss in the valley that had been her home for the last seven years and, without warning, the idea of leaving the place where she'd been happy with John moved her to tears. She blinked, and glanced through blurred eyes at Philip, grateful now that he was sound asleep. But somehow she managed to work her way through the conflicting emotions of the day and she arrived home satisfied with what she'd achieved so far.

She was also pleased when, the week before she finally moved, she was given a strong indication of her success as a trainer. A journalist from *Horse & Hound* came to Stonewall to interview her, which gave her the chance to announce to the racing world that the next season she would be at a much more accessible yard in Gloucestershire.

Since her offer for Edge Farm had been accepted at the beginning of May, Jan had been searching for a good-sized mobile home that she and the children could live in while she earned enough money to build a new house there. She had found a serviceable second-hand one on a holiday site down by the River Wye.

The owner recognized Jan from his days at the races. He knew her circumstances and insisted that she pay only for its transport to Gloucestershire. In return, he suggested, she might like to give him a call some time when she had a runner she fancied. Jan was deeply impressed by such generosity and couldn't think what she'd done to deserve it from a complete stranger.

The caravan arrived at the new yard a few days before she was due to move. Leaving the children with Olwen, she drove over right away to prepare it and organize the electricity supply. Towards the end of the afternoon she found herself standing in the cramped living area, wondering if, after the rambling space of Stonewall, she'd been rather too optimistic in thinking she could live there with two small children and all their clutter. It was at this low moment that Annabel arrived, bringing with her a bottle of wine and a bunch of flowers to cheer Jan up. She had also brought a present for Megan – an exquisite doll's house, eighteen inches high and filled with miniature furniture and tiny Persian rugs.

'I hope you don't mind,' she said, putting it on the table and opening it up to show Jan. 'I know you're pushed for space, but I thought Megan might be really upset about leaving Stonewall and this could be a little house of her own.'

'Annabel!' Jan said, moved by her kindness. 'It's wonderful and she'll love it, but you can't give it to her. It must be worth a fortune.'

Annabel shrugged her slender shoulders with a smile. 'That doesn't matter. I haven't played with it for yonks and I want her to have it.'

'But you should keep it for when you've got a daughter of your own.'

Annabel, who had been rearranging some of the tiny furniture, paused and said nothing for a moment before closing the front of the house.

Jan looked at her closely. 'What's the matter? Don't you want to keep it for your own family?'

Annabel glanced up at her. 'No, it's OK,' she said quietly. 'I'll worry about that when the time comes and it would make me so happy to give it to Megan.'

Once Jan and Annabel had spruced up the caravan, they went out to take a look at the buildings. As they strolled around the farm, it came home to Jan just how much she was going to have to do to make the place work.

'It's all very well Dad saying I just need to knock up a few partitions and sling a tarpaulin over the roof, but how the hell am I going to find a builder I can trust to do it before all the horses arrive? What are the owners going to think, seeing their horses housed like that?'

Annabel put a hand on her forearm. 'Jan, stop fretting. There are no more races this season. There's no reason why all the horses can't go straight out. There's masses of grass in the paddocks.'

Jan nodded. 'I suppose so, but looking at this—', she waved a hand at the derelict barn, 'it suddenly all seems a bit much – the idea of living in a caravan with the children among all these ruins.'

'It'll be great, Jan! You know you can do it. I tell you what – why don't we go to the pub in the village now and start asking around for someone to come up and do the work for you?'

As they drove down the deeply rutted track to the road, Jan spotted several pieces of broken fencing. 'They'd better start with replacing some of these knackered rails,' she said gloomily.

The Fox & Pheasant had been a pub since the seventeenth century and hadn't changed much since that time. When she saw the people in there – healthy Gloucestershire faces like her own – she guessed that most of them were descended from the men who'd used the inn for the last few hundred years.

A tall girl in her twenties with chubby cheeks, big breasts and spiky black hair was behind the bar when Jan and Annabel walked in. She gave Jan a quick, shrewd glance with her chocolate brown eyes. 'Hello, I'm Julie,' she said. 'You're the people moving into Edge Farm, aren't you?'

'She is,' Annabel disclaimed. 'I'm not, but I'll be helping out there and I'm looking for a cottage to rent in the village.'

'Oh well, you want to talk to him, then,' the barmaid nodded at a well-dressed, somewhat forbidding man sitting alone with his pewter mug on a settle in a dark corner of the pub.

'Thanks, I will.'

While Annabel walked over to talk to the unlikely looking landlord, Jan perched on a stool and told Julie that she needed a builder. A few minutes later she was being introduced to Gerry.

A local lad of twenty-five, Gerry was six foot three with a red face and hands like shovels, one of which he thrust forward shyly for Jan to shake.

'You're a builder, are you?' she asked.

'Joiner,' he mumbled. 'But I can do pretty much anything.'

'And you wouldn't try to stitch me up, just because I'm a woman?'

Gerry looked shocked at the thought. 'No – just the opposite, I should think, for someone as . . . someone like you.'

Jan smiled and wondered how he had been going to describe her. 'That's good, because once I've got my stables up, there's a whole house to build.'

She told him what had to be done first and he didn't need much persuading to come up and price the job. Doing his best to overcome his embarrassment, he was still thanking her for the opportunity when Annabel came back from her discussion with the old man on the settle.

'I think I might have found a cottage already,' she said. 'Mr Carey seems to own half the village.'

Julie, earwigging beside them, nodded. 'He does, and Stanfield Court. He's a miserable old git, though,' she added under her breath.

'Well, he's very kindly offered me', she glanced at the piece of paper where she'd written the address, 'Number Two, Glebe Cottages.'

'That's a nice little place,' Julie said, 'but he'll want an arm and a leg.'

'Judging by the way he was looking at her,' Jan said, 'it's not her arms he's interested in.'

'Oh, he's all right like that,' the barmaid said. 'Just bloody stingy.'

'Will you come and look at it with me?' Annabel asked Jan. 'He says he'll go and get the key now if I want.'

A quarter of an hour later they were inspecting the cottage, which was freshly painted but hadn't been modernized in the previous twenty years. 'I expect I can manage without a Poggenpohl kitchen.' Annabel laughed and turned to Jan. 'Do you know, this is the first time in my life that I'll be living on my own? Apart from school, I've only been away from home for a short time when I went to London, and for a few months in a hall of residence at Bristol, before that all went wrong too,' she murmured.

'You've never told me what happened there,' Jan said quietly.

'I was on the rebound – a lecherous don. I was so gullible—.' Annabel shook her head. 'I suppose I was trying to get back at my father.' With an effort, she smiled. 'I don't want to start banging on about it now. I love this place.'

And within ten minutes she'd made up her mind to take the cottage.

They had decided to go back to Stonewall that evening, where Annabel would stay the night. Annabel drove them in her Golf, promising they'd get back half an hour quicker than they would in the Land Rover.

On the way home Jan laughed at the ease with which Annabel had been accommodated. 'It's just not fair the way men fall over backwards to do favours for tall, skinny, beautiful women, when people like me have to work so hard at it.'

'What are you talking about?' Annabel grinned back. 'You had that lumbering great builder eating out of your hands and you know it. He looked besotted the minute he clapped eyes on you.'

'That's just because he thought I might be a good punter,' Jan said with a cynical grunt.

Jan wondered, though, if that was the only reason, when she and Annabel arrived back at the farm next morning and found Gerry had already been up and repaired all the broken fencing he could find.

'Least you'll be able to keep your horses in when they gets here. I thought that was the most important thing,' he said gruffly.

'It was, Gerry. Thanks very much. Now, have you had a look at the barn? I've drawn up a sort of a plan for what I want. I've got it in the caravan.'

By 12 June, Jan's moving day, Gerry had already made a good start on a run of solid stables within the stone walls of the barn and every square inch of the roof had been covered in old-fashioned khaki canvas tarpaulins. They didn't stand out too harshly against the hillside and the puddles in the barn had already disappeared. Reg had been over with his chain harrow to breathe some new life into the pasture, and with his billhook to repair the hedges. He was delighted to be useful and he was as excited as Jan at the imminent arrival of the horses.

At Stonewall in the morning Matthew was too young to understand the significance of the journey they were making that day, but Megan knew she was leaving the only home she'd ever known. Jan was aware that she still hadn't got used to losing her Dad and guessed that she didn't want to lose her home as well. Until then, Megan had never even spent so much as a single night away from Stonewall.

'Mum,' she said, as she refused to eat her cereal in the empty, echoing kitchen, 'how can I sleep if I'm not in my own room?'

'Meg, don't worry. You'll be fine after all the excitement of moving and seeing our new home. It'll be really nice to go to bed in our caravan, just you wait.'

Megan's face puckered, and the slits of her eyes filled with tears. 'I don't want to live in a stupid caravan! I want my dad! I want my friends. I want to stay here – this is my house!' she wailed.

Jan picked her up and hugged her. 'You'll soon find new friends, I promise, and you'll like the caravan after a few days. Please try, for Mummy?'

'There's another house over there, too,' Annabel said. 'And it's only this high.' She put her hand a foot and a half above the ground.

Megan stopped crying as her little mind absorbed the tantalizing prospect of a miniature home. 'Whose is it?' she sniffed.

'It's yours,' Annabel said. 'I hope you like it.'

'I think I will,' the little girl said, looking more confident.

By the time they dropped in at Olwen Hardy's bungalow on their way out with the children and the first load of horses, Megan was already looking forward to being at Edge Farm, if only to take possession of her own new household.

Olwen was less happy. 'Do you know what you're doing?' the old woman asked, with her dark eyes flaming. 'There's been Hardys at Stonewall for a hundred and fifty years.'

'I'm sorry, Olwen. I know you're going to miss the children and I will bring them over as often as I can, but I'm doing what's best for them. I've told you why. I don't know how to make a living up here – so I have to go where I can.'

'It's terrible to think of Hardys living like tinkers in a caravan!'

Jan sighed. 'It won't be for ever. We'll build a beautiful house there, just you wait and see.'

At midday Jan followed the removal lorry up the track to Edge Farm. While her furniture and boxes were being stacked in the Dutch barn, she and Annabel unloaded the first four horses and loosed them into the paddock beside the barn. Then Jan climbed back into the lorry and headed straight back to pick up the last four of her charges. Harold Powell had decided it would make sense for his horses to summer with her where she could keep an eye on them, though he'd driven a hard bargain for their keep.

Gerry the carpenter had already recruited a stable hand to help Jan and Annabel. Roz Stoddard was Gerry's cousin and lived in the village. She was a large, loud, laughing girl, whom Jan liked on sight. She had worked in her mother's livery yard and had hunted since she was eight. She said she didn't mind what she had to ride or how many hours she worked in the yard, she just loved horses.

Annabel, Roz and Gerry were still in the yard with Reg as the sun dropped down behind the Malverns and Jan arrived with the three dogs and the remaining horses. When these were settled and quietly grazing in their new surroundings, Jan felt that now the move was complete; her new life was about to begin.

Understanding this, Annabel had gone down to the village with Roz and made a large casserole, which they brought up to the caravan for Jan's first dinner at Edge Farm. Gerry came back with a couple of bottles of wine and the four of them sat with Reg, crammed around the table in the mobile home, while the children dozed in their beds at the other end.

'Here's to you, Jan,' Gerry said, holding up his glass, 'and all the winners that are gonna come out of this place.'

Within a week of moving, Jan was already feeling at home. The dogs had helped by quickly finding their way around their new territory. Fly and Fred had been allocated the main barn as their dormitory, while Tigger, the terrier, had been favoured with a basket in the caravan. Fred, the lurcher, and Tigger had soon discovered that there was sport to be had in the warrens at the top of the farm, and old Fly had found the best way to pick up a titbit was to hang around the tack room when the humans were having their tea breaks.

Although she had eight useful horses in her paddocks, Jan hoped fervently she would have at least double that number by the start of the next point-to-point season. Besides Harold Powell's four geldings – Mister Mack, Lenny's Lad, Lazy Dove and Rear Gunner – she had Eddie Sullivan's horse, her own mare, Gale Bird, a horse called Derring Duke, who belonged to Owen Tollard, an electrical contractor in Brecon, and the skinny chestnut she'd bought at Doncaster but hadn't yet named.

Jan didn't intend that any of the horses would start work again until August at the earliest, and until she had recruited a few ailing or wayward animals for treatment she was going to devote all her attention to cleaning up her yard.

Despite haggling over the move and his disappointment that Jan hadn't yet found him another high-quality hunter-chaser, Harold had lost none of his enthusiasm. He came to see his horses at Edge Farm twice in the first week, which was more than when they'd been on his doorstep. Jan was very glad he'd chosen to send them with her, for she was now beginning to wonder whether she'd been kidding herself to think she would start picking up new owners in the first few months.

A week after the horses had arrived at Jan's farm, Colonel Gilbert, her father's landlord, phoned to ask if he could come and have a look at her set-up on Sunday morning.

When the day came, Jan was almost quivering with apprehension as she watched the colonel's Jeep bounce up her track. He had owned several good National Hunt horses and was a longstanding member of the Jockey Club, as well as a steward at several local race courses. When she'd been a small girl, she had met the colonel often with her father. Then he had always seemed a distant, somewhat unreal figure to have such a strong influence over the life of a small tenant farmer on his large estate. Later, she had seen much more of him when he'd sent horses to the big racing yard where she'd worked and, as a result, she'd ridden River Rocket for him to win the ladies' Open at the Heythrop point-to-point.

He parked outside the gate of a stable yard that was unrecognizable from the mess it had been when Jan and Reg first came to look at it. Gerry had painted every stick of timber and Annabel and Roz had swept the yard with so much gusto that there wasn't a wisp of straw out of place.

The colonel climbed out of his car and limped across the yard with a rigid leg which Jan had forgotten about. Following him was a tall, thin girl in her late twenties; Jan clearly remembered her angular frame, sharp elbows and pointed nose, but she hadn't seen her in the flesh since the day of River Rocket's win.

'Good morning, Colonel.' Jan flashed her impish smile.

'Hello, Jan,' he grinned back. 'It must be five years since we've seen you round here.'

Jan nodded. It was nearer eight.

'I was very sorry to hear the sad news about your husband.'

'I got your letter. Thank you, Colonel Gilbert.'

'Sorry it was just a couple of lines. Always so difficult on these occasions. Look, I hope you don't mind, I've brought Virginia along. She's decided that she's going to take up training too.'

Probably after her miserable performance as a jockey, Jan thought, and immediately chastised herself for a knee-jerk reaction to someone who happened to be younger and more privileged.

'Not at all,' Jan said. 'Hello, Virginia.'

Virginia was gazing around the yard with an expression of incredulity on her bony face. 'Are you really able to train from here?'

'I think so,' Jan said.

'Mrs Hardy won fourteen point-to-points and a good hunter chase last season,' the colonel said, although it was clear that Virginia knew all about Jan's record.

'I couldn't train from a yard like this; I've just applied for a public licence and I'm damn sure the Jockey Club wouldn't issue one for here.'

You snotty bitch, Jan thought, as she tried to smile. 'Best of luck. That's a bit out of my league, I'm afraid.'

'I don't see why it should be,' Colonel Gilbert grunted, 'but I'll gladly send you a useful old pointer for next season.'

Jan saw Virginia stiffen; she wondered if there was a subtext to this visit which had nothing to do with her. But she was grateful for the promise of the horse, and ecstatic at the thought that this eminent and knowledgeable man believed she was capable of getting a public licence. Up until now, she hadn't even dared consider it.

She decided to defuse her instinctive resentment of Virginia. She had always known that there was no such thing as a level playing field in racing – especially as a trainer, where a talentless man from an old racing family, with a big house, money, strong connections and a public school background stood a far higher chance of attracting well-bred horses with real potential than a gifted but skint, comprehensive-educated, widowed mother of two who lived in a caravan. But, even if she had to start this competition with both hands tied behind her back, she was determined that in the end the talent that she knew she had would show through. And at least Virginia shared the disadvantage of being female.

Jan showed Colonel Gilbert and his daughter everything that she had done to make her small plot of sloping land and its dilapidated buildings function as a place to keep and train racehorses.

The colonel was full of admiration.

'Your father told me how busy you'd been up here. I gather you've been working him pretty hard, too.'

'He volunteered,' Jan replied. The colonel had been so encouraging that she thought of asking him and Virginia into the caravan for coffee, but remembered in time that she hadn't cleared up after the kids' breakfast. Annabel was just walking back up the hill with Megan and Matthew and she could hear the baby grizzling already. 'Here are the kids now, so unless you want to stop and help me change Matty's nappy, you'll have to excuse me.'

'I think we'll leave you to it, Jan,' Colonel Gilbert laughed. 'Thanks for showing us everything you've done. We'll be back – at least, I will be.'

A few minutes later, Jan glanced up from the table where she was dealing with her son's disposable and watched the colonel's Jeep being driven cautiously down the hill. She still thrilled at his throwaway words.

He didn't see why a licence to train should be out of her league.

Until that morning the pinnacle of her ambitions had been to win one of the big hunter chases – either of the Foxhunters' or the Horse and Hound Cup. But now the idea had been planted in her mind, she felt sure that if she wanted a serious chance of a secure future for her children, she would have to get herself a licence to train under rules. Suddenly, her uncertain future looked bigger, brighter – and more daunting – than ever.

7

By the end of her second week, Jan was already feeling settled and happy at Edge Farm and ready to look beyond her immediate horizons. On a warm evening, at the end of a perfect summer's day, she decided to walk with the children down to Stanfield. Tigger came with them, hunting in and out of the hedgerows, while Jan pushed Matthew's buggy and sang songs with Megan. In the quiet village, the air was fragrant with the scent of flowers and privet blossom in the gardens as they made their way slowly up the main street to Glebe Cottages.

Annabel had moved in a few days before, after staying at the Fox & Pheasant while various small jobs were being done at the cottage. Jan hadn't asked how much rent Mr Carey was charging, but she suspected it was rather more than Annabel was earning as an au pair.

The cottage was a simple semi in the middle of the quiet village, built as a worker's home two or three centuries before. Ancient rambling roses and rampant honeysuckle clambered all over its rough-hewn golden stone walls. Inside, there was a sense of peace and contentment which seemed to reflect past happy lives that had once been lived there.

Annabel had already installed some curtains and good old furniture plundered from her indulgent parents' house. Jan felt a twinge of envy that she had been able to make everything look comfortable with such ease.

Annabel had made a tasty pasta salad and welcomed them warmly. When they had finished eating and the children were sleeping in the tiny spare room upstairs, the two friends settled down over a bottle of wine to talk about their plans for the yard.

Annabel had been told about a vet from Chipping Campden called James McNeill, recommended to her by a horse-owning friend of her father's.

'He sounds the sort you might get on with,' she said. 'He does everything – from racehorses to shires and gypsy ponies. Apparently he's quite a character.' She suggested Jan should contact him, and all the other vets in the area, to promote Edge Farm Stables as a recuperation home for injured horses, and a centre for schooling young or wayward ones.

The next morning Jan was being ushered into a drab, boxy little office in James McNeill's surgery on the edge of the Cotswold market town six miles away.

The vet was a large man, who made an unforgettable impression on anyone he met. His bright emerald eyes sparkled beneath a thick fringe of curly brown hair and he seemed able to look right into the mind of the person he was talking to. For a big man he had a surprisingly busy manner. He spoke so fast in his faint Scottish accent that Jan thought he would have been more at home behind a market stall than a desk in a surgery.

'I've heard a lot about you,' he said, nodding his head.

'Oh?' Jan was genuinely surprised.

'Colonel Gilbert seems to think a lot of you, but then that could just be compared to his daughter.'

'What do you mean?' Jan asked sharply.

James put a finger on the side of his nose. 'Sorry, I can't say more. A vet's surgery is like a priest's confessional.' It would be some time before Jan realized that James was in the habit of offering and withholding knowledge as a weapon. 'But I'm told we should expect great things and I saw that fine win you had at Ludlow in March.'

Jan couldn't help swelling with pride at this appreciation of what, to date, had been her greatest moment in racing. 'He's a super horse, Rear Gunner, and I'm fairly sure he'll still go on improving next season.'

James looked at her sharply. 'Take my advice, if that's true. Keep it to yourself, or you'll just inflate the owner's hopes and shorten the odds when the horse runs.'

Jan winced. He was right, she knew, but she wasn't sure she liked being picked up quite so assertively.

'Anyway,' the vet went on, 'tell me more about what you're doing at Edge Farm – what a terrible old place, by the way. I hope you've managed to tidy it up.'

'Yeah, well,' Jan said, a little put out, 'it did look pretty awful, but like my dad said, it was bound to be a bit of a bargain because of it. Anyway, it was all I could afford. I only had a hill farm in Wales to sell and that just made its reserve.'

'I heard about that, too,' James said.

'What did you hear?' Jan asked sharply.

'Just that – it only made its reserve.' James shrugged. 'Still, that's better than not selling at all.'

Jan looked at him and tried to ignore a tremor of uneasiness. After all, she told herself, it was perfectly possible, even likely, that someone from this part of the world might have gone up to the sale in Hay to see if they could buy a cheap farm in Wales to run sheep on in the summer, and an experienced buyer could often tell from an auctioneer's body language when a lot had reached its reserve.

'It left me quite short of cash, though,' she answered, 'and I need some lodgers in my yard for the summer. I'm pretty good at repairing injured horses and I was hoping you might know of some that needed a bit of tender loving care.'

James opened his eyes a little wider. 'Were you now? Well, I expect we might be able to find a few tenants for you, but I'd better come over, hadn't I, to look at what facilities you can offer.' He gave Jan a completely unexpected beaming smile which seemed to light up the dingy little room.

Jan found herself glowing with gratitude at this optimistic response. 'Yes, please do. Come and have a meal,' she heard herself say before she'd considered the difficulty of entertaining guests in her caravan. Oh *God*, she thought, as she tried to hold her smile, *I'll have to borrow Annabel's microwave and park the kids somewhere for the evening.*

'Nonsense,' James laughed. 'I'll come and look at the place. Then I'd be delighted to take you out to dinner.'

Jan was filled with absurd relief at not being held to her rash invitation. 'Oh, thanks so much,' she gushed. 'That would be wonderful.'

James raised a ginger eyebrow. 'Let's hope so.'

Jan drove home rejecting a faint question mark over James McNeill's motives in offering her help. It was quite likely that, if he did send her any customers, he would want a cut. She would have to take that into consideration when she was working out her charges. Perhaps there was no reason why she shouldn't take him at his word and, anyway, there was nothing phoney about that lovely smile of his.

As she rumbled up the track to Edge Farm in her Land Rover, she thought that now she was inviting outsiders to the yard she really must do something about the ruts. As she neared the top, the sun flashed a sharp reflection off the sleek, silver bodywork of a convertible Mercedes. She recognized the number plate at once and felt a quick flutter of pleasure at the thought of seeing Eddie Sullivan again.

She parked beside his car and found him, evidently only just arrived, outside her caravan waiting for someone to answer his impatient knocking.

'Hi,' she said. 'You won't find anyone in there. The kids are down in the village with Annabel and I've been visiting the vet.'

'No problems with Russian Eagle, I hope?'

'No, thank goodness,' Jan laughed. 'He's not the sort of horse that has too many problems. I've just been drumming up a bit of business for the yard.'

'How's it all going? I'm sorry I haven't been before.'

'I was wondering what had happened to you,' Jan said sternly.

'I've been in Italy for three weeks, trying to buy paintings.'

'I bet!' Jan snorted. 'Chasing those little Italian *signorinas* all over the place, I should think.'

Eddie drew himself up. 'Now look here, Mrs Hardy, I never chase women—'

'Yeah, I know. They chase you,' she finished for him.

'I wasn't going to say that.'

'Maybe, but you were thinking it.'

Eddie laughed and shook his head. 'Look, I've come here to be schooled over fences, not to be psychoanalysed.'

'Not today you haven't,' Jan said. 'All the horse were roughed off three weeks ago and I won't be bringing them back in till August at the earliest.'

'Oh,' Eddie said. 'Of course, I wasn't expecting you to be able to do anything today, but I had hoped, you know—?'

Jan couldn't help smiling at his disappointment. 'I suppose we *could* ride yours from the field to do a bit of schooling. But no galloping or anything like that until he's as fit as a flea.'

'You're the boss, Jan. By the way, I haven't had a bill yet.'

'It's the last day of the month, so you will tomorrow. I like to pride myself on the fact that mine is the first letter that pops through an owner's letterbox on the first day of the month. In the meantime, would you like a cup of coffee?'

'I'd love one.'

Sitting on the padded benches in the caravan, with a cafetière on the small table between them, they talked about Russian Eagle.

'Are you serious about wanting to ride him in the Foxhunters' at Aintree?' Jan asked.

'Deadly.'

'And it could be – if you didn't know what you were doing. Don't forget it's one and a bit circuits of the actual Grand National course.'

'I know,' Eddie nodded. 'That's why I want to do it.'

Jan shook her head. 'How many point-to-points did you say you'd won?' she asked sarcastically.

'Now, don't let's be defeatist about this. That's why I'm here. You're going to teach me how to do it properly.'

'You do realize that you – or at least the horse – has to win at least one open point-to-point to qualify to run in the Liverpool Foxhunters', and you'll have to get an amateur rider's permit from the Jockey Club to ride under rules?'

Eddie nodded. 'I looked up the race he won in Ireland and he beat a couple of good horses. I did wonder why they hadn't hung on to him a bit longer.'

Jan shrugged. 'That's not what they do. They like to turn them into cash.'

Jan and Eddie went to inspect Russian Eagle and the other horses grazing in the sloping fields. He was intrigued by the past performance and prospects of each one.

'I'd love to see round the whole place, if you've got time?' he asked as they left the paddock.

'Sure,' Jan agreed.

As they walked, in between telling him what she planned to do with the barns and the house, she took the opportunity to find out more about him.

'If you don't mind me asking,' she said, 'how come you seem so much posher than your dad?'

'What do you mean "seem"? I ought to be posher than my father. He spent a small fortune sending me to Harrow and supporting me through university.'

'Did you go to university?'

'I thought everyone did these days, now every college of further education seems to be called a university.'

'I didn't.'

'You obviously didn't need it. But I spent three years in Exeter playing tennis, learning seduction techniques and studying history of art with a lot of Sloane Rangers.'

'On whom you practised your seduction techniques, no doubt.'

'The lucky ones, yes,' Eddie nodded, his eyes twinkling as he struggled to keep a straight face.

Jan laughed. 'So your dad made his fortune building houses, but decided his son was going to be a toff?'

'That's about it.'

'Doesn't it embarrass you, being so different from him?'

'Not in the slightest. He and I get on really well, though our personalities are utterly dissimilar; he has a tendency to be a control freak – which, thankfully, he's given up with me – whereas I'm very relaxed about what anyone else does. He likes to work his bollocks off getting down to his office at seven o'clock every morning, whereas I couldn't look at a column of figures before ten. But it doesn't worry me in the slightest that he still talks and dresses like the boss of an East End mob. In fact, I used to love it at school when he came to see me. The other parents all gazed in horror as he clambered into his Turbo Bentley. I must admit, though, my mother's more of a lady. I think that's why Dad was so keen – to show her family that, whatever he might have been, his son was going to be a bloody sight smarter than they were.'

'Didn't you mind?' Jan asked, appalled at this apparent abuse of a son.

'No. There are still ridiculously unfair advantages in looking as though you come from some old land-owning family, and I don't suppose it does anyone any harm.' Eddie shrugged. 'But that's enough of me; I'd like to hear more about you.'

When Eddie had left, after driving very cautiously down the track in his low-slung car, Jan was surprised to see how long he had been there and how easy she had found it to be with him. But when Annabel appeared at the gate with Megan and Matthew, she realized that she hadn't asked him anything about his friendship with her and he hadn't mentioned it. She wondered how Annabel would take the news that he had finally come to see his horse.

Annabel's first visible reaction was a sharp wince.

'I thought you'd be pleased,' Jan said.

'Well, I'm not. I told you, I made a real fool of myself over Eddie. I don't really know why now, but I threw myself at him and the poor guy just didn't know how to cope with it. In a way, I wish he'd been older and more of bastard. But when my father got involved, with my mother turning up at his little flat, and going round to see his mother – it was all so bloody embarrassing. Besides, I'm not really Eddie's type and I never was; all he talks about is pictures and racing. I shouldn't think he's ever read a book in his life. I'm sure he's much more into trendy, glamorous It-girls. But listen, Jan, I promised I wouldn't let him spoil it here for me, and I'm not going to. Just don't talk about it and I expect I'll be fine, OK?'

'Annabel, haven't you ever dumped a man?'

'Eddie didn't dump me,' Annabel came back sharply.

'All right.' Jan could see her friend was getting twitchy as she sometimes did if one probed too far. 'Like I said, if he comes again when you're here, at least be civil to him.'

'Of course I will. Anyway, if you think he's so terrific, why don't you go out with him?'

'Firstly, because he hasn't asked and I'm certainly not going to ask him. And, secondly, I'm not sure he's my type either – his old man may sound like one of the Kray brothers, but Eddie's probably a bit posh for me; I like my men more earthy. And, thirdly, it's less than six months since John died and I certainly don't feel like starting a relationship with anyone at present.'

'Yes, I know, but you could still have fun teasing Eddie,' Annabel grinned.

'Don't be such a bitch,' Jan remonstrated. 'One of the rules of Edge Farm Stables is that we never tease the owners – OK?'

'All right. What shall I do with Matthew?' She nodded at the baby sleeping in the buggy.

Jan leaned down and sniffed. 'I'd better sort him out. Come on in and have something to eat.'

When Jan had dealt with Matty at the other end of the caravan, she came and sat down to eat the sandwiches Annabel had made.

'You are an ace butty maker,' she nodding, with her mouth full.

'Thanks. How did you get on with the vet, by the way?'

Jan swallowed her mouthful. 'Pretty well. He says he's happy to come over and have a look at our set-up, and he could certainly send a few patients here.'

'What's in it for him?' Annabel asked.

'I suppose if I said "Nothing", you'd say I was naive to think any man would do something for nothing?'

'It'd be rare, let's face it.'

'As it happens, although this guy puts on a salt-of-the-earth sort of image, I wouldn't be surprised if he thinks he could be in for a useful cut. Nice for him – just sends the horses along to us and takes his ten per cent for doing nothing, as well as charging his client for coming over to look at the animal from time to time.'

Annabel nodded. 'But then, at least you'd know what you were in for – and you'd know where you stood.'

The first of July was a sizzler. Jan spent most of the day helping Gerry, who was dripping with sweat as he tried to mend a pump designed to fill the water troughs from a spring at the top of the long field. She wouldn't have known where to start without him.

Roz and Annabel had gone already and Jan and Gerry were cooling down with a bottle of cider, when Eddie's car appeared at the gate for the second time in two days.

'Gosh, you must be keen to drive over here in this heat,' Jan called once he'd parked and was walking up the hill to where they sat on some upturned logs outside the caravan.

Eddie was carrying a large cardboard box. He shrugged his shoulders with a one-sided smile. 'Not with the roof off. Besides, I come bearing gifts, and I'm not Greek, so you needn't worry.'

Jan saw Gerry look disdainfully at this interloper, and she feared that he already resented Eddie as a rival. She wondered how she would break it to him that she wasn't interested in either of them.

Eddie put the box on the ground by Jan's feet.

'Cider?' Jan asked.

'Very rustic, but probably the last thing you need in heat like this.' He opened the box and took out a handsome antique brass and glass oil lamp, and a bottle of champagne wrapped in a cold sleeve. He felt the neck. 'Just about OK. Where can I find some glasses?'

Jan told him and a moment later he emerged from her temporary home with full three tumblers.

Some time later, after Roz had agreed to babysit, Eddie took Jan down to the Fox & Pheasant for supper, where Julie the barmaid greeted her warmly.

Eddie was impressed. 'You've only been here a month and they already treat you like a local.'

'Well, I *am* nearly a local. I was only born and brought up eight miles away. But everyone here's been really helpful.'

'Enjoy it while you can. Once you start getting successful, they'll find things wrong with you.'

'You're very cynical for a young man.'

Eddie laughed. 'Sorry, mother.'

Once they'd ordered and were sitting at a table with a bottle of wine between them, Jan looked Eddie straight in his innocent brown eyes. 'And just why, by the way, have you asked me out tonight?'

'You're my trainer, for God's sake!' Eddie affected surprise. 'Isn't it part of the deal to buy one's trainer dinner every so often?'

'As long as it's just that.'

'It is. Well, mainly. When I arrived with that champagne, I admit I was more interested in sharing it with you and the beautiful Annabel than the truculent Gerry.'

'Ah!' Jan said knowingly. 'Poor Gerry; you mustn't upset him.'

'I did and said nothing to upset him. But why not tell him I came looking for Bel? I'm sure that would mollify him a little.'

'I don't know that you'll get a better response from Annabel, to tell you the truth.'

Eddie leaned back in the small chair on which he was perched. 'I dare say you're right. There's a lot of work to do there.'

He smiled at spiky-haired Julie, who was bustling across the bar towards them with a fistful of cutlery, which she plonked down on the table.

Jan thought about asking Eddie what had gone on between him and Annabel when they'd first met, but decided that she didn't really want to know, and used the arrival of Julie with their food to change the subject.

'Talking of work to be done, you must promise me not to upset Gerry. He's been absolutely brilliant and he works like a slave. He's even offered to start work on the house, though God knows how I'm going to afford the materials.'

'What sort of things are you going to need?'

'Everything – oak timbers, floorboards, roof tiles, flagstones – and I want them all old. I couldn't bear to live in a place that was all shiny and new.'

'I know what you mean; maybe I can help. If you give me a list of what you want, I'll keep my eyes open around the sales and scrapyards. I've often picked up stuff like that for myself.'

Jan didn't mind admitting that she was happy to make use of any help a man was prepared to offer; besides, she was still uncertain what Eddie's motives were. There were no hints in his body language that he was flirting with her and his eyes shone with warm-hearted friendliness rather than red-hot passion.

She was no wiser after dinner when he dropped her outside the caravan and lightly brushed his lips across her cheek before he left.

Jan let herself in, and was surprised to see it was only half-past ten. The children were asleep and Roz was quite happy to sit and gossip for a while before she went home.

Roz had already got herself wrapped up in the lives of all the animals at Edge Farm, as well as the people. 'I can't wait to start doing some work with the horses,' she said.

'Eddie's raring to ride his, too,' Jan laughed. 'I've told him he'll just have to wait until August. But I've got a vet coming round to inspect us in the next few days and I'm hoping he might send us a few animals for running repairs or a dose of TLC.'

'Which vet's that?'

'James McNeill.'

Roz's eyes shot open. 'He's got a terrible reputation. They say there's not many men'll leave their wives alone in the same room as him.'

'Oh, God!' Jan groaned. 'A randy vet – that's all I need!'

Two days later, waiting for James McNeill to come up after a brief, businesslike phone call, Jan couldn't rid herself of the trepidation she felt. But when he arrived, he shook her hand as if she were another man, said no to coffee and asked if she could show him round right away.

He looked at her boxes and paddocks, then questioned her closely about her knowledge of horse health and welfare.

'I'm no bloody shop egg!' Jan told him.

Finally, when he'd seen enough, Jan asked him into her caravan, under the alarmed gaze of Annabel; Roz had already told her about James McNeill's rumoured sexual antics. But Jan felt that he would expect her to discuss charges with him in private.

He studied the official-looking tariff Annabel had typed out for Jan and nodded his approval. 'That seems fair enough for the kind of care you're offering,' he glanced up at her with no hint of humour in his eyes for the moment, 'provided you really can deliver it.'

'If you use Edge Farm, you won't be disappointed, Mr McNeill, I can assure you.'

'James,' he corrected. 'Please call me James. Let's hope you're right. I'll certainly try you. In fact,' he suddenly treated her to one of his big, beaming smiles, 'I may have something to send you the day after tomorrow.'

'Great,' Jan said, excited to think she might start earning more than a little keep money. Now that the yard was just about shipshape, and all the horses happily turned out, she was concerned that Roz and Annabel were under-employed.

The first patient at Edge Farm Stables arrived as promised and was installed in one of the new boxes Gerry had built. It was the first time any of them had been occupied, and Jan couldn't help popping her head into the barn every so often to see the evidence that she really was in business at last.

The horse had pulled a muscle in his back and, though James had repaired most of the damage, he still needed a lot of rest and very gentle exercise, as well as regular manipulation.

Jan was delighted to see how well Roz handled the animal and she found herself increasingly confident about the kind of service they could provide. Despite Roz's deeply cynical view of James McNeill's ultimate aims, Jan hoped that if they did a good job on this patient, a lot more would follow from the same source and, besides, whatever the stories about the vet's behaviour, he hadn't tried anything on with her.

It was Matthew's first birthday on 7 July and Jan held a tiny party for him, consisting of her parents, her three staff and two toddlers from the village whom she'd met with their mothers.

'You can be really proud of him,' Mary said as they sat outside the caravan and watched Matthew play with the giant plastic tractor Reg had given him. 'He's already walking really well, isn't he?'

Matty had just staggered to his feet and was reeling around on his chubby legs, blowing raspberries back at Gerry.

Jan laughed. 'He'll probably be an Olympic runner, Mum.'

'We always knew you were going to be a rider,' Mary defended herself with a smile. 'Anyway, it's lovely to have a little party like this, specially as you didn't do anything for your own birthday last month.'

'What?' Gerry exploded. 'You never told us. What day was that?'

'June the eighteenth, just after we'd moved,' Jan said. 'Quite frankly, I had so much going on, I almost forgot about it myself.'

'We didn't, dear,' Mary said.

'I know, Mum. Thanks, but I really didn't feel like making a fuss. I mean – thirty-one! What sort of an age is that?'

'Thirty-one. Cor!' Gerry shook his head. 'You don't look it!'

'Thanks, Gerry. You sure know how to make a girl feel good.'

Later, towards eight, when everyone else had gone and Annabel had helped Jan to put the children to bed, they went out and sat at a picnic table in front of the caravan in the warmth of the sun, still high above the Malverns.

'It sounds as if you've been lucky James McNeill hasn't tried to seduce you yet,' Annabel said.

Earlier in the day, before the birthday party, the vet had been to check on his patient's progress.

'Not really.' Jan shook her head. 'I think he just doesn't fancy me. Who'd be interested in a widowed mother of two who smells of horse all day long and hasn't got two beans to rub together?'

'Well, Eddie took you out the other night for a start,' Annabel said encouragingly.

'Yes, but not for that. He never touched me.'

'Did you want him to?' Annabel asked.

Jan glanced at her friend. 'To be honest, I don't know. I haven't been near another man since I met John, and even the thought is a little scary. Besides, I told you, Eddie's not my type.' Jan grinned. 'But it would be nice to be offered the chance to say no.'

'I don't think Eddie takes those sort of chances. Oh, look.' Annabel was pointing at the bottom of the track. 'You've got a visitor.'

A car had just turned in from the lane and was creeping up the hill like a shiny black beetle. It was a new BMW, which stopped beside Jan's lorry, thirty yards from where they sat.

'Do you know who it is?' Annabel asked.

'I haven't got a clue.'

They watched the driver get out. He was a slim man, mid-forties, five feet ten, with wavy dark hair a little too long and a gold ring glinting in the lobe of his left ear. He stood looking around for a few seconds before he saw them and started to walk towards the caravan.

'Hello there,' he called. 'They said in the pub I should find Jan Hardy up here. Is that one of you two?'

Irish, Jan thought. They were never far away in the racing world.

'Hello? I'm Jan Hardy and this is Annabel.'

'Good, good,' the man nodded. 'I was going to ring, then I thought, what the hell? I was on my way from looking at a club in Cheltenham and here y'are.'

'And who are you?'

'Jesus, I'm sorry. Did I not say? Eamon Fallon.' He held out a hand and solemnly shook Jan's, then Annabel's.

'Sit down,' Jan invited and he slipped onto the bench beside Annabel, opposite Jan. 'Would you like a drink?'

'No, thanks. I didn't come here for drinkin'.'

'What did you come for, then?' Jan asked.

'I saw a horse of yours win at Ludlow.'

'Rear Gunner?'

'That's it. It was very impressive. I've a couple of horses of my own in a little yard up by Droitwich, running in the point-to-points. Dingle Bay and Posy's Pride.'

Jan nodded. 'I've seen them both run. They look nice horses.'

'They are very good horses and they should have been winning for me, but I made the mistake of putting them with another Kerry man. I don't know what he's been doing, but sure as hell he's not been training 'em.'

'I was surprised they didn't do better,' Jan ventured, 'given their form in Ireland. They should be running under rules over here.'

'You may be right there, but I've always loved the points back home, and I wanted a good crack at it here.'

'Do you live in England?'

'I do – in Birmingham. I've a couple of little clubs, you know.'

Jan tried to imagine what kind of clubs, but she didn't want to clutter the conversation with irrelevancies at this stage.

'So what would you like me to do?'

'I'd like you to train my horses for me.'

'To go pointing?'

'Of course. You don't have a public licence, do you?'

Jan laughed. 'They don't give licences to penniless hill farmers' widows.'

'Well, maybe they should, but I want my two to run between the flags – for the moment. So, would you have them?'

'I'd have to look at them first.'

'But you've seen them.'

'That was months ago. Anything could have happened to them since then. There's no point you sending me something with a leg that's never going to mend, then getting all hot and bothered when it doesn't run.'

Eamon's left eye and shoulder twitched in a fleeting display of impatience, which Jan didn't miss. 'All right, then. You'd better go and have a look at them. But would you ever slip in there without letting y'man know what you're doing?'

Jan decided that she might as well look at Eamon Fallon's horses the next day. She rang the trainer, Jim Partridge, to make sure he'd be there. Then she left Annabel in charge of the children and set off in the Land Rover on what was a fine summer's morning.

Just after midday she turned into a grassy lane off the Kidderminster road and drove a few miles down it until she found a collection of ramshackle barns and stables partly hidden by woods. Surrounding the unpromising buildings were two paddocks, thick with docks and thistles, and fenced with rusting pig-wire. The half-dozen horses standing in them seemed too busy flicking the flies off their faces to get their heads down to eat.

Jan parked in the yard and stepped out onto a surface of ruptured concrete that looked as if it hadn't seen a broom for years. She stood there for a moment, listening to a thrush and a flock of scavenging starlings that had fled the yard on her approach. There was no sign or sound of any human presence.

'Hello?' Jan called, already disapproving of Jim Partridge for keeping horses in such squalid surroundings. 'Is there anyone in?'

There was an answering cough from a shed wedged between two of the barns and a small wiry man, unshaved and wearing grimy jodhpurs, emerged and blinked watery eyes in the sun.

'Oh,' he said with surprise, 'it's yourself, is it?'

Jan attempted a friendly smile. It hadn't occurred to her that she might be recognized. 'I'm Jan Hardy. I rang earlier.'

'But you didn't say who you were.'

'I never say who I am when I'm coming out to buy.'

Jim Partridge stiffened his short back defensively. 'To buy is it? How d'you know I've anything to sell?'

'I've never known an Irishman with horses who didn't and you were running a few nice-looking animals from here last season.'

He glowered at her suspiciously. 'I've only six horses here at the present, and none of them's for sale.'

'Well, you never know. Why not show me what's here, anyway? I've got a couple of punters prepared to pay good money for something that'll win for them.'

Jim eyed her hesitantly. 'Oh, all right. You may as well have a look. I'll get a lead.'

He disappeared into the nearest building and came out a few seconds later with a length of plaited bailer twine. He led Jan out of the yard and through the gate to the first paddock, where five of his six charges were clustered under a vast horse chestnut tree, flicking their tails and stamping their feet. Jan walked among them and wondered why anyone would send a horse to a place like this. From a quick assessment of their qualities, Jan decided that she could plausibly be interested in two of them.

'Who's this?' she asked, stroking the nose of a small bay gelding with four black feet. She knew he was neither of the horses she had come to see.

'That'd be Carlton Breeze – a very talented animal.'

Jan looked blank. 'What's he won?'

'He didn't do much this season, owing to a bit of a leg. He struck into himself badly and it went septic, but he's as right as rain now.'

'Would you trot him up the yard for me?' Jan asked, wondering how helpful that would be on ground that looked like the surface of the moon.

'Sure.'

She watched the horse's action from front and back as Jim ran him back and forth along a strip of level ground at the back of the stables.

'You're right,' Jan said. 'He's sound now. What do you suppose his owner would let him go for?'

'As a matter of fact, this horse is my own and if I were to sell him I'd be looking at fifteen thousand for him.'

'Fifteen thousand?' Jan asked, with a hint of incredulity, but not enough to be offensive.

'That's right,' the little man said.

'Who's that in the other field?' Jan asked, seeing a big, gaunt chestnut mare on her own, standing on a patch of dried mud and shaded from the sun by a hedge of runaway thorn.

'That's Posy's Pride. She'd not be for sale.' He turned away to lead the bay back to the field.

Jan carried on studying the mare, noting her lack of condition and stary coat. 'She doesn't look well,' Jan said.

'Well, we've had one or two little problems with her.'

In the first paddock, Jan thought she had identified Dingle Bay, a big rangy bay, as his name suggested. He looked a great deal better than the chestnut in the other paddock.

'He's a nice individual. Could I have a look at him?'

Jim shook his head. 'No, he wouldn't be for sale either.'

'Why?' Jan asked lightly. 'Who does he belong to?'

'An old friend of mine up at King's Heath. I used to do the dogs with him. I'd bring them over and he ran them at Perry Barr, before they closed it.'

'You must have been young then.'

'We were, and wild,' Jim cackled.

'What's he called?'

Jim hesitated. 'Eamon Fallon, but he'd never sell a good horse. Even if he did, he'd not be an easy man to negotiate with.'

'Trot him up for me anyway, just in case,' Jan cajoled. 'Then I'll have another look at Carlton Breeze.'

Jan left Jim Partridge's yard confident that he didn't know why she'd been there.

When she got home, she dialled Eamon's number and was answered by a woman with a strong Birmingham accent, who was evasive until Jan explained exactly why she was calling, after which she was finally answered by Eamon's own soft Kerry vowels.

'I saw those horses,' Jan said, feeling that despite his own easily delivered charm, any flannel would be wasted on him. 'The chestnut mare, Posy's Pride, looks dreadful – like she's got red worm, ringworm and a few other worms besides. I don't think she'll be doing a lot next season. But the other horse, Dingle Bay, looks useful. He doesn't look as if he's been made to do much work for some time, though. I talked Jim into trotting him up for me and the horse moved nice and straight.'

'Do you think you could train him?'

'Oh yes.'

'To win?'

'You might be able to make those kind of predictions about greyhounds, but you must know there's always an element of uncertainty with racehorses – especially jumpers.'

'I'd prefer less chat about the dogs,' Eamon said quietly. 'But you go and pick up Dingle Bay as soon as you can. I'll ring Jim and tell him you're coming to collect him, OK?'

'Yes, that's all right. But if you want me to pick him up, I'll have to charge you for the transport.'

'That's fair enough,' Eamon said. 'And maybe you should tell me how much you'll charge for training him.'

When she'd told him her rates, he gave a satisfied grunt. 'That'll be fine.'

Jim Partridge was expecting Jan when she arrived back at his yard with her lorry two days later. Dingle Bay was already in a stable, looking well groomed and with a clean head-collar.

'I don't know what the hell you did to get him to part with the horse,' Jim muttered under whisky breath.

'What do you mean?' Jan asked as she led Dingle Bay towards the ramp of her lorry.

'How did you persuade him to sell him to you?'

'I didn't. He hasn't sold it. He's sending him to me to train.'

The little man's shoulders collapsed abruptly. 'To train? The bastard!' he sniffed. He seemed already resigned to the loss.

Jan was almost sorry for him, but another glance across the paddocks quickly dispelled the feeling. She led Dingle Bay into the box and tied him up. She walked down the ramp and swung it up with a little half-hearted help from Jim Partridge.

'I'll get the papers,' he muttered, still smouldering with resentment and walked across to the shed, which was evidently his office. Jan followed him into the gloomy little cabin with dirt-smeared windows and piles of dusty papers everywhere.

'I'm sorry you're losing the horse, but at least Mr Fallon's leaving you with Posy's Pride,' she said.

He grunted. 'We both know she won't be doing a lot next season, but', he suddenly pleaded, 'don't for pity's sake tell Eamon.'

Jan winced with regret. 'I'm afraid I already told him I didn't think she'd be ready to run for some time. I'm sorry, but, look, is he all paid up and everything?'

Jim glanced at her quickly as he handed her the horse's passport and certificates. 'What do you mean?'

'I mean does Mr Fallon owe you any money on the horse's keep? I wouldn't want to take a horse from a yard before it was paid up – otherwise you've no collateral.'

'It's all right about the money; he owes nothing.' The little man dismissed the problem with a backward wave of his skinny hand and Jan had the impression that it was probably Jim who was owing.

She nodded. 'Well,' she held out a hand. 'Thanks for getting the horse ready for me.'

He heaved a shoulder as they went back out into the yard, where he stood and watched while she walked to the cab of her lorry.

Jan started the engine and glanced in the wing-mirror at the forlorn figure, who didn't move as she drove up the short track to the lane.

On the motorway, heading back for Gloucestershire, she caught sight of herself in the mirror – the light blonde hair flicking in the wind, the innocent blue eyes – and hoped she wasn't guilty of overloading Jim Partridge's burden of woes.

She talked to Annabel about it when she got back to Edge Farm.

'But surely,' Annabel said, 'if Eamon hadn't sent the horse to us, he'd certainly have sent it somewhere else. There's absolutely no reason why you should feel bad about it. In the end, Jim Partridge's failures are his problem, not yours.'

Jan sighed and tried to push aside the memory of the pathetic look in the man's face as the best horse in his yard had been driven away.

8

By the end of July James McNeill had sent three more patients to Jan. Another horse had come in from a local farmer's wife for some schooling and there were still nine healthy racehorses in the paddocks – in all, just enough to cover the wages of her two girls, but not enough to deal with the ongoing costs of Gerry's building work.

The only way that she could see of financing this would be to take out a large mortgage, but she had no intention of jeopardizing her fragile business in order to make the repayments. She made up her mind to bite on the bullet and on a Friday evening towards the end of July she asked Gerry in for a drink.

When she told him that she would have to put the building work on hold, at first he looked shocked and turned pale. He quickly recovered, though.

'It's OK, Jan, I'll just carry on, and you pay me when you can, when things pick up. As soon as you start getting them horses to the races, there'll be people knocking the door down to send theirs here.'

'Gerry, be realistic. It's six months before there's any racing. I'm sure I'll pick up a few more owners before then, but let's face it, there aren't going to be many, and I'm not going to have much more money coming in than I've got now.'

'That don't matter. I've got a few other jobs I can fit in to keep me ticking over.'

'I've still got to buy the materials.'

'Eddie's been bringing in most of what you need and he won't mind waiting; he's got plenty of money.'

'Gerry, I'm not going to build this house on charity. I can't be owing money to you and everybody else – not until I know I'm going to be earning some. The house will just have to wait.'

'You can't spend a winter up here in this place.' Gerry waved a disparaging arm around the mobile home.

'Why not? We know it's waterproof after that awful storm last week, and we've got a couple of radiators to keep us warm.'

'But Jan,' Gerry urged, desperate at the thought of not working up at Edge Farm, 'what about them kids?'

'I promise they'll be all right,' Jan put a hand on Gerry's. 'And to be honest, if it did get really bad, Annabel's always said we can move into the cottage.'

'She would,' he said sulkily, knowing he was beaten. 'But I can still come up here and help out, can't I?'

'Of course you can, if you want to.'

Jan watched him walk back down to his van, sad to see him so despondent. He'd already started putting in the footings, working on his own with the help of a mini-digger he'd borrowed. He'd been a tower of strength since she'd arrived at Edge Farm, and she knew that he was more than just interested in helping her out, but it was hard not to encourage him; besides, she couldn't help being touched by his gentle infatuation.

The following Sunday Jan took Megan and Matthew back to Wales to see their grandmother for the first time in five weeks. Olwen had made it clear she was no more reconciled to the loss of Stonewall than she had been when Jan had sold it and, although she still drove her own small car, it was highly unlikely that she would condone Jan's decision by visiting Edge Farm. Despite that, Jan owed it to her children to maintain contact with their grandmother, who was, after all, the only remaining member of their father's family.

She wasn't looking forward to lunch with Olwen, but she couldn't suppress a few pangs of nostalgia as they drove up from the Wye valley over the hills to Stonewall. The sun appeared sporadically between piles of cumulus that had drifted in from the Irish Sea. It bathed the curvaceous heathered contours in a seductive glow and reminded Jan of the excitement she had felt the first time she had ridden across those ridges.

'That's where Dad is,' Megan sang out when she saw the tiny white church of St Barnabas tucked in a fold between two hills. She leaned forward from her child's seat in the back of the Land Rover to see her mother's face. 'Do you think he's happy there?'

Jan was cheered by the question, which seemed to confirm that the little girl had positively come to terms with her father's death. 'Yes, darling,' she said. 'I think he is. It's a really peaceful place.' She didn't suggest going to see the grave; she would do that on her own later.

The farmhouse which had been the centre of her universe for the seven years of her married life looked abandoned and forlorn, although it was only seven weeks since they'd moved out. Jan had been back several times to collect a few last items in the week following their move, but she hadn't ventured up the drive since then. She wondered why the Davieses who'd bought the farm hadn't moved in. Someone had taken a cut of hay off the lower meadow, and the higher fields of permanent pasture were full of big, lowland sheep. She found she didn't want to look. She began to have an inkling of how it must have been for Olwen and she felt a little more sympathy for her.

Olwen opened the door and, without glancing at Jan, held out her arms to greet her granddaughter. In one hand she held a bag of Megan's favourite sweets.

'How's my beautiful little Megan?' she asked in her strong Cambrian accent. 'Come to see your Nana at last?' Jan didn't miss the side-swipe of accusation in the old woman's voice, but she stifled her urge to defend herself.

When Olwen had finished making a fuss of Megan, she turned her attention to the baby boy in Jan's arms, pointedly avoiding eye-contact with his mother. 'And how's Master Matthew Hardy?

My goodness, you look more and more like your dad! He looked just the same as you at your age.'

Jan sighed to herself and offered the boy for Olwen to hold. Olwen took him and turned to carry him into the bungalow.

In the spotless living room, two mats had been laid out on the floor with toys. Without being told, Megan rushed straight towards a selection of dolls and My Little Ponies. The old woman sat Matthew on his mat and watched with satisfaction as he started immediately to play with a big, bright plastic activity centre.

Jan was getting fed up with Olwen's self-satisfied smirk. 'You haven't got anything a little more advanced for him, have you? He's a bit past just making squeaks.'

'He's happy enough with it,' Olwen growled; and Jan knew he was.

'How have you been, Olwen?'

'As if you cared,' the old woman muttered.

'Of course I care. You're the only family the children have on John's side.'

'There's not a lot more on your side, is there, with your brother gone missing.'

'He hasn't gone missing,' Jan started, before she remembered how many times Olwen had tried to provoke her with Ben's absence and the implicit flaw in her family. 'After he left California, he went to Australia.'

'That's as good as missing,' Olwen retorted.

'I think he might be making a bit of money out there.'

'Oh yes?' Olwen asked sceptically. 'Then perhaps he'll come and buy this place back.' She nodded her head with a circular motion to indicate the old family farm that surrounded them.

'Olwen, it's just been sold. The new people have already got stock on it.'

'No they haven't. That's Bryn Morris's sheep. He's just took the grazing till the end of August. Stonewall Farm's back on the market.'

Jan was in the process of taking Matthew's nappies from a

carrier bag she'd brought in with her. She stopped abruptly. 'Are you sure?'

'Look, here, in the *Hereford Times*, if you don't believe me.' Olwen picked up the local weekly, already open at a page of farm sales, with a photograph of Jan's old home prominent, and in bold print at the bottom of the advertisement, an asking price nearly a hundred thousand pounds more than it had been sold for at auction in April.

Jan felt the blood drain from her face. 'My God!'

'It's a bit late asking him,' Olwen grunted. 'You've been took to the cleaners by them auctioneers.'

'Don't be daft,' Jan said, more forcefully than she felt. 'They sold it for as much as they could get on the day; I was there. Harold Powell only just nudged it up to its reserve price. If there had been a buyer there, they'd have taken on the Davieses.' Jan knew she was trying to convince herself as much as Olwen. The almost invisible, niggling suspicions she had had from time to time seemed suddenly magnified into a major catastrophe.

If, by bad judgement or being too hasty, Jan had sold the one asset John had left her for nearly a third less than its value, she would never be able to forgive herself for depriving her children of what would ultimately be theirs. Or, so help her, she was going to have to work like hell to make up for it!

'It's just the way the market goes, Olwen. Who could have known it would pick up so much in three months?'

'The man that stole our farm most likely did.'

'Look, if anyone has done anything crooked, I can promise you I'll find out who, and have them sorted.'

Olwen, looking Jan straight in the eye now, lifted one, cynical eyebrow. 'And how would that be?'

The sweet Welsh lamb that her mother-in-law served for lunch tasted to Jan like mouthfuls of straw tainted with some bitter sauce. She couldn't fight off the nausea she felt at having been so easily duped and she was now convinced that she'd been deliberately misled. By whom, she hardly dared to guess.

Driving back, the beauty of the evening sun didn't move her at all as she tried to plan what she should do next. She was determined not to rush in and scare her adversary into a defensive position. The farm had been openly back on the market now for about ten days, and the fact that she hadn't already been in touch with the agents might suggest to them that she knew and simply thought she had been a victim of a surge in the market.

She was about to turn up the last hill before dropping down to the Wye valley, when, abruptly, she thought of John.

'I think we will go and see Daddy after all,' she told Megan, 'and make sure that he's got some nice flowers.'

There was only a small bunch of freesias in a tiny glass vase on the grassy tump which marked John Hardy's grave; Jan had been told she couldn't put up a headstone for another year, to allow the earth to settle.

Jan guessed the flowers were Olwen's and was grateful to her for leaving them, but she promised herself that she would come back as soon as she could to put her own there. She stood with Matthew in her arms and Megan, wide-eyed but composed, beside her, clutching her hand, and thought of the cold damp day they had laid John to rest. She gazed at the grave and tried to see him lying deep beneath the surface, calm and thoughtful as he'd always been.

Gritting her teeth, she closed her eyes.

Dear John, she said silently, *you wouldn't have let this happen with the farm. You would have been calm and sensible about it. I was too hasty, I know, because I just wanted to get the whole business over and done with. Now I've lost so much! Please help me. Tell me what to do, if you can.*

Reg and Eddie were in the yard when Jan got back, sitting side by side on a small bale of wheat straw. It was one of a thousand that Colonel Gilbert had sent over from Riscombe Manor that week. He had phoned afterwards. 'They're fifty pence each, and you can knock the cost off your training fees when I send you Sorcerer's Boy.'

Jan had been more than grateful. Both for the straw, which she was already using for some of the ailing horses who couldn't be bedded on shavings, and for the commitment the colonel had made to sending her a horse – Sorcerer's Boy had chalked up two good wins the previous season.

When Jan saw a bottle of cider resting precariously on the straw between her father and Eddie, she detected Reg's influence. These days, there was nothing he liked more than to swig cider and have a good gossip, preferably in the open air within scenting distance of livestock.

'Can I get you some glasses?' she asked, walking across the yard towards them.

Eddie stood up. 'Don't be so fussy. We've done very well sharing the bottle up until now. Anyway, I'm off. Did you have a good time at your mother-in-law's?'

Jan stared at him, wishing he knew the trauma she'd been going through since she'd heard how she'd been conned over Stonewall. She wanted to blurt it all out. She needed to tell someone, as soon as possible, but her dad was there and he would want to hear it on his own first. She pulled herself together. 'Not too bad, thanks. Olwen spoiled the kids as usual, but that's no bad thing now and again.'

'Good,' Eddie smiled down at Megan, who had trailed across the yard behind Jan. 'I love spoiling them myself; it makes me feel like a king. I was just telling your dad I was coming over next weekend. Any chance I might get my leg over—', he paused with a grin, before adding, 'my horse?'

Jan tried to focus. 'Yes. You could ride him from the field gently. He's got plenty of weight on him.'

'Great! I'm looking forward to it already. I'll see you then.' He turned to Jan's father, who was still sitting contentedly on his bale. ''Bye, Reg. See you soon.'

Jan waited for the Mercedes to set off before she sat down where Eddie had been beside Reg.

He looked at her. 'What's the trouble, Janine? You look all washed out.'

At the sound of his soft, sympathetic voice, Jan burst into tears. 'Oh, Dad. I feel terrible – such a fool.'

'Why? What's that mother-in-law of yours been up to now?'

'Only pointing out the truth.'

'What truth?'

'That I've been a bloody fool, Dad, a complete fool, and it's cost me a fortune.' She told him all about the new advertisement in the *Hereford Times* for Stonewall Farm.

'Oh dear,' he murmured when she'd finished. 'I can see why you're so upset.' He shook his head. 'But you know there's nothing you can do about it, don't you?'

'Dad, there must be, if someone's taken advantage of me.'

'Not legally. The place was sold at public auction', he shrugged, 'and that's that.'

'But I'm sure it was kept cheap deliberately. It only just crept up to my reserve price.'

'Did anyone make a fuss when it was knocked down? Did anyone jump up and say he was still bidding?'

Jan looked at him, knowing he was right. 'No,' she said quietly.

'There it is then,' Reg said. 'Allus you'll do by worrying about it is get yourself wound up and fretting like a young heifer, and that won't do you no good at all.'

'But, Dad, if people have cheated me, it must be people I know and I don't think they should get away with it.'

'Revenge? Is that what you're after?'

'No,' Jan shook her head vigorously. 'No, but justice. I can't just stand by and do nothing.'

'Then you're going to need some help.'

'Oh, Dad, you're very kind, but what could you do?'

'I wasn't thinking of me. I was thinking of your chum who's just gone. Master Eddie.'

'Eddie? Why do you call him my "chum"? He's a client.'

'Maybe, but he'd do a lot for you. He thinks the world of you, I can tell.'

'I don't know about that, but what do you think he could do?'

'He's a clever boy, and bold. Take my advice – you tell him what's happened and he'll help you get to the bottom of it.'

'But don't you think it's a bad idea for me to tell my customers about my problems, especially when I've made such a prat of myself?'

'He'll understand and he certainly won't take his horse away because of it.'

When she had put the children to bed that evening, Jan sat on her own in the lounge of their mobile home and watched the sun dropping over the dinosaur's back of the Malverns in the west.

While she and Roz had got on with the evening tasks around the stables, she had thought about what her father had said. And she knew now for certain that it wasn't revenge she wanted. But if people she had trusted had abused her, she bloody well wanted them to know that she knew.

She also knew that Reg was a reliable judge of character: that he approved so strongly of Eddie came as a surprise to her. She wouldn't have thought that the younger man's charm would have made any impact on him. But Reg had taken to Eddie from the start and trusted him. And he wouldn't have recommended him lightly.

Her hand hovered over the telephone for what seemed like minutes, while she stared at Eddie's phone number in the book.

There were other things to take into consideration as well. She didn't want him to think that she was pursuing him, or asking him to help her as an excuse to bring him closer to her. He also had to know that she was asking a favour with no strings attached – either way. She wondered if he would understand.

Her finger dropped to the keypad and few seconds later she heard his lazy, deep voice.

'Hello?'

'Hello, Eddie. It's Jan here.'

'Hello!' He sounded pleased to hear her. 'You OK? Or has there been a disaster? Has Eagle dropped dead?'

'No, no.' Jan couldn't help laughing. 'Eagle's fine. I'm sorry to ring you so late, but I've got a favour to ask.'

'Great. I love doing women favours.'

'Look, I've got no right to ask this. There's nothing in it for you,' she added, trying not to sound too stern.

'A selfless favour? I don't often do those, but I could try. What is it?'

'I can't tell you over the phone. When could you come over? I'd come to your place now, only I can't leave the kids.'

'I can't come right now, either. But I could get over first thing in the morning, if you like.'

He arrived at the caravan just after seven, and a few minutes before Annabel on a grey Monday morning.

'What on earth are you doing here so early?' Annabel asked suspiciously, seeing him drinking coffee while Jan helped Megan to get dressed.

'I just popped in for a word with my trainer,' he answered blandly. Jan hadn't yet told him what she wanted to talk about.

'I was going to ask Eddie if he could do me a favour,' Jan said, not meeting Annabel's eye.

'Oh, do you want me to disappear? I could get on with the feeds for the three invalids if you like.'

'Yes, please. The list's above the feed bins.'

'I know,' Annabel said, disappearing through the door.

When Annabel was out of earshot, Jan wondered whether it would matter if she talked about her problem in front of Megan, who had developed a habit of absorbing almost everything she heard.

'Do you want to pop down and help Bel?' Jan asked her.

Megan's eyes lit up, and a few seconds later Jan was watching her trot down to the yard behind Annabel's slender figure.

She noticed Eddie was watching too.

'What is it between you and Annabel?' she asked before she could stop herself.

He turned back to look at her and smiled ruefully. 'It's not easy. I wasn't going to talk to you about it, but I suppose she's already told you. We had a bit of a scene, five or six years ago. She ran away from school and turned up at my flat. She wasn't under-age or anything, but her father sent the police round – God knows why. Frankly, I think his archaic attitude was the cause of her problems in the first place. And even now she still seems a bit in awe of him. Otherwise why did she carry on living at home so long?'

'I think that was more to do with her mother,' Jan said. 'And the fact that she didn't want to go back to London.'

'There's more to it than just her dad, though. I don't know what, but something's left her insecure and with very little self-esteem for someone as bright and beautiful as she is.'

'She is very beautiful, isn't she,' Jan said with only a hint of envy.

'Yes, I think she is,' Eddie mused. 'In fact, I'm sure she is, but somehow she's not very – I don't know – sexy, I suppose is the only way you could put it. I'm very fond of her, she's lovely to look at, but I just don't fancy her.'

'Well, be kind to her, won't you?' Jan sighed.

'I should think kindness is the last thing she wants from me. But I certainly wouldn't want to do anything unkind,' Eddie promised. 'I can see what an asset she is to the yard and I don't want anything to upset that.'

'Good, because I've got another favour to ask you.'

'What's that?'

Jan picked up the paper, folded open at the page which contained the advertisement for Stonewall Farm, and pushed it across the table to him.

He took a few seconds to absorb the details before he flicked a curl of black hair from his eye and looked up. 'Oh dear,' he said, in the much same tone Reg had used.

'"Oh dear"! Is that all you can say?' Jan asked more sharply than she meant.

'It's just my restrained way of saying, "Bloody hell",' Eddie replied mildly. 'Obviously I realize that something's gone wrong in a big way. It looks as though you're about a hundred grand out of pocket.'

'Actually, a bit more than that. They're offering twenty acres less than I sold – the ground next to the bungalow. I suppose they think it might be worth sitting on that until my mother-in-law dies and I sell the bungalow, so they can flog off the land to the new occupants at an inflated price.'

'You're probably right,' Eddie agreed. 'Do you know who's actually selling it now?'

'No. I only discovered the place was for sale yesterday when Olwen tried to rub my nose in it, so I haven't been in contact with the agents since it came back on the market.'

'These aren't the people that sold it for you, are they?'

'No, of course not! They wouldn't be that stupid.' Again, Jan regretted her brusqueness. 'I'm sorry, Eddie, I shouldn't take it out on you. It's just that I feel such a fool for trusting certain people.'

'I understand. So what do you want me to do?'

'I want to know who really owns it at the moment – who's going to make the profit on it.'

'If they do make a profit. One thing you've got to bear in mind is that they haven't actually sold it yet. They may have misjudged the market.'

'I wish they had, but I don't think so. If you look at prices round here, they've been going up all the time and that's going to ripple out towards Wales. I've been reading, there are more and more Londoners selling their houses for fortunes and thinking it might be nice to have some of the good life and take up a bit of hobby farming – so long as they've plenty stashed away to live on,' she added sourly.

'Jan, you can't blame people for being lucky, and I'm bloody sure you won't be living on a shoestring for ever. But I'll see what I can do. Don't tell me your theories about it now, though,' he nodded at the paper. 'I don't want to start with any preconceptions.'

'When can you start?' Jan asked eagerly.

'Hang on!' Eddie laughed. 'And remember, whatever I discover, the chance of you getting anything back out of it is very slim.' He stood up. 'I've got to go. Thanks for the coffee. I'll be in touch as soon as I hear anything.'

Jan watched Eddie walk back to his car, glad that at least she now had a committed ally, but she didn't get much reassurance from this as she walked to the paddock behind the caravan and leaned over the rails. Gloomily, she looked at Rear Gunner, strong and with a big grass belly on him. He'd be ready to come back in soon to start his preparation for one of the really prestigious hunter chases the following spring.

Eddie still hadn't rung by Thursday morning and Jan's frustration was almost at breaking point. She'd spent the last few days full of guilt about her mishandling of the sale of Stonewall. She wasn't naturally a greedy woman – maybe that was why she'd been so thoughtless in disposing of what was her biggest financial asset – but, living in the caravan, she was constantly reminded that she was the sole parent of two young children in a complicated, costly world with a very small income. Whether she liked it or not, money mattered, and her sense of grievance was so strong that, despite her father's pessimism, she was sure she should get her fair share of the profit if Stonewall were resold for more than she'd received.

She was also confused about whether she wanted to hear from Eddie for news of any progress, or because she just wanted to hear from Eddie.

But while she was trying to deal with these problems in her head, and for the most part on her own, she and her two helpers were getting on well in the yard. The horses who had been sent to her to convalesce were already showing signs of improvement and Jan felt confident that she hadn't attracted them there under false pretences. Her confidence was confirmed when James McNeill turned up shortly after midday and inspected the three animals under his care.

'It certainly looks as though you women have got the magic touch. Mind you.' He grinned. 'If I was being massaged by you lot every day, I'd pretty soon perk up.' He looked around at the three of them, to be met with Roz's distrustful glower. 'I'll tell you what. As a treat, I'll take you all out to lunch at the Fox!'

'We can't all go, we're expecting a new patient, any time now,' Jan said.

'That's OK,' Roz said. 'I'll stay.'

'And I'm meeting my mother in Cheltenham for lunch,' Annabel added.

'I don't think Roz is very keen on me,' James said when he and Jan were sitting at a table in the pub.

Jan laughed. 'She thinks you've got a bit of a reputation.'

'Have I?' James looked surprised. 'What for?'

'Seducing clients' wives, apparently.'

'Well then, you lot haven't anything to worry about, have you? None of you has a husband. Anyway,' he said, changing his tone, 'I'm really glad you're doing so well. I see you've got three or four other patients in and a nice-looking new racehorse in the paddock.'

'Yes,' Jan nodded. 'He's called Dingle Bay.'

'I think I saw him run – a little disappointing, I seem to remember. Whose is he?'

'He belongs to a businessman from Birmingham.' Jan said, thinking that was a pretty inadequate description of the voluble Eamon Fallon.

'As it happens, I may have another Brummie businessman for you,' James said thoughtfully. 'A bloke called Bernie Sutcliffe. He'll need a bit of working on; he's got piles of loot but he's as tight as a duck's arse.'

'Why does he want a racehorse then?'

'He doesn't, but Sandy, his girlfriend does and poor old Bernie's looks don't match up to his bank balance. He's got the body of a toad and a head like a blighted spud,' James said with the smugness of a man who had complete faith in his own appeal.

Unjustifiably so, Jan thought to herself. 'What's that got to do with it?' she asked.

'Sometimes he has to spend money to keep her interested in him. Sandy's an old friend of mine; she introduced me to him, and he asked me what was the cheapest way to own a racehorse. I told him to start with pointing.' James shrugged. 'And I *could* tell him that the best young trainer round here is you.' He leaned back in his chair and smiled.

Jan wondered if she was expected to grovel with gratitude. She lifted her left shoulder an inch. 'You must tell him what you think best.'

And, whatever his motives, James didn't refer to the potential owner again. He and Jan spent the rest of the hour they were in the pub discussing remedies for the various horses they were treating.

It was only afterwards, when he dropped her back at the stables with a businesslike farewell, that he added, 'I'll tell Bernie Sutcliffe to get in touch, if that's OK?'

Jan hadn't been back long and was checking a poultice on a strained tendon when the phone in her pocket rang.

'Hi, Jan. It's Eddie.'

'Hello?' Jan said hoarsely, and held her breath.

'I've got a bit of news. Will you be there in half an hour?'

Jan stopped what she was doing as soon as she heard a car turn into the drive. She walked round the end of the barn and saw the Mercedes. She waited by the new parking place Gerry had made while Eddie drove in.

'What did you find out?' she asked, even before he got out of the car.

'The place is already under offer at the full asking price,' Eddie said, straightening himself and putting a hand on her shoulder in a way he hadn't done before.

Jan bit her lip. 'Oh bloody hell! I *knew* they would get the money for it. Do you know who's selling it?'

'Davies and Company – a small agricultural engineers in Talgarth. They don't turn over a lot, but they own a few freehold sites in the town. They bought Stonewall from a farmer called Terry Davies, who just happens to be Rhys Davies's brother. He'd bought it at the auction. In fact, I gather he simply passed his contract straight on to them. According to Companies House, there are two equal shareholders in the firm. Rhys Davies and Harold Powell.'

Jan felt the blood drain from her face. 'The bastard!' she hissed.

All her muscles tensed and she clenched her teeth at the thought of Harold sitting with her in the pub in Hay, acting like a kind old uncle when she'd gone to see him after hearing the will read, and then later when she'd specifically asked him about selling Stonewall. He must have felt like a spider catching a half-crippled fly. He'd even pretended to discourage her from selling so soon at auction. And after all she'd done for him with his horses!

'Take it easy, Jan,' Eddie was saying. 'Shall we go up to the caravan and talk about it there?'

Jan looked across at Roz and Annabel in the yard. She nodded and silently they walked up the bank.

Inside, Jan asked, 'Do you want a drink?'

Eddie nodded. 'A beer, if you've got one.'

Jan took two stubby bottles from the fridge and emptied them into glasses before she sat down opposite Eddie.

'I just don't believe it!' she sighed. 'How could he do something like that to me? He knew my circumstances.'

'I don't suppose he feels he's done anything particularly wrong – certainly not illegal. It would be hard to prove that he'd talked you into selling it through him.'

'He didn't,' Jan said. 'That's what makes me so sick. He just watched me walk into it. He even tried to talk me *out* of it. The way the auction was run was totally straight, too.'

'No, it wasn't, at least not entirely. I've checked back and found that it was very lightly advertised.'

'They certainly put an ad in the papers,' Jan said. 'I saw it.'

'One small, low-key advertisement with no photo in the *Brecon & Radnor Express*, which only circulates in mid-Wales, where people don't buy farms unless they're being knocked out with no reserve. Compare that with the massive colour ads they've done this time.'

'The bastard!' she said again. 'He pitched it just right, didn't he? No wonder he was sweating the day of the sale, worrying that a real buyer might turn up.'

'He'd have told his accomplice to bid quietly, and if the bidding dried up too far below the reserve, he could just go on taking bids off the wall until he got there. He had to take the chance that a real buyer wouldn't come and run him up, and he'll have had his own limit. If he wanted to do it legally, there had to be a certain amount of luck involved.'

'But surely it can't be legal for an auctioneer to buy things he's selling?'

'There's no reason why he shouldn't. Anyway, it wasn't Harold Powell who bought Stonewall, it was Terry Davies.'

Jan took a deep breath. 'Right, I'm going to ring him.'

'Why? What are you going to tell him?'

'I'm going to ask him to give me some of the profit he's made, or I'll take him to court.'

'What's the point of that? It'll cost you money and you won't win.'

'We'll see. I'll sue him for incompetence and the publicity in a place like that won't do him any good at all. People need to be able to trust their auctioneers.'

'Well, whatever you do, I wouldn't ring him. You'll do a much better job if he's totally unprepared when you confront him with it. If you can, just sit it out until the next time he comes over. Do you know when that'll be?'

'He said he was coming on Saturday morning, about ten.'

'Oh, good. I'll be here too, then.'

9

On Saturday morning Harold Powell bowled up the track to the stables in a new Range Rover. Jan and Eddie watched as he parked beside the Mercedes and climbed out. He looked around at the yard and the paddocks with a faintly proprietorial air, in the way owners sometimes did when visiting their trainer, Jan had noticed, as if, without their horses in the yard, none of it would be possible.

He sauntered up to the caravan. Jan opened the door when he was still a few paces from it.

'Hello, Harold. How are you?'

'Fine, couldn't be better! Full of the joys of spring. How are the horses?'

'You can see for yourself. Rear Gunner's as fat as a barrel and ready to come in to start some light work.'

'And so is that great big thing over there,' Harold, said, pointing at Russian Eagle.

'Yes, he's going to be ridden today for the first time this season. He belongs to Eddie.'

As Harold climbed into the caravan, she waved a hand in Eddie's direction, 'Eddie Sullivan, this is Harold Powell, my major owner and benefactor.' She smiled at the irony.

Harold preened himself. 'It's been a real pleasure helping you, and watching you do so well,' he said: odious and patronizing, Jan thought. 'That your Merc, is it?' he asked Eddie.

''Fraid so,' Eddie admitted.

'Lovely car,' Harold said approvingly. 'And what sort of business are you in?'

'Pictures – eighteenth-century sporting. That sort of thing.'

'Really?' Harold pricked up his ears. 'I'm senior partner in a firm of auctioneers over in Hay-on-Wye. We have a few good sales of antiques and paintings each year – a lot of nice stuff, too. We had a Herring through a couple of months ago.'

Eddie nodded. 'Though that one turned out not to be right, if I remember correctly.'

'Well, as it turned out, it was a contemporary copy,' Harold blathered, 'but, of course, we could only go on the expert advice we'd been given.'

Eddie nodded and caught Jan's glance. 'And do you ever buy in any pictures on you own behalf?'

'Oh no. Neither buyers nor vendors like it much. They always think you're up to something.'

'But you do in property sales.'

'Excuse me?' Harold asked, as if he couldn't possibly have heard correctly.

'When you're selling property by auction, you do sometimes buy on your own account.'

'Certainly not,' Harold said sharply.

'No, of course not,' Eddie agreed smoothly. 'That would be terrible PR for a small-town auctioneer, but if you were instructed to sell a farm that you thought might be offered at a lowish reserve, and you could keep the sale as low-key as possible, and fill up the saleroom with any old cronies who could be bothered to come in for a bit of a drink afterwards, and you managed to knock it down to a farmer who could sell it on to a company with no overt connection with yourself, but in which you had a substantial equity, you might acquire it that way. If you'd done particularly well and the market was going your way, you might be tempted to make a quick return on it, sometimes making as much as a hundred grand without touching the place.'

As Eddie spoke, the colour in Harold's face increased and the veins on his temple began to stand out. He looked at Jan, trying to keep a lid on his panic, and still wondering if he might be able to bluff it out. 'What the hell are you talking about?' he blustered.

'What are you getting so excited about?' Eddie asked with a dry smile. 'I was speaking hypothetically.'

'Oh no he wasn't.' Jan spoke at last in a low even voice. 'He was talking about Stonewall.'

'Bloody hell, Jan!' Harold turned on her indignantly. 'You don't think I'd do a thing like that to you, do you?'

'I know you did it! The farm was bought by Terry Davies, who sold it straight on to a company run by his brother Rhys, with fifty per cent owned by you!'

'I don't have anything to do with the running of that company,' Harold protested.

'So it was just a coincidence?' Jan laughed scornfully. 'Isn't that amazing? I ask you to sell my farm, a company you happen to own buys it and three months later puts it back on the market for a hundred thousand pounds more than I got? You must be bloody cocky to take a risk like that!'

'Listen, Jan, I'm telling you, it *was* a coincidence,' Harold stammered. 'I'd no idea Rhys had bought it until it came back on the market a fortnight ago.'

'And you didn't think of telling me? I know I was bloody stupid the way I sold that place, but I'm not that daft. I'm suing you for negligence and professional what's-it-called.'

Harold's normally affable features had hardened into an ugly mask. 'If you start anything like that, I'll be taking all my horses away from here, I warn you.'

Four horses – half her existing string, such as it was. But Jan was already prepared. 'You didn't think they were staying here, did you?'

Jan opened the door of the caravan, jumped down over the two wooden steps and almost ran down to the yard. 'Roz, Annabel,' she yelled, 'can you get head-collars for Rear Gunner, Lazy Dove, Mister Mack and Lenny's Lad? Catch them all, bandage their legs and load them into the lorry. Then collect up all tack that belongs to Mr Powell.' She put her hands on her hips and turned back to Harold, who had followed her down to the yard. 'All right, Harold,' she said before as he opened his mouth to speak, 'where would you like them to go?'

Five hours later, Jan watched her lorry turn off the lane and creep back towards the stables.

Eddie had insisted that he should drive Harold's horses back to Wales. She hadn't stopped him. She realized what a hell of a journey it would have been for her, disposing of four horses – including the best in her yard – and half her training income.

It had been bad enough staying behind and seeing the gaps on the tack-room wall where the head-collars had been and so few horses in the paddock. But she felt better just seeing Eddie draw up and jump down from the cab with his usual grin.

'That was fun,' he said. 'I've never driven a truck before. It gives you a great feeling of power, doesn't it, bearing down on some poor little car in a narrow lane.'

'Haven't you got an HGV licence, then?' Jan asked, appalled.

'Good God, no.'

'You're mad! You should never have driven it! It's totally illegal and you were uninsured.'

'It's lucky I didn't hit anything then, isn't it? Anyway, I'm back now and I promise I'll never drive it again.'

'When you said you'd drive, I never dreamed you didn't have a licence!' Jan tried to moderate her exasperation at the unnecessary risk. 'But like you said, you're back, so thanks a lot. I think I'd have kept wanting to turn round and bring them back.'

'I guessed you might regret chucking them out.'

Jan shook her head. 'I'm not regretting it one iota, the twisting bastard! How could I have gone on training for someone who did what he's done to me? And I tell you, Eddie, I *am* going to sue him.'

'It'll cost you, Jan. If money was tight before this, it's going to be a hell of a lot tighter now.'

'Don't I know it,' Jan sighed. 'And I could have done brilliantly with Rear Gunner next year.'

'Poor Jan, there is a horrible irony to the fact that not only has Harold cost you a fair price for your farm, but he's cost you his horses as well.'

'I always knew it was bad thing to end up too dependent on any one person. It's always difficult in my situation, with all the bills to pay at the end of every month, but I'll never let one owner dominate my yard again.'

'Brave words,' Eddie murmured, 'though you may find them hard to stick to. Now,' he went on with a change of tone, 'I seem to remember arriving here hours ago to ride my horse for the first time.'

'Come on then,' Jan said. 'We'll get him in and I'll come and watch you. We'll use the bottom field, that's the flattest.'

Jan threw herself into the job of improving Eddie's riding to a level where he might be expected to win races. For a while, she even managed to forget Harold Powell's treachery and the fact that she was currently down to four horses for the following point-to-point season.

She saw right away that, despite his enthusiasm, Eddie was an inexperienced rider. He sat too far back in the saddle and didn't keep contact with the horse's mouth through the reins; but he was athletic and supple enough to be taught and he seemed to get on well with his horse.

Eddie was also a quick learner and after a while Jan felt more optimistic about his riding. At the same time, she was delighted with Russian Eagle. Despite having been on grass for at least two months, the horse showed a liking for work that was very encouraging, as well as a healthy wish to please. These might not mean he had the will to win, but he could be a surprisingly easy horse to train.

'OK, that'll do,' Jan called after an hour of flat work. 'I don't know who's more knackered – you or the horse.'

Walking back to the stables to untack, Eddie seemed quite bullish.

'I know it's early days, but given that we know the horse has won a good point-to-point in Ireland, what do you think about the Foxhunters'?'

Jan laughed. 'Ask me again in a couple of months and I might be able to give you an opinion.'

'OK, but what about my riding?'

'Right now, you couldn't win a donkey derby, but if you work at it, you might get there. At least you aren't carrying any surplus body weight.'

'Maybe, but I'm still over twelve stone. I'll have to lose at least seven pounds to get to the right weight.'

'Well, don't overdo it.'

When they'd rubbed the horse down and let him back into the paddock, Eddie said he had to go.

'It's been a hell of a day for you,' he said. 'Will you be OK?'

'I should be,' Jan said, more confidently than she felt.

'Don't do anything hasty about Harold Powell, will you? It's bad enough losing the horses.'

'No,' Jan agreed. 'I won't do anything until next week, when I've had a chance to mull it over.'

Eddie climbed into his car and drove off with a wave. Feeling very grateful for his support, a smiling Jan walked back up to her mobile home.

Annabel was ready to leave.

'I've got their tea ready,' she said, 'and I've read Megan the first half of *Charlie and the Chocolate Factory*. I promised her you'd read her the rest.'

'Thanks,' Jan said. 'Actually, that's probably just what I need after today.'

Annabel made a sympathetic face. 'Poor Jan. Are you going to be able to afford to carry on without those four horses?'

'Well, I was only getting keep money for them, but if I don't get some replacements and a few more in by September, it could be tricky. In the meantime, we'll just have to try and build up the horse repair side of things.'

'Now I know what Harold did to you, I'm sure you did the right thing. It must have taken a lot of guts, though.'

Gerry came up on Sunday morning and carried on with various jobs he'd found for himself. Roz and Annabel weren't due in, so Jan brought Megan and Matty down to the yard while she dealt with the horses' feeds and treatments.

Her mother and father had arranged to come over for lunch, which Mary was bringing with her to save Jan cooking. Reg helped Mary up the hill to the caravan, where she happily got on with preparing the food she'd brought, while Reg came down to look at Jan's tenants.

He studied the animals in the paddocks for a few minutes before he turned to Jan with a worried face. 'What's happened to your Mr Powell's horses?' he asked.

She swallowed. Her dad would probably take it as hard as she had.

They sat down opposite each other on two straw bales, and she told him the whole story, up to the point where Eddie had driven the horses back to Wales.

'I knew Eddie would help you', he nodded, 'and I think you've done the right thing, but it must have been hard.'

'What else could I do?'

'I suppose you might have thought to yourself that you were never going to get any kind of compensation for what he did, and the thing to do was just pretend you didn't know what had happened. At least then you'd have kept the good horses and the training fees.'

Jan looked at him. 'Would you have done that?'

Reg smiled and shook his head. 'No, my little Jan, I'd have done exactly what you've done, and bugger the money.'

'You don't think it's irresponsible of me, then? After all, I've got hardly anything coming in as it is. I'm beginning to think I'd have been better off staying at Stonewall. I've worked out that even if I had a dozen decent horses to go racing, I couldn't make more than a couple of hundred quid a week after all the costs, and that's without trying to build a new house. It's lucky we're building up the convalescent side a bit.'

'Well, Jan, you're a hard-working girl; you know what you're doing, and you've got plenty of determination. Things may look pretty bad at the moment, but your mum and I aren't too worried; we know you'll be all right in the long run.'

Jan spent a comfortable afternoon with her parents. Her mother was sewing the initials '*JH*' onto half a dozen exercise sheets Reg had bought Jan as a birthday present. They talked about one of Ben's rare letters that had arrived that week, posted in Australia, where he said he was touring with a band, though he didn't say which.

'What I say is', Mary sighed, 'at least he's alive. He can't be too gone on them drugs or he wouldn't be able to write these letters, would he? And he's doing what he loves.'

Jan and the children waved goodbye as her parents disappeared down the lane in Reg's old green Daihatsu, and she went back in, feeling that whatever the world chucked at her she could take it. In the morning she would go into Broadway to ask her solicitor if she had any chance of successfully suing Harold Powell's firm for mishandling the sale of her property.

She put the children to bed and they were already asleep behind the flimsy partition which separated their makeshift bedroom from the rest of the mobile home when she heard a car drive onto the new hard standing. When she looked out she saw James McNeill's Volvo.

As soon as he got out, she could see that something wasn't right. He stopped twice, then almost fell over as he carried on up towards the caravan.

She didn't need the blast of wine-laden breath that met her when she opened the door to know that he was very drunk. Suddenly uneasy, she was alarmed that a man like James McNeill should have lost control of himself.

At first, although obviously drunk, he seemed fairly normal.

'Just been having lunch with some clients at a stud near Ford', he said, 'and thought I'd check my patients on the way home.'

He stepped back unsteadily from the caravan; Jan came out and closed the door behind her. She didn't like leaving the children for long in case they woke up and panicked, but she didn't want James wandering around her yard on his own in the state he was in.

She walked briskly down the hill in front of him and waited outside the barn for him to follow. When he'd caught up, they walked in. Jan tried to open the first stable door, but the foot latch was stiff and she couldn't budge it without leaning down to push the door in a little.

She was bending over thinking she would have to ask Gerry to look at it for her, when she felt a pair of hands clutch her behind and squeeze. She shot upright and spun round, almost tipping James over.

'What the hell do you think you're doing?' she asked sharply.

The vet shrugged his shoulders defensively and shook his big curly head. 'Don't be like that; I'm only giving you a cuddle. It must have been a long time for you.'

Jan gritted her teeth. She didn't want a second showdown in two days. 'Oh, that's what you were doing was it? Well, thanks very much, but I really don't want a cuddle right now.'

'All right, I'm sorry,' James said without any visible remorse and pushed past her, through the stable door which was now open.

'How's this little bugger?' he turned to her.

'That's the mare,' Jan answered coldly. 'I don't think she's feeling a thing on that hock now. Frankly, she might just as well go home.'

'Oh, the owners won't mind if she stays here another week or so,' James said conspiratorially, 'especially if I tell them she must.'

'I don't want to keep any horses here under false pretences, James. That's not how I operate.'

James shrugged a shoulder and leaned against his patient's quarters. 'It's up to you, but I heard you lost a few horses yesterday.'

Jan was amazed, as she had been before, by how quickly news travelled in the racing world, even at her lowly level.

'I didn't lose them, I told the owner to shift them.'

'Why on earth did you do that?'

'Because he cheated me out of a lot of money over a property he sold for me.'

'Poor old Jan,' James slurred. He put out a hand to touch her arm, but she shrugged it off. 'May I suggest', he went on, 'in future you don't let your principles get in the way of making a profit, or you won't last long in this game.'

Jan could hardly believe that this was the same man who had been so businesslike in all their dealings up to now. She walked to the door of the stables. 'James, I'm sorry to say this, but you seem far too drunk to make any judgement about these horses. Why not come back in the morning or next time you're passing?'

James's eyes seemed to glaze for a moment, then a big, uncontrolled leer spread across his face, which was nothing like his usual charming smile. He pushed himself away from the mare and walked carefully from the stable. As Jan shut and bolted the door, she felt his arms wrap themselves right round her waist, meeting in front of her stomach.

She turned as far as she could, to be met with a waft of sour, winy breath as his face lurched towards hers.

'You're so good,' he muttered. 'You deserve a little kiss.'

Jan moved sharply to avoid his lowering mouth and banged her head hard on the angle of the door frame. For a few moments of semi-consciousness her world went dark, with flashes of brilliant light. When she came to, she found herself lying on the shallow stack of straw bales inside the door of the barn. James McNeill's face was just above hers. There was a lecherous gleam in his eyes.

'All right, Jan? God, you're lovely!'

His cold, damp mouth descended on hers, and she gritted her teeth as he tried to jab his tongue against them. A sudden nausea welled up in her and she could hardly breathe from the pressure of his body on hers. Suddenly she was desperate; she wanted to scream, but she had no breath to do it.

She felt him shift his body over her. Taking the chance the movement gave her, she brought her knee up with all the force she could find and drove it straight into his genitals.

The effect was instant.

He howled and fell sideways away from her, slipping off the bales and crashing to the ground. She quickly rolled off the straw and ran to the door, where she stood, panting with fear and rage, and looked back as the dogs ran in and started barking at the commotion.

James was doubled up, foetus-like and groaning. Slowly, he unfurled himself and pulled himself up until he was sitting with his back against the bales.

He looked up and saw her. He seemed suddenly sober. His eyes were filled with anger and he breathed deeply through quivering nostrils as he tried to regain control of himself.

Neither he nor Jan spoke. Slowly he pulled himself to his feet and walked towards her. She stood rigid, determined not to show any fear, but shaking inside.

He walked straight past her, out into the yard. She didn't move as she heard him walk away towards the gate. His footsteps stopped.

'My lorry will be here in the morning to collect the four horses I consigned. Have my bill ready, give it to the driver and it'll be settled by return.'

Jan didn't reply or turn around. The footsteps resumed, echoing from the building opposite, until James reached the gate and his car.

Jan still hadn't moved from the stable door when she heard the car reverse and move off down the drive. Her shoulders heaved and large tears welled up to sting the corners of her eyes and trickle down her face as she thought of the two small children asleep in the caravan.

Jan leaned against the sturdy oak stanchion of the barn door frame. Her back slithered slowly down the smooth old timber until she was sitting on the ground with her legs hunched up in front of her. Fred came up, sniffed and licked her ear. She put a hand out to stroke his bony back and gazed around through blurred eyes at the buildings, the spotless ground between, the new half-barrels of her favourite orange-red geraniums, which Gerry had brought up in a show of devotion.

She thought of all the extravagant expectations she'd had for her yard until just a few days before. All her dreams of building up a busy racing stables, turning out a string of winners, perhaps one day – she had dared to think – going on to train National Hunt horses, had completely collapsed. Even her short-term aim of building up the best convalescent home for horses in the Cotswolds was looking dicey if James McNeill's patients were to be removed next day.

If she was going to make anything out of the place to support herself and her children, she might even have to abandon this ambition and revert to the unglamorous, low-paid drudgery of keeping hunters at livery.

She closed her eyes, thought of the kids and sighed. If that was what she had to do to survive, so be it. She pulled herself together, got to her feet and walked from the yard back up to the caravan. Letting herself in quietly, she checked that the children were asleep and put the kettle on to boil. She heaped two self-indulgent spoonsful of sugar into a mug of tea and sat down at the table. From the shelf above her head, she pulled out a dog-eared file she had kept since first planning her yard at Edge Farm. She opened it and ran through her list of outgoings for the twentieth time to see which of them could be cut.

As she considered the options, she felt her tears returning. She shook her head desolately and wished that John was there, standing behind her, to guide her with his quiet, unhurried advice. The only people she could turn to now were her parents and she had no intention of upsetting them with an account of what James McNeill had just tried to do. Even if she lied to them about his reasons for removing the horses and, presumably, not sending any more, they would worry about her. They would want to help out with money, when she knew they had little enough of their own.

A couple of times, though, her hand strayed to the telephone, wanting to hear her father's reassuring voice, but she resisted. She thought about ringing Eddie; she could have told him exactly what happened, knowing he wouldn't be too shocked and would understand her reactions. But she felt she had asked more of him than she'd intended over the Harold business. She had already used up her share of his good will, given their principal relationship was that of owner and trainer, whatever additional undercurrents she might sometimes have sensed between them.

In the end, she picked up her handset and dialled Annabel's number. She listened, imagining the phone ringing in Annabel's pretty cottage kitchen, until an answerphone clicked in.

'Sorry I'm not here. Please leave a message after the beep and I'll call you back.'

'Annabel, it's Jan. Where are you? Something's happened and I need to talk to you. Call me if you can, any time up till midnight. Otherwise, see you in the morning,' she added bravely.

Jan barely slept that night. Annabel didn't ring, and half a dozen times Jan came close to dialling Eddie's number. But she held back, even harbouring a nagging and illogical idea that Annabel was with Eddie, and feeling confusingly ambivalent about it.

Annabel came in next morning, fresh and keen as always, but as soon as she saw Jan, a worried frown creased her brow.

'Jan, you look terrible! What's wrong? I've only just picked up your message. I'm sorry I wasn't there last night. I went to have dinner at my parents' and decided to stay the night.'

Jan tried to smile. 'I don't pay you enough for what you do as it is, let alone expecting you to be on call the whole time.'

'What's happened?' Annabel pressed.

Jan sat down and felt her face collapse as tears welled up in her eyes. 'I'm afraid we're losing four of our patients today.' She went on to describe James McNeill's drunken arrival the previous evening and what he had done to her. She concluded that, without Harold's horses and no immediate prospect of others to come, she would have to advertise for hunting liveries. Failing that, she would just have to let Roz go; she and Annabel could manage the children and the horses between them.

Annabel, sitting opposite, put a hand on Jan's and shook her head. 'Jan, I know what James did must have come as an awful shock, but I'm afraid it's something that some men do, isn't it – more than you'd think, actually. And at least you gave him a good kicking.'

Jan couldn't help smiling a little at the thought. 'I tell you what, I certainly made his eyes water!'

'Yes, and you got rid of him. It seems the rumours Roz heard must have been true. But it'd be a terrible shame if he stopped sending us horses.' Annabel's mouth tightened in a regretful wince.

'He's stopped all right,' Jan said. 'Anyway, I wouldn't have them.'

'Jan, this is your business; you can't be like that or take these things personally. It's your livelihood, whatever you think about him. And he certainly won't try to molest you again.'

'Yes, well, it's a bit hypothetical, isn't it?'

'OK, but there are several other people who have talked about sending you horses – Colonel Gilbert, and even old skinflint Mr Carey was muttering something about maybe sending us a horse for a bit of interest next winter.'

'Your landlord? I'll believe that when I see it,' Jan snorted.

'Funnily enough, I think he might. He's really rather nice, once you get to know him.'

'Hmm,' Jan grunted. 'That's not surprising. Men always tend to be nice to slim, beautiful girls. Anyway, thanks for listening. I suppose we'd better get on with some work.'

'Here's Roz,' Annabel said, seeing her car juddering up the track. 'Don't say anything about letting her go just yet. See how things are for the next week or so and you needn't pay me for August. I've honestly got all the money I need for the moment.'

'Of course I'll pay you. But you're right about Roz. I won't make any hasty decisions; I've made enough of those already.' Jan spoke ruefully, thinking of what John or her father might have done. 'But I'm still going to see the solicitors this morning to see if there's anything I can do about Harold Powell.'

Morris, Jones & Co. was a small, old-fashioned firm of solicitors in Broadway who had looked after Reg Pritchard's uncomplicated affairs for the last thirty years. The senior partner, Mr Russell, had known Jan since she was born and had seen her ride in her first point-to-points when she was a teenager.

Jan sat in front of his big mahogany desk in an office that smelled of musty paper and pipe tobacco. After a brief chat about the horses in Jan's yard and her prospects for the next season, she handed over her dossier of correspondence with Harris & Powell regarding Stonewall Farm. The old solicitor leafed through the sheaf of papers until he came to a newspaper cutting of a small advertisement for the sale. He took off his gold-rimmed glasses and leaned back in his chair.

'I'm afraid it looks as if Mr Powell's firm fulfilled all the normal statutory and professional obligations in the way they offered your property for sale. You could argue that they didn't do it all that well, but this would be terribly hard to prove and, undoubtedly, the case would be fought by their professional indemnity insurers.' A look of regret on the lawyer's face, rusty and wrinkled like an old iron roof, expressed his view of the inevitable outcome. 'If you lost, you would have to pay all their costs and I'm afraid you would find that you'd spent a great deal of money for absolutely nothing. In my opinion, legally, there's no point in pursuing this matter. I'm sorry.'

Jan stared at his kindly face, feeling almost sick with frustration at his passive attitude, but grateful for his desire to avoid wasting money that she didn't have.

'But surely', she said, 'the publicity would be very bad for a firm like theirs in a small town?'

The solicitor looked unconvinced. 'I don't suppose it would

worry them much.' He glanced at a letter from Harris & Powell. 'I expect they've got a monopoly in the town and people soon forget small legal cases, if they ever bother to read the reports in the first place.'

'Well, I know Harold Powell, and I reckon he *would* be worried at the thought of bad publicity. Couldn't we scare him a bit and see what happens – let him know that we intend to take the matter further?'

Mr Russell nodded. 'We could certainly write him a strong letter to that effect. That wouldn't do any harm and, once in a while, it can produce a result.'

'How much would it cost?'

'To send one letter? About fifty pounds, I should think.'

Jan repressed her instinctive reaction to what seemed an exorbitant charge for one letter. 'All right,' she said. 'Would you do that? And make it very strong – as aggressive as a solicitor's allowed to be.'

The lawyer smiled. 'All right, Mrs Hardy.' He leaned forward over his desk. 'We may look mild and docile, but we do know how to bark when we have to.'

As James McNeill had threatened when he left the night before, a lorry arrived for his patients soon after Jan arrived back from Broadway. She watched with mixed emotions as the horses were driven away. It was a real blow that such a useful source of income should have dried up after only five weeks, but she knew she could never again be comfortable dealing with a man who had tried to abuse her in the way McNeill had.

With only four horses left, the farm had a distinctly empty feel to it. Sounds seemed to echo more loudly around the buildings and Jan's depression began to infect her two helpers as well.

As the week wore on, Jan felt no better and nothing appeared to alleviate her gloom, besides receiving a copy of an unexpectedly blunt letter Mr Russell had written to Harold Powell on her behalf. She prayed, without much hope, that it might have some effect.

Looking at her list of possible owners, she wondered what she could do to conjure up more. Angrily she crossed off the name Bernie Sutcliffe, the man James McNeill had said he was going to send to visit her yard.

She wondered if Eamon Fallon might be persuaded to buy another good horse. He looked as if he had the money, but he hadn't been to the yard since Dingle Bay had arrived.

She was sure that Colonel Gilbert would stick to his word – after all, he'd paid in advance with the delivery of straw. And Gwillam Evans, the farmer who had bred Rear Gunner and still owned his half-brother, Barneby Boy, had rung the week before to say he would at least come and look at her set-up, although it was over seventy miles away. That was all very well, she told herself, but in the meantime she couldn't live on fresh air and promises.

On Saturday morning, Reg and Mary called in on their way back from a shopping expedition to Evesham. While Reg immediately spotted the absence of some of Jan's injured tenants, Mary had other concerns.

Sitting in the caravan, where Megan was showing her the doll's house, Mary turned to Jan with a worried face. 'What's happened to Megan's shoes, Jan? They're practically falling to bits!'

'Nothing's happened to them, Mum. Just normal wear and tear.'

'But they shouldn't be that worn out. Where did you get them?'

'I can't remember now,' Jan said, pretending she hadn't realized the child's shoes were as bad as they were. 'Oxfam in Tewkesbury, I think.'

'You mean they were second-hand to start with?' Mary asked, appalled.

'They'd hardly been worn.'

'Well it's time you got her some new ones.'

'Mum, they're all right. Do you know what kid's shoes cost

these days? It's a total rip-off, when they only fit them for a few months.'

'A child's feet are very important, Jan. I made sure that whatever else you had to go without, you always had good, solid shoes, and you always had lovely feet.'

'All right, all right, Mum. I'll get her some more, but right now, you know, I've got a few other priorities.'

Mary suddenly realized she had pushed Jan too far. 'Oh, I'm sorry, my duck. I know it's been hard for you. Your father said it must be with losing those horses of Mr Powell's. Look, if money's a bit short, let *me* get her the shoes.'

'No! No, Mum, I can cope!' Jan tried to soften her indignation. 'I don't want you to be worrying about me when it's hard enough for you to look after yourselves.'

'Your father and me would rather see you and Megan and Matty well and happy. We want to help you.'

'I know you want to help', Jan said, trying to stay calm, 'and I'm really grateful, but I promise you, I can manage on my own.'

'It's not as though you've a man to help you now.'

'For God's sake, Mum! I can manage without a man, you know – I'm bloody determined to. I'll cut the grass verges with nail scissors if I have to!' Jan heard her voice rising and regretted it at once. 'I'm sorry,' she mumbled

'That's all right, love,' Mary said gently. 'I know what you're like, and you always have been, but don't be too proud. Don't forget that we're always there if you really need us.'

As she watched her father's Daihatsu trundle away, she was glad she had been strong enough to turn down their offer of help, and she felt almost strengthened by it in her determination to pull herself through this early crisis in her new life at Edge Farm.

When Eddie appeared later in the morning for another schooling session on Russian Eagle, Jan didn't want him to see how hard the week's events had hit her. But after they'd done a good two hours' work, they went up to sit outside her caravan with a drink and Eddie took a long, thoughtful slug of his beer. He looked at her with friendly concern in his eyes.

'Jan, it's no good you bottling things up and being all retentive, you know – not with me. What's been going on?'

Jan lifted one shoulder. 'It was a bit hard, losing Harold's horses, I admit, but—'

'You've lost more than Harold's,' Eddie interrupted. 'You had seven horses in for repair last week and I've noticed there are only three now.'

Jan grimaced and nodded. 'James McNeill came round last Sunday; when he left, he told me he was sending a lorry to collect them.' She sighed. 'They went on Monday.'

Eddie's eyes widened at what this must have meant to her. 'What on earth did you do to let that happen?'

'What did I do? It was more what I *didn't* do!' Jan said. She took a gulp of cider and started to describe the vet's drunken attempt to have sex with her the previous Sunday.

As he listened, Eddie's face wrinkled. 'The bastard! I have to say, on the one occasion I met him, I thought he was dodgy, specially after Roz told me how he puts it about all over the place.' He leaned forward and topped up Jan's glass from the bottle beside him. 'Anyway, you're better off without a two-faced shit like that for a client.'

'I shouldn't take it so personally, though.'

'I should think it's bloody impossible not to. Anyway, there are plenty of other vets around who are also decent human beings.'

'I know, but I wish they'd just send me a few horses.'

'Have you asked them, or told them what you can offer?'

'I phoned them all when I first came here,' Jan said defensively.

'They'll probably need reminding and you should get in touch with the big racing stables round here, too; it might suit them to send young and injured horses here, rather than have them clogging up their yards – especially now they're bringing horses back in from their summer break. What you need is a really good professional-looking brochure printed which you can mail to everyone you can think of who might be a potential customer.'

Jan sighed. 'I know; you're right, but, as always, it's a question of money. Which comes first, the chicken or the egg?'

'Don't worry about that. I'll get it done and you can knock it off my training fees at the end of the season. And I tell you what,' he went on as if he'd had a sudden inspiration, 'I happen to have a dollop of cash at the moment from a big picture I sold, so why don't I pay you now for Eagle's training fees up to the end of the year? It would suit me if I didn't have to think about bills again for a few months.'

Jan drew in a quick breath. 'Oh, Eddie, I don't know. What if something went wrong with the horse and I couldn't go on training him?'

'He'd still be here while he was convalescing, wouldn't he? And if, God forbid, he was so badly hurt he had to be put down, he's well insured and I'd want you to find a replacement for him right away. I don't know of anyone else who could do a better job than you.'

'Well, if you're sure . . .'

'I am,' Eddie urged. 'It really would suit me, I promise.'

'All right,' Jan nodded, praying that she wouldn't regret the subtle change in their relationship that this would make. 'Thanks a lot. It would be an enormous help right now.'

'Fine. I'll bring the cash round . . .', he paused, Jan guessed, for a mental scroll through his diary, 'tomorrow evening. I know it's a Sunday, but if you can find a babysitter, I'll take you out to dinner as well, if you like.'

'Now you're spoiling me. You mustn't make a habit of it!' Jan smiled, very relieved by the removal of her immediate cash-flow problems, as well as Eddie's vote of confidence in her. But she found it hard to believe that, although he was three years younger than her, Eddie was ready to offer so much support without a more physical motive, and she was concerned not to let her gratitude turn into any other kind of emotion.

'Does that mean yes or no?' he asked.

'Yes, please. I can always drop the kids at my mum's if I can't get Roz or Annabel to sit.'

'I'm sure Gerry would do it for you,' Eddie said with a twinkle in his eye.

Jan shook her head. 'He already does more than he should for me. It wouldn't be right to encourage him.'

'You could look on it as a way of rewarding him for all he's done – he'd probably love to hang around here for an evening, feeling close to you, even if you weren't here.'

'Don't be unkind, Eddie. He's just a bit shy.'

'I know. He's a lovely chap. Now,' he said, looking at his watch, 'I'll have to go soon, but if you give me an idea of what you want to say in this brochure, I'll take a few digital shots of the place and put together some layouts on the computer.'

When he'd left, Jan admitted to herself how much Eddie's visit had cheered her. Her pressing cash-flow problems were all but resolved and, suddenly, everything she'd dreamed of now seemed possible. But it wasn't just the money and the encouragement Eddie had given her. Quite against her will, she'd also found herself comparing him with John – until she realized it was an impossible comparison. As men, they were poles apart and their individual appeal for her couldn't have been more different.

Jan began to enjoy the rest of the day, massaging a horse's back, lunging Gale Bird and walking round the fields checking all her other tenants with Megan, while she gave Matty a ride on her shoulders, pretending to be a horse herself.

After tea with the children, she still felt optimistic enough to pull out the plans of her house which she'd had drawn up – the house which she hoped to see rise from the rubble-strewn patch where once the old Edge Farm house had stood.

Beside the outline, already dug by Gerry, stood piles of stone blocks and tiles. Under a tarpaulin were several old oak beams, recycled pine rafters and floorboards – all found and sent over by Eddie over the last few weeks.

After gazing at the plans for a while, Jan went out and walked around the site, imagining how each room would be – where Matty and Megan would sleep, and where her kitchen window would look out across the broad sweep of the Severn Valley to the Malvern ridge.

She sat on a big hunk of golden limestone to watch the setting sun, chuckled to herself then sighed. It was going to be a bloody long time before any of the house was real, but now, at least for this evening, it felt like it might actually happen one day.

10

On Sunday evening, Eddie arrived as promised with a bag full of cash to cover his bills for the next five months. He also produced the draft of a professional-looking brochure – *Edge Farm Stables, Equine Recovery Centre*. Jan was delighted with it, so Eddie confirmed that he would have it printed and sent to everyone they could think of who might be interested in Jan's expertise.

When they'd finished drawing up a comprehensive list of addresses, Eddie took Jan to a noisy Italian restaurant near Cheltenham. All the waiters there seemed to be his best friend and Jan didn't miss the nudging and winking that went on between them. She wondered how many women Eddie had taken there before. Looking at him laughing and smiling, with his eyes twinkling, she found herself thinking what he'd be like in bed, though she dismissed the thought almost as soon as it had entered her mind. Besides, she thought, nothing he said or did suggested he wanted any more from her than her company and the chance to talk about horses.

Later, he dropped her back at the caravan and said goodnight with his usual fleeting kiss on one cheek. He promised to be back in a few days with the finished brochure.

The following day Jan went to her bank in Broadway to pay in the cash Eddie had brought and drove back buoyed up with renewed confidence.

On Thursday, though, when Annabel had gone home after work, leaving Jan alone with the children in the caravan, her depression seeped back.

Around nine, the evening turned gloomy. Lights had started to twinkle across the valley and the sky was turning thick black when a car's headlights swept off the lane and two powerful beams lit up her drive. She couldn't see what kind of car it was and she waited curiously to see who had come to visit her this late. She was not averse to some company to take her mind off things. It was only when the driver had parked and walked halfway up to the caravan that Jan saw it was Harold Powell.

Instinctively she shrank back and thought about locking the door, but she detected a hesitancy in Harold's approach which suggested he hadn't come aggressively.

Nevertheless, she waited until he knocked on the door.

'Who is it?'

'Jan, it's Harold. I've driven all the way over from Hay to see you. Can I come in?'

Jan opened the door and looked at him without displaying any emotion. 'How did you know I'd be here?'

'I phoned earlier and your girl, Roz, said you would be. Didn't she tell you?'

Jan thought back. 'No, but I was up in the top paddock when she left. Anyway, as you're here I suppose you'd better come in.' Jan pulled the door open a little wider and beckoned him up.

He climbed the two wooden steps and sidled into the caravan.

Jan closed the door behind him and waved him to one of the padded benches. He sat and slid his knees under the table.

Jan didn't join him. 'Well, why are you here?' she asked.

'Look, Jan. I can understand what you must have thought when you saw Stonewall on the market for so much more than you got, but the simple fact is the market's hardened a hell of a lot in the last few months, and I did warn you at the time not to sell in a hurry. Whatever your solicitor says, we did everything by the book when we were selling the place.' He looked up at Jan, who still hadn't sat down. She said nothing and didn't react. 'Believe me,' he went on with a hint of desperation, 'I had no idea Davies bought the place just to turn it for a profit; I thought he was expanding, but I can see why you think it looks a bit iffy, and obviously we don't want clients feeling they've been ill-treated. So, we thought we should talk to you about it.'

'I don't want to talk about it. I want the extra profit you made out of my property.'

'If you'd waited until the summer, like I said, you'd have had it. It was your decision to sell when you did, not mine.'

'And it was your decision to put just one ad in the *Brecon & Radnor Express* and nowhere else.'

'Any serious buyer for a Welsh hill farm would always check the *Brecon & Radnor* – you know that.'

'Don't bullshit me, Harold. I've known you too long. You know damn well you wanted as few people as possible to see that ad. I can't think why I didn't complain at the time, but John wasn't long dead; I had other things on my mind and you took advantage of that; you knew I wanted to get away from the farm as soon as I could.'

'Like I say, Jan, it was your decision, not mine.'

'All right, so because my solicitor's sent you a letter you've decided to talk to me about it. What exactly did you want to say?'

'After all our expenses, and assuming the new buyer doesn't back down, we will make a profit of about fifty grand—'

'Harold! Don't talk rubbish! You'll make closer to a hundred.'

'Jan, calm down,' Harold said mildly. 'Think about all the expenses and the opportunity cost.'

'More bullshit,' Jan reorted. 'I see you've let the grass keep already.'

'At a very low rent, just to keep the fields grazed off.'

Jan uttered a cynical grunt. 'All right, then. What are you suggesting?'

'We propose, and this is completely without prejudice, mind—'

'What's that?'

'Any offer I make to you this evening is no admission of liability and would have no bearing on any subsequent court proceedings.'

'Go on.'

'We'd like you to sign this letter.' Harold pulled a folded sheet of paper from the pocket of his tweed jacket, opened it and put it on the table facing Jan.

She picked it up. It was a typed letter, addressed from Edge Farm with her name at the end, confirming that, in handling the sale of Stonewall Farm, in her opinion, Harris & Powell had acted properly and with professional integrity throughout. Jan looked up at Harold. 'Why on earth would I sign this?'

'Because, to show our sincerity in not wanting you to feel aggrieved, we would make you an ex-gratia payment of ten thousand pounds.'

Jan felt herself flush with satisfaction that her lawyer's letter had produced a result, but she felt deeply indignant that Harold thought she could be bought off so cheaply.

To avoid eye-contact with Harold, she looked down at the letter again. 'To sign this letter, so that you can avoid all the hassle and embarrassment of being sued by me, I'd want half the profit – fifty grand and not a penny less!'

'I told you, Jan, that's about all we made, and we could easily prove in court that we'd behaved properly.'

'Really? Well, the bad publicity would kill your business stone dead.'

Harold shook his head with a supercilious smile. 'I don't think so, Jan. Not when it comes out that you wanted the place sold as quickly as possible. Your mother-in-law would testify to that.'

Jan gulped. She knew it was true that if Olwen took Harold's side, the local community would trust her more than an outsider like herself.

'No,' Harold went on. 'Our offer is based on our sense of fairness.'

'It's because you don't want the hassle, Harold, let's face it. Or the legal bills.'

'Look, Jan. You can think what you like, but the bottom line is, if you sign that letter, we'll give you ten grand – cash.'

'All right, Harold,' Jan said. Harold's eyes gleamed triumphantly before Jan went on. 'You leave me the letter and I'll think about it.'

The brightness in Harold's eyes dimmed. 'Look, Jan, we don't want this dragging on and on.'

'It won't; I'll let you know what I think by the end of the week, OK?'

Harold took a deep breath and scrutinized Jan's face in an attempt to read her mind. 'All right,' he said, sliding himself along the bench to stand up. 'But just remember it's a very generous offer, which we are under no professional obligation to make, but we *are* honourable men.'

'I'm sure you are,' Jan said, opening the door to let Harold out. 'Thank you for thinking of me,' she added deadpan.

Harold paused for a moment, apparently to say something, but he seemed to think better of it and dropped down the two wooden steps before disappearing into the darkness towards his car. 'G'night Jan,' he called back when he reached the Range Rover.

Jan closed the door and picked up the letter Harold had left. She folded it and, with steady hands, tore it slowly into a handful of tiny squares and dropped them into her swing bin.

Although Jan had grown close to Annabel, she didn't tell her everything that went on in her life. She sensed that it could be dangerous or, at least, leave her potentially vulnerable, to expose too much of herself to any one person.

She sometimes felt, though, that this was a wasted exercise with Annabel, who seemed to have an uncanny knack of identifying her problems even before she was aware of them herself. The morning after Harold had been round, Jan told her little more than he'd come to offer some kind of recompense for any grievance she might have felt over the sale of Stonewall Farm. Annabel was sitting with a cup of coffee, brewed from freshly ground beans she'd bought for Jan in Cheltenham. She looked up and nodded. 'I was at a dinner party near Hay last weekend,' she said. 'Someone asked me why Harold had taken his horses from you. They couldn't understand it. And a woman said she'd asked Harold about it. Apparently he was really cagey, so now everyone thinks you had some kind of row, and, seeing the price that's being asked for Stonewall, they've put two and two together. Not that they know Harold has any connection with the new vendor, but, you know—'

'Yes, I know,' Jan said. 'And the smarmy creep was trying to kid me he didn't know his partner in the engineering firm had bought the farm.'

'Is there any chance he'd offer to send his horses back?'

'I've no idea,' said Jan, and meant it. She hadn't even considered that Harold would want to after the way she'd sent them home to him. 'Anyway, I wouldn't have them.'

'But, Jan, you know you'd have more winners next season with Rear Gunner. He'll easily qualify for the Foxhunters'.'

'Harold Powell would need to crawl on his hands and knees across a bed of burning coals to this caravan before I'd even think about training for him again.'

'Jan,' Annabel said with sudden sharpness, 'I've told you before, you mustn't take these things so personally. You're not offering to be an owner's best friend, you're just agreeing to train whatever horses they send you, however useless they are.'

'Well, I'll just tell you something, I'm not interested in training useless horses. It's far easier to train good ones and miles easier to get winners from them. I don't intend to take on any old rubbish, just for the training fee, which barely covers my costs anyway.'

'But Harold's aren't useless,' Annabel pointed out quietly.

'Too bad,' Jan said.

On her own, Jan wondered how far she could carry these principles and how much they would cost her. They were bound to cost, either financially or emotionally, or both, but were they worth it?

In the last fortnight she'd lost seven horses whom she desperately needed to provide cash-flow for her business, and yet it was the same desire not to compromise that had made her tear up Harold's letter.

Later that day Jan felt gratified when, through an ironic twist of fate, a new owner arrived at Edge Farm – an owner with little apparent knowledge of horses and all the trappings of big money. He had phoned in the morning to ask if she would be there, saying no more than he wanted to see her yard.

He drove up Jan's track in a brand-new Jaguar, and seemed to hesitate before committing himself to parking it among the collection of untidy vehicles on the hard standing. As soon as Jan caught sight of him, she decided that he was a very unattractive individual.

She and Roz watched him from the yard as he got out, locked the car and picked his way gingerly towards them, as if wary of contact between his black Gucci shoes and the naked earth.

'Cor!' Roz said. 'He looks a right pleb.'

'Shh,' Jan said, grinning.

As he came closer, Jan saw that his shoes were the only thing about him that shone. Everything else was grey and lustreless, especially his skin. Although Jan guessed he was in his mid-forties, there was already a patina of age on his deeply furrowed face. He had a long, thin head, topped with a covering of scanty, dull grey hair. He was about five foot eight, slightly hunched and wearing a jacket of tiny black and white checks. Close to, though, he smelt expensively clean and his shirt looked as if it was new out of its packaging that morning.

'Hello,' she said, meeting him as he reached the gateway into the yard.

'Are you Jan Hardy?' he asked with a lack of charm which would, in time, become familiar to her.

Jan nodded.

He held out a bony, light grey hand. 'I'm Bernie Sutcliffe. James McNeill told me about you.'

'Did he?' Jan asked. 'I'm very surprised. He took all his horses away at the beginning of last week.'

'I know. He told me. And that was when he told me not to come near you, but I like people who stand up to big bastards like McNeill. He tried to get his dirty paws on my girlfriend last week

– thinks just 'cos he introduced us it gives him some kind of rights.' He spoke with a nasal whine and a strong Black Country accent.

'Ah,' Jan nodded, thinking she was beginning to see what had happened. 'He did mention you to me a few weeks ago.'

Bernie wagged his head up and down with quick, jerky nods. 'Did he tell you what I want?'

'He just said you might be interested in owning a racehorse and he'd suggested you try pointing first.'

'Yeah, well. Sandy, my girlfriend, she fancies it. I know nothing about it, but I'm a quick learner', he added sharply, 'and I can smell when people are trying to tuck me up.'

'You won't smell anything like that round here, Mr Sutcliffe, I can assure you,' Jan said and wished she hadn't sounded quite so haughty.

'We'll see,' Bernie said ambiguously, before changing his tone. 'What would you suggest if I want a horse to win a few races?'

'First of all, whatever I suggest or do for you, there's absolutely no guarantee you'll have a winner. We can do a lot to shorten the odds; we can go out and find you the right horse with the right pedigree; we can enter it in the right races and in the right company. We can make sure we've got the best pilot on board. But we never cheat and we only play with a straight bat.'

'I've been told there's a lot that don't,' Bernie said.

'I wouldn't have thought so, Mr Sutcliffe, not in pointing. There'd not be much purpose to it. The prize money's pretty pathetic and it's almost impossible to get a large bet on.'

'Call me Bernie,' he grunted. 'I meant on the proper race tracks.'

'I wouldn't know. I don't have a professional licence so I can't run on National Hunt courses, except hunter chases, which are open to point-to-pointers, but they take a lot of winning.'

Bernie glanced at Roz, who was hovering near them. 'Haven't you got an office or something, where we can talk business?' he asked Jan.

'Only the caravan where I live.' She nodded up the hill.

'You live in that?' Bernie asked, not even trying to disguise his horror.

'I take my job seriously, Mr Sutcliffe—'

'Bernie,' he interrupted more impatiently, and Jan noticed for the first time that he was looking at her closely. He seemed pleased with what he saw.

'There was no house with this place when I bought it, but I need to be near my horses as much as possible; there's always things that can go wrong and the earlier you can catch them the better.'

Bernie nodded appreciatively. 'Let's go up there, then.'

Jan led him from the yard and up the bank. As they walked, she turned to look at him and saw his eyes flashing all round the place, taking in everything that was there.

'What's your business?' she asked conversationally.

His eye shot back to hers. 'Investments', he said with deliberate vagueness before evidently deciding that was too unspecific to satisfy anyone. 'Salvage and property,' he added.

'Developing?' Jan asked, out of curiosity.

'Developing a bit. Letting mostly and a few other things.'

'Where are you based, then?' she asked as if it weren't obvious from his accent that it could only be in the Black Country.

'Brierley Hill.'

'Oh, right,' Jan said, not knowing where that was. They'd reached the caravan and she led him up the two steps. Inside she offered him a seat and a cup of tea.

He sat down and squeezed his legs under the table. For the next half-hour he grilled Jan on what sort of horse and service he could expect for the amount of money he wanted to spend. It wasn't a big budget and Jan told him if he wanted a good chance of winning anything beyond a member's race, he'd probably have to spend more.

'And to give yourself a realistic chance beyond that, you would really need two or three horses because any horse can go wrong. The bones, ligaments and muscles of a horse's legs are amongst its most vital assets. They're highly specialized limbs and when a horse is racing fit and tuned right up, it doesn't take a lot to damage them – sometimes just in their stable they can give themselves a knock that'll put them off for a month or so. And, of course, their lungs and their heart are all sensitive, particularly when they're under pressure.'

'All right, all right. You'll put me off the whole thing if you go on. Say I told you to spend ten grand, then could you get me something?'

'I should be able to find you a horse capable of winning. Then it's a hundred and thirty quid a week, plus shoeing, vet's bills and transport.'

'You're not using that slimy bastard McNeill for a vet are you?'

'No.'

'Good. How come he took his horses away from you?'

Jan took a deep breath. 'They weren't his, they belonged to his clients; they were here to be nursed back to full health – backs, legs, coughs – stuff like that. And he took them because he turned up here drunk, about ten o'clock at night, two Sundays ago and molested me in the barn. I'm afraid I had to give him a serious kick in the balls.'

Bernie's eyes lit up, and he uttered a harsh cackle. 'The dirty bastard. Serve him bloody well right! Good on you, girl! Well, if you see him again, you tell him Bernie Sutcliffe's having a horse with you, and let's rub his bloody nose in it, right?'

Annabel told Jan she wanted to take her and the children to the pub for supper that night, using Bernie's promise of a new horse as an excuse.

'But, Bel,' Jan protested, 'I think we should wait till he's bought and paid for one before we celebrate. He looks the type that could mess me about before anything happens.'

'Oh well, come out anyway. You've had a bloody awful couple of weeks and it's about time things turned around for you.'

Jan didn't argue. Before they went, she fed Matthew, loaded

him into a papoose and wondered how long it would be before he was too heavy for her to carry.

It was a sunny evening and the pub was packed. A lot of people there seemed to know Jan and greeted her warmly. Julie behind the bar coochi-cooed at Matthew, who looked at her spiky hair and howled.

When Annabel had bought the drinks, they sat at a table looking at the menu. Jan noticed that Annabel kept glancing around the room and guessed that she was expecting someone to join them. She wondered if it was a man, but after a few minutes, a young woman emerged from the crowd and came up to the table.

'Hi, Annabel.'

'Hello, Penny; have a glass of wine,' Annabel offered, as the girl hovered before sitting down to join them.

'This is Penny Price,' Annabel told Jan. 'She comes from near my parents' home up at Kington.' Penny was in her late twenties, short but heavily built with stout arms and big breasts that filled her shirt. Her straight black hair and big, forthright brown eyes were typical of the country girls Jan knew from the Welsh borders. 'This is Jan Hardy, and Megan and Matthew.'

The girl nodded at Jan and the children with a shy grin. 'Yes, I know.' She shook Jan's hand. 'I recognize you from the races. I saw Rear Gunner's win at Ludlow and Lazy Dove's. I never saw horses so well turned out at the point-to-points.'

'I don't like to take them looking like ragamuffins.' Jan laughed. 'Do you go racing much?'

'Every time I can, to the points, mostly, and the big hunter chases.'

'Do you ride, too?'

'Not in races.' Penny laughed with a shake of her long hair. 'I used to hunt, but it got so expensive I couldn't keep it up once I went out to work and had to rent a flat of my own. But I kept my mare; she's a thoroughbred, by Oats,' she added proudly.

'What do you do with her now?' Jan asked.

'I put her in foal to Gunner B six years ago, but only once since then. The first foal was a colt. I was really worried because he got so big; he's only just grown into himself. But I had him gelded as a yearling, broke him in and backed him myself. He's going really well now.'

'Well done,' Jan said, seeing how much the whole process meant to Penny. 'It must be very satisfying. I've never bred a horse myself. My dad once had a foal from an old mare Colonel Gilbert gave him, but it had a bog spavin and was never quite right. What are you going to do with yours?'

Penny glanced at Annabel, as if for support, then back at Jan. 'Well, I was hoping you might train him for me if you thought he could go pointing.'

With a twinge of guilt, Jan wondered how she was planning to pay even her modest fees if she already found hunting too expensive. 'I'll certainly have a look for you. He's a five-year-old, is he?'

Penny nodded.

'And a bit backward?'

'He's more or less caught up with himself now. He's a big horse – about seventeen hands, but I've had him jumping some small hedges and tree trunks, and he loves it.'

They talked a little more about the horse, until a girl came to take their order and Annabel suggested Penny should eat with them.

'Oh, no thanks,' Penny said, suddenly embarrassed. 'I mustn't interrupt your meal. It was really kind of you to let me talk to you about my horse. And whenever you can come up and see him, just let me know. Annabel's got my number.'

'Yes, I will,' Jan smiled, appreciating the girl's enthusiasm.

'And you needn't worry about the money,' Penny said. 'I'm taking a night job at Sun Valley Chickens to pay for his training.'

Jan shook her head. 'I wasn't worried about the money. I just hope I like the horse because I'd love to train for someone who cares so much.' She stood up to say goodbye to Penny, and watched as she squeezed her broad hips through the crowded bar.

'Thanks,' Annabel said when Jan had sat down. 'Her mother

works for my parents and when Penny heard I was working for you, she came up to ask if I'd introduce her to you, but she was adamant that I shouldn't say anything first.'

'I really do hope I like the horse. I meant what I said – I'd like to train for someone like that – someone who really loves their horse.'

Three days after she'd met Penny Price, Jan drove the lorry over to west Herefordshire to look at the horse she wanted her to train. He was living with his mother and younger sister in a small, steeply sloping paddock which Penny rented, beside a river on the edge of Kington.

'He's called Arrow Star', Penny said proudly as she led Jan into the field, 'because he was born right beside the River Arrow.'

Arrow Star certainly was a big horse. Jan was concerned because horses of his age and size could still be too narrow and gangly. But as she walked up and examined him, she was relieved to see that he had already broadened and developed a good, deep chest to match his height, with fine sloping shoulders, big-boned, well-shaped hocks and a nicely rounded behind.

Jan also liked the look of him overall; he held himself well and had a big, kind eye. She turned to Penny who was waiting eagerly for her opinion.

'Without seeing him do some work,' she said, 'I'd say he's got all the makings of a useful horse. I'd be very happy to train him. The only thing is he's a big baby and we may find he just isn't ready to race this coming season. Alternatively you could leave him in the field for another year, carry on riding him out a bit and school him over some proper hurdles.'

'But I'd like you to start with him now,' Penny said. 'I think he's ready and I'm prepared to take the gamble.'

'Just as long as you know it is a gamble. Unfortunately, I'll have to charge you either way, until I can say for sure that there's any sense in racing him next season.' Jan saw Penny's disappointment and tried to steer a course between reality and the girl's ambitions.

'Look, it should be OK. He's got the rest of the summer and he'll be six in the new year. But, in the end, you're paying. You must decide.'

'Yes please,' Penny's eyes were shining now at the prospect of her pride and joy going away to be trained by a woman she admired and whose career she had followed avidly through every local point-to-point.

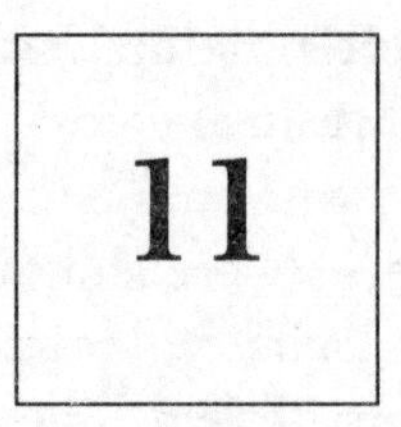

As the summer came to a close and September crept by, Jan allowed herself to think back to those two weeks in August when everything had seemed so against her. She had been at her lowest point and now she felt she was finally through it.

Eddie had gone to Italy for a fortnight – to buy paintings, he said – but before he'd gone, he and Jan had posted the glossy new Edge Farm brochures to every possible customer within a seventy-mile radius. Enquiries and visitors had started to flow in almost at once, to the point where Jan now had all eight of her boxes in the barn filled with invalids and a waiting list. As soon as she'd asked him, Gerry had rushed to finish another run of ten timber boxes along the northern side of the yard.

Gwillam Evans had finally got around to making the journey over from Wales. Once he'd seen Jan's new yard, he had decided it was worth sending his horse all the way over to Edge Farm for her to resume training him, so Barneby Boy was now back in her charge.

Jan had also found a horse for Bernie Sutcliffe. Arctic Hay was a ten-year-old from the big racing stables near Stow where she'd worked as a teenager. Jim Hely, a larger-than-life character from Limerick was head lad there, an old friend, and a firm believer in her talents. The horse had won several respectable chases in his time, but had lost his form. In a new environment and the less competitive arena of pointing, it was likely he would regain his enthusiasm for the job and win more races.

Bernie was thrilled when Jan told him she'd only spent six

thousand pounds, not the ten he had rather reluctantly promised, and as soon as the horse was installed at Edge Farm, he appeared with Sandy, his girlfriend, who had persuaded him to buy a horse in the first place.

Sandy was a tall, loud girl, with implausibly peach-coloured hair and doll-like make-up. Everything about her suggested she liked having money spent on her and she made it clear that she felt short-changed by Bernie only buying a point-to-pointer for her to lead in to the winner's enclosure. Nevertheless she seemed determined to indoctrinate Bernie thoroughly into the mysteries and joys of horse racing and saw this as a starting point. At the same time she didn't want to encourage him to get too interested in Jan or, more to the point, Annabel.

As soon as the new stables were ready, Sorcerer's Boy arrived from Colonel Gilbert and a few days after that Annabel's landlord, Mr Carey, rang to say that he had a mare he would like her to train. Jan went with Annabel to look at her, alone in a field at the furthest point of Mr Carey's large estate. She hadn't been touched for two years, he said, but had shown some promise as a youngster. In her current wild and unruly condition, she didn't look much at all, but Jan agreed to tidy her up and see what she could do.

From having had just three owners at the start of the summer – Eddie, Owen Tollard and Harold, who'd left – Jan now found herself with six more, Colonel Gilbert, Eamon Fallon, Penny Price, Bernie Sutcliffe, Gwillam Evans and Mr Carey. Then, at the end of September, one of her old owners from Stonewall, Alan Preece, who originally hadn't wanted to have his horses so far away, rang her and asked her if he could buy the chestnut she'd bought at the sales in May. She had ten horses now, which wasn't as many as she wanted, but it was a start, and with the recuperating animals she had all the work she and her two helpers could manage.

So it was that she found herself in a more optimistic frame of mind when Colonel Gilbert next came to see his horse and, having planted the seed of the idea in the first place, sat down with her and seriously urged her to think again about applying for a public trainer's licence.

The following day she went to discuss this potential quantum leap with her father.

Reg was sitting outside his house on an old oil drum, forking pet food from a tin into enamelled dishes for the tribe of semi-feral cats that now inhabited the old farm buildings.

Jan sat down beside him, as she had so many times in the past when she had things to discuss with him. She knew Reg found it easier to say what he was thinking if they weren't sitting face to face.

'Dad, Colonel Gilbert was round yesterday to see Sorcerer's Boy and have a look at the yard. He was really nice about it all and said he'd heard good reports about what we've been doing with the sick horses we've had in. But he said that now the season's starting I should concentrate on training, and he didn't see how I could ever make a living just training pointers; there's a limit to the amount of money involved. He thinks I should look at getting a licence, like Virginia.'

'Virginia!' Reg snorted with unusual cynicism. 'She don't know nothing and I reckon the colonel knows it too.'

'But why should he be encouraging me?'

Reg shrugged his shoulders. 'I dunno, but he's a good bloke is Frank Gilbert; he wouldn't want to tell you to do the wrong thing.'

'I'd love to train National Hunt horses, Dad. I just don't have a clue if I'd be any good at it.'

'I should think it's much the same as what you do already. Feed 'em right, get 'em fit; look after them; find the right races.'

'The trouble is the Jockey Club make you give them a bank guarantee for thirty-five thousand quid before they'll give you a licence!'

'What's that for?'

'Just to make sure everybody gets paid – your staff, farriers, vets, feed merchants and everybody else – if it all goes wrong.'

'Thirty-five thousand!' Reg sighed. 'You may as well forget it, then. That's too much risk and, anyway, we've none of us got that kind of money.'

'Oh Dad, I wouldn't dream of asking you for it! But I might be able to find someone to put it up for me. I've also got to produce a CV to show what I've done; I've got to get pledges from twelve different people saying they'll keep horses with me, but I've only got eight owners at the moment.'

'You'll get more as the season gets going, I should think.'

'I need them now, though.'

'What's the rush, Jan? Why not get another season's pointing under your belt and get everything right before you go for this licence?'

'Oh, Dad! I've done five seasons already. Can't you see, if I *can* get a licence, I want to get on with it!'

Reg sighed again. 'You always did want to do everything in a hurry. I don't suppose you'll ever change. Still, good luck to you.'

Jan thought she was due a little luck, so on Monday morning she rang the Jockey Club and told them she would like to apply for a public trainer's licence. The forms arrived the next day and Jan spent a long time studying them, wondering what her best strategy for finding a suitable guarantor would be. She considered putting an advertisement in *Horse & Hound* or the *Racing Post*, but shied away from dealing with the unknown quantities it might produce.

Later, she found Eddie in the tack room cleaning his bridle and asked him what he thought. He stopped what he was doing for a minute and his dark brown eyes focused on Jan's for a little longer than usual. 'Why don't I put up the bank guarantee?'

It had vaguely occurred to Jan before then that Eddie could be a potential backer but, not believing he was rich enough, she hadn't seriously considered him. She stared back at him, trying to see what lay behind this unexpected and very generous offer. But, as always, she saw no more than friendliness. 'I wasn't asking you,

Eddie. If I was going to ask an owner, I'd have tried Eamon or Bernie, or someone like that. After all, why should you?'

'I've got just as much reason as those two – more really. And, anyway, let's assume that I'll never have to cough up; the money can sit in a high-interest account as long as it needs to. I've seen how you operate, and people like you don't go bust. Quite apart from that, I believe in you as a trainer, just seeing how the horses have come on in the few weeks since you brought them in and the way you've schooled me and Eagle.'

'Even so, you could still lose the lot if I got ill or something – I mean, you just never know – and you shouldn't do it unless you're prepared for that. Can you spare thirty-five thousand quid?'

Eddie grinned and lifted a hand. 'I'll let you know when the time comes. You get the papers for me and I'll do the rest. When are they likely to come and inspect your stables?'

'If I send the application right away, they said about the middle of next month.'

'Then we'd better all pull our fingers out and have this place looking as beautiful as it can be. It's a pity about the barn roof, but there it is. We can't do anything about that in such a short time.'

'What's wrong with the barn roof?' Jan asked indignantly. 'It doesn't leak, which is more than you can say for some of the professional yards I've seen.'

Eddie smiled at her indignation. 'Don't be so defensive. They'll be much more interested in what your horses look like and the results you get.'

'And what other people say about me.'

'Why should anyone say anything bad about you?'

'Oh, I don't know,' Jan shrugged. 'I sometimes get the feeling that not everyone wants a woman on her own to make it in this business, especially if you don't bow to their wishes.'

'Who are you thinking of?'

'James McNeill for a start. I'm bloody sure he'd try and put the boot in if he got the chance once it leaks out that I've applied for a licence. Even if he writes in telling them total rubbish, he's an established vet and they'd take it seriously.'

'Then for God's sake get in first with a pre-emptive strike,' Eddie urged. 'I thought you should have done at the time.'

'But I didn't want to start causing hassle when I'd only been here five minutes.'

'Look, Jan. The man's a bloody menace. If you hadn't been strong and quick enough to kick him in the balls, he'd have raped you. I think you should put in a formal complaint to the Royal College of Veterinary Surgeons and do it right away.'

'But it happened six weeks ago.'

'Just do it, Jan.' Eddie frowned angrily at the injustice.

Jan looked at him, and nodded. 'You're right. I will.'

The evening before the Jockey Club inspector was due to visit Edge Farm, Jan looked around her yard, hoping that she and her team had done all they could to make her premises acceptable. The children were in the tack room, watching a fuzzy old television Roz had brought in to keep them amused while Jan worked in the yard.

Jan had checked everything she could think of, making sure the horses and their stables were all looking their best, when Julie from the Fox & Pheasant drove up in her old pick-up.

'Hi, Jan,' she called, climbing out and banging the driver's door. 'How's it going?'

Jan walked across the yard to the parking place. 'OK, but I've got a bloke from the Jockey Club coming round tomorrow and I'm dead nervous about everything he'll find wrong.'

'Gerry told me you were having your inspection. He's even more worried about it than you are, I think.' Julie grinned. 'Poor Gerry, he's obsessed with everything up here.'

Jan felt a twinge of guilt that she might have been taking advantage of the young builder's obvious crush on her. 'He's been brilliant. I couldn't have done it without him.'

'That's why I came up. We've had a bit of a disaster down in the cellars and we need him urgently to sort out the drains. I can't find him anywhere and he's not answering his mobile. I thought he might be up here.'

'No,' Jan said. 'He went about an hour ago.'

'Yeah,' Julie nodded. 'I saw his car wasn't here. Oh,' she said, reacting to another car creeping up the track in the dark, 'perhaps this is him.'

Jan looked at the headlights until the car was close enough to see. Her heart pounded angrily when she recognized Harold Powell's Range Rover.

She hadn't contacted him since his last visit, although several times she'd thought about asking her solicitors to write to him to demand point-blank the money she considered she was owed. She'd held off only because she thought it wouldn't do Harold any harm to stew for a while, and she would rather apply the energy needed to pursue him and his partners after she'd dealt with her licence application.

Jan saw that Julie, who was naturally curious, was watching to see who would get out of the vehicle and she realized that she couldn't have any kind of conversation with Harold in front of her.

'It's Harold Powell, one of my owners,' she said quietly to her. 'He'll want to talk privately.'

Harold climbed down from the Range Rover and walked towards them. It was clear that, outwardly at least, he was trying to appear conciliatory.

'Hello, Jan. How are you?' he said in his warm, silky voice.

Jan raised an eyebrow. 'All right, thanks. Julie, this is Harold.'

'Hello,' Julie said. 'I'm just off. I'll see you Jan, and if you see Gerry before I do, tell him we need him, like now!'

'OK, Julie. 'Bye.'

Jan and Harold watched as the girl jumped into her pick-up and spun it noisily across the loose, gritty surface of the parking space. As her headlights bounced down the track and swept out onto the lane below, Jan turned to Harold. 'Well, what do you want?'

'To talk,' Harold shrugged. 'I hadn't heard from you, so I assume you're still feeling aggrieved. I was wondering if there was anything I could do to help.'

'You've got a nerve. I've told you what I want, and when I've got it I'll sign your letter.' She thought of the letter, in a hundred shreds as she'd tipped it into her bin.

'Jan, don't be unreasonable. Fifty thousand? That's crazy. But I have thought of something that might sway you to accept the offer we've already put on the table. I see you've got plenty of boxes here now, and very good it all looks too. So how about if I send those four horses back to you, right away, on full fees? That'd bring you in another six hundred a week.'

'Huh!' Jan snorted. 'You must be joking! The profit margin on my fees is tiny, and anyway, right now, I've got all the horses I can take. What I suggest you do is go back home and empty your piggy bank. If I haven't heard from you soon, my solicitors will be in touch and this time they'll mean business. And as you're driving home now, I want you to think of three things, Harold. First, how much I did for you with your horses over the years. Second, how much money you made out of me just because I trusted you. And third, how much harm the bad publicity would do your firm if I have to take you to court. Now, I've got things to do,' she said curtly and, turning her back on him, walked into the tack room.

Inside, she leaned tensely against a saddle rack and listened. For a few seconds there was no sound of movement outside, and Jan wondered what Harold was thinking of doing, until, abruptly and telegraphing his anger through his footsteps, he marched back across the yard, got into his vehicle, banged the door and skidded off the parking place.

Jan let out the breath she'd been holding in. She didn't care how long it took; she would get there in the end.

Damn it! she thought. She was still offering to let them keep half the profit they'd made on her farm! What she was dealing with now was pure, unadulterated greed. And if Harold thought she was just going to give up simply because she was an impecunious widow, he should know better.

When he came the following day the Jockey Club inspector looked at everything in Jan's yard, inside and out, carrying out his duties with a quiet, uncommunicative smile. He looked at the horses, the stables, the bedding, the condition of the tack, the feed room and veterinary supplies, the gallops, the accident records and the wages books.

Before he left, Jan asked him what his conclusions were, but he said no more than that he would write and let her know in due course.

That evening, bursting with frustration, she sat down with Gerry, Roz and Annabel and held a post-mortem.

'They can't turn you down, not on the stables,' Gerry shook his head. 'They look bloody tidy, perfect actually.'

'Thank God the gallop doesn't look too muddy at the moment,' Annabel added.

'Yes, but supposing he comes back next month when they're all cut up?' Roz asked.

'Colonel Gilbert said I could tell the Jockey Club I can use his big field that runs up the side of Barton Wood and always drains well – the one Virginia sometimes uses.'

'Wouldn't Virginia make a fuss about that?' Annabel suggested.

'Too bad,' Jan said. 'It's not *her* field.'

They were all still there when Eddie arrived to hear how the inspection had gone. As usual when he was around, Annabel sank into the background while Jan told him what their impressions had been.

'It sounds as if you've done all right. Anyway, I've filled in all these papers for you and I've asked the bank to endorse the guarantee form.'

In the week that followed three invalids went home, fully recovered, and two new horses arrived to be trained. They'd been sent by Frank Jellard, a wealthy fruit farmer from Evesham. Both horses, Supercrack and Cambrian Lad, had had promising form, and Jan was hopeful of improving on it. This increased her string of horses to twelve, including her own Gale Bird and the unnamed chestnut gelding.

Jan had to decide now how many more convalescing horses she was prepared to take in, for although they brought in almost as much in fees as the racehorses, they tended to get in the way of the training schedules. She also had to take on another girl and a lad from the village to help with riding out. That hadn't been difficult; there was a waiting list of eager young kids wanting to work in her yard, and it was mainly a matter of judging which ones were serious and useful and which weren't. Emma Collins was a friend of Roz Stoddard's, with similar experience. Joe Paley was a traveller who was lodging with the Stoddards and, though he was a little too relaxed about his time-keeping for Jan's comfort, he was an excellent rider.

The yard was settling into a businesslike routine and Jan was beginning to enjoy being greeted in the lanes around Edge Farm as she headed up her small string of five or six. She liked to give her horses plenty of road work early on, to harden their legs before they started any serious work.

A week after the Jockey Club inspector had been, there was still no sign of his report. Jan tried not to think about it, but she knew that if he demanded any substantial changes she had no way of paying for them. However, she thought, as long as they hadn't turned her down, there was still hope.

But on the third Monday in October Jan's future plans were hit by a hammer blow.

It was a foul, grey-black morning, with wind howling down the broad sweep of the Severn plain from the north-west, spitting and blasting bursts of needle-sharp rain.

Megan had recently started at the primary school in the next village and Jan set off to take her there. She drove down the track, now gushing like a brook, and peered through the rain bucketing onto the windscreen. As she reached the bottom, she was startled to see that the gate to the lower paddock on the right was hanging open. The previous evening she had left three recovered horses there in New Zealand rugs.

She stopped the Land Rover and jumped out into the deluge. She ran into the field, praying that she would find the horses standing in a corner on the far side, in the lee of a tall hedge. But even as she ran, squinting through the downpour, she knew they wouldn't be there.

It took her less than thirty seconds to be certain and the fresh hoof prints in the mud around the gateway confirmed her worst fears. She ran back to the Land Rover with rainwater pouring off the brim of her hat and coursing down the folds of her waxed coat. She tried to grin at the little girl strapped wide-eyed in the passenger seat. 'I'm afraid you'll be late for school today, Meggy.'

'What's happened, Mum?'

'Someone's left the gate open and the horses have got out. They haven't come up to the farm, so they must have got onto the road, but I don't think they've been gone long.'

Jan hesitated at the bottom of the track. After an instant's thought, she decided to turn right towards the main road, where they would have got into the most trouble. Half a mile up the lane, at the junction with the Evesham road, she didn't know which way to turn until she spotted a blue light, blinking through the rain four hundred yards to her left. She spun out into the main road and raced up to where a small queue of cars had formed. Beyond the cars were two police vehicles and an articulated lorry, which had slewed off the road from the opposite direction. It was resting in the ditch at a forty-degree angle, while most of the three hundred sacks of potatoes it was carrying were scattered all around, ruptured and spilling their contents over the road.

A moment later, Jan saw one of the horses, with its New Zealand rug all twisted, tugging nervously at the end of a makeshift rope. It was being held by an anxious man who looked as if he was wondering what on earth to do with it. She drove on past the stationary cars until a policeman in a Day-Glo yellow jacket flagged her down fiercely. Jan lowered her window. 'That's my horse,' she bellowed over the wind.

'What about the others?' the policeman asked, nodding beyond the squad car.

Jan's heart almost stopped. She closed her eyes and grasped the steering wheel, trying to get to grips with what had happened. Taking a deep breath, she opened her eyes again and turned to Megan. 'I won't be a minute, Meg. Don't worry and don't move, all right?'

'I'll keep an eye on her, madam,' the policeman said, opening the door for her.

Jan ran down the road as fast as she could in wellingtons and knelt down by the first horse. There was a slight movement in the animal's ribcage and his eyelids flickered as Jan leaned down to find if he was still breathing.

With a faint whinny, he tried to raise a leg that twisted grotesquely, unmistakably broken in at least two places. Feeling suddenly weak, Jan looked up at the nearest of the two policemen. 'Have you called the vet?'

'There's one on his way from Chipping Campden. Should be here in about ten minutes. Are these all your horses?'

'Not actually mine, but I'm looking after them,' she gasped and felt sick as the full horror of what had happened began to overwhelm her.

'I'm afraid the other one was hit full on by the artic; he's in a terrible mess,' the patrolman said. 'I think he's already gone.'

Jan staggered to her feet. She felt strangely light-headed and had to force her legs to carry her to the other horse. She took one look at his mangled chest and head before she closed her eyes to fight the nausea welling up in her, but she made herself crouch down beside the animal.

One horse dead; another so badly damaged he would have to be put down. Jan squeezed her eyes tight shut, as she tried to make the stark horror of it go away, while she searched her mind over and over for a reason why the gate should have been open.

She knew she hadn't done it. She and Roz had led the three horses down to the field and she'd closed the gate behind them herself; she was absolutely certain.

Besides, the animals must only have escaped within the last hour or so and it was very likely they would have left soon after the gate had been opened. A dozen different reasons for it happening, with or without human assistance, spun around her head.

The sound of a plaintive whinny above the continuous howling of the wind reminded her that the third horse was still standing. The man holding him had led him away from the scene of the crash, maybe hoping he might pick grass on the verge, fifty yards beyond the articulated truck, past the queue of traffic that had built up behind it.

Jan walked briskly towards them. The man nodded. She didn't know him, but his face was familiar from the Fox & Pheasant.

'Thanks so much for catching him,' she said, seeing that the horse was being held by a piece of twisted orange binder twine lopped through his head-collar.

'He didn't take much catching. He was just standing there quivering with fright, but at least he wasn't hit.'

Jan nodded, quickly running her hands up and down the animal's legs and along his back, then soothing him with a steady flow of comforting words, before she turned back to the man holding him. 'There should be a vet here any minute to deal with the other two horses and I'll call the hunt kennels to take them away. I've got to ring my yard too and ask someone to come and collect this one. Would you mind hanging on to him for a few more moments while I go back and use the phone in my Land Rover?'

'No, that's fine,' he said.

When Jan opened the door of the Land Rover and leaned in, Megan was sitting quietly, not distressed but well aware that something serious was going on.

'What's happened, Mummy?'

'Some of the horses have been a bit hurt and I've just got to phone someone to come and take them home,' Jan said, plucking the phone from its cradle. 'I'll do it outside,' she smiled at Megan, closed the driver's door and walked round behind the vehicle, out of the wind.

First she dialled her yard. Annabel answered.

'Bel, it's Jan.'

'Hi, Jan. Everything all right? We thought you'd be back from school by now.'

'We never got there,' Jan said, bracing herself. 'There's been a major disaster.'

'Oh no! Is Megan all right?'

'Yes, she's fine. It's not her. Somehow the gate to the bottom paddock was opened. The three horses in it got out and ran up to the main road and I'm afraid there's been an almighty accident.' She shut her eyes, and suddenly all the strength which she'd summoned up to deliver the news without getting hysterical deserted her. Her shoulders collapsed as she sobbed into the phone. 'One's dead,' she choked. 'The other's so badly damaged it'll have to be put down.'

'My God!' Annabel gasped. 'How horrible!'

'Yes,' Jan tried to get herself together. 'Someone's got to get down here and collect the one that's OK. Bel, can you bring the trailer? I'll ring the kennels for the other two and there's a vet coming from—'. Abruptly, Jan put a hand to her mouth. 'Oh God, the police said the vet's coming from Chipping Campden. I've only just thought – I bet it's James McNeill! Oh God, that's all I bloody need. He'll tell the whole world what's happened – especially now I've lodged that complaint about him!'

'No, no,' Annabel said urgently. 'He doesn't have to know they've got out from here. Roz can go down and ask Gill, her mother, to collect the horse in her lorry and say they're all hers. He doesn't know who she is.'

'What about the forms and everything? For the insurance and things?'

'We can worry about that afterwards,' Annabel said. 'Tell me where you are, and I'll tell Roz.'

'Turn left on the main road, about four hundred yards.'

Two hours later Jan was still shivering as she sat in the caravan with a large mug of tea.

When the vet – a man she'd never met before – had reached the scene of the crash, she had almost collapsed with relief that it wasn't James McNeill or his partner, and she'd stood in the rain while he'd despatched one horse and confirmed the other dead. Feeling sick and helpless, she'd watched the Evesham Vale huntsman winch the carcasses into his trailer.

Mrs Stoddard had arrived with her lorry only minutes after the vet and told him the horses had escaped from one of her fields, before she loaded the one remaining horse and brought it back to the yard, where it was now in a stable being pampered by Roz.

'What do you think happened?' Annabel asked.

Jan shook her head. 'God knows. I'm thinking maybe the latch was faulty and the wind did it. It was gusting like hell last night – the whole caravan was shaking.'

'Let's go down and have a look,' Annabel urged.

Jan nodded, and gulped down the rest of her mug. 'Come on, Meg,' she said to the wide-eyed little girl. 'We'll look at this gate, then I'll take you on to school.'

At least the rain had eased for a bit as they walked down to the Land Rover. They climbed in and drove down to the gate, which was still hanging out towards the track.

It was made of galvanized iron with a corrugated zinc panel fixed over the bottom three bars to stop horses putting their feet through and getting them stuck. It was normally opened inwards, into the field, but it could be secured only with a bolt which shot through a large staple on the outside of the eight-by-eight timber post, which made it easier to secure.

Where the staple should have been, there were two rusty slits in the wooden post. Jan looked down. The big black wrought-iron loop was lying, half hidden by long grass, a couple of feet in front of the post. She picked it up and tried to fix it back in the holes in which it had been lodged, but they had been enlarged when the staple had been torn out and it would have taken a hefty hit with a hammer to refix it.

'It looks like you were right,' Annabel said.

'I don't know. It really must have been blowing hard to have dislodged this thing. Look at the spikes on it.'

'But that wrinkly tin would have really caught the wind.'

'Oh hell!' Jan groaned. 'People will say it's my fault because I didn't check the bloody staple, or I should have had it fixed on the other side or something.'

'Jan, it was an accident, for God's sake! Real accidents do happen. Just because all these lawyers are always trying to persuade people to blame someone else. There's no way you could have known that a strong wind would blow hard enough to yank the bloody thing out.'

Jan looked at her, grateful for her support. 'Let's hope the owners and the insurers take it like that. After all those brochures Eddie and I sent out – if everyone starts saying we can't even keep a horse in a paddock, it'll have been a total waste of time!'

'Relax, Jan; you're getting paranoid. I'm sure the insurance will be OK.'

'I don't think we'll get away with it.' Jan shook her head and put the big staple in her coat pocket. 'I'll get Gerry to replace this with an eye that bolts right through the post.' She looked at the rain which had started to pour heavily again. 'I'd better drop you up at the yard before I take Megan on to school.' She started walking towards the car.

'Hang on, Jan!' Annabel said sharply.

Jan turned. Annabel was staring at the ground in front of her. 'When did you last drive up to this gate?' she asked.

Jan looked down at a distinct set of tyre tracks, which showed that someone had driven up onto the broad, muddy verge, as if they'd been going to carry on into the field, but had stopped a couple of yards short of the gate. 'Not for weeks,' she answered. 'I've only walked horses down here.'

'Me too. And Gerry hasn't worked here recently has he?'

'No,' Jan said. 'Those tyre marks are very fresh anyway, or the rain would have washed them away more.' She glanced at Annabel. 'Are you thinking someone's given the wind a bit of a hand to push that staple out?'

'Well, why else would anyone turn here? Look, you can see, they've driven up, then they must have reversed up the track to drive back down again.'

'Someone might have been lost?' Jan suggested, without much conviction.

'I don't think so. And, anyway, I just don't see how the wind could have shoved that bloody great staple out. It looks to me as if someone's been having a go at you.'

'Oh God.' Jan didn't want to believe it, but she knelt down and gazed closely at the zigzag tread pattern in the soft earth, which she was sure couldn't be more than a few hours old. And she thought how absurdly vulnerable she was – simply by opening a gate someone had caused the death of two of the horses in her care. She turned her head and looked bleakly up at Annabel. 'I'm afraid you might be right.' She straightened her legs and gazed at the track, wondering whose malice had led to this.

'Who do you think it was?' Annabel prompted her.

Jan sighed. 'I don't know; perhaps it was James McNeill.'

'Because you complained about him to the RCVS?'

Jan nodded. 'I had a letter from them a few days ago asking for more details. He probably got a copy of it, too. I wish I hadn't done it now, but Eddie suggested I should, to stop McNeill saying anything negative about me to the Jockey Club.'

'He was right,' Annabel insisted. 'And anyway, why should the disgusting bastard get away with it? He would have raped you if he could.'

'That's what Eddie said.'

'But there's not a lot you can do about this,' Annabel went on. 'You'll simply have to see if he follows it up. If it was McNeill, he'll show it in some way or other, I'm sure of that. In the meantime the best thing to do is carry on and treat it as an accident, like we first thought.'

'But I was going to get the police up.'

'Don't bother, Jan. It'd be a complete waste of time. Even if they could match this tyre tread to McNeill's car – and he probably didn't come in his own – there's no way anyone could prove he'd broken the fixing.'

'I suppose you're right, but it's bloody frustrating. I don't know how I'll contain myself, doing nothing.'

'Just carry on as normal and get it repaired. That's what I suggest.'

'OK, but I'll put a bloody great padlock on here in future, though that wouldn't have stopped this happening,' Jan added ruefully.

Jan apologized to the head teacher for dropping Megan off late, though she didn't tell her why, then she raced back to Gerry's house in the village. His mother told her he was working on an extension at the pub. She found him there and told him what had happened, without telling him about the tyre tracks and the possibility that James McNeill or someone else had done it deliberately, and then explained what was needed to repair the gate.

He nodded gravely, patently glad to be in Jan's confidence. 'There's some old iron eyes like that at Mr Carey's; they'll be a bit rusty, though.'

'That's fine, as long as it's sound, but when you've got time, buy a new one on my account to replace the one you take. I don't want to be pinching stuff from Mr Carey.'

Without asking why the job had to be done so urgently, Gerry immediately abandoned what he was doing. He went off to find the ironmongery he needed and Jan went back to the yard.

Annabel was waiting for her in the tack room.

'You never told me who the vet was,' Annabel said.

'I don't know, but it wasn't James McNeill or his partner. Gill's got his details.'

'What about the police?'

'Oh hell! I wasn't thinking; I told one of them they were my horses!' Jan punched a bag of nuts in frustration. 'What a bloody mess!'

Annabel sat down beside her and put an arm around her shoulder. 'Don't worry about it, Jan. It was an accident, pure and simple. Just calm down first, then you can decide what to do, and how to tell the owners.'

'But, Bel, I haven't even had the Jockey Club inspector's report. They haven't turned me down yet, but there's still a long way to go, and if they get to hear about this, it really could go against me. That must be why McNeill did it.'

'Jan, I know that – if it really was him. But you're not going to solve anything by panicking.'

'You're right,' Jan sighed. She knew she was lucky to have Bel with her at a time like this.

During the days following the accident and the death of the two horses, Jan couldn't believe that she wouldn't be blamed or penalized in some way for what had happened, despite the fact that she and Roz's mother, Gill, had not yet encountered any problems handling the formalities with the vet. So far, no official had been to ask Jan how the horses had got onto the road.

Nor had James McNeill, until four days after the event.

He arrived in the middle of the morning. Jan was in the yard on her own, mucking out and keeping an eye on Matthew while the others were out exercising. It was the first time she'd seen James in two months. She fought back her fear and walked up to him, still holding a muck fork, though she felt a sudden contraction in her guts at the thought that he might have been responsible for the death of the two horses.

Whether he was or not, she was sure he'd come to gloat.

'Hello,' she said. 'What do you want?' She made no move to invite him into the yard.

He stopped and looked at her as if nothing unusual had happened the last time they'd seen each other. 'I'd been thinking about sending a few horses here again, but I heard some got out the other day – and there was a bit of a disaster.'

Jan tried not to let her complexion change, nor to allow McNeill to see her urgent swallowing. 'From here?'

'I know exactly where they were,' James said quietly. 'And, of course, I realize these things happen. Gates wear out in time and without warning. No one should blame you. But then, not everyone is so understanding. Bernie Sutcliffe, for instance, might be a little pissed off to know that sort of thing goes on here.'

Without stopping to think about it, Jan came off the defensive and squared up to him. 'Oh, so this is what it's all about, is it? You've finally heard that I've bought a horse for Bernie and you're annoyed about it.'

'It would have been normal to let me know, since I recommended you to him in the first place.'

'You told him not to touch my yard and you know it. It's pathetic – because I wouldn't let you screw me!'

McNeill raised one of his thick, ginger eyebrows. 'I gather you've shared your thoughts on that incident with my professional body,' he said, as if it were a matter of complete indifference to him. 'I can't imagine what you think you're going to achieve. I also hear you've applied for a licence to train.' He allowed himself a brief, cynical smile. 'I don't suppose the Jockey Club inspector will be too impressed if he hears what happened to those horses and how you tried to cover it up.'

Looking at his big round face and the bland, false smile he was wearing, she felt like ramming the muck fork into it.

'Look, James, I've been asked to write a report on what you tried to do to me last time you came here. There were two witnesses to back it up,' she bluffed, 'and if you don't want me to send it back to the RCVS, I suggest you get yourself out of this yard – right now!' She didn't wait for his reaction, but turned and walked straight back to the stable she'd been mucking out when he'd arrived.

It seemed like an eternity before she heard the door of his car slam, the engine start, and the car rumble off down the track.

Once she was sure he'd gone, she found she was shaking at the thought that the Jockey Club might hear about the three horses who had got out. She'd been only too aware, since the day it had happened, that it would be a simple matter to confirm that two of them, both registered at Weatherby's, had died while technically in the charge of Edge Farm Stables. And it seemed unlikely now that her official complaint to the Royal College of Veterinary Surgeons would be any deterrent to James McNeill.

Jan was also conscious of the fact that it was she who had first rung the kennels, and it was possible that someone had mentioned this to McNeill. What chilled her most, though, was that the vet seemed to know how the horses had escaped and, as far as she was aware, apart from herself, only Annabel and Gerry knew the precise details. Nevertheless, his manner had left her with the strong impression that he had come to gloat: that he had heard about what had happened after the event, not that he had caused it himself.

After this encounter, the shadow of the accident hung over Jan like a dark cloud. Annabel and the others did what they could to cheer her up and tried to reassure her that no lasting damage had been done. At the same time Jan didn't want to worry them more by telling them about James McNeill's threat to draw the Jockey Club's attention to the incident.

12

Unexpectedly, and at short notice, Annabel received an invitation from Virginia Gilbert's brother, George, to a dinner party the following Saturday at Riscombe Manor. The next morning, when they were exercising Gale Bird and Russian Eagle, Jan asked her if she would be going.

'I don't particularly want to. I know who'll be there. George has got a whole lot of his friends coming down from London to shoot. One or two will bring girlfriends, but he needs some women to balance the numbers. Half the men will be drunk before dinner starts and they'll all talk about nothing but shooting.' She sighed. 'I suppose I'll have to go, though; it's just one of those evenings you have to put up with unless you want to be thought of as a complete outcast.' Annabel gave a short laugh. 'Sometimes I think I wouldn't mind that much if I was, by that lot.'

'I don't understand you, Bel,' Jan said. 'You're very attractive; there's no shortage of men after you. You could pick and choose as much as you liked.'

'That'd be fine if there were ever any men around who were the sort I wanted.'

'Well, what sort is that?' Jan asked, a little impatiently.

'Someone thoughtful; someone whose ego isn't bursting out all the time like most men's. Not an academic type necessarily, but not one of these air-head friends of George's who work in the City and just talk about money, cars and shooting, and who they slept with last night.'

'Definitely not Eddie any more, then?' Jan glanced at Annabel, who looked away.

'Jan, I told you, I got Eddie out of my system a long time ago. You know what I think of him now. Besides, I'm sure he's more interested in you.'

Jan laughed before she could stop herself. 'In me? You must be joking. For a start, I'm hardly his type, am I? I mean he's a sort of deb's delight, even if his old man *is* a cockney builder.'

'Funnily enough, Eddie was always quite clever about that – not making any attempt to disguise his parents makes him, like, a bit of rough you could take anywhere.'

'You think he does that deliberately?' Jan was disappointed.

'No,' Annabel said. 'Not really. He's far too genuine for that. But I still think he's interested in you.'

'A bit of rough for a bit of rough, eh?' Jan laughed. 'Well, for a start, he's a bit young for me; besides, I haven't been anywhere near another man since I met John. The very thought of it makes me feel quite odd. I must admit, though, Eddie's been a great friend. He always seems to turn up just when I need him with some plan to solve one of my problems.'

Annabel nodded. 'Yeah, I know that, but he and I . . . well, it ended more or less in disaster, but I'm not going to let that get in the way of my work for you, especially as he comes here so often.'

When Annabel arrived at Edge Farm the morning after the dinner party, she picked Megan up and gave her a quick squeeze before flopping down onto the bench. 'God, I need more sleep!'

'What on earth's happened to you? Did you give in to one of the City slickers?'

Annabel made a face. 'No, I did not, but I did sit around far too long talking with quite a nice, rather tubby man who's interested in horses, and I think I may have got you a new owner. That's why I've come up. He said he'd be over here about twelve.

The only trouble is . . .' Annabel seemed reluctant to say whatever was on her mind.

'The only trouble is what?' Jan pressed.

'Virginia was at dinner last night, too, trying to put him off – telling him it was a waste of time and money owning pointers.'

'Well, that's for him to decide. We've been through all that before with owners.'

'Yes, but when I told him you've already applied for a licence, Virginia looked furious and said they don't just hand them out to anyone, and you wouldn't find it easy because the Jockey Club would take a dim view of the fact that some of your horses had got out, two had been killed and you'd been a bit evasive about them coming from your yard.'

Jan felt the blood drain from her face. 'Virginia said that?' she whispered. 'The bitch! And how the hell does she know?'

'She said her vet told her, and her vet—'

'Don't tell me – James McNeill,' Jan finished for her.

Annabel nodded. 'Did you know he's been talking about it?'

'I sort of did. He came round here last week and said he'd tell the Jockey Club, but I told him I was sending a report to the RCVS about him trying to rape me; I thought that might put him off.'

'It looks like he's found an indirect route then, doesn't it.'

'Do you think Virginia will tell the Jockey Club?' Jan asked, already sure of the answer.

'She's very jealous of you and not just because you've already got more horses than her. I've a horrible feeling she might.'

The potential new owner, Toby Waller, was as affable and rotund as Annabel had described him. He came, expressed his enthusiasm for Jan's yard and left with a promise to be in touch.

'I think he was just being polite,' Jan told her father when she arrived with Matthew at her parents' the following morning.

'Why should he be?' Mary asked.

'Because Virginia Gilbert was trying to put him off at a dinner party on Saturday night, Bel said.'

'Was Bel having dinner up at the Manor?' Mary asked, impressed.

'Yes; she knows George, poor girl, and he was having the first shoot of the season.'

'I know,' Reg nodded. 'Bloody useless most of them, the keeper said.'

'But why was Virginia trying to run you down?' Mary asked.

'That's easy,' Reg answered. 'She's worried our Jan might turn out a bloody sight better at training horses than she'll ever be, and she doesn't want to be shown up in front of all her posh friends round here. D'you remember what a fuss she made when Jan won that race on Rocket?'

'Why do people have to be like that?' Mary asked and shook her head in puzzlement, before bustling off with Matthew to pick apples in the small orchard behind the house.

'What's the matter, Jan?' her father asked when they were alone. 'I can see summat's up.'

Jan sat down in the deep moquette armchair that had been in the front room of the house for as long as she could remember. She nodded and bit her lip, trying to stop the tears that wanted to flow.

'I got the Jockey Club inspector's report at last. It arrived this morning.'

'Bloody hell, they took their time, didn't they?' Reg said, already defending her because he'd guessed what was coming. He sat down in an old rocking chair opposite her and pulled his pipe from a pocket of his battered tweed jacket.

'They say the stables are no good as they stand – at least, the stables in the barn aren't because the old asbestos sheets are flaking and causing dust. On top of that, because it's got a canvas roof over the asbestos and we keep hay and straw there, they say it would be too great a fire hazard if I wanted to stable horses for the public!'

'What do they expect you to do, then?'

'Keep the hay and straw somewhere else, I suppose, and reroof the barn – which is cobblers as it's all made of timber anyway. Dad, there's no way I can afford to do that and build a new hay store. I mean, they make it virtually impossible for someone like me, who doesn't have a lot of money or rich friends to sponsor the yard.' Jan sniffed. 'And there's worse: they said they'd heard about the two horses getting killed on the main road and that puts a "question mark" over my competence. They don't say who told them, but I bet it was Virginia, who got it from James McNeill.'

Reg nodded. Jan had told him at the time, without going into too much detail, about the vet's attack on her before he'd taken away all his horses back in August. 'Oh Jan, I'm really sorry – just as things were looking up for you.'

'I know. I've had loads of enquiries recently, too. I've turned away some of the repair work because we haven't got enough time to do them all and keep the other horses fit as well.'

'Well, my little pet, you're just going to have to be patient, aren't you, and write to them with what happened over the horses that got out. They'll understand if you tell it to 'em straight. And if you have a good season next time, you'll be able to do that roof to their satisfaction, I'm sure, so don't go getting yourself into a state. At least that Eddie Sullivan's agreed to put up the bond for you.'

'Yes, he's been great, but I haven't seen him for a week or so. I tried to phone him this morning to tell him about the inspector's report, but I couldn't get hold of him and the dopey girl at his shop in Stow said she hadn't heard from him herself since last Thursday.'

'Oh well, you know what they're like, these young chaps – all over the place they are. Look at our Ben.'

'That's a bit different, Dad. Eddie's supposed to be running a business.'

'Well, it don't matter too much at the moment, does it? You can't go ahead, anyway, till you can afford the work that needs to be done. Don't worry. Eddie's not going to go away.'

'No, he's not,' Jan agreed confidently and smiled at her father's attempts to cheer her up.

Jan had arranged to leave Matthew with her mother for the rest of the morning so that she could drive over to Lambourn to look at a couple of horses Frank Jellard had been offered. As she drove across the Cotswolds, over the Vale of the White Horse and the Berkshire Downs, Jan tried to come to terms with the idea that she would have to put her dreams of training under rules on hold for some considerable time. Her father's advice, as always, was level-headed and practical. Besides, she admitted, she didn't have any choice.

She tried to convince herself that she'd just have to do the best she could with the horses she had and make enough of a mark on the point-to-point scene to ease her transition to National Hunt racing the following year.

The trouble was, all her instincts were screaming at her to get on with it now, telling her that every season spent outside the world of 'real' racing was a season wasted. Driving for the first time into the Lambourn valley, lying comfortably among rolling green hills, which was home to several hundred racehorses, only increased her ambitions. The sight of strings of top-class animals being ridden through a village dedicated to horse racing, making their way to the gallops on the downs, made her mouth water.

But she wasn't going to let the authority of the place affect her judgement. She told herself that she might only be a point-to-point trainer from the back end of nowhere, but she wouldn't let anyone talk down to her or bully her into taking any horses she didn't want. Nor, when she arrived at the stables, did she let herself be blinded by the displays of affluence in the pristine stone yard, the immaculate lawns and massive troughs planted with geraniums. And when the head lad, barely glancing at her down his long nose, led out the two horses on offer and trotted them up for her, she didn't have to look long to realize that someone was trying to offload their rubbish onto her owner. She politely but firmly rejected both horses and drove away from the Mecca of National Hunt racing empty-handed, but knowing she'd done her job well.

As she reached the top of the hill on the road north, she glanced back at the village of Lambourn and vowed to herself that one day she'd be back, leading her own string up onto those broad, white-railed gallops.

That evening Jan phoned Frank Jellard and told him the horses in Lambourn he'd been offered were unlikely ever to see a race course again, but if he was serious about wanting more, she would carry on looking for a couple that might give him some fun around the points. Jan had already recognized that Jellard was one of those difficult owners who thought he knew a lot more about horses than he did, and she put her views as tactfully as she knew how. In the end, after a nerve-racking, twenty-minute conversation, he agreed.

She put the phone down, delighted, and glanced outside, where the wet, black night was being pierced by a pair of flickering headlamps. She couldn't see what type of vehicle had just pulled up, but a few moments later there was a knock on the door of the caravan. Jan opened it and found Eddie standing at the bottom of the steps with rain dripping from a shapeless waxed hat.

'Hi!' She smiled, pleased to see him. 'You look a little damp.'

Eddie stepped up and through the door. 'I'm more than a little damp,' he said.

Jan looked at him sharply. She'd never heard him so gloomy. 'Why, what's happened?'

'Have you still got any of that Bushmills the Irishman gave you?'

'Yes,' Jan said, closing the door behind him and taking his wet hat and coat. 'I'll get a glass.'

Eddie slipped onto the bench and pulled a packet of cigarettes from his pocket. 'Smoking?' Jan asked. 'Since when did you take up smoking?'

'Since this weekend,' Eddie said stonily.

Jan put the glass of whiskey on the table in front of him. 'For God's sake, Eddie. Has someone died or what?'

'Not quite. My father—', Eddie glanced at Jan with large, apologetic brown eyes, 'my father has just been made totally, comprehensively, balls-achingly bankrupt. He went down so fast, he didn't even touch the sides. And it looks like he's taken me with him.'

Jan felt her jaw sag as she suddenly realized how much she had been relying on Eddie; his disaster seemed to affect her almost as much as him. Slowly she sat down opposite him.

'How come he's taken you with him?' she asked huskily.

'Any assets I had were all tied up in his various companies. I just used them as security for any funding I needed, for the business and so on. The banks called in my overdrafts. My cottage is part of the estate and my father's bankers have already foreclosed on the lot. I've got to be out at the end of the week. And the Merc's had to go back.'

'Oh, Eddie. That's awful!' Jan wailed, loud enough to bring Megan sleepily from her end of the caravan.

'What's the matter, Mummy?' she asked.

'Sorry, darling. Did I wake you? Mummy's just had a bit of a surprise, that's all. Do you want a drink?'

Jan felt there was something surreal about the sense of normality which she was trying to convey to her daughter, knowing the little girl's antennae were finely tuned to calamity. But she managed to keep up the charade until Megan was back in bed and the door closed between them again.

'God, I'm sorry to drop a bomb like this when you've already got all the problems you need,' Eddie grunted.

'Don't worry.' Jan tried to laugh. 'I haven't even told you the latest news here.' She gave him the salient points of the Jockey Club inspector's report and its various implications. 'I'm going to have to wait until I've had quite a lot of work done before I reapply,' she said.

'I'll find someone else to put up your bond,' Eddie said.

'God, don't worry about that now! At least you've still got your business.'

'What there is left of it,' Eddie groaned.

'Why, what's the problem there?' Jan couldn't help wondering who would be paying for Russian Eagle once the advance Eddie had given her had been used up.

'No money; too much stock, not enough sales. Business has been lousy – anyway for the last couple of months; there's the staff wages and the ridiculous rent I'm paying. I'm locked into a terrible seven-year lease which I'll never shift, and I've got a massive VAT bill to deal with at the end of November from that big sale I made in the summer.'

Jan was finding it hard to handle a deflated, despairing Eddie. Until now in their relationship it had always been he who had been the solid, immovable rock. Now that he needed support, she was conscious that she had little to offer in return.

'Well, at least Eagle's keep is paid up to the end of the year, I'll school you for nothing and you should have some fun on him when the season gets going.'

She was glad to see how much this made Eddie perk up.

'Do you really think I might win on him?'

'I'd say there was a good chance, though you've got a lot more work to do on yourself. You'll need to lose that last half stone and get into a gym to tone up your muscles. You'll never race three and half miles if you're not as fit as a flea.'

'What about the Aintree Foxhunters'? Do you think I might get somewhere in that?'

Jan laughed. 'Anything's possible, I suppose; he could even win it, but we've got to get you and him to win at least one open point-to-point, just to qualify to run in it.'

'But you do think he could do it?'

'I couldn't be sure, not till I've seen him doing more fast work. But he's won over that distance in Ireland, so he must stay. The trip wouldn't be a problem for him.'

Eddie took another slug of whiskey and grinned at her. 'I'll bloody well do it!' he laughed. 'They can take what they like, the thieving bastards, but they're not having my horse!'

Eamon Fallon stood beside Jan in the middle of Colonel Gilbert's big field. A broad strip of well-kept turf curved along the edge of a dense wood of mature oaks on two sides of the field, making a gentle rising gallop of five furlongs. He lowered his binoculars, turned to Jan and shook a long skein of wavy black hair from his forehead. His blue eyes shone with delight.

'Dingle looks brilliant. I'd barely recognize him from the horse in Jim's yard last winter. You've done a grand job.'

'So far,' Jan warned. It was really too soon for a horse to be doing much fast work and she didn't encourage over-optimism in her owners.

'And that big horse, behind,' Eamon nodded. 'He looks useful, too. Who's he?'

'He came over from Ireland for the Doncaster sales. Eddie Sullivan bought him. He wants to ride him in the Foxhunters' at Liverpool next April.'

'Eddie Sullivan? Would that be Ron Sullivan's boy?'

'Yes,' Jan said guardedly. She was already wary of telling one owner anything about another.

'Does he have any money left?'

'Why do you ask?' Jan said, as if she didn't know what he was talking about.

'Did you not hear? Ron Sullivan went bust last month in some order. It was in all the Sunday papers. He made a load of money from building houses, but he must have got greedy or careless. For the last few years he's been piling money into one of those software companies making video games, then they got sued in the States for a few hundred million for causing some juvenile to turn on his family. The whole lot's crashed, leaving Ron holding the baby for over thirty million.'

Jan hadn't asked Eddie any of the details of his father's downfall, mainly because it wasn't any of her business and she hadn't really wanted to know. She'd heard a little about Ron himself and his colourful history from Toby Waller, Annabel's friend, who had come again to talk to Jan about training a horse he had found himself.

Toby had been at Harrow with Eddie and had seen the succession of Bentleys and Ferraris with which Ron had tried to impress the other parents at the school. But, Toby had added, there had always been something engaging about Ron's naive flamboyance and most people thought Eddie was a perfectly presentable human being, despite his outrageous father.

'I don't train horses for his dad, so I wouldn't know,' Jan said. 'And Eddie's prepaid his bill up to the end of the year,' she added, scotching any ideas Eamon might have had that Eddie was getting a free ride from her.

'I wonder if that's the horse A.D. was talking about,' Eamon said thoughtfully.

'Do you mean A.D. O'Hagan?'

'I do.'

With a jolt, Jan remembered the Irish tycoon's comments when she'd given Eddie her first appraisal of Russian Eagle. 'In which case, it could be,' Jan said. 'He was standing behind me when we were talking about it. I'm amazed he remembered, though.'

'A.D. remembers everything. That's one of the secrets of his genius. As a matter of fact, I think it's inherited from his forefathers. They were big horse dealers, and illiterate, so they couldn't write anything down. A.D. says his father could remember the size, age, colour and price of every horse he ever sold.'

'How do you know him, then?' Jan asked.

'Oh, I used to do a little work for him some years ago,' Eamon said with a vagueness that Jan realized marked a dead end. 'So,' he went on with a change of tone, 'do you think we might win a few with Dingle?'

'I hope so.'

'I heard you're thinking of training National Hunt horses.'

Jan wondered who he'd heard it from, although she was getting used to the way information and, more often, misinformation flew around the racing world. 'I might apply next year,' she said.

'Get me a winner at the points and I'll put a couple with you when you get a licence.' Eamon turned to her with a grin and the morning sun glinted on the big gold hoop that dangled from his left ear.

Since she'd started training, Jan had been struck by the extraordinary variety and shapes in which owners came, and the range of motives which attracted them to keep race horses, even at her modest level of the game. People like Colonel Gilbert and Eamon, despite their different approaches, were both in it for the sport and nothing else. At first she thought Eamon was a gambler, but it was obvious that if he did want a serious bet he wouldn't bother with the restrictions of the point-to-point betting market.

Frank Jellard liked horses, but he also liked impressing his friends, whereas Bernie Sutcliffe seemed to have no affinity whatever with the animals, although he liked telling people about his racehorse, too, and had already brought a few of them to see Arctic Hay.

At first, Jan had been concerned that for him horse-owning was just a weapon in his campaign to keep his girlfriend, Sandy, compliant, but in the last few visits Sandy hadn't been with him and his interest seemed to be more concentrated on Annabel and, to some extent, Jan herself, than on his horse.

She was fairly sure that Annabel was also the reason Toby Waller came back for a third visit. But Jan didn't feel any resentment, especially when he asked her if she could find him a horse. The one he'd told her he was going to look at had turned out to be sold already.

He appeared on foot at the Saturday meet of the Evesham Vale Hunt, where Jan and the others had taken five horses for one of their qualifying days, and followed by car for most of the time they were out. When they all got back to the yard, he was waiting for them.

While they were sitting in the tack room discussing his budget, Jan noticed that he couldn't take his eyes off Annabel, who was busy cleaning tack. Later, when she and Toby had gone up to the caravan, Jan took the opportunity to ask if he knew anything about Annabel and Eddie.

'No,' Toby shook his head vigorously. 'I wouldn't have thought he was her type at all. Eddie's a nice enough guy, but he's a total playboy really. That picture business of his is just a front for pottering about Europe and staying in big country houses. At least, it was,' he added wryly. 'I fear that now Dad has gone belly up, Master Eddie is going to have to be a little more serious.'

Jan couldn't square this view of Eddie with the good advice and commitment he'd given her over the last few months, but she said nothing. Instead, she suggested that Toby might be interested in buying Gale Bird, who was already beginning to look like a useful racehorse. 'If you bought her from me, I'd be able to redo the roof of the barn and get rid of those horrible old tarpaulins.'

'But what about your house?' Toby asked, looking at the undisturbed stacks of stone and timber beside the footings.

'That'll have to wait,' Jan laughed. 'Even if I had the money to crack on with it now, it wouldn't be ready until March or April, so the kids and I might as well get through the winter first. We'll think about the house next year.'

Toby phoned two days later and said he'd decided to buy Gale Bird. He told Jan he was still in Gloucestershire and suggested that he should come round for a drink to complete the formalities. At midday he arrived with Eddie, who was at the wheel of a much-dented Land Rover, already well into its teens and a stark contrast to the Mercedes.

Jan watched curiously as he drove up towards the caravan and parked on the slope outside. Then he and Toby started to manhandle a bulky, black object out from the back.

As they staggered towards the caravan with it, Gerry arrived in his van and climbed out with a tool bag and a heavy-duty welding torch.

'Morning, Jan,' Eddie called as they got closer to the door.

She opened it to find the three men grinning up at her.

'If you're going to live in this bloody tin can all winter,' Eddie said, 'we've decided you've got to have some heat.'

On the ground between them was a small wood-burning stove.

Eddie had done his homework. Jan realized he must surreptitiously have taken dimensions and worked out how the stove would fit in. Within minutes Gerry had cut a hole for the flue in the roof of the caravan, and the other two were bolting the stove to the floor. Within an hour the new fire was functional, and in a small ceremony accompanied by a bottle of champagne they lit some kindling and filled the fire box from a load of split oak logs they'd brought, storing the remainder under the caravan where Jan could easily get at them.

She was delighted, not just with the heat, which filled the small space almost at once, but also with the combined generosity of three men, who owed her no more allegiance than pure friendship. After they had christened the stove, Toby produced another bottle to celebrate his formal acquisition of Gale Bird.

While they were drinking his champagne, they talked about what they might expect Gale Bird to do when the point-to-point season started in two months' time. Toby glanced out of the window just as Julie was driving up to the yard in her pick-up. She parked and climbed out.

'Good God! Who on earth's this?' Toby asked, unfamiliar with the sight of Julie and her hair, more outlandish than ever since she'd had it dyed bright purple a few weeks before.

Eddie laughed. 'That's our village barmaid. Now you're an owner at this yard, you'll have to get used to seeing her down at the Fox & Pheasant.'

'Impressive shape,' Toby said, seeing her unashamedly large breasts as she walked up towards the caravan.

Jan got up and opened the door. 'Morning, Julie. What brings you up here at this time of day?'

'Nothing really. Monday's my day off, so I thought I'd look in and see how it's all going.'

'You're just in time for a glass of champagne to celebrate a new owner,' Jan said, standing back as Julie climbed into the cramped space around the stove. 'This is Julie,' she introduced. 'And this is Toby Waller, who's just bought my mare Gale Bird from me.'

Toby got to his feet with an old-fashioned display of good manners which had Julie tittering.

'He only wanted to come round today to see Annabel,' Jan went on with a grin, 'but I didn't tell him she'd gone to her parents for the day.'

'I did not,' Toby protested unconvincingly.

Julie sat down and the conversation reverted, as it usually did, to horses. Seeing a large framed photograph that Jan had recently found space to hang on the wall, she asked which horse it was.

'That was my first hunter chase winner, at Ludlow last March – Rear Gunner. I haven't got him any more,' said Jan with a pained face.

'What happened to him, then?'

'He was one of Harold Powell's.'

Toby glanced at her. 'Was that the chap Eddie was telling me about – the auctioneer who bought your old farm and sold it a few months later for nearly a hundred grand more?'

'That's the man. Bloody crook. He pretended to be a friend of mine. I'd trained his horses and done well with them for four or five years. Then he took complete advantage of me just after my husband died.'

Toby nodded and turned to Eddie. 'Were those his horses you had to drive back to Wales?'

'That's right.' Eddie grinned at the memory of it and told the others about Jan's rage at his not having an HGV licence.

'But', Toby looked at Jan, 'aren't you trying to sue this chap?'

'The solicitors in Broadway wrote to him; then he turned up here with a pathetic offer and I told him to get stuffed. He came back again last month, wouldn't up his offer, and not a lot's happened since. Mr Russell, the solicitor, doesn't think I've got much of a chance because technically they did it all by the book. But I still reckon they might not want the publicity of a court case, even if they didn't lose.'

'I'm sure they wouldn't, but the trouble is no lawyer is going to work that hard for you because they'd know there's a limit to what you can spend, and they'd be up against some big firm acting for this chap's professional indemnity insurers, who'd want to fight it all the way.'

'Yes,' Jan nodded ruefully. 'That's what I thought.'

'I'll put you on to my London solicitors. They're real heavy-weights. They'll get the ball rolling for you again.'

'Harold Powell?' Julie asked. 'Wasn't he the bloke who turned up when I was up here one evening about four weeks ago?'

'Yes, that was him. That was the second time he came to persuade me to take a few thousand in settlement for what he'd done to me. I told him to get lost and I haven't heard a squeak from him since.'

'I saw him again', Julie said, 'a few days after that. Where did you say he lives?'

'In Wales, between Hay and Brecon. Were you up there?'

'No way. I was at the pub in the next village, the Star. The girl there's a friend of mine and she does my hair. She's done this colour for me.' Julie proudly shook her head of purple spikes. 'I was up in her room while she was doing it and I saw that bloke in the car park. He'd just come out of the pub and he stopped to have a chat with one of them pikey boys – a cousin of that kid Joe Paley that works for you.'

Jan stiffened. 'How long after you'd seen him here?'

'No more than a couple of days. Why?'

'It doesn't matter, but what was he called, the boy he was talking to?'

'I don't know.'

'Would Joe know?'

'I should think so.'

'Jan,' Toby asked, 'what do you think he was doing?'

'I don't know. Maybe it's just me being paranoid,' Jan said quickly, not wanting to air her suspicions.

'OK, but if you think there's the remotest chance it could have something to do with your dispute with him, you've got to tell your lawyers. Would you like me to sort out this London firm for you?'

Jan dithered for a moment. London lawyers, insurance companies with bottomless coffers – it all sounded way out of her league. And yet there was no way she wanted to see Harold get away with what he'd done to her.

'Yes, all right,' she said. 'That would be a great help.'

When Toby, Eddie and Julie had gone, Jan settled down to give Matthew his lunch. While she watched him eat, she thought about what Julie had told her, and before she went back down to the yard to get on with her afternoon chores she rang Gerry on his mobile. She asked him if he could drop in that evening.

Gerry arrived early, ready, as always, to do whatever she asked.

Discreetly, during the afternoon she'd asked Joe Paley if he had a cousin who used the pub in the next village.

Joe admitted that he knew Amos Smith, the boy whom Julie had described, but he claimed to be only a distant blood connection with the sixteen-year-old, who came from one of the more disreputable families in the area.

Jan confided in Gerry – with a stern warning it mustn't go any further – that she thought Harold Powell had recruited Amos Smith to let the horses out of the bottom field, which had resulted in them being killed on the main road.

'What do you want me to do about it?' Gerry asked, twitching with eagerness to see justice done.

'See if you can find him, on his own, and ask him how much Harold Powell paid him to open that gate.'

It was two days before she saw Gerry again; he arrived late in the evening and put his head around the door of the caravan with a shamefaced smile.

'Sorry, Jan,' he said right away. 'It looks like I've blown it.'

'Come in out of the rain, Gerry; I won't eat you.'

Gerry squeezed his large frame into the confined space.

'Sit down, for God's sake,' Jan smiled. 'You make the place untidy standing around like that.'

Gerry sat on one of the small benches, while Jan got him a can of Stella, which she knew he liked.

'OK, so how did you blow it?' she asked.

'I found him easily enough in the Star, but he wouldn't come out and talk to me. I couldn't get him on his own, so I just had to say in front of his mates I wanted to talk about a bloke he'd met in the car park there a few weeks ago. I could see he knew what I was talking about, like, but he said he didn't. He said he hadn't met a bloke in the car park, any time. I told him he'd been seen, but I didn't say who by; then he and his mates just told me to piss off.'

'Did they threaten you at all?'

'No, but they would have done if I'd pushed it any more. Anyway, I went back there tonight and some of the same blokes are there, playing pool and drinking like hell – I reckon they pulled off some scam – but this young lad, Amos, he wasn't with them and they said he'd gone.'

'Gone? Gone where?' Jan said in frustration.

'They said they didn't know – maybe apple-picking over in Herefordshire; but they sure as hell weren't going to tell me. So it looks like I scared him off before I got anything out of him.'

Jan sighed. 'It does, but never mind. Maybe we should have done it some other way. I suppose I should have got the police to check those tyre marks when they were there.'

'I doubt that would have helped. He probably came in a stolen vehicle anyway. I'm sorry I blew it, Jan.'

'You did what you could, Gerry. Thanks. I may be barking up completely the wrong tree, but I've got a hunch that Harold was involved in letting the horses out – if anyone did. Could you keep your eyes and ears open and tell me when Amos turns up again?'

13

As autumn crept inevitably towards winter, Jan began to feel that her first half year at Edge Farm had been some sort of psychological trial, as if God had decided to test her skill and stamina.

She'd had to face Harold's treachery over Stonewall and, maybe, his attempt to undermine her reputation by organizing the escape and death of two of her horses; James McNeill's sexual forays; the Jockey Club inspector's damning verdict on her premises, and her principal backer's financial collapse. But she recognized that the route to a Jockey Club licence might well be a two-circuit race and she was now better prepared for any more obstacles that might crop up.

At least it now looked as if McNeill's threat to report her to the Jockey Club for the lost horses had been neutralized by her own warning that she would follow up her complaint with his professional body. She was sure that, otherwise, she would have heard something by now, which gave her more time to establish who the real culprit was.

At the same time, despite all the disasters and setbacks, the underlying strength of her yard had been growing. Every one of her staff – the girls and the lads – had committed themselves to Edge Farm Stables, backed up by people like her mum and dad, Billy Hanks and Gerry. Even Darren and Tom, the two boys from the village who came up every Saturday to earn a little money cutting docks and thistles in the paddocks, had developed a fierce loyalty to Jan. They both dreamed of being jockeys and swore that as soon as they were big enough they'd be up and riding out for her every day.

Jan's owners, although very different, all seemed to have become devoted to the cause. Hardly a day went by without one or other of them dropping in to see their horse and chat about their prospects. And they had each promised to support Jan's application for a public licence by pledging to keep a horse in training with her when she turned professional.

With the caravan now permanently warm, even the thought of spending the rest of the winter there was bearable, and Jan felt less guilty about her shortcomings as a mother in using the money from the sale of Gale Bird to pay Gerry to put a new roof on the barn instead of building the house.

Also, in a subtle reversal of roles, she'd found time to give Eddie some support in his unfamiliar state of penury.

He told Jan that he'd managed to keep his small shop going in Stow with the help of a couple of part-time pensioners who didn't need so much money. The sale of a large picture would cheer him up for a few days, but it was obvious that he was fighting a losing battle. He had, though, found somewhere to live after he'd been evicted from his cottage in the grounds of Windrush Grange, his father's old house.

Jan had never been to the cottage, by all accounts pure Cotswold chocolate box and, given the change in Eddie's circumstances, she was glad she hadn't, but he had asked Jan round to see his new home a few days after he'd moved in.

She rang him and said she could drop in on her way to the saddler's at Stow one Saturday morning. He sounded pleased and more cheerful than he had for quite some time, but when she arrived there, although he'd warned her that Old Ford Mill was fairly dilapidated, she wasn't prepared for what she found.

It was hidden behind a long, high wall and ancient gates of paint-peeled timber. When she pushed them open and drove onto a weed-covered circle of broken cobbles, she found the mill house was built of the local sandstone, like every other house in the village, and three hundred years on marshy ground beside its millpond had given the stone a faint coating of green moss. A massive wisteria, which must have been clambering up the building for over a hundred years, covered most of the front and dangled like a curtain over the small windows. Although undeniably picturesque, the place looked as if it had been uninhabited for years. Wild creepers and saplings seemed to have taken root in every available crack in the side walls and a lot of the stone roof tiles showed signs of slippage.

Jan parked her Land Rover beside Eddie's much older model and was relieved that she'd decided to leave Megan and Matthew with Roz for the morning – Eddie's mill house looked like a death trap for inquisitive children.

As she climbed down from the Land Rover, the big oak front door opened and Eddie came out.

'Morning,' he called, 'and welcome to Old Ford Mill. What do you think of it?' He had reached Jan and leaned down to kiss her cheek. 'Isn't it beautiful?'

Jan laughed. 'It's like something out of an old painting by Constable. Is there any electricity?'

'God, no. This is seriously archaic living, and very green.'

'I can see that,' Jan nodded at the weed-infested walls. 'What about water?'

'There's a hand pump in the kitchen and a range that must be a hundred years old. I've also got a few lodgers', Eddie grinned, 'of the furry variety.'

Jan shook her head in disbelief as he led her through a dark, low-beamed hall into a kitchen where nothing appeared to have changed in the previous century. 'Eddie, how can you live in a place like this?'

'That's what my dad said when he stayed last night,' Eddie laughed. 'As a matter of fact, he's only just popped out to get the papers. He won't be long. I told him you were coming round and he's looking forward to meeting you, so you must stay until he gets back.'

Ron Sullivan was a legendary character, one of the most colourful racehorse owners in recent years, and ever since she had met

Eddie Jan had wondered about the relationship between father and son. It would be strange finally to meet Ron in these bizarre circumstances, but she thought she'd enjoy it more than if he'd still been living up at Windrush Grange, surrounded by flunkeys, limousines and all the trappings of big, new money.

'What's he like, your dad?' she asked.

Eddie had taken a big iron kettle off the range and was pouring boiling water into a cafetière. 'We'll have some coffee and I'll tell you.'

When Eddie had filled the two mugs, he sat down with Jan at a large scrubbed table and leaned back in his chair.

'When you meet Dad, you'll find he's an out-and-out Londoner, born in the East End and never pretended he wasn't. He left school at sixteen back in the fifties without a qualification to his name, but he went out and became an apprentice brickie. And though he never passed an exam in his life, he's a clever old bastard, always a very quick learner. I should think he soon knew every dodge in the book and found he could make a lot more money handling men than bricks. He did really well in the building boom in the sixties and by the early seventies he'd moved away from East Ham and was employing a couple of dozen men as a subcontractor on the big new housing estates going up around Dagenham. It was then he discovered what he likes to call his natural sense of style.' Eddie grinned. 'You'll see what I mean, but he started getting a few bigger jobs out in Essex. The size and the price of the houses he was building began to rise, and he managed to get a lot of very good guys onto his payroll. Some of them were still working for him until a fortnight ago and that's really upset him.

'Anyway, when there was that big property crash in the early seventies, he was still in his thirties, but he was already running a big building company and he'd made an awful lot of money. That gave him a fantastic chance to snap up some bargain sites after the crash in seventy-four, when most of the big property companies got buried under massive stocks of land. Then he just took his time and developed them as prices slowly recovered.'

'But when did he marry your mum?' Jan asked, not so concerned with the business history of Eddie's family.

'That was back in sixty-two. He always says it was a great time then. The Beatles had just released "Love Me Do", and all the girls were starting to take the pill. I think Dad enjoyed himself, but not my mother. Still, she managed to persuade him to build their first big house, a great lump of a place on the edge of Harold Hill. That's where I was born, but I can hardly remember it because when I was about four Mum made my father buy a place on St George's Hill, the smart side of London. And that's when one of his posh chums persuaded him to put me down for Harrow.' Eddie laughed. 'I'm not sure he doesn't regret it, though we still get on really well.' He cocked an ear at the sound of a car coming through the gate. 'That'll be him now, so you can see for yourself.'

Ron Sullivan made his presence felt with a bellow at Eddie as soon as he walked through the front door. When he came into the kitchen, Jan saw he was a big man in his early sixties. There was something about him that seemed to announce the fact that he'd made his first million back in the seventies and, like an old institution clinging to tradition in the hope of averting change, he still wore his silver grey hair, which framed his large tanned face, in a short-topped, long-tailed style, like a footballer of the period. To complete the statement, he was wearing chunky gold rings with a neck chain to match, a lime green jacket and canary yellow trousers.

'Dad,' Eddie said with what sounded to Jan like genuine affection, 'I want you to meet Jan Hardy, my trainer. Jan, this is my dad, Ron Sullivan.'

Jan took the big hand extended to her and sensed a latent power in Ron that wasn't present in his son.

'Pleased to meet you,' Ron growled. 'Though I don't know how the bloody hell Eddie thinks he's going to pay your wages now. I mean, look at this place!' He raised his brows as his eyes swept the ancient room.

Jan shrugged a shoulder. 'He's already paid his training fees up to the end of the year and I'm schooling him for nothing.'

'He'll need some bloody schooling,' Ron laughed. 'They taught him bugger all at that toffs' school. After all that wonga I spent, he's still only a bleedin' shopkeeper!'

'Now then, Dad. Don't get too excited. There's not a lot you can do about it now and at least I know something about pictures. You never know, I may yet restore the Sullivan millions.'

Ron looked at his son, not without affection, but with no illusions about his money-making talents. 'Listen, son, for all you'll earn in that little shop of yours, you might as well urinate into a hurricane. Just try and scratch a living, Ed, that's all I ask. I was worth thirty million a couple of years ago.' He laughed bitterly and shook his head. 'And now', he glanced at the Rolex Oyster on his wrist, 'at midday precisely my beautiful house, Windrush Grange, five hundred acres and half a dozen cottages, becomes the property of Mr Cyril Goldstone.'

He sat down and for a few moments, his whole face collapsed, which gave Jan an inkling of how it must feel to have fallen so far, so fast.

Eddie filled a mug with coffee and pushed it to his father across the old deal table. 'Cyril Goldstone, the bookie? You lost that much to him?'

'No, of course I didn't, but the official receiver accepted his offer for the house, the land and everything in it.' Ron heaved a shoulder. 'I'm sorry, son.'

'That's OK, Dad. I've had a good run with your money and I think I'm going to like this place anyway.'

Ron scowled around the dilapidated kitchen. 'Dump, more like. How much are you paying for it?'

'Nothing, I've just got to do it up slowly and in return I have it for ten years.'

Ron shook his head. 'It's hard to tell who's conning who, isn't it?' He turned to Jan and smiled. 'What do you think?'

'I'll tell you in ten years,' Jan replied.

'Well done! Spoken like a true trainer,' Ron laughed. 'I used to have a few horses in training myself, you know.'

'Yes, I remember,' Jan said. 'Have you any more?'

'No, Jan, I haven't. When I tell you I'm boracic lint, I mean totally bloody skint.' His face clouded again.

'But how could someone like you, who's made so much and knows so much, end up like that?'

For a moment Ron looked up, his eyes blazing and Jan thought he was going to chew her out for her cheek; but, with a visible effort, he eased the tension. 'Yeah, well, it must look bloody odd, I know. I suppose you could say I got seduced. They said I'd turn twenty million into half a billion.' He shrugged a shoulder to emphasize his own gullibility. 'Of course, I didn't believe the numbers. I'd have been quite happy to turn twenty mill into a hundred, and I thought there was a good chance of that.'

'What were you punting on?' Eddie asked.

'A bunch of villains, as it turned out – slimy little City slickers I could have eaten for breakfast if we'd been dealing in property. They knew they were cruising for a bruising in the States, they wanted their money out and they saw me coming. But I'm not blaming anyone except me. I can barely switch on my own computer, so what the hell was I doing getting into software when the whole world was already in for the ride? But that's not the point. It don't really matter why it happened, does it? That's history. The banks have gone for everything, I haven't an effing shred of a counterclaim, not without spending a bleedin' pile on briefs who won't get out of bed for less than ten grand. And there's another bunch of villains that wants the half a mill off of me I borrowed to keep things goin' a bit longer. They were round a couple of days ago – said they wanted to remind me that health's important.'

'What other bunch of villains?' Eddie asked shakily.

Hearing the worry in his voice, Jan could tell he was dreading the worst.

'They call themselves a bank.' Ron shrugged. 'I knew what they were when I dealt with them, but I was sure I'd be out of the shit in time to settle up.'

'But they can't go after you now, can they, if you've been made bankrupt?'

'As it happens, I haven't yet. It's not till tomorrow I'm formally declared totally and utterly boracic! Don't you think the hacks would have got onto it by now if it'd already happened? Anyway, they couldn't give a monkey's about the laws of bankruptcy, or any other laws for that matter.'

'Jesus, Dad! What are you going to do about it?'

Ron managed to pull a grin across his broad face. 'I'll think of something – I always have. And your lovely little trainer doesn't want to hear all my personal problems, does she?' he said, giving Jan a big grin. 'Don't get excited about it, son.' He stood up and shook his yellow trousers back into shape. 'Right, I've got to go. I'll see you in a couple of weeks when I've got it sorted.'

Ron said a brief goodbye to them both and gave Jan a farewell kiss on the cheek.

She and Eddie watched him walk from the house to a small Ford, which she guessed was hired.

Jan looked at Eddie. 'He's a hell of a bloke, isn't he, your dad?'

Eddie nodded; she saw that there was the hint of a tear in his eye. 'He's a rogue, though. He doesn't want anyone's sympathy; and, frankly, he doesn't deserve it. He was always the winner in everything he did and for a man like Dad who's made it all himself this is the ultimate humiliation. He hates the fact that he got so comprehensively shafted when he really should have known better.'

'But you're worried about him, what he said about that loan, aren't you?'

Eddie bit his lip and nodded again. 'It's not just him I'm worried about. My mother's house in London is still technically half his, and if anyone cottons on to that she'd end up getting booted out too and that would break her heart – on top of everything else that's happened. And she's still very fond of my dad.'

'Why did they split up then?'

'Well, it's hard to understand your own parents' relationship, but I think she'd just lost interest in sex and, in a funny sort of way, he was too honest just to go out and get a mistress. She wasn't too bitter about it when he said he wanted a divorce and he found her this beautiful little Georgian house in St John's Wood ten or eleven years ago. She gets on with loads of charity stuff that keeps her busy and nags me about why I don't take any girls back to meet her,' Eddie grinned.

'Why don't you?'

'I don't think that's the sort of thing a trainer should be discussing with her client, do you? I asked you over to look at my historic residence, so let me show you round.'

After Eddie had proudly shown Jan the full extent and dilapidated condition of the mill house, he suggested lunch at the White Horse, his village local. Jan arranged for Roz to stay with the children a little longer and tried not to feel guilty about having a few hours to herself without the children.

The landlord and regulars in the White Horse were intrigued to meet Jan. They'd heard a lot about her – not only from Eddie, but also from Billy Hanks, who lived in the village. They were encouraging, but Jan couldn't help feeling some resentment at always being compared to Virginia Gilbert; as far as Jan was concerned, all she had in common with Colonel Gilbert's daughter was her gender.

When they had their drinks and a plateful of sandwiches on the table in front of them, Eddie asked Jan what progress she'd made with Harold.

'Gerry went to find this lad that Julie saw him talking to,' Jan said, 'but he wouldn't admit to anything. He had a crowd of his mates with him so there wasn't a lot poor Gerry could do. Then, when he went back next day, Gerry was really mortified because this kid, Amos Smith, had done a runner – at least, his mates said he'd gone off apple-picking somewhere and wouldn't be back.'

'I'm not surprised, but if we can't talk to him, maybe we should go and ask Harold Powell what he was up to in that car park.'

Jan nodded. 'That's what I was thinking.'

'Then let's do it,' Eddie said. 'There's no point hanging about while the trail goes cold. We could go over there this afternoon.'

'No.' Jan shook her head doubtfully. 'I must pick up the kids.'

'Bring them with you. You could always drop them at their grandmother's.'

'OK,' Jan said, making her mind up. 'We're bound to find him somewhere and it would be better if he had no warning we were coming.'

Eddie insisted on going in his Land Rover, which added to the journey time. But it was a bright autumn day and Olwen had sounded pleased when Jan had phoned to ask if she could bring Megan and Matty over for tea.

'What are you doing over here?' Olwen asked, eyeing Eddie suspiciously when they arrived.

Jan couldn't see any benefit in discussing her mission with her mother-in-law. 'We've come to see about a horse,' she said, with a vague grain of truth. 'We'll be a couple of hours. I hope that's all right?'

'You know I'm always very happy to have my son's children,' Olwen said stiffly.

Harold lived in a handsome Edwardian stone house about fifteen minutes from Stonewall Farm, in a small village just above the River Wye, north of Hay.

A long drive approached the house between iron-railed paddocks. Jan recognized a few of the horses grazing in them.

'He must be trying to train them himself,' she remarked.

'That's what he said he was going to do, with a couple of girls,' Eddie confirmed. 'I thought it was just sour grapes.'

'There's no reason why he shouldn't try, though I don't think he has a prayer of getting the feed and the exercise right. I can't see Rear Gunner here, though.'

'I wonder if Harold is.'

'It looks like it,' Jan said as they turned into a sweep of gravel in front of the house, where Harold's new Range Rover stood, sparkling clean in front of a handsome weeping ash.

Eddie parked beside it, switched off the engine and turned to Jan. 'Here we go then.'

'How are we going to play this?' Jan asked, suddenly scared now they were here.

'Keep cool. He'll be worried too. We'll hit him head on, as if we had positive proof that he did it.'

They climbed out and crunched with confident strides across the gravel towards a light oak front door.

They mounted two broad, smooth stone steps and Eddie pressed a large china bell push.

The door was opened by Sheila Powell. Her eyes narrowed at once, though Jan wasn't sure if it was from the sunlight or at the sight of her.

'I didn't know you were coming round,' she said, revealing that she was used to her husband not telling her what was going on.

'Nor does Harold,' Jan said. 'We just dropped in on the off-chance. It looks as though we're in luck,' she added, nodding over her shoulder at the Range Rover.

'He's watching the rugby – Llanelli–Bath,' Sheila said.

'I'm sure he'd like to talk to us, though. I just heard on the radio Llanelli is taking a bit of a drubbing,' Eddie said, putting on a convincing smile.

Sheila shrugged, in the certain knowledge that whatever she did would be wrong, and opened the door to let them in. 'You'd better wait in there,' she said, pushing open the door of a small formal drawing room off the dark front hall.

Jan and Eddie looked at each other, both slightly nervous in the cold, anonymous room. A few moments later Harold came in. He was wearing a bland, inquisitive smile as he walked through the door.

'Hello, Jan, and Mr Sullivan, isn't it?'

'That's right,' Eddie nodded.

'Sorry to interrupt your rugby, Harold.'

'No problem,' Harold said, affably. 'What can I do for you?'

Jan looked at him, sensing that his friendliness was a sure sign of insecurity. 'I've already told you that, Harold, but I haven't heard from you lately.'

Harold's lips straightened and the flesh round his jaw became firmer. 'I've told you what we can offer, bearing in mind that we're not obliged to offer anything at all. But as you're an old friend I persuaded my partners that we should, in the interests of good will. Are you sure you want to discuss this in front of Mr Sullivan?'

'Certainly,' Jan said. 'He knows what's been going on. In fact he can tell you a little more about what we know already.'

'Oh, really?' Harold said, looking coldly at Eddie, but Jan didn't miss his Adam's apple jerk as he swallowed.

'There's one thing Amos Smith didn't tell us before he went missing,' Eddie said, impressing Jan with his calm delivery, 'and that's how much you paid him to open the gate and let out Jan's horses, two of which, as you'll have heard by now, were killed.'

Harold didn't answer at once, but his face seemed to darken in colour as his eyes darted from Eddie's to Jan's. 'What the hell are you talking about?' he spluttered suddenly. 'Why would I want to kill Jan's horses? How would that help me?'

'I expect you thought it would put her off pursuing you through the courts for the money you robbed her of.'

'I think, Mr Sullivan, you should keep your nose out of other people's business.'

'I asked Eddie to help,' Jan interjected. 'And I trust him completely.'

'Let's hope he's a bit more trustworthy than his father, then,' Harold sneered.

Jan saw Eddie wince. She glared at Harold. 'I hope you could say the same about your own kids,' she snapped.

'Look, if you've just come here to insult me with fairy stories, you may as well leave. I don't know what the hell you're talking about, or any Amos Smith.'

'You don't remember the young man you talked to in a pub car park on October the sixteenth, less than four miles from Edge Farm?'

'I remember some young bloke – a right chancer, by the look of things – asking if he could clean my car. I had some good tack in the back and I told him to clear off, but I didn't ask his name.'

Jan looked away, at a gold carriage clock ticking quietly on the mantel-shelf. Harold's indignation and explanation seemed totally plausible.

'What were you doing in that part of Gloucestershire, anyway?' Eddie pressed, ignoring Harold's denial.

'I'd had a bit of business in Oxford on behalf of some clients. I was on my way back and I thought of visiting Jan, to see if we could work out her grievance over the sale of Stonewall, and I stopped for a bit of lunch to think about what we could do. Then, given the reception I had last time, I thought better of it and carried on home.'

Eddie stared at Harold, without saying anything for a moment. 'You had that answer all nicely worked out, didn't you? But, unfortunately for you, Amos told us about your conversation with him and what you asked him to do.' Eddie shrugged his shoulders, to convey the futility of Harold denying it.

But Harold was smiling now. 'Look, Mr Sullivan,' he said soothingly, 'I don't know where on earth you got your information from, but I can assure you this lad never told you anything like that, or, if he did, he was making it up because he thought there might be a few bob in it. And, believe me, I understand that Jan feels unhappy that the farm fetched a great deal more money a few months after we sold it for her, but anyone will confirm that the market hardened a hell of a lot last spring. We'd like to help: we've made an offer and I don't see how we could be expected to do more.'

'You could have offered more, to make up for my loss through your bad advice alone, never mind deliberately keeping the price down so you could buy it cheaply and make a nice turn for yourself.'

'Look, Jan, I've said I can understand you grievance, but we're just going round in circles now. I had nothing to do with your horses getting out and I take great exception to you coming here with Mr Sullivan to accuse me of it. I think we may as well bring this meeting to a close. Our original offer still stands. All you have to do is sign the simple document I left you and that'll be that.'

Jan glanced at Eddie. 'Let's go.'

Eddie raised a shoulder. 'Mr Powell, we know what you did, and when Amos Smith reappears the police will be talking to him about it.'

Harold said nothing; he just waited for them to leave the room. Jan went first, but as she reached the door she couldn't stop herself from turning back once more. 'There's something else I'd like to know, as I put a hell of a lot of work into him. What have you done with Rear Gunner?'

Harold raised his eyebrows. 'You did well with him, I've always said so,' he agreed, 'but to see him achieve his true potential I've sent him to a professional yard. He's with Virginia Gilbert now; she wants to run him in a few good hunter chases.'

'The bastard!' Jan gasped as soon as they were back in the Land Rover and Eddie had started the noisy diesel engine. 'He's done exactly what he knew would really annoy me.'

'Then don't give him the satisfaction of seeing it,' Eddie said quietly as he swung the car round in front of the house and headed back down the drive towards the main road.

'As for that cock-and-bull story about Amos wanting to clean his car—'

'I think he's seen Amos since Gerry did.'

'Yes,' Jan nodded. 'He was so confident that we didn't really know anything, and his mates said Amos had gone to pick apples in Herefordshire. He could easily be somewhere out this way; there's loads of orchards still being picked.'

'He knows there's nothing we can do, I'm afraid.'

'But do you really think he did it?'

'Frankly, I just don't know.'

'Oh God!' Jan groaned. 'It's horrible, being so sure you know one minute and then having to accept you may have got it all wrong.'

'Have you been in touch with those solicitors Toby Waller suggested?' Eddie asked.

'No, not yet. But I will, first thing Monday morning. I'll get them to send Harold a final warning that we're going to go after him for the difference between what I got for Stonewall and what he got for it.'

14

'You've done what!?' Jan's shoulders collapsed and her mouth fell open.

Three days after they'd been to see Harold in Wales, Eddie was sitting opposite her at the small wooden table in her caravan. Between them were the remains of a Chinese takeaway, a vase of flowers and a bottle of wine, most of which had been drunk by Eddie. The light from a pair of fat, flickering candles on wrought-iron brackets gleamed off a few silver trophies and framed photographs of winning horses squeezed onto the tiny shelves.

'What happened was', he said, 'I went back to the Grange to see Cyril Goldstone, to sort of welcome him into our old home. He didn't take it too well, but as he's a bookie and I had to make conversation, I asked him what price he'd give me on Russian Eagle to win the Aintree Foxhunters' with me riding. He just laughed at first, but when he offered me a hundred to one I had to go for it.'

Jan shook her head. 'But five thousand quid? Eddie, you're barking mad.'

'Look Jan, my father owes this dodgy Italian bank half a million. If he can keep them off his back somehow until next spring and we can win this race, I can get him off the hook and Mum can keep her house.'

'But where did you find five grand?'

'Ah, well,' Eddie winced. 'That's the tricky bit. I'd been keeping it on deposit at the bank to pay my VAT next week.'

'For God's sake – how are you going to pay it now?'

Eddie shrugged. 'I don't know – pray, I suppose.'

Jan couldn't believe anyone could do anything so utterly foolish. She had been thinking what a good evening they were having until then.

'You must be out of your head having a ridiculous bet like that.'

'But, Jan,' he said with a puzzled smile, 'you said you thought Eagle could do it.'

'For Christ's sake, Eddie! Where have you been all your life? There's a mile of difference between "could" win and "will" win.'

Eddie refused to be shaken. 'Do you still think he could win?'

'Like I've said before, all we've got to go on is his form, which says he can do the distance; so far his jumping looks reliable, though I don't think he's got a lot of speed. In a poor contest, with the right conditions and a competent jockey – yes, it's just *possible* he *could* win.'

'That'll do for me.' Eddie grinned and topped up their glasses.

Jan pushed hers away. 'No. That's enough for me – and for you, if you seriously think you're going to come in and ride work at seven tomorrow – especially if you want to nudge your chances below a hundred to one.'

Eddie looked at her steadily for a moment, as if he were trying to spot a chink of softness or invitation in her firm blue eyes.

'It's no good looking at me like a dog at a bone,' Jan said, suppressing a smile. 'You're going home to bed.'

Eddie nodded with a grin and stood up. 'Goodnight Jan.' He leaned across the narrow table top and lightly kissed her forehead. 'Do you know, I do believe you're the best-looking trainer in Gloucestershire.'

'That's not saying much, Eddie. You've had far too much to drink, you're looking at me by candlelight, and the only other female trainer in Gloucestershire is Virginia Gilbert. Get on home, you berk, and leave me alone.'

As he stepped down from the caravan, she flashed a smile at his back. He turned, just in time to catch it lingering on her lips. 'Eddie,' she said more gently.

'Yes?' He put a foot back on the first step.

She put her hands on his shoulders and gently pushed him back. 'Promise me you won't ever have any more big bets on horses in my yard without talking to me first?'

Eddie was more muted the next few times he came to Edge Farm to be schooled on Eagle. But Jan also noticed a new determination in his efforts and she realized that, crazy as it seemed, he was completely serious about winning the Aintree race.

One morning, after he'd gone, she talked about it with Annabel, without telling her just how dire Ron Sullivan's predicament was.

'The trouble is,' Annabel said, 'whenever Eddie got into trouble in the past, he would just go to Ron, who bailed him out, or the bank would lend him what he needed against his shares in Sullivan Homes. Now Ron's in trouble, Eddie wants to help him, but he actually hasn't got a clue how to deal with the pressure. I don't suppose he's ever been seriously tested in his life.'

'I wish I could do more to help,' Jan said. 'I never told him he had a *good* chance of winning, just that he *could* win if he's very lucky and he gets a good run. That's one of the dangers of training. If someone's pestering you about whether their horse might win such and such a race, you say it could be possible and they take it you're predicting a win. I mean, Eddie's horse is coming together all right and he's really worked on his riding – I'm pretty confident he'll win a few point-to-points if we enter him in the right ones, but', Jan sighed, 'we'll be very lucky to do more than that.'

'Are you OK, Jan?' Annabel was looking more closely at her. 'You seem a bit wiped out.'

'I am. Matty was up half the night coughing, and I was thinking that we shouldn't still be living in a caravan, though I don't think that's what's causing it. But then there's everything else. We all work our backsides off here; you do it for half what you should, Gerry never sends in all the bills he should, and I still can't really get ahead of the game enough to start building a proper house or anything. I need that licence badly, but what with the Jockey Club turning me down and everything else—'. Jan shook her head, 'I sometimes feel like giving up. OK, I think we might be passed on the fire risk next time, but they weren't that happy about the gallops either. Then Virginia's complained about those horses getting out and now I don't even have anyone to put up the guarantee.'

'You could always ask Bernie,' Annabel said. 'He'd do anything for you.'

'I think it's you he comes to see, actually.'

'Oh no, it's not; you should try him.'

'Frankly, I'd rather not be in hock to someone like Bernie, when you look how he uses his money to keep Sandy interested.'

'That's all she's interested in, anyway,' Annabel said.

'I don't think he'd do it,' Jan said. 'The fact of the matter is there aren't that many people prepared to stick their necks out for people like me, especially being a woman.'

'Oh, Jan,' Annabel gave her arm a squeeze, 'don't sell yourself short. You've got a lot of support. Of course, I know it's been tough this last few months and you're still getting over John; there's been James McNeill and Harold and all that to deal with, but at least all the horses in the yard look great.'

'Thanks, Bel.' Jan smiled wanly. 'I suppose you're right, but sometimes I wonder if it's worth all the worry and the stress, and spiteful people ganging up against you, when all you're trying to do is make a living.'

'By the way, I forgot to tell you, Mr Carey came round last night and invited me and you and anyone to do with the stables to a bonfire party tonight. Apparently he does it every year on December the first for all the village. Julie says it's something to do with him being Catholic and not believing in Guy Fawkes Night. He provides most of the fireworks and the pub lays on some booze.'

Victor Carey, Jan was learning, was a man with two distinct sides. Since she'd had his horse, August Moon, in the yard, he'd been up a few times. He'd shown a good knowledge of horses and racing and he was looking forward to seeing his mare run. Mr Carey had never married, no one knew why, and there was no obvious reason. Jan concluded it was because, under his curt manner, he was very shy. But despite regular displays of astounding meanness, there were occasional flashes of great generosity, of which the firework party was a good example.

Jan decided to take her children; all the people who worked for her were coming and she told a few of the owners whom she'd spoken to that day about it. So, as darkness fell, she arrived at the paddock, which was surrounded on three sides by woodland and facing the heavy stone features of Stanfield Court, where a massive bonfire had just been lit.

Julie from the pub was standing behind a trestle table, serving mulled wine in plastic mugs and pop for the children.

Eddie Sullivan was already standing at the temporary bar.

'Hello, Jan. Have a drink.' He handed her one and got another for Megan. 'Is Matthew up for anything?' he asked.

Matthew was gurgling from a sling on Jan's back. 'He's quite happy at the moment, but I shouldn't think that'll last long once the fireworks start. I may have to make a hasty exit. Anyway, what brings you here?'

'I thought I might find you. The thing is, I've got a major problem. I sent off my VAT return with a cheque for just over five grand and, unless there's a miracle, when it hits my bank next week it's going to bounce like a *Baywatch* boob and I'll be in deep manure. They'll start sending in the bailiffs.'

It was obvious to Jan that Eddie had already had a few drinks. 'Look, there's not a lot I can do about it, I wish there were, but—'

'Good God, I'm not expecting you to lend me the money or anything, but there is something else you could do; I may have to sell Eagle in a hurry to raise the cash. He'd be worth five grand, wouldn't he?'

'More, probably, but not if you want to sell him quickly.'

'As long as I can get enough to cover this bloody cheque, but the trouble is I've got to sell him to someone who'll let me ride him in the Foxhunters'.'

'That would narrow the field considerably. A lot of people want that sort of horse to ride themselves.'

'But can you try to think of someone, maybe someone who's told you to look for a horse?'

'All right, Eddie, but if you're serious about wanting to keep the ride, it's going to be bloody hard to find someone who'll commit themselves into letting you do it.'

'Look Jan, I've *got* to keep that ride. I've told my father that I think I can pull something out of the hat for him. He doesn't believe me, and of course, I didn't tell him what it was, but I really want to do this for him.'

Jan looked at him with fondness and frustration. 'Eddie, for God's sake, how many times have I told you, even if you keep this ride, your chances of winning the race aren't a lot better than Cyril Goldstone's given you.'

'But I've got a really good feeling about it so, please, do what you can.'

She looked at him and sighed. 'All right, Eddie. But I wish you could think of some other way of finding this money.'

'I'm looking, believe me, I'm looking,' he said gloomily.

Annabel had just arrived. Eddie spotted her and, Jan noticed, managed to transform himself in an instant into the carefree, life and soul of the party he liked to seem. Jan watched curiously as he walked over, planted a kiss on Annabel's cheek and greeted her with his usual joking banter.

Her thoughts were interrupted by Victor Carey, who came up and greeted her with a quick, tight-lipped smile.

'It's very kind of you to ask us all, Mr Carey,' Jan said, seeing how the firelight deepened the furrows in his pasty, wrinkled face. 'Though I'm not sure what he's going to do when the fireworks start.' She nodded over her shoulder at Matthew, slumbering on her back.

'There'll be quite a show, but you could always take him into the house. You could still see them from in there.'

'Thanks.'

'By the way, I wanted to tell you; I've seen how dedicated you are up at that yard and I'd very much like to see you get your licence. I just hope the incident with the loose horses hasn't gone against you.'

Jan was surprised that Victor Carey knew about the accident and its repercussions, but she was touched by his evident wish to see her succeed.

She wondered if this might be a time to talk to him about the other problem she had, of finding a suitable backer to pledge the thirty-five thousand pounds the Jockey Club demanded. But her instincts warned her that this was probably beyond the limits of his generosity.

When Mr Carey leaned down to light the first of the fireworks ten minutes later, it was not Matthew but Megan who hated the flashes and bangs and howled loudly. Jan thought of taking up Mr Carey's offer and retreating to the house, but she decided it would be easier just to take her daughter home and calm her there. She slipped away while everyone was still gasping at a series of monster set pieces, which must have cost a small fortune, defying the popular view of Mr Carey's stinginess.

Bernie Sutcliffe rang in the morning to say he was passing and could he drop in around midday.

The dogs announced his arrival. They always seemed to bark more at Bernie than at anyone else. Roz used to joke about it: 'It's like he's got a particular smell to a dog and I don't mean all that pongy aftershave he wears.'

Jan was thinking of it as she went out to greet him.

'Hello, darling, what are you smiling about?' he asked when he saw her, and a big grin distorted his long, bony face. 'Or are you just pleased to see me?'

'Always pleased to see owners,' Jan replied. 'Sorry about the dogs, though.'

'Oh that's all right. I expect they can just smell my new one.'

'I didn't know you were a dog lover, Bernie.'

'I'm not. But I've got a warehouse where I keep all sorts of good stuff, down by the canal in Brierley Hill and the alarms there are always packing up, or the villains know how to get round them. I thought the best thing would be to get a really fierce dog, so I went along to this place where they take in strays, and give 'em away if you want them and there was this great big sort of Dobermann thing. If you just walked near him, he growled like a lion. So I said, like, I'll have him, and they put him in the back of me car. But when I got home I was a bit worried because when I opened the door, he didn't bloody growl at all. And when I get him into the warehouse he turns out to be a pussy cat.'

Jan tried to keep a straight face as she listened to Bernie's whingeing tale of disappointment.

'Still,' she said, 'at least he'll bark when anyone turns up.'

'Oh, no. He doesn't bark!' Bernie said resentfully.

'What does he do then?'

'He just sort of sniffs. He's bloody useless; the trouble is I've got quite fond of him and I can't send him back, and he eats about twenty quid's worth of meat every week.'

At that Jan couldn't stop herself from grinning. She already knew Bernie hated to see money spent unnecessarily. He'd been through the first two bills she'd sent him with a magnifying glass, suspiciously demanding an explanation for every item. Jan had got herself in the habit of keeping a record card for each horse in her care, so that she could keep a check on any medication and treatment they'd had. As a result, she'd been delighted to provide documentary evidence of every single item she'd charged for.

'Anyway,' he went on, 'I wanted a word with you.'

Jan wondered what was coming as they walked across the yard to the tack room, where she tended to conduct most of her business.

'So, what is it you want?' Jan asked.

'I thought I might treat myself to another horse. I like the way the other one you got for me is coming along.'

'What sort of horse?'

'You know, something that'll win a few good races, maybe one of these hunter chases or whatever they call them when point-to-point horses run on proper tracks; that's what Sandy really wants to see.'

For her own sake and Annabel's, Jan was relieved to hear that Sandy's opinion was still a factor. She thought for a moment and took a deep breath. 'What about Russian Eagle?'

'You mean Eddie Sullivan's bloody great horse?'

'I do.'

'Huh,' Bernie grunted. 'I thought he might be feeling the pinch a bit after old Ron hit the skids,' he said, as if he were thinking, *There, but for the Grace of God* . . . 'How much is the horse worth?'

'If we entered him at Doncaster Sales, he'd probably make six or seven, the way he looks now and on his Irish form. But I should tell you, there's one proviso: Eddie's determined to win the Aintree Foxhunters' on him. I think he's had a bit of a bet, but he *must* be riding the horse himself, so whoever buys him would have to agree to that.'

'That's not a problem. I'm not going to bloody well ride him, am I? And if he thinks he can win . . . Do you think he can win?'

'Like I told Eddie, if all the conditions suit him, he could.'

'What do you mean all the conditions? You mean if all the other horses fall over?'

'No. He's quite capable of jumping round and as long as he doesn't have to quicken too much at the finish, he really does stand a chance.'

'Will he win anything else?'

'He ought to win a few points,' Jan said with complete confidence, 'and some smaller hunter chases. He's not the sort of horse that's likely to go wrong and I should think he'll stay three and a half miles, no trouble.'

'OK. I'll give him four grand for it.'

Jan shook her head. 'No you won't. He needs five and he won't take less.'

'Well it may not be his choice. Tell him I'm offering four and he can ride the horse. If he wants it, tell him to ring my office.'

At midday the next day Jan sat opposite Eddie in the caravan and watched him dial Bernie Sutcliffe's office number. She felt almost as jittery as she had before Rear Gunner had run in the Shropshire Gold Cup at Ludlow.

Although Eddie's chances of winning his bet were pretty slim, it might just be possible; she also knew it meant everything to him and she really cared. For Eddie, she guessed, it was a way not only of helping his father and showing his appreciation for all he'd been given over the years, it was also a means of proving to Ron that he, too, could pull off a spectacular coup.

It followed inevitably that Eagle winning the Foxhunters', hazy prospect that it was, had become all-important to Jan as well.

'Hello,' Eddie said in his deep, comfortable voice. 'Can I speak to Mr Sutcliffe, please?'

He looked up, put his hand over the mouthpiece and grinned at Jan. 'What on earth is Sutcliffe Industries?'

'I don't know,' Jan said. 'Eamon Fallon says he's into scrap metal and recycling paper and makes a packet out of it. Four or five grand would be absolute peanuts to him.'

'Yeah, well, some people get very possessive about their peanuts. Hello?' he said, turning his attention back to the phone while he fiddled with a pen and doodled on the note pad on the table in front of him.

'Bernie! Good morning. It's Edward Sullivan . . . No, no, I haven't got the bailiffs in yet, but thanks for asking . . . I was just ringing to thank you for your offer for Russian Eagle, but I'm afraid I've accepted a higher one . . . Good Lord, no. I just wanted to let you know, out of politeness . . . Not at all . . . Where am I now? I'm at Edge Farm, in Jan's caravan . . . Yes, of course I've got all my clothes on.' Eddie tried to laugh while screwing up his face and shaking his head at Jan. 'Fine, if you want. I'll be here for a while I expect . . . OK. Goodbye, Bernie.'

Eddie put down the phone. 'Good God, he's a dirty-minded little sod. For some reason, he seemed really excited at the idea that I might have been in here naked with you.'

'Urgh,' Jan grunted. 'Anyway, what did he say?'

'He said he would call me back.'

Jan grinned. 'He'll take it then. Well done; you're acting is very good – which makes me a bit worried, actually. I've noticed: you can turn on the charm more or less at will, can't you?'

'Not all the time', Eddie said seriously, 'and I think you know that too.'

'Why don't you ever show your real side to Annabel?'

'If by that you're saying I'm only real when I'm feeling gloomy and sorry for myself, you're wrong. I'm lucky; most of the time I really enjoy life, though I admit it's been a little tough recently. And anyway, look what a brave face you put on things when they've all been going wrong for you. I don't jump on you and accuse you of being bogus, do I?'

Jan held up a mollifying hand. 'All right, I'm sorry. But, even so, you did a great job on Bernie. If he'd thought you were just trying to talk him into having the horse, he'd have backed off. Now he just thinks he's lost a bargain.'

'I know. I may not be the deal king like Dad, but I wasn't born yesterday.'

'If you shut up, I'll get you a drink', Jan said, 'because there's something else you might be able to do for me.'

'You can always ask. Is there any of that Irish left?'

'Not much.' Jan reached behind her and took a bottle from a shelf. From a cupboard, she took a glass tumbler, poured half a finger of whiskey into it and slid it across the table like a barmaid in a Western saloon.

Eddie eyed the paltry measure with disdain. 'Never mind. So, what can I do for you?'

'I would do it myself, but I wondered if there was any way you might be able to sound out Victor Carey about my bond. He was talking to me at the firework party; he's very pleased with the way August Moon's coming on and he seemed quite interested in what I'm trying to do here. He said he'd like to see me with a licence.'

'I think he'd be far more likely to consider a request for a guarantee if it came from you directly,' Eddie commented.

'I will ask him myself but, before I do, I wouldn't mind if you sounded him out first. It would be just as embarrassing for me as for him if he wanted to turn me down.'

'Isn't there anyone else who you think might be easier and more committed?'

'Possibly, but the truth is I don't want anyone who's going to interfere all the time and feel, because their money's on the line, they've got the right to tell me how to do my job or to put their oar into my accounts and things.'

'You mean, someone like Bernie?'

'Yes, or Frank Jellard or Eamon Fallon, for that matter. And, of course, I can hardly ask Colonel Gilbert; Virginia would go bananas.'

'You're right there. OK, I'll find some excuse to talk to Carey and, if it leads into it easily enough, I'll bring the conversation round to your licence application and how difficult everything is because you just can't raise the guarantee. Frankly, I should think he'll smell it's a put-up job, but I'll do my best.'

'Thanks, Eddie. You're a good mate. You can have the rest of this whiskey; there's only a tiddly bit.' Jan poured the last few drops of the spirit into Eddie's glass. He downed it in one slug and stood up.

'OK, Mrs H. I'm off.'

'Hang on, what about Bernie?'

'Tell him I've gone, but he can ring me at home later.' Eddie thought for a moment. 'I think I'll leave the answerphone on.'

'Don't push your luck,' Jan said and gave him a grateful smile.

The following day was a Tuesday and Jan had to take a lorryload of horses hunting to catch up on their qualifying days in time for racing in the New Year. She arrived back at the stables fully expecting to have heard something from either Eddie or Bernie about Russian Eagle. But although there were five messages from Bernie, there was nothing from Eddie.

On Wednesday Jan rang Eddie's home number. She smiled as she listened to the message on his answerphone before leaving her own: 'Listen, Eddie, I hope you return this call, even if you're not returning Bernie's. He's going mad; says he can't get hold of you anywhere. He's so desperate he even asked me if I knew how much you'd got for the horse. I said I didn't know, but I thought six, and he said he'd match that if I could talk you into it. So, call me back to confirm what you want to do, though I expect I know already.'

The third week before Christmas was a much better week for Eddie, and for Jan.

Ownership of Russian Eagle was transferred to Bernie, and Eddie paid into the bank five of the six thousand pounds Bernie had given him, just in time to cover his VAT payment. He also told Jan to keep the three weeks' training fees he had already paid for Eagle, saying that she deserved it as commission on the sale.

Jan had also found two more suitable horses for Frank Jellard. One, Nuthatch, came from the same yard as Arctic Hay and the other, a small horse called Rhythm Stick, Jan bought from a local farmer's widow who had no interest in racing. Both were animals Jan considered very trainable. They had cost a little more than Frank had said he wanted to pay, but he didn't grumble and wrote out a cheque as soon as he'd seen them.

Fortunately, during a dry spell over the preceding ten days, Gerry had abandoned his current customers and rushed up to Edge to finish the barn roof in green, galvanized iron before the prevailing wet weather returned. With Frank Jellard's two new horses and two invalids still in, the yard was now at its full capacity of sixteen.

At the end of the week, Eddie arrived for a schooling session as Billy Hanks came back from riding out a couple of Jan's horses. The amateur jockey, who had a day job in Gloucester market, was in demand from several trainers in the area, but he had taken to coming to Jan's more than the others. He stood by her to watch

Eddie for the first time as she was schooling him over the steeple-chase fences.

Jan knew Eddie had improved but she found it hard to be objective about his performance.

'What do you think of him?' she asked Billy.

'I tell you what, I've known Eddie Sullivan for a long time and if you'd told me a year ago he was going to try and ride in races himself, I wouldn't have believed you. Not that he isn't a fit-looking bloke, it's just that he was always on the piss and chasing women.'

'Eddie? Chasing?'

'Well, maybe not; he's too bloody lazy for that; but he was definitely screwing them.'

'Oh, Billy, I don't want to hear about that.'

Billy laughed. 'All right, all right, but what I'm saying is I didn't think he had it in him to stick at it, but fair play, he's lost a bit of weight and you've taught him well. He's definitely seeing a stride into his fences and helping his horse.'

'What about the horse?' Jan asked.

'He's a good sort, isn't he – quite athletic for his size. What distance do you reckon he needs?'

'No less than three miles, I should have thought, probably three and a half. I suspect in the shake-up he could be a bit one paced.'

'He jumps nicely, though, and he'll make ground in the air. What does Eddie want to do with him?'

'Unfortunately, it's not up to him; he sold the horse to Bernie Sutcliffe, but I'm pretty sure Bernie'll let him ride it in the Fox-hunters' at Liverpool.'

'Why the hell did he sell him?'

'You'd have to ask him that.'

'I think I know,' Billy said. 'I see he's had to get himself a rich girlfriend, too.'

Jan turned sharply to look at him, wondering if, finally, Eddie and Annabel had got it together and been too coy to tell her. She hesitated before she asked, as casually as she could, 'Oh? Who's that? Annabel?'

'God, no! I said rich, not posh. Sharon Goldstone.'

For a moment, Jan couldn't make the connection. 'Who's she when she's at home?'

'Cyril's daughter – you know, that bookie who bought the Grange from Ron. They were saying in the White Horse she's really gone after him, and she's only eighteen.'

Jan felt slightly sick, although she was well aware she had no right to resent the fact that Eddie didn't tell her everything about his private life. 'Oh well,' she tried to say lightly, 'so long as it doesn't affect his riding.'

Later, when Billy had gone to work and Eddie was drinking coffee with Jan in the tack room, she restrained her immediate impulse to ask him about Sharon Goldstone. As they talked about the day's work, she began to open the bundle of envelopes the postman had left. Most contained bills, but there was also a cheque from Bernie and a letter from Toby's lawyers in London. She read it twice before handing it to Eddie.

With Eddie's help, a few days after they had seen Harold Powell at his home, she had sent the solicitors a full account of what had happened, with copies of her correspondence and the advertisements that had been published each time Stonewall had been sold, and asked them to approach Harold.

They had immediately fired off a letter informing Harold's solicitors of their intention to recover the fraudulent profit gained by their client and his associates. Now they were writing to say that they had received a reply to the effect that Mr Powell denied any liability, with details of how his firm had followed rigorously all the statutory procedures for selling property by auction. Any public suggestion that their client had acted in any way dishonestly or unprofessionally would be treated as a serious libel.

Toby's lawyers added that it was unfortunate that Mrs Hardy

no longer had the letter, or a copy, in which Mr Powell had proposed an ex gratia payment of ten thousand pounds. They took the view, however, that it was still possible that Mr Powell's firm would rather avoid the publicity of a messy case, with a possible reference to the DPP's office.

Eddie read the letter and looked up at Jan. 'At least they'll run with it a little further.'

'As long as they think I can pay. I dread to think how much even these first two letters have cost.'

'I'd say it was worth pushing it a bit further before you settle for Harold's ten thousand.'

'There's no way I'm going to settle for that. I'd rather have nothing,' Jan said fiercely.

'That's all very well, and highly principled, but you can't feed Megan and Matty on nothing.'

'All right. I'll risk another letter,' Jan said, more firmly than she felt. 'Oh, by the way, did you have a chance to go and see Mr Carey?'

'Yes, I did, yesterday. I said I'd come to see him about some of your owners getting together to give you a decent Christmas present.'

'Oh, Eddie, you shouldn't have done.'

'Don't get excited; we didn't come to any decision about that, but at least it meant we could talk about you, so it was comparatively easy for me to mention that you were determined to get a licence as soon as you could but a lot of things were getting in the way. I left the thirty-five grand bond until last. He may have smelt a rat, I don't know, but he didn't seem too put off by it.'

'What did he say?'

'He didn't say anything; he just nodded.'

'He nodded?'

'Yes.'

'That means "yes",' Jan said excitedly.

'Take it easy, Jan; it could just mean he was listening to what I was saying. I know I said I'd help you find another backer, but frankly, with Victor Carey, it's up to you to talk him into it. I've sown the seed, though; I don't imagine he'll be that surprised and I'm sure he'll listen.'

The day turned more wet and blustery and by the evening, when everyone else had gone home, and Jan was giving the children their tea, the prospect of venturing out to ask a man she hardly knew to put up a considerable amount of money as a guarantee for her business was not inviting. But she felt that if she allowed anything to stop her now, all momentum in her pursuit of a career as a National Hunt trainer would dissipate. Time would move on, another year would pass, and she would still just be training pointers for peanuts, with no money to pay for a house or the growing needs of her two children.

She picked up the phone and dialled Victor Carey's number. When he answered, her throat went dry and her words came out in a croak.

'Hello, Mr Carey. It's Jan Hardy here. I was wondering, if you were in, whether I could pop over and have a quick chat with you about something?'

'What would that be?' he answered dryly.

'It's to do with the running of the yard.'

'I see. And what exactly do you want to talk to me about?'

'Well, as you know, I've been applying for a full licence to train, and one of the things the Jockey Club want is—', she paused, 'a dozen people to give pledges that they'll send me horses to train.'

'There's no need to come and see me about that. I'd be quite happy to confirm that I would go on using your services, even though, of course, my horse hasn't run from your yard yet.'

'Oh, thanks.' Jan desperately cast around in her head for a way of broaching the real topic. 'But there was something else—'

'And what is that?'

God, Jan thought, *this man is not making it easy.*

'D'you know, I think I'd prefer to come and talk to you about it face to face, if you don't mind, rather than over the phone.'

'I see. When do you want to come?'

'I thought, perhaps, this evening? About half-six? If you're not busy?'

Mr Carey didn't answer for a moment, then with what sounded to Jan like a sigh, he said, 'Come round by all means. I'll expect you at six-thirty, then.'

Jan phoned Annabel next, to ask if she could leave the children with her. Annabel agreed, but Jan thought she sounded subdued, much quieter than normal. Her impression was confirmed when she arrived with Megan and Matthew. Once the children were happily crawling all over Annabel's small drawing room, she had time to ask her about it.

'I'm going to have to take a day or two off next week,' Annabel said, 'if that's OK?'

'Of course it is. You never take time off and I sometimes think you should – better now than when racing starts. What are you going to do?'

'I have to go to London.'

'What for? Shopping? A man?' Jan grinned.

'No. I've got to go into hospital for a few tests.'

'Oh Bel, no! What for? What's the trouble?' Jan gazed at her friend with concern.

'It's OK, Jan. It's not what you think, or anything remotely life-threatening. It's just something I have to do.'

Jan could tell that Annabel didn't want to tell her more at this stage and curbed her usual thirst for detail. 'Of course you must have the time off, though I'll miss you, even for a couple of days.'

Annabel nodded. 'Why are you going up to see Mr Carey? He's not worried about August Moon is he?'

'No, not at all. In fact, I think he's quite excited about seeing her run again – not that he likes to show it much. I was going to talk to him about my licence application.'

'Ah.' Annabel looked doubtful. 'Best of luck and thanks for being so good about the time off. I'll see you later.'

Jan parked the Land Rover by the back door of Stanfield Court. Before she got out of the vehicle, she sat for a moment listening to the rain drumming on the roof.

Why? she thought. *Why am I having to go through this humiliating performance, going round with a begging bowl, just so that a bunch of pompous stuffed shirts in a big office in Portman Square will allow me to do what I already know I can do perfectly well?*

She hated having to depend on others to achieve her aims. But she had to accept that in the career she had chosen, and in her circumstances, she had absolutely no option. She took a deep breath, let herself out into the rain, and ran across to shelter under the big stone arch of the back door, while she tugged at the old iron bell pull beside it.

Jan had no idea if anyone else lived in the rambling Victorian mansion with Mr Carey, but she wasn't expecting him to open the door himself. However, he did, and greeted her crisply.

'Evening, Jan. Come on in. Foul night.' He showed her along a corridor to a musty library, where a few coals glowed in a small iron fireplace. He waved her into an armchair by the fire and walked across the room to a sideboard in front of the heavily curtained windows, where a single bottle of sherry stood with two glasses.

'Sherry all right?' he asked over his shoulder.

'Yes, thank you.'

He filled both glasses carefully and carried them back, placing one on a small table beside Jan's chair.

Still standing, he took a sip and appeared to savour the sherry for a few moments, while Jan tried to decide how she was going to present her case.

'So,' he said suddenly, 'the Jockey Club, in its wisdom, thinks you should lodge a guarantee of thirty-odd thousand pounds before they'll let you have a public licence?'

Jan felt slightly breathless, as if all the wind had been taken from her sail. 'Well. Yes, actually, I was going to—'

'I guessed as much. And I have looked into this particular requirement. I understand it's to provide a fund from which any workers or suppliers would be paid if you were to cease trading.'

'Yes, that sort of thing,' Jan said.

'Hmm.' Carey took another swig of his sherry. 'Presumably you don't have liquid assets of that amount?'

Jan shook her head.

'Nor your family?'

'No, Dad doesn't even own his own place and their total savings wouldn't be half that, I shouldn't think.'

'Yes, well, it has been hard recently.' He lifted his eyes. 'I haven't made a profit on this farm for five years now.'

Jan felt her stomach sink.

Carey sat down in a chair opposite and looked hard at her. 'Tell me, what horses do you have at the moment and how many do you think you might be able to train next year?'

Jan took a few minutes to describe each horse in the yard, what she thought she might be able to do with them in the coming season and which could, possibly, go on to run under rules, including Mr Carey's own August Moon.

He listened carefully, nodding as she spoke.

When she had finished, he downed the rest of his sherry and stood up again. 'Right. I think I've got the picture. I realize you are hoping I might put up an appropriate guarantee to support your licence application. I've heard what you have to say and I'll let you know in due course if I can help.'

Jan got up too, with her knees shaking. She had no idea whether or not he was interested in helping her. He would let her know 'in due course'! 'When?' she wanted to scream.

'Thank you,' she said, as mildly as she could. 'If you do decide to, I'd be ever so grateful.' She noticed her hand was shaking as she reached down to pick up her glass and finish her drink.

Jan went to bed that night feeling more alone than she had done since the day John Hardy had died.

Annabel was away for three days. Jan felt her absence more acutely than she'd expected, even though Roz, Emma and Joe rallied round to take over the extra work. They were helped by Billy Hanks, who, by now, was coming up two or three times a week. Jan took Billy's frequent visits to be a direct reflection of his opinion of the horses in her yard, most of which he would be riding when the season started in five weeks' time.

Mid-December was always a tricky period in a pointing yard. The animals were fit and nearly ready for the job, but bringing them to their peak too soon would have them wiped out before the season was half over. Jan was convinced that, despite the absence of Rear Gunner, she had a better string than she'd ever had. At least, as her father had suggested, she might make an impression on the point-to-point world while her next licence application went in, but her pleasure at seeing the horses coming on so well with so few problems was soured by a complete silence from Mr Carey. He had called in a couple of times, and only once broached the subject, as if it were something trivial that he was looking into.

Her equilibrium wasn't helped the evening before Annabel was due back. She was reading *The BFG* to Megan when the phone rang. Still with a smile on her face, she answered.

'Hi, Edge Farm Stables.'

'It's Harold here.' There was none of the old friendliness in his voice.

Jan cleared her throat. 'What do you want?'

'I just want to tell you that if you see that young chap around – the one we talked about when you came to see me with your friend – and I hear there's been any suggestion I was in any way responsible or knew anything about those horses of yours getting out, I'd have to protect my reputation.'

'I should think it needs protecting,' Jan returned sharply.

'I mean it. If anyone suggests I was involved in deliberately causing the death of those horses, I'll have no alternative but to do you for slander.'

'What do you mean "do" me?'

'I mean take you to court. I've been very reasonable with you, Jan. I've made you a fair offer for the sake of our former friendship, but I'm just warning you, don't go asking questions or making allegations, or you'll find yourself in court and my offer will be withdrawn.'

'You can withdraw what you like, Harold, but I still want the money you helped yourself to from Stonewall.'

'I expect you do, but I wouldn't count on anything from that particular source if you're planning your budget.'

After this conversation, Jan wondered if Joe Paley's cousin, Amos Smith, would ever reappear in the district. Twelve days before Christmas, the next time Eddie came to ride out, she told him about her conversation with Harold and Eddie suggested that he and Gerry keep an eye out for the boy. He was also keen to tell Jan about his plan for an impromptu Edge Farm Christmas party at his house. Although Jan was grateful to him for the idea, she found she couldn't work up much enthusiasm for it.

'What's the matter, Jan? Things aren't that bad, are they?'

'They aren't that good either.'

'Haven't you heard anything from Carey yet?'

'No.' Jan was deliberately non-committal.

Eddie didn't press her.

'OK, so you don't feel like holding a Christmas party yourself; then I'll have one anyway and invite everyone who's got anything to do with the yard.'

'What? All the owners? Even Bernie?'

'Even Bernie and his sniffing Dobermann, if he likes.'

'What about Cyril Goldstone?'

Eddie raised a quizzical eyebrow. 'Cyril? Does he have a horse in this yard now?'

'No, but I hear you're pretty chummy with his family.'

A smile spread slowly across Eddie's face. 'Jan, are you a bit jealous, or what?'

'No, of course I'm not; but I wouldn't mind being told about things.'

'If we sat down and I told you about all the women who come chasing after me, you'd soon get very bored.'

Jan couldn't help laughing. 'You arrogant bastard! You've got such a big head! I heard she'd made most of the running, mind,' she conceded.

'Sharon Goldstone may look like a slightly fleshed-out version of Barbie, but she also wears pink fluffy slippers, leopard-skin leggings and drives a Japanese convertible; she and I are hardly likely to be soul-mates. Besides, she's only eighteen and frankly she doesn't know a lot.'

'But you might be charitable and teach her?'

'Look, the only reason I went out with Sharon was to keep her old man happy. If she'd gone running back to him saying I'd stood her up or turned her down or whatever, he might have got nasty.'

'So what? Why should you care if some horrible old bookmaker doesn't like you?'

'Jan,' Eddie said with a rare display of honest self-analysis, 'I should have thought you knew me well enough by now to know that I don't like being disliked by anyone. Some may consider this a weakness; I consider it a strategy for life.'

'In other words, you can't say "no" to anyone.'

'That's about it,' Eddie laughed.

'Well, I have to say I think that's pretty pathetic.'

'And as I want you to go on liking me too, I won't say what I think of what you're thinking.' He gave her a big, bland smile. 'Anyway, I'd rather you didn't mention Sharon to Annabel.'

'Why on earth not? Annabel's not interested in you.'

'Maybe not, but I still crave her approval.'

'I *will* enjoy this party,' Jan said, 'seeing which of the women you end up with in a dark corner.'

'Dark corner? The whole of my house is dark. I've only got lamps and candles to light the place, remember.'

Jan relaxed. 'I'm sorry, Eddie; I was just teasing. Thanks for suggesting the party. I'll tell everyone, if that's what you want. What day?'

'Friday, the twenty-first. I expect a lot of people will already be doing something, but that's too bad. By the way, where's Annabel?'

'She went to London for a few days.'

'What for?'

'I don't know.' Jan shrugged. 'She said she needed to go and I wasn't going to stop her.'

'Oh.' Eddie looked surprised. 'When's she due back?'

'Tonight.'

'I'll give her a ring later, then.'

That evening, Jan thought that if Eddie had tried to ring her, he was out of luck because Annabel had driven straight to Edge Farm on her way back from London and stayed to have supper in the caravan.

Jan had seen that she was feeling very sorry for herself as soon as she'd walked through the door.

'Let's have a bottle of wine,' she suggested and Annabel, not normally a drinker, nodded keenly.

When they each had a glass in their hand, and the place was lit only by a small lamp and the glow of the wood-burner, Jan asked her what had happened.

'I'm afraid this is going to sound pretty pathetic from a girl of twenty-three, but the fact is for some time I've been pretty sure I'll never be able to have children.'

Jan closed her eyes, suddenly understanding, knowing that this answered a lot of questions about Annabel and her behaviour.

'Oh, Bel,' she said and reached out to take the girl's slender hand in hers. 'It's not a bit pathetic to feel bad about it at your age. For God's sake, in the old days you'd already be well into child-bearing and all that. And I know bloody well how I'd feel if I hadn't or couldn't have any. But what did the hospital actually say?'

'They said my tubes and my uterus malfunction so badly that I'll never ovulate properly or be able to retain a foetus.'

'So even *in vitro* wouldn't work?'

Annabel shook her head. Her pale chestnut hair shimmered in the lamplight and for the first time since she'd known her, Jan saw she was crying. Jan leaned over and put an arm around her shoulders.

'Believe me, Bel, I *do* understand. I see now why you gave that beautiful doll's house to Meg and why you seem so distant with men you like. It explains why you love the horses so much and are so good with them.'

'That's not the only reason why I'm wary of men. The fact is the two relationships I've had so far both went wrong pretty quickly, and my father's always treated me and Charley like a couple of junior squaddies. Charley's gone, and I've made up my mind I'm not going to take any more stick from Dad, even though Mum didn't want me to leave. I've known for ages I had problems, but to be told point-blank that I'll always be infertile was devastating.'

'Oh God,' Jan groaned, her own eyes damp with sympathy, 'why is life so bloody unfair?'

Annabel was in a completely different mood when she arrived at Jan's caravan an hour before they'd planned to set off for Eddie's party.

During the week since Annabel had been back from London, Jan had tried to help her come to terms with the devastating diagnosis. 'There are other ways of having a family,' she'd told her, 'and being able to have babies isn't the only thing men are looking for in a woman. You've got masses to offer and you should make the most of it if you want to meet the kind of man who'll appreciate you for your intelligence and kindness, as well as for being a stunning woman.'

'Being stunning, as you call it, isn't much of an advantage really,' Annabel answered morosely. 'So many men are just interested in you for sex, it takes a lot of wading through the dross to identify the ones who see you as a person.'

'Hm,' Jan grunted. 'I don't know too many women who'd complain.'

On the evening of the party Annabel arrived early, keen to help Jan with her hair and make-up.

'I'm a bit scared about this,' Jan admitted. 'John and I were never asked to parties, if they even had them in mid-Wales.' It must be at least eight or nine years since she'd been in a room full of young stags, all drinking and dancing in an atmosphere charged with testosterone. 'I don't think I'm ready for it yet,' she said. 'I really don't want to go.'

'Look, I don't want to go much, either,' Annabel said, 'but you never know, there might be a few interesting people and Eddie must have gone to an awful lot of trouble.'

'No, he hasn't. Believe it or not, he's had his mum down helping him.'

'Gosh, I can hardly imagine Eddie's mother,' Annabel said. 'I've never met her, but she's probably rather sweet. And she must have a bit of character to have married someone like Ron Sullivan in the first place.'

'Eddie told me the break-up was fairly amicable. He thinks she'd just gone off the physical side of their relationship, and of course men can't seem to understand that it's not particularly unusual for some women to lose their sex drive once they've had a few babies.'

'Oh,' Annabel asked with a grin, 'have you?'

'That's unfair. I suppose it depends who's offering but, frankly, I haven't felt like being close to anyone since John died.'

'There are plenty of men interested in you, though.'

'It's just as well I'm not interested in them; I simply haven't got the time for a relationship while I'm trying to build up this yard.'

'Even so, tonight I'm going to make you look absolutely fabulous.'

'You'll be lucky!' Jan laughed. 'Still, Eddie did once say I was the best-looking trainer in Gloucestershire.'

'Compared to who – Virginia Gilbert?' Annabel said, screwing up her face.

'That's what I said. Not saying much for me, was it? Mind you, Eddie *was* pretty drunk at the time!'

They stopped off to drop Jan's children at their grandparents in Riscombe and Mary asked them in for a cup of tea. She wasn't sure how to handle Annabel – a friend of their landlord's son, but also their daughter's employee. But Annabel made it easy for her, and agreed that Jan was looking 'like a little angel'. They left Riscombe late deliberately, so they would arrive an hour after the party had started. When they were nearly there, Jan was more grateful than she would admit that Annabel was with her.

It was all very well for Eddie, she thought, and, for that matter, Roz and Emma, who were off at parties or discos every weekend. For a thirty-one-year-old widowed mother of two, it was bound to be a different experience.

There were cars parked up the banks and all over the verges for twenty or thirty yards on either side of the gates to Old Ford Mill.

'Gosh,' Annabel said. 'Eddie seems to have invited the whole of Gloucestershire.'

'Billy Hanks said he was coming with a lot of his racing friends.'

'And he's sure to have asked the Gilberts,' Annabel said, 'and a few from the other big houses round here.'

It was a clear, starry night, and Annabel parked her Golf down the lane, out of harm's way. As they walked towards the house, she and Jan heard music and laughter drifting through the crisp, still air and the drone of a petrol generator Eddie had hired to power the disco. Jan struggled to control another dose of panic as they walked between the high stone gateposts and across the cobbles towards the open front door. Once inside the hall, though, they were met with welcoming smiles by a group of friendly faces and she felt herself relax a little.

'Let's find Eddie first and tell him we're here,' she said.

Annabel nodded. They made their way to the kitchen and walked into a freshly painted room, lit entirely with candles and oil lamps. To give him his due, Jan thought, Eddie had made the large room very inviting. Clusters of holly, ivy and mistletoe and a few traditional decorations made it look as it might have done at Christmas a hundred years before. There were a couple of dozen people in the room, picking at canapés, but there was no sign of Eddie. On the pine table in the middle stood a capacious terracotta bowl full of spicy wine cup, being ladled out by a tall, handsome woman, aged about sixty.

Jan guessed at once from her firm features, wavy dark hair and chocolate brown eyes that this must be Eddie's mother.

As she took a glass, she asked, 'Are you Mrs Sullivan?'

The woman nodded with a smile. 'I'm afraid so. Eddie needed someone to come and clear up after this is over.'

'I'm Jan Hardy. I . . .'

'I know exactly who you are,' Mrs Sullivan said. 'Edward's told me all about you.'

Annabel leaned over Jan's shoulder. 'Would you like me to take over, serving that drink?' she asked Mrs Sullivan. 'You might like a chat with Jan.'

'I'm sure I would. Thank you, dear.'

Jan followed Eddie's mother, squeezing through the crowd back into the hall. Mrs Sullivan looked over her shoulder and almost had to shout over the sound system, 'There's a quiet place – a sort of study at the back of the house.'

Last time Jan had seen the small room it had been full of packing cases and dust. Now there was a big kilim rug on the polished floorboards and fat candles burned in wall sconces, flickering off the oak linen-fold panelling. Two small sofas had been placed on either side of a big log fire. Otherwise, the room was empty.

'This is a big improvement since I last saw it,' Jan said.

'I sent him up a bit of furniture. What he had in the cottage only filled a couple of rooms here. Of course, the whole place has got to be practically rebuilt before he can decorate or furnish it properly.'

Jan detected Mrs Sullivan's London background in her voice, but it was much less obvious than Ron's. And from her manner and her clothes it was clear that she'd put her origins behind her long ago.

'I told him I thought he was mad to take this place on,' Jan said, as they sat down opposite each other in front of the fire, 'but he just laughed. He's been really good about getting materials for the house I'm building, though. I'm sure he'll make something of this place and at least he's not paying any rent.'

'Poor Edward. He's not used to poverty. He's never known it, not like me and his father.'

'Don't worry, Mrs Sullivan, he's tougher than you might think.'

'Do call me Sue, please. But you're right, he is quite tough. He was a big support to me when his father and I split up and he comes to see me whenever he's in London. But I've never felt he was achieving much. He's just been playing with this gallery. In a way, what's happened to Ron could be the making of Edward. His father spoiled him really, at least financially. Edward told me he had to sell the horse he was keeping with you. I think he was quite upset about it, but he says he's still going to ride it.'

'I hope so.' Jan assumed that Eddie hadn't told his mother about his ridiculous bet with Cyril Goldstone. 'His riding's improved a lot and I think he's really determined to win because of what's happened recently.'

Eddie's mother looked at her. Jan took in her strong features and gentle, intelligent eyes.

'But I'm still worried about him,' Mrs Sullivan said. 'He's quite capable of going off and doing something stupid if he thinks it will get him out of trouble in a hurry.'

Jan nodded. 'I know what you mean,' she said, truthfully, 'but he talks to me quite a bit, so I usually know what's going on.'

'He thinks a lot of you.' Mrs Sullivan looked at Jan thoughtfully. 'And he listens to what you say, which is more than he does with most people, including me.'

'I haven't got much advice to give him about anything, except racehorses, but at least he's really committed to getting a result with Eagle – we both are. I just hope he gets the chance.'

'You realize, I suppose, that he was quite involved with Annabel Halstead a few years ago, when she was still very young.'

'I thought she was seventeen then,' Jan said.

'That's young enough, especially coming from the kind of rigid discipline her father seems to dish out.'

'Poor Bel. She's over it now and she's getting on fine.'

'What about Edward, though?'

'You mean his love life?'

'Yes.'

Jan shrugged her shoulders. 'I don't know. He never says.'

'Well, whatever you do with him, keep him focused.' Mrs Sullivan gave Jan a warning look. 'He's always had a tendency to lose interest quite quickly once he's achieved anything,' Mrs Sullivan said. 'His father's just the same, that's why he's ended up bankrupt.'

Jan wondered if the fact that Sue Sullivan's home was still partly owned by Ron was causing her any nightmares, or if she even knew about the existence of the Italian bank Ron owed money to. She didn't think she could ask, so she changed the subject back to Eddie.

'If he loses interest in his riding, that's his problem, not mine. But I hope he doesn't; at least it gives him some kind of discipline.'

Susan leaned forward confidentially, although there was still no one else in the room. 'You will keep an eye on him for me, won't you? I can see you've got your feet firmly on the ground. If I give you my number in London, you could always phone me if you felt like it.' She fished a card from her small handbag and handed it to Jan.

'Thank you,' Jan said. 'I think he'll be fine, but if he seems to need a mother's guiding hand, I'll give you a ring.'

Susan stood up. 'Now, you ought to go and mix with the young things. I've monopolized you long enough.'

Eddie was holding court in the hall at the bottom of the stairs and greeted Jan with a lot of fuss and a kiss on the cheek.

'If you want a laugh, have a look in there.' He nodded towards the music. 'Bernie's dancing with Sandy, but I'm not sure he's too happy.'

Before Jan had a chance to go and watch, the drama spilled out into the hall when Sandy walked out with her peach-coloured hair flying round her head like stuffing from a burst cushion. She was followed by Bernie, dressed in an absurdly baggy Armani suit.

'You nasty little bastard!' she was shouting in her sharp Birmingham voice. 'Spying on me like some dirty old pervert!'

'And finding you with your knickers round your ankles and

your skirt over your head being shagged by some penniless little jockey,' Bernie shouted back at her as she stormed towards the front door.

Billy Hanks emerged from the dance room behind Bernie with a look of sheepish triumph on his face.

Sandy, who was taller than Bernie, spun round and glared at him. 'He may be penniless, but he's a bloody sight better at it than you, so you can stuff all your money up your arse!' She flounced out of the front door with her turquoise and gold chiffon skirt swirling round the top of her long brown legs.

After a moment's hesitation, Billy went too, with Bernie's eyes blazing after him.

'Oh dear,' Jan murmured to Eddie. 'Do you think that's the end of Bernie's horse-owning career as well?'

To Jan's surprise, Annabel wanted to leave first.

'There's nobody left who's sober enough to talk to,' she said.

'There's more to life than conversation,' Jan said with a grin.

'Don't start that; you know I'm not a party girl. Though I have enjoyed seeing some of these people, and watching Jimmy Hely dance with Virginia Gilbert was a real laugh.'

'She's not very sexy, is she.'

'It's hard to say if you're not a man, but I doubt it.'

'Did you talk to Eddie's mother at all?' Jan asked as they crunched along the icy lane to the car.

'A little. I though she was very charismatic. Extraordinary to think that her parents were first-generation Italian immigrants selling ice cream around London before the war. She said she loved it when she and Ron first moved out here with Eddie – the pure Englishness of the houses and the landscape. I think she misses it, poor thing, but when she and Ron divorced she decided to throw herself into two big charities in London. Now she's such a successful fund-raiser everyone wants her on their committees. It's strange because I'm sure she didn't deliberately turn her back on her family, but somehow she's turned into a real English lady.'

Jan nodded. 'I was always a bit puzzled how someone like Ron had produced Eddie, but meeting Sue explains it. Anyway, he's lucky to have a mother who'll come and help out at a do like this.'

'It was a good party, you must admit,' Annabel said.

'And nearly everyone who has anything to do with Edge Farm was there, weren't they, except for Allan Preece and old Gwillam Evans.'

'And Mr Carey,' Annabel added.

'Well, I didn't expect him to come. It's two weeks since I saw him about putting up the guarantee for my licence. He said he'd think about it, but he still hasn't let me know and he must realize I'm waiting every day to hear. My whole career's at stake.'

'I'm sure he's not doing it on purpose, he's very shy.'

'I know he's interested in my getting a licence and at least he's agreed to pledge a horse, but I don't think he understands what it's like to be a mother on your own, trying to make a living with two small children.'

'Well, I'm sure he'll be up before Christmas to see his horse; ask him again then.'

Victor Carey did come up – the next morning. Jan was tacking up Eagle, Dingle Bay and Colonel Gilbert's horse, Sorcerer's Boy, when he arrived.

He walked across the yard to look into the paddock, where most of the horses had been turned out in their New Zealand rugs for a few hours of freedom. Having inspected them, he came over to the box where Jan was putting a saddle on Eagle. 'My mare's looking well. How's she working?'

Jan looked up from the girth she was buckling. 'Fine. She gave me a good feel this morning when we did a bit of fast work up at Colonel Gilbert's.'

'How often do you use his gallops?'

'Once or twice a week, to give the horses a change and so our own gallop can have a rest.'

'Will the Jockey Club be happy with that arrangement when you apply for your licence?'

'I think so. Colonel Gilbert said they would be.'

Mr Carey nodded. 'He ought to know.'

Jan closed her eyes, and prayed for him to get on with it, to put her out of her misery.

'I've been thinking about that guarantee you asked me to put up.'

Jan nodded, but didn't trust herself to say anything.

'I'll do it—', he paused, 'when I've seen how you get on this season. It seems to me that if you're asking me to take this risk, I should have a good idea of how well, or not, you are likely to do.'

Jan quivered at the prospect of another delay. 'But Mr Carey,' she said, trying not to sound wheedling, 'I *do* have a track record. I was champion point-to-point trainer in my region last year.'

'But this is a new area and a different yard. It simply may not work as well for you.'

Jan took a deep breath. 'So when do you think you might be in a position to make a definite decision?' she asked.

'Oh, I should think towards the end of February. You will have had a fair few runners by then, weather permitting.'

'OK, fine. Thank you,' Jan said, casting around in her mind for other options, although she realized that there was some justification for Mr Carey's attitude. And he probably had no idea how much it mattered to her. She let herself out of the stable and walked back to his car with him, making polite conversation as best she could, whilst trying to hide her bitter disappointment.

As Mr Carey drove out, Eddie's old Land Rover turned into the drive and the two vehicles crossed. Eddie parked and jumped out, wearing jeans and jodhpur boots. He was carrying a pair of suede chaps. Billy Hanks emerged from the passenger door.

'Morning, boys,' Jan called. 'I've tacked up the horses, though I didn't really think you'd make it after last night.'

'I wasn't up too late,' Billy said.

'No? I bet that Sandy kept you awake, though.'

'No she didn't.' Billy laughed. 'She realized she couldn't get back to Brum without Bernie, so she went back to the party and made him drive her home.'

'And my mother woke me up with a cup of tea this morning,' Eddie groaned. 'Thank God I was on my own.'

'Hmm,' Jan grunted. 'I don't think she has any illusions about your activities.'

'I'm glad you've met her,' Eddie said, 'as you're my sort of surrogate mother up here.'

'Shut up, you cheeky brat,' Jan said, 'and go and get your horse out of his stable. We're late enough as it is.'

Eddie was on Russian Eagle, Billy on Dingle Bay, and Jan rode Sorcerer's Boy. The colonel's horse was a big rangy twelve-year-old bay and a very experienced chaser; Dingle Bay at nine had a couple of point-to-point seasons behind him and two years' hurdling in Ireland. Jan wanted Eagle and Eddie to get used to jumping in company and planned to school them all together after they'd ridden to the top field and had a good half-speed gallop up to the ridge.

On the way out, in bright winter sunshine, they talked about the party, the incidents, the accidents and the damage, emotional and physical.

'Fortunately,' Eddie said, 'there's very little to break in the house and as far as I can see, apart from a bit of wax on the carpets, according to Mother no real harm's been done, though I don't suppose she knows about Sandy, Bernie and matey, here.'

'It seemed like a really good party,' Jan said. 'I didn't think I was going to enjoy it at all, but I had a good laugh with a lot of people.'

'They all liked meeting you, too,' Eddie nodded. 'Especially the ones who hadn't seen you since you first rode pointers round here ten years ago. You might find you've got yourself a few more owners.'

'I could only take horses that were almost fit, though,' Jan said, 'or we'd have no chance of getting them ready in time to do much this season.'

'I tell you one person who wasn't pleased to see you,' Billy laughed, 'Virginia Gilbert.'

Jan shook her head. 'I don't know what her problem is. You'd have thought she'd be quite happy getting Rear Gunner, who was my best horse last year. Never mind her, though. Let's give these horses a bit of a blow.'

She rousted Sorcerer's Boy into a canter until they reached the broad strip of well-seasoned turf that swept up to the top of the field for just under four hundred yards. She squeezed hard with her legs and gave him more rein until he was really stretching his neck. To her great satisfaction, Dingle Bay soon cruised past her, and Russian Eagle kept right up on her horse's tail.

At the top, she called over to Billy. 'How did he feel?'

'Bloody great! He's got plenty more in the tank.'

'How did Eagle feel?'

'In my very amateur experience, absolutely brilliant,' Eddie called back, 'and I still had a good hold of him.'

'We'll work him with Gale Bird at Colonel Gilbert's after the New Year and that'll give us a better idea of his pace. Now let's get back to the schooling fences and see how your jumping is coming on.'

Later, when they were hacking back to the yard, Billy turned to Jan. 'D'you know, if you'd bet me last spring that you were going to get young lover boy here to jump horses like that over fences, I'd have taken as much dosh as you wanted; but now he's doing a great job – as good as anyone riding pointers and better than most.' He turned to grin his approval at Eddie, too.

'You'd better watch out then, Billy,' Eddie said. 'I might nick the championship off you this season.'

'There's more to it than schooling at home,' Billy laughed, 'and I ain't going to tell you what that is.'

16

Christmas Day started like any other for Jan, mucking out and feeding, but only two horses were going to be exercised that day.

Roz and Emma had volunteered to come up and help. The three women got through the jobs in a cheerful mood despite a heavy grey sky hanging over the top of the ridge.

After she'd given the children their breakfast, she put on their warmest coats and piled them into the Land Rover with a collection of hastily wrapped presents. First, she drove down to the village, where she joined the congregation in the big, fifteenth-century church of honeyed stone. Within its quiet, reassuring walls, she tried to pray. Although she was uncertain about the value of prayer, deep down she sometimes felt a need to communicate with a supreme being whom she understood to be God. She was also glad to be there to show her children that there was a side to Christmas which did not involve presents and material things.

Seeing Mr Carey sitting in the front pew like an old-time squire, she tried to quell her bitter disappointment at his procrastination over her guarantee, and prayed that it would be all right in the end. After the service, touched by the friendship shown to her and the children by other churchgoers, she drove on to her parents' house in Riscombe.

This would be the first Christmas for years that Jan had not spent with John and Mary had wanted to make it as special as she possibly could. The house was a riot of bright tinsel, with a massive Christmas tree and piles of beautifully beribboned gifts for Jan and the children.

Mary was a good, simple cook and she had made a great effort to create a traditional Christmas Day for them all. The sense of celebration was enhanced by a card which had arrived from Jan's brother on Christmas Eve.

Without actually saying so, Ben hinted that he might be returning to England during the coming year; he really was getting somewhere in the music business at last. He didn't say exactly what he was doing, or why he would be coming back, but the thought of seeing him again three years after he'd left had made Mary look ten years younger and, as Megan observed bluntly, she didn't seem to hobble as much as she had.

Inevitably, most of the conversation at lunch was taken up with Jan's progress at Edge Farm and her frustration at trying to put together everything she needed for a successful licence application. Mary admitted that she didn't really see why it was so important. Reg understood, though, but he repeated his advice that Jan should be patient, that if she was as good at the job as he knew she was, it would only be a matter of time.

After lunch they played games with the children, and Reg volunteered to act the horse for little Matthew. 'By God,' he exclaimed to Jan as Matthew urged him on, 'I can tell you've already taught the little fella to use his legs and heels.'

And it was true that, where Megan had always been rather uninterested in the idea of sitting on a horse, tiny Matthew had already demonstrated a healthy fascination with them.

'You'll have to get him a little pony, like we got you,' Mary said. 'You can see now he's going to be keen.'

'He's going to have to be bloody keen before I start filling up my yard with ponies, I can tell you.' Jan laughed, disguising her fervent hope that at least one of her two children had inherited her enthusiasm.

Back in the caravan that night, tucked up under her duvet with the stove still glowing, and content to be on her own, Jan thought about the year that had just passed. Despite the obstacles in her way, her disastrous mishandling of the sale of Stonewall and the subsequent deadlock with Harold, she felt that she had made some good decisions and had achieved a little measurable success. She had established a presence in her new yard, albeit unproven, as Mr Carey had so bluntly pointed out. But whether her horses were good enough to win, when push came to shove, she would only know once they'd raced the opposition.

Most of her owners were new and had lodged their horses with her entirely on trust. She still found it amazing that they had shown such loyalty before the season had even started. They had, as Eddie had hinted, clubbed together to buy her a new set of exercise tack and sheets to add to the half-dozen Reg had given her for her birthday.

But after six months of running a point-to-point yard, she was certain that if she was ever going to make any kind of living, and a life for her children, she had to get a professional licence and get it pretty damn soon.

Before she slept, her mind drifted from happy anticipation at maybe seeing her brother again to less comfortable thoughts about the trip she and the children would be making to Olwen Hardy at Stonewall in two days' time, which led on inevitably to Harold Powell and his excessive greed. Despite Gerry's vigilance, with some help from Eddie, no one had seen Amos Smith, so there'd still been no chance of hearing his version of the conversation with Harold. His cousin claimed that Amos hadn't been seen since Gerry had first spoken to him. Jan knew the loose ends of the incident were a potential time bomb unless they could be tied up, especially before her next licence application came up for review should Victor agree to back her. The thought that, in the meantime, Harold had deliberately sent Rear Gunner to Virginia Gilbert to compete against her, made her blood boil.

Thinking of Virginia, James McNeill and Harold, she found it extraordinary how easy it was to make enemies she felt she'd done nothing to deserve, and before a single runner had been sent out from her new yard.

On a brighter Boxing Day morning four horses from Edge Farm were going to the meet of the Evesham Vale Hunt on the wide, grassy margins of Broadway's main street in front of the Amberley Arms.

Jan had fond memories of the event from the years before she'd gone to live in Wales; she'd always enjoyed being part of a profoundly English tradition in such a pretty setting, and she was really looking forward to putting in an appearance again.

Edge Farm had been sending out horses to hunt regularly since the start of the season because each horse had to have a card signed by the Master of the Hunt to confirm that it had been out with them at least seven times before it was allowed to run in point-to-point races the following season. And Jan had always felt that hunting provided horses with such a natural environment in which to jump, plus all the excitement of being with others, that it went a long way to preparing them for the more artificial circumstances of the steeplechase course.

She was up at seven to give the horses a small feed before plaiting their manes and tails. Edward, Annabel and Roz came in soon after nine to tack the horses and get them loaded onto the lorry. They were all looking forward to the day's hunting and bantered competitively about who was going to do what if the hunt really took off. Jan felt a surge of pride, seeing fit and obviously well-kept animals being so beautifully turned out from her yard.

Reg and Mary arrived in their Land Rover to take the children to the meet. Afterwards they were going to follow the progress of the hounds as best they could from the road. Reg had always enjoyed doing this; although he'd never followed a hunt on horseback, he had been following 'on foot' nearly all his life. Now, in retirement, it provided most of his social life for the winter months.

Since Jan had come back to Gloucestershire, it hadn't taken her long to become a recognized member of the hunt. There were still a number of followers who'd been hunting ten years before, whom she'd known since she'd last been a regular. There was also a big contingent of newcomers, mostly from London, who believed the best way to integrate with their new rural environment was to hunt across it.

A lot of the locals suffered from a knee-jerk prejudice against these rich townies who could afford all the best horses, but Jan took them as they came. She had soon concluded that, if they were genuine with her, she was ready to reciprocate. As a result, she'd already had some enquiries about training their pointers the following season. When she told them she was hoping to train National Hunt horses, most people had still been interested, mainly because her horses always stood out anywhere as the fittest and the best turned out.

Virginia Gilbert didn't hunt often; she didn't have to qualify her horses and she was nearly always racing on a Saturday. But on Boxing Day she was there with an entourage of friends and hangers on, and making it very clear that, in the pecking order of racing people out with the hunt that day, she ruled the roost.

Jan refused to be intimidated and smiled at her as she rode past from the lorry to the meet.

Scattered among the large crowd of people on foot who had come to enjoy the traditional spectacle, hotel staff were handing round glasses of mulled wine, ginger cup and port, with trays of small sausage rolls that flaked all over the horses' plaits and the riders' coats as they ate them.

Jan looked at Eddie and smiled at the splendid picture he made in a gleaming top hat he was wearing specially for the occasion. He was obviously planning to make the most of the day and walked Russian Eagle around the gathering. A lot of people there seemed pleased to see him, although, Jan was amused to see, some kept their distance, presumably not willing to be tarred by association with the recent demise of the Sullivans. Jan was well aware that there would always be a few old-fashioned snobs who resented a man with Ron Sullivan's working-class origins buying a house like Windrush Grange, and living there for twenty years without making any effort to blend with his neighbours. As far as they were concerned, Ron's son was no better, however popular he might be with the girls in the area.

Reg walked Megan among the horses to where Jan and Annabel stood side by side, as quietly as they could on horses who were now stamping their feet and rattling the bits in their mouths, impatient to move off. He lifted the little girl up to Jan, who straddled her across the front of her saddle for a few moments. But Megan didn't enjoy it, and wriggled vigorously until Jan handed her back down.

'I'm afraid she's not going to take to it, Dad,' Jan laughed.

'Don't you believe it. We'll get her hunting soon as she's big enough – so long as they don't ban it,' he added with a disparaging cough.

At that moment the huntsman tootled his horn at the hounds, who gathered around him as he moved off up the main street among a sea of waving tails. When the master followed, Jan and her party tucked in close behind. If hounds started to hunt early on, they had no intention of getting caught behind a field of people whose horses wouldn't jump. Unlike a lot of other point-to-point trainers, Jan truly believed in hunting her horses properly, not just putting in an appearance at the meet then lurking out of harm's way until one o'clock when the master would sign their cards. She also believed that a horse who was nervous in company or who had gone a little stale could be very effectively cured with a season's hunting.

It was only as they were moving away that Jan first noticed Bernie Sutcliffe among the onlookers. She heard him shout across the road to Eddie. 'You look after my horse, mind.'

Jan wondered how Eddie would take it, or how many people knew he'd had to sell the horse, but, to his credit, she thought, he shouted back cheerfully. 'I'll make sure he has a great day. I'll bring him back safe and sound, don't you worry.'

A moment later, both she and Eddie spotted a young blonde

girl standing just behind Bernie, who turned to her and pointed at Russian Eagle as they rode past.

'I see Bernie's got himself a replacement for Sandy. That's lucky.'

'I'm not sure it is, as a matter of fact,' Eddie said, more quietly. 'That's Sharon Goldstone and I really don't think she can see much in Bernie to attract her. After all, she's got lots of money of her own.'

'And she's already sampled the charms of Eddie Sullivan,' Jan added with a grin.

Eddie was about to answer when a terrier on a long lead shot out and snapped ferociously at Russian Eagle's legs. The big horse, normally reluctant to make a fuss, half reared and covered the next fifty yards in a high-stepping, fretful canter with Eddie trying to sit still and keep his dignity.

Jan laughed. 'If you fall off, that topper won't be much help to you.'

'Of course I'm not going to fall off,' he hissed back in embarrassment.

Russian Eagle behaved beautifully for the rest of the morning. Eddie kept him near the front with Roz and Annabel, and Jan was delighted to see that the horse didn't look twice at any of the hedges or post and rail fences they came across over the next few hours.

At a long break outside a dense covert, Jan and her team gathered to eat the sandwiches they had brought and chat about the morning's hunting. But the moment was spoiled for Jan, when Annabel suddenly exclaimed, 'Oh, God! Jan, you're not going to like this. Look!'

Annabel nodded towards the gate of the field the hunt was standing in. A group of three horses and riders had just trotted through, led by Virginia Gilbert.

Eddie didn't understand what the fuss was about. 'Virginia's been out all morning,' he said. 'She was at the meet. I've been chatting to her a bit, winding her up that I might move this chap to her yard.'

'She probably believed you,' Jan said. 'She's really rubbing my nose in it today. She's just gone and changed horses, though we haven't done nearly enough to justify it.'

'So?' Eddie said. 'Maybe she's qualified one and wants a bit of fun now.'

'I don't think so. The horse she's on now is Harold Powell's. That's Rear Gunner.'

The week between Christmas and New Year was a busy one at Edge Farm. Jan had a lot of work to do with horses who were getting close to full fitness. She was pleased to find that seeing Virginia out on Rear Gunner had simply sharpened her determination. Furthermore, Eddie had come back at the end of the day and announced that he had found himself next to Virginia late in the afternoon. He had asked her point-blank if she was planning to run the horse in the Foxhunters'; she had said she was.

That's it, Jan thought. *The gauntlet's been thrown down.*

After a couple of busy days, Jan managed to squeeze in a trip to Stonewall with the children to see Olwen.

Over a strained lunch, her mother-in-law questioned Jan sharply on what she was doing about Harold Powell. Jan didn't intend to tell her what she and Eddie suspected and the confrontation they'd had at Harold's house the last time she'd brought the children over. It took all her patience to explain that solicitors had been instructed and she didn't want to rush matters. She also kept off the subject of her licence application, knowing this would be treated with barbed scepticism.

However, she recognized that Olwen had made a great effort for the children and had bought them some beautiful presents. Jan tried to keep their normal antagonism to a minimum and, as they left, she promised they would come again soon.

Jan didn't see Bernie again until the end of the week, when she saw at once that Sharon Goldstone wasn't with him, nor was any other candidate to replace the flighty Sandy. Jan prayed that he wouldn't decide to home in on her.

Most of the people involved with Edge Farm had gone in a minibus to a New Year's Eve party at one of the clubs Eamon Fallon ran on the outskirts of Cheltenham. For the first time, Jan began to get an idea of Eamon's business. The club was more sophisticated than Jan had expected and it was clear that he was held in awe by some of the people who worked for him.

After they'd eaten dinner, which she found surprisingly good, Jan still didn't feel comfortable and was unable to relax. She wasn't enjoying herself much when Bernie Sutcliffe, who'd been hovering all evening, finally sat down in an empty chair beside her and draped his arm around her. 'It's time you and I got better acquainted,' he said.

Jan's heart sank.

'I feel I know you pretty well already, Bernie,' she said lightly. 'You come down to the yard often enough.'

Bernie stiffened. 'And why shouldn't I? I'm paying you to look after my two horses.'

'It's OK, Bernie, I wasn't complaining. Of course I like owners to take an interest in their horses and I know you'll have great fun with yours.'

'Do you think it's safe to let Eddie go hunting on Russian Eagle, though?'

'As safe as anyone else and the horse has to be hunted to qualify him to run. Anyway, Boxing Day was his last day, so from now on we'll be concentrating on serious work. He'll probably run for the first time on the nineteenth.'

'As soon as that? Will he be ready?'

'He's not far off being ready now.'

'And you're happy about Eddie riding him?'

Jan looked Bernie straight in the eyes. 'Completely. You ask Billy Hanks what he thinks of Eddie's riding.'

Bernie looked back. 'I will. I will.'

Jan felt a nervous twinge. She had promised Eddie he would keep the ride on Eagle, but in truth, if Bernie felt like it, he could have anyone on the horse and he had to be convinced that Eddie had a better chance than any other amateur jockey.

Bernie stood up abruptly. 'Right. It's time you and I had a dance,' he said with a leer that Jan couldn't believe he thought was attractive.

Trying not to show her reluctance, she got to her feet and tried to smile compliantly. At least the disco wasn't playing anything slow and smoochy.

Bernie's dancing looked very uncomfortable. He contorted himself into a series of bony, angular shapes, grimacing and clicking his fingers randomly and out of time with the music. Jan was fit and lithe from her regular riding and in good shape for dancing. When she'd danced with Eddie at his party she'd really enjoyed it. But tonight, with Bernie, she couldn't. She was almost certain that Bernie was going to make a move on her and she dreaded having to fend him off.

When the record came to an end, she flashed him a big smile. 'That was great! I'm just going to the loo. See you in a minute.' She walked off the dance floor and headed for the ladies' without looking back. When she emerged, she saw Eddie and some of the others sitting round their table. She caught a glimpse of Bernie's back at the bar so she went and sat down next to Eddie. 'Look, I don't want you to take this the wrong way, but would you mind dancing with me if Bernie looks like he's going to ask me again?'

'Sure,' Eddie grinned. 'It would be a pleasure, but you could try Billy, as well, otherwise Bernie might think I'm your favourite.'

From then on, each time Bernie came up Jan made sure she was dancing with either Billy or Eddie. In between, Bernie was drinking from two magnums of champagne he'd insisted on buying and sat hunched sulkily in his chair, staring at the dancers. It was after one o'clock, and his fifth failure to get Jan to dance, that he finally lost it.

He marched across the floor and pushed himself between Jan and Billy. 'You can't do this,' he shouted. 'You're taking the piss, aren't you? I can see you all laughing. How the hell would you pay the bloody bills on your place if I wasn't paying you all that money? I've had enough of you lot, all thinking you know so bloody much. Well, if you do, why haven't you got more money?' He was spitting as his voice rose and everyone had stopped dancing to watch the row unfold.

'Calm down, Bernie,' Jan said. 'I'm only having a dance.'

'Having a dance? With that randy young sod? He's not interested in dancing.'

'Well that's all he's getting. You're out of order, Bernie. This is meant to be a celebration. Nobody's laughing at you.'

'They won't now, not now I'm taking both my horses out of your yard.'

Eddie was standing behind Bernie. He'd been looking apprehensive, signalling to Jan to ease off. Now his face fell and he paled.

'Hang on, Bernie,' he said, coming round to face him. 'You'd be crazy to move them now, just before the season starts. I promise you, I wasn't laughing either.'

'You, you toffee-nosed, potless prat!' Bernie turned on him and snarled. 'Do you think I'm going to take any advice from you?' Shaking with rage and, it seemed, with fright at his own anger, he looked back at Jan. 'I'm telling you, them horses are going. You'll be hearing from me.'

He continued to glare at her for a few moments with his jaw quivering, before he turned abruptly and walked off the dance floor, to a ripple of applause from some of the drunken revellers.

Jan hardly slept. The party had broken up as soon as Bernie left and the journey back in the minibus had passed in almost total silence. When her alarm clock finally woke her at seven-thirty, she reckoned she'd been asleep for no more than twenty minutes.

Feeling sick and weak, she made herself a cup of tea before the children woke up and sat at her table in the caravan, looking out at a grey dawn trying to seep through the blanket of clouds draped over the Cotswolds' edge.

Somehow, she knew, she had mismanaged the whole affair yesterday. She was beginning to realize that if she had to rely entirely on the whims of people who sent their horses to her, she must learn to handle them with kid gloves.

It wasn't as if Bernie was one of those owners who was going to tell her what to do, or when she should or shouldn't run their horses. Up until now, he'd been prepared to let her guide him, accepting his own lack of knowledge. But because she hadn't given enough thought to the party at Eamon's club, which she hadn't even enjoyed, it looked as if she'd lost one owner and badly upset another. Eamon had looked extremely annoyed about the fracas, although no damage had been done. For the next two days, every time the telephone rang, Jan picked it up expecting Bernie to tell her that a lorry was on its way to collect his horses.

The call came eventually on 3 January.

'Hello, Jan? It's Bernie here.'

Jan held her breath for a moment. She could detect no aggression in the five words, only a hint of self-effacement.

'Hi, Bernie. Still got a headache?'

'Not now. But I did have. I don't usually drink a lot.'

Jan waited. She didn't trust herself to say the right thing next.

'Look,' Bernie went on. 'I made a bit of fool of myself, I realize that. And I know it would be daft to take the horses away before you've even had a chance to run them.'

Jan expelled a long breath. 'Well, it would really,' she tried to say calmly.

'So,' Bernie sighed. 'I'll leave them where they are. I'll be down some time to see them.'

'Whenever you like, Bernie,' Jan said. 'You're always welcome,' she added and, at that moment, she meant it.

For the next two weeks only a few mild frosts upset the rhythm of Jan's training regime. The horses were working so consistently that she found herself almost waiting for the next setback. In the meantime, she had qualified them all with the Evesham Vale and could concentrate on bringing each one to the boil, ready for their first race.

The earliest point-to-point Jan planned to go to was on 19 January, a Saturday meeting in Wiltshire where she'd entered four horses, including Russian Eagle in the men's Open race. When she rang Eddie at his shop to tell him he was overjoyed.

He came round that evening. 'Thank God, we're going to be under orders at last!'

Jan knew what his priorities were. 'How's your dad getting on with his cash-flow problems?'

'He's managed to keep the Italians at bay with a little bit of dough. He says he's convinced them that there's more to come. As long as they believe him, they won't go over the top and, thank God, they haven't sussed his connection with my mother's house.'

'Why don't the other banks he owed money to know about it?'

'There's no reason why they should. Even if they did, the proper banks couldn't do anything about it because she owns half the house and never gave her consent for it to be mortgaged.'

Jan knew that, for Eddie, Russian Eagle's race was the first step in his campaign to save his father from unscrupulous creditors. She also knew he was placing unjustifiable hope on winning the Foxhunters' at Liverpool, but she'd made up her mind that her best strategy, as a friend, was to support him. She couldn't see that any good would be done by constantly reminding him that it was, at best, a very long shot. After all, every once in a while, long shots did win, if not always for the right reasons.

17

The night before her first race of the season was one of Jan's worst since the weeks immediately after John's death. She was conscious that it was just over a year since then, and she had vivid memories of his last, horrendous weeks and of watching his coffin being lowered into the black peaty soil of St Barnabas's churchyard.

She was woken by her alarm after she'd barely slept and she felt horrible for the first half-hour of the morning. Somehow, though, as she always did and with the help of a few cups of strong tea, she managed to kick herself into action and every time her jitters returned she quashed them.

The anxiety of knowing that, if she was to get her licence, she had first to prove to Victor Carey she hadn't lost her touch as a trainer, combined with all the other trials she had endured over her first seven months at Edge Farm, had brought her close to paranoia, she thought. Showing not just Victor Carey but the world that Edge Farm Stables was a fully functioning racehorse training establishment had become almost an obsession, far more than it had ever been at Stonewall. Now so much seemed to hang on its success.

But she made sure she didn't let her fear show to Emma, Roz and Joe, who were coming with her to the races.

Having set off with an hour to spare, they arrived early and Jan drove her lorry into an empty field reserved for horseboxes beside the race course of ten fences. The track was laid out between flags below a crest of beech trees on a gentle, south-facing chalk down near Devizes.

She looked around at a scene that made her heart beat faster and felt at once the familiar pre-race tightening of the guts, that dread of the start mixed with a yearning for her horses to come home safely.

The cloud cover was high and only a mild wind stroked the top of the winter corn in the surrounding fields. There was already a large turnout of point-to-point fans, keen to see in the new season. An hour before the first race the car park was filling up with picnic parties equipped for all weather conditions and a crowd of people ebbed and flowed between the marquees and trade stands.

Stepping down from the cab, Jan breathed in the air, knowing that she truly was a part of this scene. Even when she moved on to the grown-up world of National Hunt racing, she knew she would never forget all she had learned and the joy she had known in the amateur game.

'Morning, guv'nor!' The deep, familiar voice floated among the cluster of lorries, and Jan turned to see Eddie and Billy walking towards her with broad smiles on their faces. Eddie was carrying a soft tan leather bag and Billy a black nylon Umbro, which, Jan thought, neatly summed up the differences between them.

'Morning, boys. I hope you've been behaving yourselves.'

'I can't speak for him,' Billy nodded at Eddie, 'but I was tucked up in bed well before ten last night, on my own with the *Racing Post*.'

'Give us a hand with the ramp, then,' Jan said, and shot down the long bolts that secured the tailgate to the back of the box. 'I had to put Eagle on last,' she said, 'so we'll get him off and let him have a stroll for twenty minutes while I get the others ready.'

They lowered the ramp. Jan jumped up and untied Eagle's rope. She led him down with his head held high, his nostrils flared as he lifted his knees in short, bouncy steps, looking around with quick, jerky movements. He knew something unusual was going to happen and that things were expected of him.

'Crikey!' Eddie said with a hint of uneasiness. 'He looks a bit full of himself.'

'You didn't want me to bring him half-asleep, did you?'

'But he looks like he's been on wacky baccy.'

Jan led the horse in a short circle behind the lorry. 'He's fine! What do you want in a race – a Morris Minor or a Ferrari?'

Eddie laughed nervously. 'All right, all right. It's just that I've never seen him like this; he's absolutely bursting.'

'He knows what he's here for. And I tell you what – I think he'll give you a bloody good run. What about you, though? You look a bit peaky.'

Eddie made a face. 'I didn't sleep a wink last night.'

'Oh Gawd!' Roz said with a loud groan. 'Who were you with?'

Eddie looked hurt. 'I was on my own,' he protested. 'I was staying with my mother in London and drove down this morning.'

'Were you really that nervous?' Jan asked more sympathetically. 'I didn't think anything ever worried you.'

'I'm all right now,' Eddie answered, 'but do you think I can do it?'

Billy laughed. 'You look like you're about to fill your nappy.'

'Shut up, Billy,' Jan said. 'I need to build his confidence and I won't have you destroying it. Eddie, I know you can do it.' She handed Eagle to Joe Paley, who walked away, talking to the big horse.

Billy was due to ride in the first race and headed for the jockeys' changing room while Jan and Roz led out the other two horses – Arrow Star and Supercrack, one of Frank Jellard's – who were running in different divisions of the maiden race.

While they were grooming, Penny Price arrived with her mother – a small, nervous woman, who hung back, evidently overawed by the idea of being involved with racehorses.

Penny flung her arms around her big gelding's neck. 'Hello, Arrow boy! How are you? Cor, you look well. Doesn't he look well, Jan?'

'He's been doing really nicely, as I told you, and his jumping's been brilliant. I know we thought he might need more time, but I'm not a bit worried about it now.'

'What does Billy think?' Penny asked anxiously.

'He's happy.'

Jan saw tears of excitement in Penny's eyes as she gazed at her pride and joy. 'Gosh,' she said. 'I can hardly believe that at last my baby's going racing and you've made him look so like a racehorse!'

'Thanks,' said Jan. 'I've done my best and it's what he's bred for.'

Penny looked at her watch. 'Oh, my God, there's a whole hour still to go. I don't know what I'm going to do with myself.'

'Come back to the car and have a cup of tea,' her mother suggested tentatively.

Penny nodded. 'OK, Mum.' She walked away with frequent glances back over her shoulder at her horse.

'She worships you. You'd better do bloody well,' Jan murmured into the horse's ear.

About an hour later Penny Price was hugging Arrow Star with tears running down her face as he stood in a makeshift winner's slot at the edge of the timber-railed paddock.

'I just can't believe it! I can't believe it.' She shook her head and sobbed, as her mother stood by, wondering what she should do. Penny turned to Jan with her face as white as a ghost, streaked with her tears and the horse's sweat. 'Thank you, Jan, so very, very much!'

'Just doing my job,' Jan said, more lightly than she felt, as she tried to keep her emotions under control. Of all the people who had entrusted horses to her care, she had most wanted to see Penny have a winner, and that it should be her first of the new season as well as the first she'd sent out from Edge Farm only increased her pleasure.

But the big buzz for Jan was that Arrow Star's win confirmed the state of all her other horses and her judgement as to which were ready to race.

Billy Hanks was also rather pleased with himself for getting off the mark on the first day as he bounced out of the changing room ten minutes later for his next ride on Frank Jellard's horse, Supercrack.

The brown gelding could only deliver a third in his division of the maiden, but Jan wasn't complaining. She knew he had room to improve. She and Roz led him back to the lorry and were just about to load him, when Bernie Sutcliffe strutted up.

Jan had been dreading meeting Bernie. Since his drunken threat on New Year's Eve to remove the horses and his subsequent climbdown, Bernie had been to the yard only once, a week before, to see his two horses. Then, despite his experience at Eamon's club, he had tried to persuade Jan to have dinner with him. Jan genuinely couldn't find a babysitter that evening; at least, she would have had to look further than she was prepared to for the sake of an evening with Bernie. He'd gone off with all the smouldering resentment of a thwarted teenager.

Of course Bernie had already heard about Jan's win in the second race, which he seemed to accept as normal, so he couldn't understand why she hadn't repeated the achievement in the third race.

'Bernie, there were fifteen horses in each division; one of ours beat fourteen of them, and the other beat twelve. I'm quite happy about that.'

'Well, what about this open race, then? Are we going to win that?'

'As I'm not a prophet and I don't have a crystal ball, I wouldn't like to say, but, as you can see the horse is fit and ready to run; he's schooled well at home; I've really got him lifting his feet over the tops of the fences because some of these are very solid.'

'What about him?' Bernie nodded towards Eddie, who had just walked into view.

'Eddie's well up to the job. And he's giving the horse plenty of help – they make a good combination.'

Bernie turned to Eddie, and shouted at him as he approached. ''Ere, you're not overweight, are you? We don't want him carting round a load of stuff he doesn't need to.'

'Don't you worry, Bernie,' Eddie said, trying a little too hard to sound confident, Jan thought. 'I'm right on the mark, so I won't be carrying any dead weight and I've got a decent-sized saddle.'

To see Eagle's race, Jan and her team wanted to watch from the bonnet of Eddie's Land Rover, which was parked well up the hill, giving them a view of the whole course. Bernie wanted them all to watch from his Jaguar, right on the rails by the finish, from where half the course was invisible. But, outvoted, he puffed up the hill with the others, where he perched on the bonnet of the Land Rover and grumbled about the disgusting state of the vehicle.

In the paddock before the race, Jan had taken Eddie's arm and given it a quick squeeze. 'Don't try to start winning until the second half of the final circuit,' she'd said. 'But don't lose touch with the others on the way round. Just jump him off quietly and let him keep his place, gaining a length or so each jump. Ease him back if you get too near the front. He won't need a lot of asking when you want to quicken; take a tighter grip and he'll fly. Just look at him now!'

Jan was right. Russian Eagle looked superb, striding round beside Roz as if the rest of the runners didn't exist. Bernie, unfamiliar with the scene, had wandered away across the ring to have a closer look at his horse.

'I just hope I don't let him down,' Eddie said quietly, so only Jan could hear.

She detected a faint tremor in his voice. She looked at him again and took in the pale greyness of his face. 'Don't worry! I've told you, I wouldn't let you go if I didn't think you could do a proper job. It's my reputation too, you know.'

He smiled weakly. 'You'd better be right for both our sakes, then.'

'Aren't I always?'

'Yes, Jan,' Eddie grinned. 'Without exception.'

Just then the 'Get mounted' signal was given. Roz turned the horse to face inwards and Jan legged her jockey into the saddle, squeezing his leg and giving him a last encouraging smile. 'Go for it, Eddie.'

Now, up on the bank watching Russian Eagle circle with the twelve other runners before the starter tried to get them into some sort of straight line, she could easily understand the tension Eddie must have been feeling. She gazed at the pair through her binoculars. Eagle still seemed to be on his toes, but at least compliant; he was going where Eddie was asking him to go and he wasn't throwing any silly tantrums at the short delay.

A moment later they were off.

Eddie quickly settled Eagle in tenth place as they came up to the first fence. He eased him back and gave himself time to place the horse right. He took off in a trajectory a foot higher than any of the horses beside him and flew past them in the air. It was as good a jump as any Jan had seen him do at home.

What really excited Jan, though, was that Eddie was managing to sit on the horse and stay in perfect harmony with him. He wasn't fussing him or pestering him, but keeping his hands steady, moving them forward only with the animal's neck each time he stretched for a jump. As the field passed the winning post for the first time with a circuit to race, Eddie was lying in the middle of the field. Behind him two of the runners, seemingly brought out too early in the season, were showing signs of tiredness. Pointlessly, their jockeys had already pulled their whips out.

On the bottom straight there was a row of three plain fences, handily spaced. The two leading horses took them well, a couple more fiddled and made mistakes at the first and hadn't recovered by the time they were turning the long, right-handed bend heading towards home. Eagle had taken the fences in his stride with easy grace, earning an admiring remark from the course commentator.

Jan, gazing transfixed through her glasses, waited for Eddie to pick up his horse and ask him for more.

But Eddie sat still, cruising past two more until he was lying third and just five lengths off the leaders.

'Come on, Eddie. For God's sake, pick him up!' she grunted through clenched teeth.

Bernie looked up at her sharply. 'What's wrong?'

'Nothing's wrong; it's just that he's leaving it a bit late.' But they all gasped together as Eagle stood right off the penultimate fence, flew it again with a spectacular leap into second place and started to close the gap on the leader.

Jan, Roz and Joe were all screaming their heads off; Jan felt as if her lungs would burst. She was sure the horse could hear her. Even Bernie allowed himself one discreet, plaintive, 'Come on, my son!'

Eagle reached the last fence a stride behind, made a length in the air and landed with his nose at the other's girth. The leader's jockey looked over his shoulder, lifted his stick for the first time and brought it down hard on his horse's rump. Eddie leaned forward, working his legs and starting to pump his fists over Eagle's withers. The big horse kept on, inching forward until his nose was at the other's shoulder. Two strides more and he reached his neck. And the finishing post.

Jan wanted to yell, *Eddie, you fucking idiot, why didn't you bloody well ask him when I told you to?* But she knew Bernie was beside her and she had no intention of blaming Eddie in front of him.

Jan watched for a few more seconds as Eddie tried to pull up Russian Eagle, to make sure the horse was still sound, but they galloped for another quarter of a mile before Eddie finally managed to stop him. When they had turned and were trotting back to the paddock, Jan lowered her glasses and looked at Bernie with a grin as big as she could muster.

'There you are! A brilliant race! Another hundred yards and he'd have made it!'

'But he didn't, did he.'

'For God's sake, Bernie! He ran a blinder. I'm sure he'll be winning next time out.'

'Maybe next time the jockey will know what to do.'

'Bernie, he rode him beautifully! Frankly, I'm amazed how well he did; he hardly moved on him.'

'Well, maybe he should have got his whip out like the other bloke, then he'd have got up there and won.'

'Not every horse responds to the whip, you know. It positively stops some of them. I certainly wouldn't have wanted the horse hit.'

Bernie looked at her. 'All right,' he said. 'At least we got placed, so it's not a complete donkey I've bought.'

'He certainly isn't,' Jan insisted. 'That was a very competitive race; several horses in it have won races. Did you look at the form?' She pulled out the printed yellow guide, which gave the ratings and past performances of each runner, and waved it under his nose.

''Course I did, but you always said this was a good horse. I paid six grand for it, remember.'

'At least you now know you've got good value for your money.'

'Not till he's won, I haven't,' Bernie snapped and set off down the hill towards the marquees.

Jan watched him go.

'What an ungrateful little shit!' Roz burst out indignantly, almost before he was out of earshot.

'Right, we've got to get down there,' Jan said. 'You run on, Roz – you're faster than me. Go and lead Eagle in. Do you know where to put him?'

'Next to where we put Arrow Star?'

'That's it,' Jan laughed, quite happy, despite the initial disappointment of Eagle's race, to have had a good win and a very strong second on her first day's pointing for over seven months.

On her way to the paddock, she bumped into Billy, who was carrying his saddle from the no-hoper he'd had to pull up.

'Eddie should have got up there,' he grunted.

'I know, Billy, I know, but if you'd ridden your first race as well as that, you'd be entitled to be proud of yourself.'

'That's not the point, though, is it? Like you always say, what you need is winners and lots of them.'

'Listen, I know what I need, and it's not advice from you right now,' Jan said sharply and carried on towards the paddock, where she could see Roz leading Russian Eagle into the second slot. As they reached it, Eddie jumped off with his legs buckling slightly. Jan regretted her sharpness with Billy almost at once, but she had to sustain her loyalty to Eddie. She told herself that he really had ridden a cracking race for his first time out, and she wanted nothing to detract from that for his sake. She also wanted nothing to diminish his chances of riding Russian Eagle when he finally ran in the Aintree Foxhunters'.

By the time Bernie had seen his horse clapped into the ring and half a dozen complete strangers had come up to tell him how well his horse had run, and how he was bound to win soon, he seemed mollified. 'When you've got back and put the horse to bed, I'll get you all a meal at that steakhouse by the motorway at Tewkesbury,' he offered, including everyone except Billy in the invitation. Jan guessed he still hadn't forgiven Billy for going off with Sandy. That, at least, would deter him from suggesting or, worse still, insisting that Billy should ride Eagle next time.

'Great!' Jan said, and turned to Eddie, who had just come back from the weighing room. 'Do you want to come and have a steak with all of us later? Bernie's treat.'

'Yes, please. I could do with a steak after that.'

'You could have had two steaks if you'd have won,' Bernie said.

'Next time, Bernie. Next time.'

They walked back to the lorry with Russian Eagle, patting him and telling him what a magnificent animal he was. Jan had to admit, she couldn't have asked more from him, under the circumstances.

'Well?' she asked Eddie. 'How does it feel?'

Eddie grinned. 'So bloody good – and that's just coming second! Winning must be better than sex.'

'Let's hope you get there next time, then,' Jan said with a laugh.

Once Eagle had been washed down and scraped dry, he had a

long drink and was allowed a few minutes' grazing before they loaded him with the others and heaved up the ramp of the lorry.

It was a two-hour haul home. Putting the horses away, getting themselves showered and changed took Jan and her team another hour, so it was nearly nine before they arrived at the steakhouse, where Bernie was waiting for them impatiently. They were all so tired that the dinner wasn't a great success.

Bernie sent back his steak twice, first because it was overdone and, again, when its replacement was underdone. Eddie seemed too exhausted to say much, and nobody really wanted to talk to Bernie.

Afterwards, when they'd said their thank yous and goodbyes to Bernie, Roz and Joe went off to the loos and Eddie walked back to the Land Rover with Jan, talking about the race. It was the first time they had been alone.

'Look, Eddie, you rode a great race and I don't want to take anything away from you because it was your first ride, but I really think you could have won if you'd pushed him along coming into the final bend, like I told you.'

'I know,' Eddie admitted. 'I suppose I thought that at the time. It was just that the horse was going so well, and I was so chuffed with the way he was jumping, I didn't want to do anything to upset his rhythm.'

'That's what I thought,' Jan said, 'but you did start to ride him out right at the end, didn't you, and it worked. Next time, start a lot earlier. And it wouldn't do any harm just to wave the whip, even if you don't want to use it. I did notice, too, that you looked fairly knackered when you came into the unsaddling enclosure.'

'Next time', Eddie said, 'I'll be fitter and we'll win.'

They had reached the Land Rover, which was in a dark corner of the car park. Eddie shrugged his shoulders. 'I'm sorry I let you down,' he said.

Without thinking, Jan reached up a hand and put it behind his neck. 'Don't be so stupid. You rode a great race and I'm proud of you. You've been a good pupil.'

'Thanks,' Eddie grinned. He wrapped his long arms around Jan and gave her a quick squeeze. 'And you've been a brilliant mistress.'

'What's that!?' Bernie Sutcliffe's voice cut through the air like a knife.

Jan almost jumped out of her skin. Eddie released her and spun round to see Bernie, dimly visible in the glow of a distant light, glaring at them.

'I don't believe it!' Bernie said. 'What's all that about a brilliant mistress? Are you two having some kind of relationship or what? I mean – what's going on?'

'Good God, Bernie! Don't come creeping up like that. Of course we're not having a scene. He said I was a good mistress in the sense of *teaching*, you know, as in race riding.'

'And having a good snog too, by the look of things,' Bernie snapped.

'Look,' Eddie said coldly, 'if Jan and I wanted a snog, as you put it, that would be our business and none of yours, but as it happens, we don't. I just gave Jan a thank-you hug for all she's done for me, OK? It's not such a difficult idea to grasp is it? Or do you only hug people when you're having sex with them?'

'You'd better watch it,' Bernie glared at him sharply. He turned back to Jan. 'I'll be in touch, all right?'

He spun round and walked quickly across the car park to his Jaguar.

Jan and Eddie didn't speak for a moment.

'What a horrible little toad,' Eddie said eventually. 'He deserves a good thumping.'

'Yes, Eddie, but I'm afraid he owns that bloody horse of yours, so whatever you do, don't do anything else to upset him. Right?'

'Jan! Jan! Come and look at Eagle!' Roz's voice wasn't normally short on volume, but in the tack room Jan could hardly hear it over the whine of the wind and the rattle of rain on the iron roof.

The morning after the glory of Arrow Star's win, and Russian Eagle's impressive second, life had returned rudely to the cold, wet and inglorious mood of an English winter. Jan had slept very little in her caravan the night before; even her wood-burner hadn't been enough to stop the cold wind forcing its way through cracks in the walls she hadn't known existed until then.

She was already thinking the worst as she pulled her waxed hat down over her head and wrapped John's old mac tightly around her to run across the open space to Eagle's box.

She shook most of the rain from her coat and let herself into the stable, where Roz was holding Eagle in a head-collar and rope.

'Look!' Roz groaned. 'I'll just walk him in the barn.' She started to lead the horse out. Before he had even left the stable, Jan could see he was as lame as a cat on his off-foreleg.

'OK, Roz, don't bother to take him out. I can see.' Jan walked over to the horse and ran her hand gently down the hurting leg, right to the crown of his hoof. She swore to herself. The lower shin and fetlock joint were severely swollen and positively hot to the touch. 'I wonder what the hell he's done. He's given himself a knock somehow, but it wasn't showing yesterday.'

'Poor Eddie,' Roz gasped.

'Never mind poor Eddie! What about poor Russian Eagle?'

'Well, of course I'm sorry for him too, but he'll mend and Eddie hasn't got much time to win a race to qualify the horse for the Foxhunters'.'

Jan sighed. 'Yeah; well, there's not much I can do about that.'

When Annabel came up for lunch in the caravan with Jan and the children, she brought a video of *The Sound of Music* for Megan and a bottle of wine for her and Jan.

After Roz had left that morning, Jan finally got round to opening the previous day's post. If Eagle's lameness had depressed her, one of the bills she received completely extinguished the lingering glow of victory from the day before. She showed it to Annabel.

'My God,' Annabel gasped. 'Six hundred pounds! Is this from the solicitors Toby recommended?'

Jan nodded. 'I suppose if we eventually take Harold to court and win, he'll have to reimburse me for all these charges, but if we lose or decide we haven't got a case, I'll have to pay them myself and there'll be more before we even get to that stage.'

'I'm sure Toby can't have been expecting them to charge so much. If I were you, I'd ring them and check it's right.'

'I will. The trouble is that, however bullish these lawyers are, they've got nothing to lose, have they?'

'That's right. My father always says that preachers and lawyers are the only tradesmen in the world who can tell their clients how much of their services they need.'

'Well, I think just for the moment I've had as much as I can afford. I'll let things stew for a while and see what crops up.'

The next two weeks seemed destined to go on as they had started. When Jan's new vet, Chris Roberts, had come out for his weekly visit, he'd declared that the horse must have hit a guard rail and told her to go on poulticing and hosing the leg gently with cold water to bring the swelling down as soon as possible. 'But I wouldn't do any work on it for at least ten days,' he advised forcefully.

Jan paled as she saw all those months she'd thought she had to qualify the horse for Aintree vanishing until there would be no time left to win the necessary Open race.

She also had two horses entered to run on the Wednesday. When she had them groomed and ready to go, she rang the secretary for a final check, only to be told that the course in Herefordshire was waterlogged on the bottom bend and they'd had to call it off. She banged down the phone in frustration.

After the elation of Saturday, Eddie's reaction caused her more concern. She discovered that he was by no means as sanguine as she'd always thought. He became almost morose when he saw Eagle's leg and was convinced it would take twice as long as the vet had said to recover.

'No, it won't,' Jan told him while they drank tea in the tack room amid the smell of well-cleaned leather. 'It's not that serious. It was obviously a hard knock and he's bruised the bone, which will take a while to settle down.'

'But he'll lose fitness, too, won't he?'

'A little,' Jan conceded, 'but if all goes well, we'll soon get him back on song.'

Eddie looked at Jan, as bleak and serious as she'd ever seen him. 'We've *got* to do this, Jan. I can't tell you how much it matters to me. It's not only winning the money; it's . . .' Eddie closed his eyes for a moment, Jan thought like a small boy having a dream. '. . . It's the first time I've ever set myself a real, hard challenge.' He blinked and looked at her. 'Life's always been a bit of a breeze for me, you know. At my age – quite intelligent, just about good-looking enough and fairly rich until a couple of months ago – I've never had to try too hard at anything. But now I've got to, I'll do whatever it takes.'

'I do understand,' Jan said quietly, moved that he'd chosen to reveal this side of himself to her, 'and I'll do whatever I can to help.' She shook her head. 'But don't you think you should have gone for something easier?'

'I could have done, I suppose, but this presented itself and it's all about risk and return; the bigger the risk, the bigger the reward, they say.'

Jan was thinking about Eddie's challenge and his previously hidden reserves of determination as she drove back from the races with a lorry load of runners the following Saturday. Of the four horses on the lorry, there was a single winner – Gale Bird in the adjacent hunts' race – and she was finding her own resolve severely tested.

As the following week went on, the going got heavier.

The gallops were too wet to use because of the constant

downpour and she had to accept the fact that Nuthatch, whom she had entered for a very competitive Open the following Saturday, simply wasn't ready to run.

She phoned Frank Jellard to tell him.

'But, Jan,' he replied, 'I saw him work two weeks ago and you said he would easily be ready.'

'I didn't know it was going to rain continually since then and, anyway, as it turned out, I was wrong. I'm sorry, Mr Jellard.'

'I've got four horses with you now, Jan, and I've been completely supportive. I've written to the Jockey Club recommending you, but so far this season I've had one runner who's come a miserable third.'

'Actually it was a very good third, considering what he was up against. And I'm not a wizard: if the horses aren't ready, they aren't ready, and there's nothing any human being can do about the weather; we can only do our best.'

'I want that horse to run, Jan, on Saturday. I'm sure he's ready; I saw he was with my own eyes two weeks ago, so, if you don't mind, please go ahead, and remember – I own the horse and I pay the bills.'

'I don't know if you pay your doctor's bills, but if you do, I bet you still follow his instructions when he tells you what to do.'

'Jan, you're not a doctor. You're not even a professional trainer in the real sense of the word, and I'm the customer, so the horse runs. Let that be the end of the matter.'

The morning after their phone call, Jan rode Jellard's horse out in the torrential rain to satisfy herself that she was right.

Later, drying off in the caravan before a midday snack with Annabel and Roz, she took a deep breath and rang him at the office of his big fruit-growing business.

'Mr Jellard,' she said when she'd been put through to him, 'it's Jan Hardy here. I've had another look at Nuthatch. I rode him myself to be sure, and I have to say that I strongly advise you not to run him on Saturday.'

'You've already given me your very strong advice in this matter,' Jellard answered coldly, 'and I've told you what I want. If you won't do it, you can expect my lorry round to collect all four horses next week. Is that clear?'

Jan started to mumble a reply, then stopped. 'Yes it bloody well is clear, and if the horse comes back injured, be it on your head.'

'Be it on yours, Jan,' she heard, before the line went dead.

Jan looked at Annabel and wanted to burst into tears. 'For God's sake,' she sniffed, 'what the hell am I supposed to do? I tell him he might do his horse serious damage if he insists I run it, and he just says he'll take them all away if I don't.'

'Then you'll just have to run it, Jan,' Annabel said. 'You can always tell Billy to pull up if he feels the horse is wrong. You certainly can't afford to lose four horses right now and two of them will do really well, once they're ready.'

'That's the point – once they're ready! Why the hell can't people understand that horses aren't machines? And you know I've always said that if I send a horse out to race it's ready to do its job.'

18

Reg Pritchard lowered a pair of well-worn binoculars and shook his tweed-capped head.

'You shouldn't be running that horse.'

Jan wished he hadn't insisted on coming, but they were only twenty-five miles from Riscombe and Reg had driven himself.

She was also worried it was so obvious that Nuthatch wasn't ready to run. He hadn't even looked right in the paddock. Jellard, standing beside her, was all smiles. In his ignorance, he hadn't noticed the horse's condition. Jan had told Billy earlier what to do, but there, in the owner's hearing, she'd said, 'This is a very competitive race, Billy, with two strong front runners. Don't take them on; wait till they come back to you, then have a go at them.'

Jellard had been satisfied.

Jan had been mortified. She hated the lying and the subterfuge; she hated the compromise.

Now her father was looking at her accusingly.

'Dad, I didn't want him to run. He needed at least another two weeks; he's a difficult horse to get fit anyway. But Frank Jellard said he would take all his horses away if I didn't run him.'

'What a bloody idiot!' Reg exploded. 'You should have told him where to shove 'em!'

'Dad, how could I? He's paying me a lot of money at the moment.'

Reg turned his attention back to the race, which had reached the halfway stage. 'Young Billy's pulling him up.'

'Good. I told him to.'

'That's not going to please your owner then, is it?'

'It's better than the horse breaking down,' Jan murmured through teeth clenched in anticipation at the row she was going to have with Jellard after the race.

'You're right, Jan,' Reg sighed. 'It's not an easy game, is it, this training? I don't think I'd want to try it, knowing there's always problems, with some people wanting one thing, and some another, and they've always got you over a barrel.'

'No, Dad,' Jan agreed. 'It isn't easy. If it was, everybody would be doing it, wouldn't they?'

'Still, at least you're going home with another winner,' Reg grunted with satisfaction.

'Yes, Eamon will be pleased, and he's the sort of owner who wouldn't dream of telling me what to do.'

'Hey, Jan,' Reg said suddenly, tugging at her sleeve, 'isn't that the bloke you used to train for? The one who had that good horse?'

Jan followed her father's gaze.

'Yeah, that's Harold Powell,' she said, refusing to be put out by the sight of him. 'He owns Rear Gunner. I saw he had a runner here – not one I know and it did nothing. I didn't think he'd be here, though; it's quite a long way for him.'

'Oh,' Reg said warily. 'It looks like he's seen you. He's coming over.'

'Don't worry, Dad. He's not going to attack me here.'

'And don't you have a go at him either, mind.'

'Hello, Jan,' Harold greeted her loudly with no hint of animosity as he approached. 'Sorry that last horse of yours didn't make it round.'

Jan shrugged a shoulder. 'As you know, it happens.'

'Still, that was a nice win you had,' he went on grudgingly. 'But I was hoping I might have seen that good horse of yours that came from Ireland. Russian Eagle, isn't he?'

'Yes,' Jan sighed, wondering what was coming next.

'I heard a rumour you're going to run him in the Foxhunters' at Aintree, if you can qualify him in time.'

'The owner would like to,' Jan nodded.

'Well, best of luck to him. Virginia's entered Gunner for it and he's going brilliantly now; he'll take all the beating.' He stretched his mouth into a quick, false smile, turned on his heels and walked off without waiting for her reaction.

Reg gazed after him, furious. 'What an arrogant pillock! Who the hell does he think he is?'

'Don't worry about it, Dad. It's his problem, not ours,' Jan said, wishing she meant it.

She was painfully conscious that the London solicitors, despite their large bills, hadn't achieved any more than Mr Russell from Broadway and no one had seen Amos Smith since he had moved on the previous autumn. But while she'd been focusing on training her horses and getting them to the races as well prepared as she could, she'd been forced to put the whole business on the back burner, until the boy came back or something else turned up.

She tried not to let Harold spoil her day and was delighted when Eamon rang that evening, full of praise.

'I'm just sorry I wasn't there to see it,' he said. 'I knew you'd get a win out of him sometime. I didn't know it would be so soon. I'll try and make sure I'm there next time, but I've got a few little problems to deal with.'

'He's a super horse and he really ran his socks off. Eamon, look, I've got a little problem, too. I've just sent you out a bill for January and I haven't had December's money yet.'

'Jaysus! Have you not? What the hell has that accountant of mine been up to? You take your eye off the ball for a second—'

'I do need it, Eamon. I can't feed these horses on thin air.'

'Jan, I know that. Don't say another word. It'll be dealt with.'

As Jan put the phone down, she thought about what her father had said at the races that day. She agreed that anyone going into this job needed a strong constitution to expose themselves to the frustrations and vagaries of other people's behaviour, when a lot of people who supported your business considered themselves your friends when it suited them and not when it didn't.

She was beginning to develop insights that went well beyond

the basic requirements of training horses. And one of these was telling her not to hold her breath while she waited for Eamon Fallon's cheque.

She sighed and got ready for bed. At least Jellard had accepted Billy Hanks's explanation for pulling up Nuthatch in the end, and his four horses were still in her yard.

Jan helped Annabel to carry Sunday lunch into the small dining room of her cottage. Toby Waller and Megan were already sitting at the table, with Matthew beside them in a high chair, specially brought in by Annabel.

Toby bustled to his feet. 'At the risk of appearing to demean women, may I offer my services as a carver?'

'As Bel's cooked it,' Jan said with a grin, 'and Meg and I did the spuds, you might as well do something to help. I don't feel a bit demeaned. Do you, Bel?'

'No,' Annabel laughed. 'There's a knife and steel on the top in the kitchen, Toby, so go to it.'

Jan watched unashamedly to see how Annabel and Toby were getting on. Although, physically, Toby wasn't very attractive, he was thoroughly considerate, and, she knew from her dealings with him, highly intelligent. Jan could see how his solid dependability and also, maybe, the fact that he was less attractive than Annabel might boost her confidence.

She thought back over a conversation she'd had with Annabel while they'd been riding out together soon after Toby had appeared on the scene. She had asked, 'What do you want in a man, then – a small tummy or a big brain?'

'Both, I suppose,' Annabel had answered.

Looking at Toby now, seeing him doing his able best to be charming and entertaining, Jan wondered how much his physical appearance mattered, and found herself thinking about what she was really looking for. She came, as she'd often done, to the worrying conclusion that she wasn't looking for anyone at all – worrying because she hadn't set out to make herself totally independent, she had simply found that as a woman doing the job she'd chosen an autonomous mindset was essential, and if it was this that stopped her taking men seriously, she thought, that was just too bad.

Whatever Annabel thought of Toby, as far as Jan was concerned he had turned out to be an ideal owner. Although he liked detailed reports, he left all the decisions about Gale Bird's training and running to her. He wasn't proprietorial or condescending when he came to the yard; he always paid his bills on time, and Jan knew that, unlike Penny Price, he could easily afford to. The day after Gale Bird had won, when he'd come up to Edge Farm, he had said, 'I'm sure all of you have helped to produce my mare so well,' and had left a present for everyone in the yard.

At lunch he fed Matthew, told Megan jokes and gently teased Annabel. He topped off the day by announcing that he would like to have a second horse at Edge Farm.

'By the way,' he said later, as he was showing Jan to the door, 'I've told my lawyers that I'm picking up the tab for any work they've done for you on this Harold Powell case.'

'But, Toby—' Jan started to protest.

He held up a hand. 'No, it's OK. I suggested them; I'll handle them. I think in due course they'll get a result for you. If they do, you can pay me back. And I don't want to hear another word about it,' he grinned.

After a perfect winter Sunday lunch and Toby's generosity, which she didn't think she'd done anything to deserve, Jan drove her children back to the caravan feeling more able to cope with the endless daily challenges in running a small yard. Even Bernie Sutcliffe's unannounced arrival just as she was putting Matthew to bed didn't spoil the day for her.

Bernie had brought a bottle of wine, and a bunch of surprisingly tasteful flowers – definitely not the sort that men often buy from garage forecourts as an afterthought.

'Bernie, I'm sorry,' she said, 'but if you want to look at the horse now, you can't. I'm on my own. Anyway, I don't usually have owners coming at this time of night.'

'Come on, Jan. That doesn't apply to me does it? I mean we're friends, aren't we?'

'Yes, of course. Come in, then, and thank you for the flowers.'

'Do you like 'em? My mum chose them, she said you would.'

Jan was struck by this unexpected aspect of Bernie's private life. 'They're lovely, but I still can't go down to the yard. I won't leave the children on their own at night.'

'Never mind. Just tell me how he is.'

'Who? Russian Eagle?'

'Who else?'

'He's getting there. We should be able to start light work with him again this week. Then there's a good race for him on the twenty-third; we'll try and get him ready for that.'

'Is he still entered for that big race you said, at Aintree, just before the Grand National?'

'The Foxhunters' – yes,' Jan answered carefully. 'It's two days before the National, actually, over the same course, but just one and a bit circuits.'

'Do you think he'll be able to go?'

'I told you when you bought him, he's got to win an open point-to-point to qualify. He nearly won last time and there's a good chance he will next time.'

'I wouldn't mind having a horse go up there, but only if I don't make a complete prat of myself. I thought I might ask up some of my family and friends to watch. What do you think?'

'I think, if he qualifies, he'll be as good as some of the others and a great deal better than most, but, you know, it's still a long way off and a lot can change.'

'What do you mean? He's still the same horse.'

'A horse's performance only has to vary by a fraction of a per cent to make the difference between winning and not.'

'What about the jockey?'

Jan hoped her reaction didn't show. 'Eddie's riding him very well; I've got no worries on that score.'

'I wouldn't want that cocky little bastard Billy Hanks riding him. Are there others we could ask?'

'Not really,' Jan said, 'and when you bought the horse from Eddie, you agreed he would go on having the ride as part of the deal.'

'I don't remember signing anything about that.'

Jan felt herself go pale and she hoped Bernie hadn't noticed. 'No, you don't sign that sort of thing. In racing your word should be enough. My dad always said your word is your bond.'

'Is that right?' Bernie asked, disingenuously. 'Anyway, another reason I came round was to ask you out to dinner, Tuesday week, to give you plenty of time to find a babysitter. All right?'

Jan, caught on a back foot, didn't have time to think of a plausible reason why she couldn't go at ten days' notice, but with luck something might crop up to stop her. 'That should be fine,' she said. 'Thanks very much.'

It was only when Jan looked in the stable diary that she realized the day Bernie had asked her to dinner was Valentine's Day.

From time to time, during the busy days after he turned up with the flowers, she'd tried to think of a reason not to go out with him, but she hadn't got it in her to be so cruel as to offer him a transparent excuse for not going, and now it was almost too late. Finally she resigned herself, and hoped Bernie wasn't going to take her to some tackily romantic venue. At least she would have good news to report on Russian Eagle, who had started work again and was going well.

Eddie came that afternoon to carry on schooling. Jan was glad to see that both horse and rider were improving all the time. Although they had yet to win even their one qualifying race, Jan didn't feel it injudicious to tell Eddie that she certainly hadn't written him off in the Foxhunters'.

Before he went, Jan asked him if he was doing anything special for Valentine's Day.

'Good God, is it today? I never take any notice of it,' he said brusquely. 'It's a load of rubbish invented by flower sellers for men who haven't the imagination to be romantic without a bit of help.'

'But you have?' Jan asked cynically.

'Play your cards right and one day you might find out,' he grinned.

Roz came in the evening to look after the children and watched as Jan got ready for Bernie's arrival.

'Cor, bloody hell, Jan, you don't want to look too sexy or that little prat'll be all over you.'

'Come on, Roz; you can hardly call this outfit sexy.'

'It bloody well is, with that slit up the side. You shouldn't do yourself down, Jan. There's a lot of blokes round here as fancies you.'

Jan didn't feel inclined to believe her; at the same time, she agreed that the wrap-around skirt she had borrowed from Annabel – the only garment from her wardrobe that fitted Jan – might be seen as deliberately seductive. 'Oh, bugger,' she said. 'You're right. I'd better wear that dress I got for Eamon's party.'

She went back to her small section of the caravan and came out in a modest but not unflattering silk dress that had been a Christmas present from Annabel.

'He'll still fancy yer,' Roz said, 'but least it's not like deliberate temptation. He was right brassed off, wasn't he, when you kept dancing with Eddie and Billy at Eamon's.'

'I had a dance with him too, remember?'

'I don't remember a lot, to tell the truth. That Eamon got me so drunk.'

'Eamon did?' It was the first Jan had heard of it.

'Yeah, course he did, but he didn't try anything, like; not much anyway.'

'Have you seen him since?'

'Only when he's been here. He told me he's got to sell his share in that club already; he says they've squeezed him out.'

'Who's squeezed him out?'

'The other people that owns it, he said. It's not all his, you know, but he found the place and put it all together.'

'Oh, I thought it was his, the way he was going on.'

'Probably he wanted you to think he had plenty of money to pay his bills,' Roz said candidly.

'He's left that a bit late, now, I'm afraid.'

'Why?' Roz was shocked. 'Hasn't he been paying yer?'

'Not for the last two months.'

'Cor!' Roz gasped with a shake of her unruly black curls. 'Aren't people bastards? Oh well,' she said, immediately brightening, 'it might mean you get to have his horse and he's lovely, Dingle Bay.'

Valentine's Day dinner with Bernie was as awful as Jan had feared.

He had booked them into a large, second-rate restaurant near Gloucester that specialized in 'events' and had a cabaret of unconvincing sixties and seventies tribute acts, climaxing with a Tom Jones, who Jan thought looked more like Del Boy from *Only Fools and Horses*.

Jan thought about fools and horses while she tried to look as if she was having a good evening, without yawning and looking at her watch too often. She wondered why some men were incapable of reading the signs women gave out that clearly displayed their lack of interest; she supposed their egos were to blame.

When the cabaret had finished and a disco took over, Jan danced with Bernie a few times. To her relief, he didn't force himself on her and, when they sat down for what she hoped might be a last drink, she was beginning to be grateful for his restraint.

'I was talking to your jockey the other day,' Bernie said, as if he were making a bit of light conversation.

'Eddie?'

'No, Billy.'

'I didn't think you two were on speaking terms,' Jan said with a slight smile.

'Because of Sandy? No, well, he did me a big favour really. I mean, it showed me what a right little tart she was, so I came round to thinking I was grateful to him. I mean, when there's women like you around, who needs a Sandy?'

Jan cringed, but couldn't think of an answer which wouldn't sound conceited or rude, so kept silent.

'Anyway,' Bernie went on. 'I took him out for a drink in the White Horse, and we got chatting about him riding Russian Eagle.'

Jan looked down and fumbled for something in her bag to hide her panic. 'What about him riding Eagle?' she asked, as evenly as she could.

'Well, Billy's virtually a pro, isn't he? After all, he rides all your other horses, so I got to thinking. I know there was talk of Eddie Sullivan riding my horse when I bought it, but he's had his ride; you might say he's had his chance. Billy reckons he would have won on Eagle last time.'

Jan shook her head vigorously. 'I doubt it. The thing is Eagle's not a horse to put under pressure any more than you have to. That's why I asked Eddie to ride him like that.'

'But you didn't. I heard you say, "Start going for it halfway round the last circuit", and he didn't, did he?'

'Eddie understands that horse better than anyone in the yard,' Jan hurried on. 'He's ridden him and schooled him more than anyone else and I know he'll win on him next time out.'

'Look, why's he so keen to ride the horse anyway, now he doesn't own it?'

Jan looked hard at Bernie. He didn't know that Eddie stood to win half a million if he rode and won on Russian Eagle at Aintree.

'I suppose because he chose and bought the horse,' Jan tried to say casually. 'He's put a lot into it and he wants to be part of the result. He told me', she went on truthfully, 'he's set himself this Aintree race as a sort of challenge, perhaps to get back a bit of self-esteem after what happened to him last year.'

'You mean what happened to that old bastard, Ron,' Bernie interjected.

'I suppose he's trying to show that he can stand on his own two feet and be something.'

'Well, he'll have to find another horse to do it on because from now on I want Billy Hanks to ride both the horses I keep with you and he's agreed.'

Sitting beside Bernie in the Jaguar as he drove her home, Jan couldn't speak. Her mind was in complete turmoil about what she would say to Eddie. After all, it had been her idea that Bernie should buy the horse. She'd also said to Eddie there'd be no problem over him keeping the ride.

Now she felt like a traitor for letting this happen.

She wasn't pleased with Billy, either.

In some ways she couldn't blame him. If Bernie had asked him point-blank whether he would have won the race in which Eddie came second, Jan, for one, would have had to agree if he'd said 'yes'. She'd thought it herself at the time. Billy knew nothing about Eddie's bet or how important the Foxhunters' was to him so there was, Jan had to admit, no ethical reason why Billy shouldn't have accepted the offer to ride Russian Eagle when the owner asked him.

When Jan wanted to talk to Eddie on the phone next day, she couldn't get him on any of his usual numbers. By midday she was desperate, but determined that she should tell him what Bernie had said before he heard it from someone else.

She convinced herself eventually that she had to go into Stow to see the saddler, but she finished her business there in less than five minutes and hurried round the corner to Eddie's shop. She pushed open the door underneath a sign that read, *THE SULLIVAN GALLERY* and, underneath, *E. R. Sullivan – Sporting Pictures* and walked into the small showroom. It smelled of coir carpeting and pot-pourri. The only sounds were the ticking of a carriage clock over the unused fireplace and the rustle of paper as an old man behind the desk folded up his copy of the *Daily Telegraph*. It was the first time Jan had been in the shop since the previous October and she hadn't taken much in then. It seemed to her, though, that the walls were a lot emptier.

The old man – well into his eighties, Jan guessed – smiled over the top of his gold half-moon glasses as he rose from his chair.

'Good afternoon. What can I do for you?'

'I'm looking for Eddie Sullivan.'

'Mr Sullivan's been called away to London on business, I'm afraid,' the man answered, a little cagily, Jan thought.

'You didn't tell me he was going to London when I rang earlier, you just said he'd popped out.'

'Who are you, madam?'

'Jan Hardy. I've got the racing stables over at Stanfield.'

The old man looked relieved. 'Of course. I should have recognized you. I know exactly who you are. I'm Jack Singleton, a sort of part-time manager. I'm sorry, but there are one or two people who want to talk to Eddie whom he's not very keen to see himself.'

'Do you know where he is, then?'

'Not exactly. But I know he'll be back at his house at eight this evening; he's arranged to meet his father there.'

'I tried to leave a message at the house,' Jan said, 'but I just got a funny sound on the phone.'

'I think he may have forgotten to pay the bill.'

Jan winced. If Eddie was so hard up that he was having trouble paying his phone bill, Bernie's decision would hit him even harder.

She looked more closely at the elderly shop assistant and guessed that he was on Eddie's side. 'Tell me,' she said. 'How's business here?'

Jack Singleton raised a bushy white eyebrow a few centimetres. 'I'm afraid the stock's rather low, and what there is isn't all that good.'

Jan glanced at the few pictures on the wall – a fishing scene, a group of implausible men shooting duck, and an oddly shaped racehorse being held by an even less convincing eighteenth-century groom – and began to understand why Eddie had been so pessimistic about his business future. She looked back at Jack Singleton.

'I don't know anything about pictures,' she said, 'but I think I see what you mean.'

'I fear we won't be here much longer.' He shrugged his shoulders regretfully.

'That's a shame,' Jan said, thinking this was a bit of an understatement.

'But I hear great things of his racing.'

Jan nodded. 'He's done really well. I hope it keeps going well for him,' she said, trying not to reveal she thought this was now a fairly bleak prospect. 'If you're talking to him, can you tell him I'll come round to the Mill at about eight?'

'Certainly,' Jack Singleton said. 'May I say that I think he's very lucky to have someone like you to inspire him at a time like this?'

As Jan drove to Old Ford Mill that evening, she wondered what Eddie had told Jack and if she really was an inspiration to him. He wouldn't be too inspired, she thought, when she told him Bernie was adamant that Billy Hanks should ride Russian Eagle from now on. It seemed to her that with all his other problems Eddie had been clinging to his hopes of winning the big bet like a bankrupt clutching a lottery ticket.

She drove in through the open gates and saw Eddie's battered vehicle parked outside the front door.

She took a few deep breaths and climbed out of her own Land Rover, which wasn't in much better shape, then walked up to knock on the door.

It was opened by Ron Sullivan. 'Well, well, well!' he said with a smile spreading across his big, tanned face. 'If it isn't Little Miss Donkey Walloper.' He opened the door wider and with a wave of his big hand beckoned Jan into the gloomy hall, lit only by a glimmer from Eddie's oil lamps in the kitchen.

'Hello, Mr Sullivan,' Jan replied, rather coldly. She thought that, of all the names she'd been called over the years, she liked Little Miss Donkey Walloper the least. 'Most of my friends call me Jan.'

'I'm sorry, Jan,' Ron laughed. 'It's only because I fancy you. Gawd knows what you see in that bent-nosed son of mine, though.'

'Thanks, Dad,' Eddie said coming up behind Ron. 'Hi, Jan. Jack told me you were coming. What's up?'

'Actually,' Jan said, 'I've got some bad news.'

'You'd better come into the kitchen and have a drink first.' Jan didn't miss the slight quake in Eddie's voice.

'Is this something you don't want me to hear?' Ron asked.

'I'm sure it's OK, Dad,' Eddie said, as he took down a bottle of wine from a big pine dresser that stretched along one wall. He filled three glasses and put them on the table. 'What's happened?' he asked Jan.

Jan sat down and took a gulp from her glass. 'Bernie—'. Jan started, then sighed. 'Bernie asked me out to dinner last night,' she said slowly. 'It was pretty awful, but he told me he'd been speaking to Billy Hanks; he asked him if he would ride Eagle for him in future and Billy said yes.'

Eddie's jaw slackened; he screwed up his face for a moment. 'Oh, God,' he grunted. 'Still, at least you haven't come to tell me Eagle's dead, which was what I thought first.'

'No, Eagle's fine; I'd been planning for you to ride him Saturday week at the Warwick; he stands a good chance. But now Billy will have to. I'm really sorry, but there's nothing I can do about it.'

'What's the problem?' Ron joined in. 'Ed's been jocked off, so what? There's always other horses to ride.'

Jan realized that Ron didn't know anything about Eddie's great plan to get him out of trouble. She left Eddie to answer for himself.

'I'd rather set my heart on riding this particular horse in the Aintree Foxhunters', Dad.'

'Had you, by 'eck? Well, that's what I'd call a triumph of fantasy over sanity. Since when did you think you could jump round the National course?'

'He can do it OK, Mr Sullivan,' Jan said, impressed that Eddie had kept his considerable progress a secret from his father.

'Call me Ron,' he boomed.

'He can do it, Ron. He's worked really hard at it and he's doing brilliantly. Didn't he tell you he nearly won last month?'

Ron turned to his son, visibly impressed. 'Ed, my boy! What's the point of hiding your talents from your old man?'

Eddie shrugged. 'I'm not that great yet, but I thought if I did get anywhere at Aintree, it would come as a nice surprise for you.'

'And it bloody well would have. But is this right?' He turned back to Jan. 'The geezer that owns this 'orse – he's robbed Eddie of the ride?'

Jan nodded.

'Why's that?' Ron asked.

'He thought Eddie should have won last time out.'

'The time he come second?'

'That's right.'

'What a berk! Who is he?'

'A businessman from the Black Country called Bernie Sutcliffe.'

Ron raised a shoulder. 'Never 'eard of him.'

'He's a big scrap merchant of some sort,' Eddie said.

'I'm sorry, Ed,' Ron said, shaking his head. 'In the old days, I could have done something for you, called in a couple of favours. But', he sighed, 'as it is—'

Suddenly, it seemed to Jan, Ron looked smaller.

But Eddie was putting a brave face on the problem. 'Presumably,' he said, 'the only way I'd get the ride back would be if someone else bought him from Bernie and they agreed to let me?'

'Yes,' Jan said, 'but knowing Bernie, the only time to buy from him would be when he's already decided to sell.'

'That's easy,' Ron said, pulling up a kitchen chair and sitting down. Jan guessed he still enjoyed cooking up a plan. 'The only time I wanted to sell a horse was when it couldn't win. So, don't let this one win. Simple.'

Jan looked at him and shook her head. 'Firstly, I'd never deliberately send out a horse to lose; secondly, we have to win with him to qualify for the Aintree race; and, thirdly, Billy

Hanks would go straight back to Bernie even if I did tell him not to try.'

'You don't need to tell him to do anything; you could just not train the horse well enough. That shouldn't be too hard,' Ron chuckled. 'It's what most of the racehorse trainers in this country do anyway!'

'That would still leave my first two reasons for not doing it,' Jan said.

'All right, then, the only other option's to offer this geezer a pile of dough for the animal.'

Eddie shook his head this time. 'Bernie's one of those people who, the more you offered him, the more he'd want, and you'd have to go way beyond any sensible price before he'd sell. Besides, none of us have got that sort of money.'

'No,' agreed Ron. 'Specially not me.' He stood up to mark the finality of this statement. 'But, as there doesn't seem to be much you can do about your little problem, I can tell you I have got just about enough wonga in my pocket to take us all out for a meal at that nice boozer in the village. Come to think of it, they probably owe me a few drinks in there from when I let them shoot across the Manor last winter.'

Jan thought Ron was right: there was no more to be said about Russian Eagle, and so they didn't discuss him any further in the White Horse. Despite all the frustrations and disappointment caused by Bernie's Valentine's Day announcement, and the parlous state in which Ron and his son now found themselves, Jan had a very enjoyable evening.

She was surprised how much interest her horses had generated in the pub, though she guessed that, as it was the local Eddie and Billy used, it was inevitable that her runners were widely discussed there.

But with Ron and Eddie she didn't only talk about the horses and Ron seemed to know something about any topic that cropped up. Out of curiosity, Jan asked him what he was going to do with himself – if he had any plans to rise one day, Phoenix-like, from the smouldering ruins of his old business empire. But he wouldn't be drawn.

'Let's just say I've got plans,' he said, and added more quietly, 'where the gum tree grows.'

When the conversation came back to racing, Ron was happy to talk about his past experiences. 'I owned jumpers for twenty-five years,' he told Jan. 'I've had some of the best trainers in the country look after horses for me and some of the worst – they were often the dearest. The ones I always admired most were them who didn't allow owners to run their lives. They trained on their terms and nobody else's. If you tried to tell 'em what to do, they just told you to eff off and take your horses with you. Of course, some of them smarmy, Old Etonian brown-nosers just oiled around, agreeing with everything you said provided you had enough money – bloody terrific at the old gin and tonic, but effing useless at training horses. This bloke Jellard you was telling me about, who wanted you to run a horse that wasn't ready; next time, tell him to get stuffed and take his horses with him. When it comes to it, he won't. Mark my words, there's very few serious people who don't respect a person – specially a woman – who stands up for their principles.'

Jan nodded ruefully. Next time she would take that risk with Jellard. 'What about the nice owners who don't tell me what to do, but don't pay their bills?'

'They're no good to you either. You can't run your yard on wind and three-fifths of sod all, however bloody charming they are. Put an interest charge on their bills and if they haven't coughed up halfway through the next month send a couple of reminders. If that don't work, issue a writ through the small claims court. It doesn't take five minutes and it don't cost much. That's a sort of training for them. Once they know they're going to get a writ every couple of months if they're late paying, they'll soon learn to send a cheque on time. Whatever happens, never let them owe you more than their horse is worth and never let them take a horse away if they still owe you.'

Driving home on her own after the meal in the pub, paid for by some past debt to Ron which the landlord remembered, Jan thought of all the advice Eddie's dad had given her, and she knew on the whole it was right, albeit hard-nosed and pragmatic. With Eamon and his financial problems, for instance, she came to the conclusion that much as she liked the man, she would need to follow Ron's advice.

But she still didn't know what to do about Eddie and Russian Eagle.

Although she knew Eddie was a lot more upset by the news than he'd let on, he had assured her that he realized it wasn't her fault and there was nothing she could do about it. It was always a problem, he'd said, when irrational human pettiness got in the way of one's plans and he'd admitted that if he'd handled his own business affairs properly in the first place, he would never have had to sell the horse to Bernie.

Jan was worried, though, that she hadn't seen Eddie at Edge Farm or heard from him during the week before the Warwickshire point-to-point. She wished there was something she could have done. Nevertheless, she still had her job to do and the three horses to get ready to run. The first four days of the week were bright, icy and hard as rock and without an all-weather gallop she couldn't get the work into the horses that she knew they needed. By Friday, however, the cold front had retreated and the meeting went ahead next day.

Joe was off sick and it was Roz's turn to mind the children and the horses at home while Jan and Annabel went racing. Normally, however depressed Jan became – about being without John, or without a house, or cold and broke – she could put it all out of her mind when she had horses to run. This time, though, she found it impossible.

She was doubtful that Eddie would turn up to watch Russian Eagle being ridden by Billy, so it was a great surprise when she saw him in the distance shortly after she'd arrived with Annabel. He was as bright and breezy as he'd always been and even offered to help as a supplementary groom.

Jan held her breath for a moment when Billy Hanks appeared for his ride on the first of her three runners. He obviously wasn't expecting to see Eddie.

'Morning, Billy,' Eddie greeted him affably.

Billy nodded back warily. 'Hello, Eddie.'

'Jan's got three good rides for you today; I thought I might see if anyone will give me a price on the treble.'

Billy beckoned Eddie to him. 'Look, mate,' Jan heard him say, 'I'm sorry about Russian Eagle, but the bloke had made his mind up he didn't want you to ride it; he just doesn't like you for some reason; sounds ridiculous but he thinks you're too posh to be riding for him.'

Eddie laughed. 'That's a joke, if he'd ever met my old man.'

'If I hadn't said I'd take the ride,' Billy went on, 'he'd have found someone else anyway.'

'I'm sure you're right, Billy. Don't worry about it; no hard feelings. Anyway,' Eddie added lightly, 'it's not the end of the world and you'll probably get him round Aintree much better than me.'

Jan listened while she and Annabel were getting Derring Duke ready for his first run of the season in the adjacent hunts' race. She had to admire Eddie for the front he was putting on. She would never have guessed how much it mattered to him if he hadn't already told her. She was also fairly sure that the main reason Bernie didn't want Eddie to ride Eagle was that, despite their denials, he thought she and Eddie were in some sort of a relationship.

The rest of the afternoon went particularly well for Jan. Derring Duke won his race and Gwillam Evans's gelding, Barneby Boy, won the restricted race.

Eddie came back to the lorry beaming with vicarious pride. 'Jan, you're a little genius to produce two winners in fields like that. If Eagle goes out and wins now, I'll take the thick end of a monkey off the bookies.'

'Don't count on it,' Jan said. 'He needed more work than I could safely give him this week with all the frost, and it took him a little time to come right after that leg injury he got when we last ran him.'

'God, I'm sorry about that.'

'Don't be daft, it wasn't your fault. I don't even know if he did it racing. He could have done it in his stable that night. It does happen occasionally.'

'Maybe I just didn't make him pick his feet up high enough.'

'It wasn't your fault, all right?' Jan repeated.

'Well I hope he wins today because I'll put all my winnings on him for the Foxhunters', whoever rides him.'

But Jan had a strong feeling in her innards that Russian Eagle wasn't going to win that day. She thought he really had needed that little bit of extra work to tone up his muscles.

When Bernie Sutcliffe arrived to watch his horse run, with three men who looked very out of place on a point-to-point course, Jan tried to warn him that Eagle might not be back to peak fitness yet.

But Bernie was too busy showing off to his friends to hear a word she said.

'I've changed his jockey since he last ran, and I've told him how I want the horse ridden,' he was saying importantly, as if he knew what he was talking about.

As the horses were going down to the start, the friends went off smugly to place their bets, confident that they were privy to inside knowledge.

When they came back, Jan stayed with Bernie to watch the race.

Russian Eagle jumped round perfectly, but on the last half circuit he lost touch and finished halfway down the field.

Jan wasn't too disappointed. She knew he could have done a lot better if he'd been a little fitter but, as she glanced at Bernie, she was shocked by the expression of bitter bafflement on his face. His upper lip was quivering and he wouldn't look at his friends, who, in turn, seemed totally crestfallen.

Jan didn't dare think how much they must have lost on the strength of Bernie's boundless confidence.

'The little bastard,' Bernie was muttering.

'Who?' Jan asked. 'Billy?'

'Yes,' Bernie hissed. 'He never rode him out, like he said he would, after that other idiot of yours never got after him properly.'

'Billy rode a perfect race; the horse just wasn't fit enough.'

'Why the hell didn't you tell me?'

'Bernie, don't start shouting at me. I did tell you before you all went off to have a bet. I said he took some time to get over that bad leg and I wasn't sure he was there yet. All being well, he'll be spot on next time.'

'Oh, great,' Bernie said cynically. 'That's what you said last time – the old trainer's lament – people have told me about it. You know, "He's bound to win, sooner or later." Just so long as you go on paying the bills. And when he never wins, it's a bit too late to ask for your money back, isn't it?'

'That's totally unfair, but if that's how you feel Bernie, maybe you should take the horse to another yard because I won't put up with that kind of talk.'

Bernie glanced for the first time at his companions before he turned back decisively to Jan. 'No, I won't do that. But next time we run him, I'm choosing the jockey.'

'Bernie, you chose the jockey this time.'

'Out of two? I don't call that much of a choice. No, I've got someone in mind who'll make sure he bloody well pulls his finger out.'

'We'll see about that,' Jan said, as she went down to the course to help Annabel bring Eagle back.

For the next few days, Jan wanted to pick up the phone and tell Bernie to take his horses away, rather than be dictated to about who should or shouldn't ride them.

On the other hand, the only chance she had of retrieving the ride on Eagle for Eddie was to keep the horse in the yard.

19

When Arctic Hay won for Bernie at a midweek meeting of the Radnorshire Hunt, she thought she might be able to bring him back on side, but he rang that evening and told her he'd got the man he wanted to ride Eagle next time, a well-known amateur jockey from the south-west who didn't usually venture up to the Midlands.

Jan hadn't often seen Roger Williams race, but she knew he had a reputation for hard, aggressive riding. Although she didn't particularly want him to ride Eagle, he did get a good number of winners and under point-to-point rules he couldn't use his whip excessively.

She tried to ring Eddie at his shop to tell him about it. He wasn't there, but Jack Singleton told her Eddie had managed to assign the lease on the premises and they were closing at the end of the week.

Poor Eddie, Jan thought. When she'd first met him, he had plenty of money and obviously enjoyed the illusion that he made a living from buying and selling pictures. Maybe he did have an eye for them, but it seemed to her that he'd never got to grips with the fundamentals of the business. Possibly, as his mother had hinted, his attention span was just too short.

Yet he'd shown a lot of determination in his riding, and though he'd lost the ride on Russian Eagle, there was no reason why he shouldn't carry on with other horses. If by some chance he was ever able to ride Eagle again, at least he'd then be schooled, fit and ready.

Without much hope, she dialled the Mill. To her surprise, it rang and Eddie answered.

'I'm glad you've got the phone back on,' she said.

'Yes,' Eddie laughed. 'But I haven't got a kitchen dresser any more.'

'For God's sake, Eddie. You can't just flog off everything around you.'

'It's OK. I've got a few thing coming together,' Eddie said vaguely.

Jan wasn't convinced, but she didn't say so. 'Good, but do you still have time to do a little schooling? I've got some horses here I wouldn't mind you riding in a few races.'

'Are you sure?' Eddie asked doubtfully.

Jan was touched by his lack of vanity, in this department at least. 'Yes, of course I'm sure. I wouldn't ask otherwise. I've got to win races you know.'

'I'd love to ride some more. I thought after Bernie had put the mockers on Eagle I'd be a bit superfluous around the yard.'

'Well, you won't be, so when can you come for another session?'

Eddie had always liked Victor Carey's dappled grey mare, August Moon, and Jan had him riding work and schooling her that week. After the horses were all put away and fed late on Thursday morning, she asked him up to the caravan for a coffee.

'I think I'll ring Mr Carey', she said, 'and ask him if he minds you riding his horse this Saturday, if you'd like me to.'

'Yes.' Eddie looked pleased. 'I'd love you to, if you think I'm up to it, but won't Billy expect the ride?'

'Maybe, but even he can't ride two horses at once; Sorcerer's Boy goes in the same race.'

'Are you running Eagle in the Open, too?'

'No, not this time. He's still not quite right and Bernie's insisted on giving this bloke Roger Williams the ride next time. He's a hard jockey, so I don't want him riding Eagle until he's ready – next week, I hope.'

Eddie flipped through the list of entries lying on Jan's table.

'I see Virginia's running one of her pointers in that race – looks like a bit of a superstar.'

Jan shrugged. 'I don't know why she bothers when she made such a thing about getting her licence and running under rules, but it's too bad. If Eagle's right, I've got to send him. We're getting very short of time to qualify him otherwise.'

'Bernie's never going to sell that horse,' Eddie said gloomily. 'I've been trying to work out some other way of dealing with the mess Dad's in, but I'm not getting anywhere. He's managed to buy a little more time again, but . . .' Eddie shook his head and Jan glimpsed the despair he felt.

'Look,' she said with a deal of false optimism, 'something'll turn up. It's amazing how often it does. You never know, Bernie just might give up the horse and you just might win the race. It's not all over until the fat lady sings.'

'Thanks, Jan,' Eddie said wryly. 'A little shot of bullshit goes a long way with me at the moment.'

Over the next few days Jan was concerned that Eddie's gloom might affect his riding; she knew from her own experience that for a jockey to set off with a defeatist attitude was the worst possible way to start a race, irrespective of the horse's abilities.

Although August Moon hadn't run in a race for over three years, she had been a surprisingly easy horse to train, and Jan felt that she stood a good chance, even beside an experienced old-timer like Sorcerer's Boy.

On the first Saturday in March she drove her lorry to a big, busy race meeting on the wealthy fringes of the Home Counties. There was a massive crowd on whom the sun smiled as the threatened rain was kept at bay. Jan found to her surprise that Victor Carey and Colonel Gilbert had both come to watch their horses, which were running in the same race. They were too well-mannered to show anything but friendly rivalry towards each other as they stood on either side of Jan.

'I've never seen Eddie Sullivan ride before,' the colonel remarked. 'Does he know what he's doing?'

Jan laughed. She knew he was having a good-humoured poke at Victor Carey. 'He's only ridden one race before, but he nearly won on Russian Eagle.'

'Is that the horse he was hoping to ride in the Foxhunters'?'

'Yes, but unfortunately he sold it to another of my owners, who doesn't want him to ride it now.'

'That's a bit tough on him.'

'Yes, but as he was doing so well I asked him if he'd come and ride some others for me.'

'You've certainly turned my mare out very well,' Victor Carey said, evidently not wanting to discuss Eddie's riding ability right now. Jan had told him all he wanted to know when she'd first asked him if Eddie could have the ride.

'Thanks,' Jan nodded. 'She enjoys her work and it didn't take long to get the grass belly off.'

The lightly framed, athletic horse had undoubtedly caught people's eye in the paddock. As an unknown quantity, having been off the course for so long, the odds the bookies were offering started long. But punters who thought they could tell a fit and talented animal when they saw one, especially with Jan Hardy's name beside it, had been quick to get their money on and the odds had shortened dramatically, though Sorcerer's Boy remained favourite.

In the final stages of the race, with the massive crowd roaring the two favourites home, Billy and Eddie swapped places twice at the front of the field, until August Moon's longer stride carried her a neck in front of Colonel Gilbert's old chaser on the run to the line.

The owners shook hands warmly and congratulated each other. Jan was almost boiling with excitement. It wasn't the first time she'd sent out the winner and the runner-up in a race like this, but she was ecstatic about Eddie's riding. He'd ridden a well-judged, intelligent race and made the best possible use of the mare. Coming to the finish, he'd barely used his whip, but squeezed her right up to the winning line with only hands and heels in the way he knew she liked best.

The result completely justified her professional judgement and she knew it must have gone a long way to restoring Eddie's morale. But the real prize for the day's victory arrived the next morning, a warm, damp Sunday, in the form of an invitation from Mr Carey asking Jan to go round for a drink at six that evening.

The day before he had given the lie to his reputation for parsimony by handing her grooms a hundred pounds – as a thank you, he said, for the most enjoyable race he had ever watched. Jan couldn't stop herself from thinking that maybe, at last, the pernickety old man had decided that she was worthy of his thirty-five-thousand-pound guarantee.

But she did not believe it was truly going to happen until he sat her down at a table in his library with a glass of dry sherry and placed in front of her a letter, neatly typed and already signed by him. It was addressed to the stewards of the Jockey Club, and informed them that he was prepared to act as guarantor to Mrs Jan Hardy of Edge Farm, who was applying for a professional licence to train racehorses.

Jan drove home in the Land Rover as if she were sitting on a magic carpet. All the months of uncertainty and waiting made his decision seem quite unreal now it had finally come. At home she hugged the wonderful news to herself, reluctant to tell anyone else, in case, by some crazy mischance, she had misunderstood what Mr Carey had said, or the implications of the letter he had written. Or in case he changed his mind.

She didn't let her hand stray near the telephone until eight o'clock next morning, when, having kept the news from Annabel, Roz and Joe for an hour, she was at last prepared to believe it was true.

She came back from riding out first lot and went straight up to the caravan to phone her father, determined that he should be the first to know.

By noon that day Jan's second formal application to the Jockey Club was in the post. Gerry arrived at lunchtime, following a call from Jan, who had tracked him down to where he was working in the next village. He had run out of things to do at Edge Farm over the past few weeks, when Jan had called a halt to any more work on the house until the spring. Now he was delighted to be asked back.

'Hi, Gerry,' Jan bubbled and gave the young builder a quick peck on the cheek.

'Cor!' he gasped at her news. 'That's brilliant. You'll be on the telly and all.'

'Never mind the telly. One day I'll be able to run horses in the biggest races in the country! The Gold Cup, the Grand National, the Hennessy, the King George! It's a whole different ball game!'

'Don't get too excited, Jan. You'll need the horses first.'

'Oh, I'll find them all right, don't you worry about that,' Jan laughed, not admitting that she'd lain awake half the night wondering how she would find owners prepared to buy the sort of horse capable of winning top-class races. 'Here's the list of things the inspector complained about last time. I'm pretty sure we've done them all, but could you go round and make certain? Repaint anything that looks a bit tatty. Then check every inch of fencing and double-check all the gates and their catches. They might take a special interest in that after Virginia took it upon herself to tell them about the horses that got out.'

Eddie came round later with some bottles of Spanish champagne. 'If you hold your nose while you drink it, it doesn't taste too bad,' he said.

'I wouldn't want the real thing anyway,' Jan said. 'It might be unlucky before the old fogeys at the Jockey Club have actually given me the green light.'

Reg and Mary arrived soon after Eddie.

Like Jan, Reg had reservations about premature celebration, but he was still prepared to knock back a few glasses of Spanish fizz. They sat around in the cramped little mobile home, with the wood-burner glowing and Jan's favourite candles on the table, and talked about everything they would like to see at Edge Farm Stables.

'A swimming pool for the horses,' Gerry said.

'And a horse walker,' Roz interjected; she hated all the walking that had to be done early in the training cycle.

'An all-weather gallop is what I need most,' Jan said, thinking of the few critical weeks of training that had been lost through frost.

'Steady on,' Reg said with an indulgent smile. 'What you need before any of that is owners, so you can pay for it all, and so you have the right type of horses. Winning point-to-points is all very well, but it's a big step up to National Hunt racing.'

'Well,' Eddie said, raising a glass. 'Here's to Jan. Twelve winners so far this season; let's make it twenty and the championship.'

'And I owe you one too, Eddie,' Jan replied. 'It was the win on August Moon that made up old Carey's mind. He was thrilled to bits with the way you rode him.'

Annabel laughed. 'You're not kidding. I've never seen him so cheerful. I think if I'd asked him there and then to let me off a month's rent, he would have done.'

The party carried on until Reg and Mary got up to leave at ten.

'It's another day tomorrow, Jan,' her father said.

'Yes,' Jan nodded. 'And, Eddie, if you're coming up at seven to ride out, you'd better get off home to bed, too.'

When Jan woke in the morning, her head was still buzzing. She wondered why she was so much more excited about her licence application this time than she had been when she'd applied for it back in the autumn.

Of course, now she'd sent out a good number of winners from Edge Farm and she knew that she'd dealt with all the Jockey Club's practical objections to the stables. She also had a strong guarantor and more than a dozen owners pledged. This time round a professional licence looked a far more likely prospect.

On her way down to the yard, as the sun broke out over the hill behind her, she stopped by her building site. She looked at the two-dimensional skeleton of her new house and indulged in a few minutes' fantasy.

'Soon,' she said to herself. 'Soon we'll have a yard full of quality horses and a house to live in.'

Eddie arrived just before seven, looking lean, fit and, Jan thought to herself, really quite handsome. She was still pleased that she'd been proved right in giving him the chance to ride the previous Saturday, but as much as she wanted to help him, she couldn't see the beginning of a strategy to get him back on Russian Eagle.

She talked to him about it while they were hosing the mud off the horses' legs in the yard after their work.

'You know, I can't do what your father suggested. I can't kid Bernie that Eagle's a turkey,' she said.

Eddie laughed. 'Obviously: if he's an eagle, he can't be a turkey.'

'Shut up and listen. I mean it. I'd love to do something, but I've racked my brains and so far I can't find a way.'

'Is Bernie still all right otherwise?'

'Apart from the fact that he's started making moves on Annabel.' Jan shook her head. 'I ask you, as if he had a chance!'

'I suppose someone like Bernie, who has an awful lot of money, now and again finds a tart like Sandy who'll put up with him for a bit, so he thinks that all women are susceptible to a fat wallet. But apart from everything else, Annabel's got plenty of her own dough, anyway.'

'I sometimes wonder why you haven't tried a bit harder there yourself,' Jan said.

'Listen, although I'm not mercenary, do you think I haven't? I promise you, whatever she's interested in, it's not me. A lot of man hours have been spent trying to figure out what turns her on.'

Jan thought about Annabel's chronic insecurity and wondered how Eddie would react if he knew the cause. But it was up to Annabel, and no one else, to decide who should know about it. As far as Jan knew, she was the only person Annabel had told.

'Anyway,' she said, 'I think she's managed to let Bernie know that she's not interested without being too brutal about it.'

'Hmm, I doubt it. I get the impression Bernie's not a very subtle chap. Still, I suppose Annabel's old enough to look after herself now.'

After they'd had a mug of coffee in the tack room, Eddie left for a sale, where the last of his pictures from the shop were due to be auctioned.

He hadn't been gone more than a minute when a small blue BMW purred up the track to the yard and stopped. Susan Sullivan got out and stood looking around.

'I saw Eddie's old rattle-trap up here,' she said, as Jan walked up to her, 'and thought I'd let him get out of the way first. He didn't stay the night here by any chance, did he?'

'No, he didn't,' Jan said firmly. 'He came at seven and rode out first lot.'

'I'm sorry,' Susan said. 'I can't help wanting to know about his love life, however much I tell myself it's none of my business.'

'Well, I'm afraid I can't help you there.'

'I'm glad he's so keen on this racing business, though. I hear he won a good race last week. I could hardly believe it.'

'He did very well.'

'Good. The reason I've come out here to see you is that I'm rather worried about him. I know he's found it difficult to handle what happened to his father. He wants to help and so do I, but there's a limit to what I can do. Has he told you anything about his plans?'

Jan shook her head. 'No. I don't think he wants to talk about it. I know he's been selling off the few bits he's still got, just to clear old debts as far as I can tell. And poor Ed – he sold his horse, which he was hoping to win a big race on, to a man who won't even let him ride it.'

'He told me about that. He seemed very put out.' Susan looked sharply at Jan. 'Do you know why?'

Jan gazed steadily back at Eddie's mother for a few moments, not giving anything away, until, slowly, she nodded. 'If you want to come up and have a cup of coffee with me in the caravan, I'll tell you. It's a long and frustrating story, I'm afraid.'

In the mobile home, Susan Sullivan gazed around her, clearly puzzled that a mother and two small children could squeeze into such a tiny space.

Jan made her promise that she wouldn't tell anyone else what she was about to say. Susan agreed and Jan felt she could trust her.

She was surprised to find that Susan had no idea about Ron's final, imprudent loan and the threat this now represented to him, and possibly to her own home, should they discover Ron owned half of it.

When Susan heard about Eddie's plan to deal with the debt by placing a massive bet, she laughed. 'What were his chances of winning?'

Jan felt oddly hurt by Susan's reaction to her son's heroic solution to the problem. 'He could have done it,' she said defensively. 'The horse could be good enough and he's improving generally. And Eddie's just about up to the job. Actually, after last Saturday, I'd say well up to the job.'

Susan shook her head. 'Poor Eddie.'

'It wasn't just to win the money he was doing it,' Jan went on. 'I think he really wants to prove that he can pull off some amazing deal, like his dad used to. OK, you could say he's trying to do it the easy way by gambling, but at least he was backing himself. And he knew he'd get much bigger odds out of Cyril Goldstone if he rode the horse himself.'

Susan nodded. 'I understand what you're saying. Is there no way you can get the horse back from this Bernie chap, or at least talk him into letting Eddie ride it?'

'There probably is.' Jan made a face. 'What you might call the old-fashioned way.'

'But you're obviously not prepared to do that.'

'No. I'm very fond of Eddie, but there are limits to my loyalty. And Bernie's turned his attentions to Annabel now.'

'Annabel Halstead?'

'Yes.'

'I'm not surprised, she's very attractive. She was one of the few girls Eddie ever took out that I liked, if only she hadn't been so young. Of course, I've never met most of the others, but her parents made a real fuss – at least, her father did and sent her mother round to speak to me – as if I could tell Eddie who to see and who not to see. He was already twenty-three. But, that said, I think maybe Bel was a bit too negative for him.'

'I don't know about that,' Jan said. 'She's been a brilliant friend to me. Don't ask me why, but she's always loved working with me and the horses, and she's a really intelligent girl. I'm sure she could have done almost anything she wanted.'

'Not everyone wants the glamorous life, though, especially if they've already had a taste and know they can have it any time. Where's she living now?'

'She rents a cottage in the village from Mr Carey, who owns a lot of property down there. Eddie won on his mare last week and Mr Carey's standing guarantor for my application for a professional licence.'

'You're going into the big time, are you?' Susan smiled, impressed.

'I hope so,' Jan said. 'I've got two kids to bring up on my own and I'll never do it satisfactorily by winning a few point-to-point races.'

'Well, best of luck. And thank you for telling me about Eddie's bet. I won't tell a soul.'

'If any of the girls notice you've been here, I'll ask them not to say anything,' Jan said.

Annabel's Golf skidded to a halt on the hard standing. She climbed out and banged the door shut.

'Bloody Bernie!' she snapped.

Jan had never seen her so angry. 'What's he done now?' she asked, walking down from the caravan towards her.

'That man's got a hide like a rhino! He's asked me out again tonight! He just doesn't know when to take no for an answer.'

'Oh God, is he still pestering you?'

'You can say that again! He keeps phoning and sending me flowers. I mean, I don't want to sound snotty, but he must realize that we hardly speak the same language. Yet he thinks because he's made a lot of money and I come from a wealthy family we must have something in common. It's pathetic!'

'Calm down, Bel. I'll have a word with him.'

'No, don't. There's no reason why you should do my dirty work for me.'

The two women walked into the yard. Darren and Tom, as keen as ever to learn everything they could about racehorses and earn Brownie points from Jan, had come in early to help prepare the three horses who were running at the Banbury point-to-point that afternoon. They were busy grooming Russian Eagle.

'Is Bernie coming this afternoon to watch Eagle run?' Jan asked.

'Yes, of course,' Annabel groaned.

'I wonder if he'll bring any of his dodgy-looking mates,' Jan said, 'though they were probably so disillusioned by losing all their money last time that they won't be back.'

'He didn't say if he was bringing anyone, but he's sure Eagle will win with this other jockey; I think he's promised him a huge present. It's crazy,' Annabel sighed. 'As if getting a jockey with a reputation for whacking horses was the answer! I don't think he understands the first thing about racing. He only ever wanted a horse in the first place because of that ghastly girlfriend of his and to snub James McNeill for making a pass at her. Now, unfortunately, he seems to have got a taste for it.'

'I know,' Jan sighed. 'He reads the racing papers from cover to cover every day, but he still knows nothing. I just hope

Roger Williams doesn't ride Eagle too hard today. It won't suit him.'

'Does Eagle have much of chance anyway, against this superstar of Virginia's?'

'Against Treble Up? That partly depends on who's riding him. If it's her younger brother, Harry, that'll help. He's an even worse rider than she was.'

'Actually, I think he is,' Annabel said. 'He was talking about it last time I was over there.'

'How long ago was that?'

'A week or so. Toby Waller came up and George asked me over to dinner again.'

'How's it going with Toby?'

'He's a good friend.'

'That's all?'

Annabel nodded ruefully. 'I find I can't overlook the aesthetic considerations.'

'I don't know,' Jan said with a grin. 'Compared with Bernie, he's quite attractive.'

Bernie's was one of the first faces they saw as they drove into the lorry park just before midday. He was evidently on his own and hopping impatiently from foot to foot.

'How is he?' he asked breathlessly before Jan's feet had even touched the ground.

'He's in good order,' Jan said, and watched his face change as Annabel climbed out of the other side of the cab. For a few seconds, his confidence seemed to desert him; his mouth slackened into a damp, unattractive 'O'. Jan shook her head in amazement that he had allowed himself to become so obviously besotted, and climbed up to let herself in through the groom's door into the back of the lorry. Joe and Darren had travelled in there with the horses, communicating with Jan when they had to via a baby alarm that Gerry had rigged up.

Inside, she was glad to see that the three horses were relaxed.

None of them had sweated up and they all looked comparatively docile.

'Well done, boys,' she said, giving each of them a quick rub on the nose. She lingered for a moment with Russian Eagle, fondling his big, floppy lower lip while she stroked his neck. 'Do your best today, boy. I'll tell that cocky jockey not to use his stick at all, then with luck he won't use it much.'

Eagle nodded, as if he approved of the plan.

Jan let herself out and jumped down. 'He's looking fine, Bernie. If you stick around for a while, I'll get him off and you can help groom him,' she teased.

'I wouldn't know how to do that,' Bernie protested.

'Don't you worry, I'll teach you; it's part of my new scheme for owner participation.'

'I've got a couple of other things to do,' Bernie snapped and turned sharply to walk off towards the trade stands before Jan could push him into staying and getting his hands dirty.

'How did you get on with the other horses?' Bernie asked later, after the first two had both finished their races.

'Didn't you see?' Jan asked.

'No, I hadn't got a horse running; I wasn't interested. I was in the car, watching the football on telly.'

'Neither of them troubled the judges today, I'm afraid.'

'Who was riding them.'

'Billy Hanks, of course.'

'Oh well. There you are. That little bugger doesn't know how to ride a finish.'

'You think so, do you? Well, he managed to ride the most winners in the whole Midlands area last season, so he must have got something right.'

'This bloke I've got today,' Bernie said excitedly, 'I went to watch him ride before I asked him, obviously, and he lent me some videos so I could see more. He really understands a horse and how to get the best out of it.'

'By knocking seven bells out of it, I hear. If I see him use his stick too much, I'll draw it to the attention of the stewards. I don't like having my horses bullied.'

'Jan,' Bernie said as if he were talking to a child, 'he's not your horse; he's mine.'

'Listen, Bernie; any horse in my charge I treat as my own, and I'll be mightily pissed off if this jockey of yours does any kind of damage to Eagle, OK?'

Not trusting herself to say more, Jan turned and walked as briskly as she could towards the parade ring, where Annabel had taken Russian Eagle.

Several horses were already striding around the small ring and Jan stopped for a moment to lean against the rail and look at them. There was one long-stepping, rangy individual with the yellow initials VG appliquéd on his navy sheet. Jan assumed this was Treble Up, though she'd never seen the horse before. She waited for the groom to walk by and checked the number on her arm. He was definitely Virginia's superstar, but there was no sign of the trainer. Jan guessed she was saddling other horses for more important races at a National Hunt course somewhere.

Looking round, she saw Annabel approaching with Eagle and made her way round to walk into the ring with them. While Annabel carried on leading the horse round the perimeter, Treble Up's groom whipped off his sheet and gave Jan her first proper view of the horse. Jan stood in the centre of the ring and tried to make an unbiased comparison between Eagle and Virginia's runner.

From their conformation, they were very different animals. Undoubtedly, over two miles, Treble Up would have had the advantage, although Eagle's sound jumping would be a big help. On a three-mile course like today's, she thought Eagle probably had the edge, but the records confirmed that Virginia's horse stayed as well. In truth, Jan knew that it was too hard to call here in the paddock and the question could only be answered out on the track.

She was joined now by a somewhat subdued Bernie, who had come strutting into the ring with his ungainly, unbalanced stride, and stood six feet away from her. He didn't speak until the jockeys began to spill into the ring, a sudden flurry of colour among the drab olive and khaki waxed jackets of the race goers.

Roger Williams walked over to them and placed himself tactfully between herself and Bernie. He was fairly tall and very skinny, with a thin, beaky nose and useful long arms. He turned to Jan and lifted both eyebrows for his instructions.

Jan knew Bernie had already briefed him and she took in the jockey's self-satisfied smirk. She fixed him with her steeliest glare and was glad to see him quail a bit.

'This horse stands right off and jumps big, so don't fiddle with him at the fences. Keep in touch with the leaders, but don't produce him until you've jumped the third last. Ride him out with hands and heels because if he comes back with a single welt on his arse I'll have your guts for garters. All right?' She gave him a quick cold smile.

'Sure,' the jockey said.

'You do as I said', Bernie chipped in from the other side, 'and I've told you what happens.' He nodded meaningfully.

'OK, Mr Sutcliffe.'

'Go and mount up,' Jan said. She didn't want a stand-up row in the paddock about how the race should be ridden.

Annabel drew up with Eagle and Jan legged the lanky jockey up into the saddle. The last jockey to mount – typically, Jan thought – was Harry Gilbert, an arrogant nineteen-year-old with long blond curls that dangled from under his helmet.

Jan drew in a deep breath. It would feel very good indeed, she thought, to beat him and Virginia Gilbert's hotpot.

Jan couldn't face watching the race with Bernie. She managed to slip away into the crowd as he walked down towards the winning post. She would just have to think up an excuse after the race was over.

As the runners reached the start, at the most distant point on the course, she found herself standing beside Colonel Gilbert.

'Hello, Jan,' he nodded while a smile creased his red cheeks. 'Your chap's looking nice.'

'Thanks. So's yours. The bookies seem to think a lot of him, too; hardly any of them will take money for him. Ours is only fives.'

'I know; I've just had a tenner's worth.'

'Gosh, didn't you back yours?'

'Not mine, Jan. I can assure you. Ginny runs an autonomous operation.'

'She's not here today, though?'

'No. She's got a couple of runners at Sandown.'

'Bit more important than here, then.'

'Who's to say?' Colonel Gilbert looked at her with a warm smile in his bright blue eyes. 'How's the licence application coming on?'

'I've just sent in a fresh one,' Jan said. 'I've got everything sorted in the yard now, though I had a bit a trouble finding a backer until Mr Carey very kindly said he would do it.'

'He'll be a good chap to have behind you. He's very careful, I know, but once he's committed, he won't let you down. Ah, I see they're off,' he said, raising his binoculars.

Taking a deep breath, Jan did the same.

For the first mile of the race, Treble Up took the lead; Jan knew he was a front runner and she'd been expecting him to go on. Roger and Russian Eagle lay towards the back of a closely bunched field. As they thundered past the post for the first time, with two full circuits to go, Eagle looked perfectly comfortable.

Out in the country on the far side the field began to get strung out, leaving a cluster of six horses at the front; Eagle was the last of this bunch and Jan felt quite happy about his position.

They came round a long, left-handed bend and passed the post for the second time. Treble Up was still leading, but two others had moved up beside him. Jan noticed that Harry Gilbert was beginning to bounce around on his saddle. Heading for the fence going away from the crowd, she saw his elbows come up like a pair of duck's wings and his hand reach for the sky as they cleared it.

'Oh dear,' Colonel Gilbert murmured beside Jan. 'Harry must be getting tired. I didn't think he was fit enough to ride a race, but he insisted.'

'The horse is going all right, though,' Jan said politely.

'He's not getting a lot of help, I'm afraid. Your horse looks cool as a cucumber. Why have you got that man from Devon riding him?'

'The owner wanted him and was a bit definite about it.'

'Oh, well; so far so good.'

They carried on watching in silence as the order at the front end of the field changed half a mile from home. The two horses who had been tracking Treble Up passed him and ran on strongly to the fence before the long, left-handed curve that would bring them back again to the home straight. Five lengths behind them, Russian Eagle overtook Treble Up. He put in a magnificent jump that left him in third place, two lengths ahead of Virginia's hot shot, but still behind another bay and a well-backed grey called Melon Tree.

Coming round the curve, with a jump on the apex, Eagle was beginning to close the gap to the two leaders. Jan clutched her binoculars like a vice, clenched her teeth and was scarcely aware of breathing as her horse gained ground inch by inch. Behind him, Treble Up was flagging and beginning to look like an also ran.

Roger Williams, old hand that he was, knew perfectly well how to ride a finish without using his stick, but he couldn't help waving it like a bandmaster beating time behind his back, and the horse was responding to the driving rhythm of his body.

At the penultimate fence, Eagle landed a length behind the leaders.

At the last, he was in the air as the two in front touched down. Jan thanked God that he was on the outside, where the ground was slightly higher and the going faster.

Two strides after the fence, Roger Williams cracked his whip down on Eagle's quarters. The big horse stretched his neck and visibly quickened.

The crowd roared; Jan screamed.

Eagle surged past the other bay and crossed the line nose to nose with Melon Tree.

'Russian Eagle and Melon Tree have gone past together,' the commentator said with irritating calmness, while Jan seethed with frustration. From where she was standing, twenty yards from the post, she just couldn't see which horse had clinched it.

She closed her eyes and waited for the announcement of the judges' decision.

'First, Melon Tree; second, Russian Eagle. The third horse . . .'

Jan clenched her fists.

Didn't these people know how much it mattered for Eagle to win?

She sighed. They didn't. Why should they? And, anyway, he hadn't.

But even if Eddie wasn't going to ride the horse at Aintree, Jan was determined to get Eagle there, if only to show that she could keep her part of the bargain.

She felt a moment's anxiety when she wondered what Bernie would say, coming second again by such a tiny margin. She had no complaints about Roger Williams's riding, though she didn't doubt that Bernie would find something to grumble about.

She decided she didn't give a damn. The horse had run superbly; perhaps he could have done with a couple more furlongs, but considering Melon Tree's form she was happy enough.

She wasn't sorry that Treble Up's connections had the ignominy of seeing their hotpot favourite coming home a distant fifth. At least the colonel had had the good sense not to back a horse ridden by his younger son.

'Bad luck, Jan,' he said with genuine feeling.

'Thanks.' Jan smiled wryly with a philosophical shrug of her shoulders, before setting off through the crowds to the course. She ducked under the rope which edged the track and, to her surprise, saw Bernie was already out there, walking with short angry strides towards his horse.

Eagle and Roger had just pulled up and turned to come back. Jan caught up with Bernie.

'That was a shame,' she said. 'We ran him bloody close.'

Bernie turned with his small eyes blazing. 'Jan, I'm sick of him coming sodding second!'

'Bernie, he ran a superb race and beat a lot of nice horses!'

'Next time, I want him to win, so just you make sure you find the right race.'

Jan sighed, though she knew it wasn't worth arguing. 'Bernie, I don't have that much choice. There are good horses in all these Opens.'

Eagle and Roger had reached them. Before Jan could stop him, Bernie caught hold of the reins. 'What the hell were you doing? I thought you said you'd make sure you'd get him there.'

'Mr Sutcliffe, I said I'd do everything I knew to get him there and I did, but that Melon Tree is a hell of a good horse.'

'You're all full of crap, you people!' Bernie said disgustedly and, to Jan's relief, let go of the reins. He took a last look at the jockey, glared at Jan and marched off the course.

Jan took a deep breath and reached up to take Eagle's rein.

'Well done, boy,' she said giving the big horse a vigorous pat on the neck. It was damp with sweat and his flanks were still heaving, but, although he'd had a hard race, he didn't seem at all distressed.

As she led him back towards the paddock, she looked up at Roger Williams. 'By the way, I saw that last crack you gave him, but as it was only one I'll let you off.'

The jockey grinned at her. 'I had to focus his mind on the job.'

'You did well. Never mind Bernie.'

Annabel and the two boys joined them. She led Eagle into the paddock and the slot marked 'Second'. Roger Williams jumped down and Jan quickly untacked the horse, while Darren flung a sweat rug over his back.

When they reached the lorry, Jan handed the rope to Darren

and filled a bucket with warm water from an old milk churn in the box. She put it in front of Russian Eagle, who lowered his head and thirstily sucked up a few pints in as many seconds.

'Oh my God!' Bernie suddenly wailed behind her.

Jan hadn't realized he was there. She looked round and saw him gazing in horror at the horse's head, where a tiny drop of blood had appeared in one of his nostrils.

Jan refused to panic. She'd had several horses who bled a little after a hard race, when the exertion and the consequent blood pressure caused a small vein in the upper nostril to burst. Sometimes it didn't mean anything and until now she'd never seen a sign of it in Eagle.

She was about to reassure Bernie that a small show of blood was probably nothing to worry about, when it suddenly occurred to her that it might be useful to let him worry.

'Oh, hell,' she said, sucking her teeth as she leaned down to take a closer look. 'He must have burst a vessel.'

'I knew it!' Bernie groaned. 'I knew there was something the matter with him! I've been told about this bleeding. One of my friends – he had a horse that did this. It ended up totally knackered; he had to give it away for nothing,' he said, and his former pride in the horse turned instantly to disparagement.

'Relax, Bernie,' Jan said, sensing that Bernie's horse-owning friend, whoever he was, had already done what she was trying to do. 'Lots of horses occasionally bleed a little; it may not mean a thing, so don't do anything hasty.'

'Oh, I know you'd like me to keep the horse and carry on coughing up a hundred and fifty quid a week for a dodgy animal that'll break down any minute. No thanks.'

'Just wait and let the vet have a look at him,' Jan pleaded, while the others looked on silently.

'He's just come a strong second in a very good race, too,' Annabel said.

To Jan's dismay, Bernie seemed to waver a minute at Annabel's intervention. She shot her a quick glance, and Annabel made a guilty face, realizing she'd over-egged the pudding.

Bernie straightened his back and turned away for a moment. 'All right. We'll see what the vet says,' he said, breathing deeply.

He took one last disgusted look at his horse. The thin trickle of blood had reached the end of the animal's nose. He shook his head hopelessly before he turned to Annabel. 'Am I seeing you later, or what?'

Jan watched Annabel's reaction.

'Of course,' Annabel said brightly. 'That'd be great.'

Bernie looked stunned for a moment. Jan guessed that, despite his thick skin, he'd been prepared for Annabel's rejection.

'Oh, right then. I'll pick you up from your place, about half-seven.' Bernie smirked triumphantly. He took a last look at his horse and walked from the lorry park to get his car.

Jan turned to Annabel. 'Well, that's your evening sorted,' she said sarcastically.

When the vet came in two days later, Jan told him about the slight bleed in Russian Eagle's nose and asked him to take a look at the horse.

He agreed with Jan's view that there was probably nothing much to worry about, but said that in the circumstances he would come again at the end of the week and talk to Bernie.

As they watched him drive away, Jan asked Annabel how Saturday evening with Bernie had gone.

'Pretty awful, but I think I may have made a bit of progress.'

'About what?'

'Wait and see.'

20

Over the next few days Jan had no runners, but on Saturday she had three going to a point-to-point on a picturesque meadow fringed with spiky topped willows on the far bank of the River Severn, near Tewkesbury.

Her best hope for the day was Dingle Bay, with Billy Hanks riding, while Eddie was on board Rhythm Stick, one of Frank Jellard's horses. On the way there, she felt that any one of the horses could win.

By the end of the afternoon, although one had pulled up, Eddie had come a respectable third and Dingle Bay had won for the second time that season.

Eamon Fallon had turned up unexpectedly a minute before the 'off' was called for Dingle Bay's race and he'd yelled himself hoarse beside Jan.

At the end of it, he hugged her, went off to the bookies and came back with two hundred pounds in a bundle of notes, which he handed to Jan.

'I'm sorry, but that's all I've got for you. You'll have to sell the horse now, take out what I owe you and let me have whatever's left.'

'Oh, no!' Jan groaned. 'You said you were having problems, but I didn't know they were as bad as that.'

'Yes, well, nor did I until recently. But it seems I'm a little too trusting of people who don't merit it.'

'I'm really sorry, Eamon. I can't say I wasn't getting worried about the situation, but I've enjoyed training Dingle Bay for you.'

'Don't worry about me; I just don't want you to suffer because of it. You've done a grand job with the horse and you should be able to get a good price for him.'

'Wouldn't you rather I sent him to the spring sales?'

'I'd rather the job was done privately, if you don't mind. I'd want my share of it in cash.'

'It's funny how sometimes your judgement can be completely wrong,' Jan remarked to Annabel as they were going home in the lorry. 'Look at Eamon; the minute I saw him, I thought, "I'll have to watch him." You know what he's like – all talk, flash cars and leather jackets – and when he stopped paying me, I thought, "Right, wait for it, girl. There'll be a lorry up here any minute to collect the horse," and of course I wouldn't have let him leave the yard until the account was settled. But he really doesn't want me to lose out, and he's trusting me completely to sell the horse and give him what's left. It's made me feel quite guilty for doubting him.'

'No wonder the poor chap got so seriously fleeced by these other people, then, if he's that trusting.'

'He knows I've got the horse, so I suppose he thinks he hasn't got much choice. Even so, he won't get fleeced by me,' Jan said firmly. 'We'll find a really good buyer for him; all they've got to do is promise to keep him at Edge Farm,' she grinned.

'Toby might buy him. He's really been enjoying his pointing since he bought Gale Bird.'

'You mean he's been enjoying coming to the races to ogle you.'

'No,' Annabel said mildly. 'He's not like that. He understands.'

Jan wondered, but said nothing more on the subject for the moment.

'Or', Annabel went on thoughtfully, 'maybe I could persuade Bernie to buy Dingle Bay.'

When Jan got back to Edge Farm, Mary Pritchard was waiting for her in the caravan. Roz had reluctantly taken the day off to be a bridesmaid at the wedding of one of her many cousins, and

Jan's mother had volunteered to come over and look after the children.

'Thanks, Mum,' Jan said, picking up Matthew to give him a hug. 'How have they been?'

'They've been as good as gold. Ate all their dinner, and Megan helped me make a cake for their tea. But your young builder chap, Gerry, came up here in a bit of state. He said to tell you Mr Carey's had a heart attack and they've took him in an ambulance to the Nuffield in Cheltenham.'

'Oh my God!' Jan gasped. She was shocked. It had never occurred to her that Victor Carey was getting on in years. 'How bad is he?'

'Oh, he's not too bad, Gerry said. But they had to take him in to be sure.'

'So he's not dying?'

'No. Maybe you should telephone the hospital and find out.'

'I'll go and see him now,' Annabel said decisively. She phoned the hospital for directions and within five minutes her Golf was spurting down the drive.

Jan watched her go with mixed emotions, all negative.

Since she'd begun to have more dealings with Mr Carey, Jan had become fond of him. He didn't laugh very much, if ever, and he could be frustratingly pedantic, but in his quiet way he was enthusiastic, loyal and consistent, and Jan realized she would be very upset if an untimely illness suddenly removed him.

Annabel didn't come to see Jan on her way back from the hospital, but she phoned to say that Mr Carey seemed comfortable enough and he sent his warm regards to Jan and congratulations on Dingle Bay's win. He was also anxious to know if August Moon would be running the next Saturday, as planned.

'If he wants her to run, we'll make bloody sure she does,' Jan said. 'Actually, I think she's in with a good chance.'

For the next few days Jan prayed for Mr Carey and concentrated most of her attention on August Moon, Russian Eagle, Arrow Star and Derring Duke, who were all due to run the following weekend. But all the time at the back of her mind was the thought that poor old Mr Carey had suddenly proved to be as vulnerable as anyone else. The talk in the village was that no close family had come to see him and she felt sad that, rich as he was, he should be so alone in the world.

She found she couldn't even produce much enthusiasm when Toby's lawyers wrote to say that a local investigation agency had unearthed two more cases in which Harold and the Davieses appeared to have acted wrongly and that, once they had enough evidence, they would consider taking further action against him.

In the meantime, in the wider world and a mere ten miles away, the Cheltenham Festival was being held. For the first two days Jan brought a television down to the tack room, and both afternoons she and her staff were glued to it.

'Next year we'll be running horses there, just you wait!' Roz said.

Although Jan knew this was pie in the sky, she couldn't keep her own dreams in check. Watching some of the world's best steeplechasers in action, she was more impatient than ever to be granted her own licence.

At the beginning of the week she'd had a letter from the Jockey Club to confirm that the stewards would like to interview her on Monday, 15 April. That was nearly four weeks away! She didn't know how she would keep sane until then, but, at least the news from the hospital about Mr Carey was good; he was expected home by the weekend, albeit with a full-time nurse.

On Thursday, Gold Cup Day, Jan took herself off to Cheltenham and didn't allow herself to feel one iota of guilt.

As well as her vast estate, Annabel's great-aunt had left Major Halstead a large box at Cheltenham race course. But the major wasn't particularly interested in racing and allowed Annabel to use it for this one day's racing.

She had made a great effort to cater for all the staff from Edge

Farm as well as a few other friends. Jan was very appreciative, but after lunch in the box and watching the unpredictable cavalry charge of the Triumph Hurdle, she wasn't sure that she liked this way of watching the races. She felt cocooned in the private dining room with a small band of friends, when she should have been out mixing with the eclectic band of racing nuts, many from Ireland, who made the pilgrimage to Cheltenham every year and gave the festival its unique atmosphere.

The difficulty for Jan had been finding someone to look after the yard while they were all away. Eddie, with an air of great martyrdom, had offered to, so that everyone else could go. But Annabel was adamant that he must come too. In the end, once the morning work was over, Gerry and Jan's father had been press-ganged into minding the shop until Jan got back around six-thirty to do the feeding.

As the afternoon went on, Jan found herself spending more time looking down on the saddling boxes and the pre-parade ring. She watched one race on tiptoes on the lawn in front of the stands. She watched another from the box, but her favourite spot was alongside the railed enclosure reserved for owners and trainers. She was unashamedly fascinated by the famous faces she saw in there.

She couldn't deny that she longed to be there herself one day, chatting to an eager owner who had bought the kind of horse that could win a race like this. But she hardly dared to indulge her fantasies about what she might one day achieve at this, the supreme National Hunt meeting. She found herself looking at the highest quality jumping bloodstock in the world in a different light now that she felt she was within sight of competing with them herself.

Although she immersed herself in the run-up to the highlight of the festival, the Gold Cup, it was inevitable that she should relate more to the big amateur chase that was run later in the afternoon on the same course. The Christie's Foxhunters', though worth more and slightly more competitive, was run under similar

She told him what had to be done first and he didn't need much persuading to come up and price the job. Doing his best to overcome his embarrassment, he was still thanking her for the opportunity when Annabel came back from her discussion with the old man on the settle.

'I think I might have found a cottage already,' she said. 'Mr Carey seems to own half the village.'

Julie, earwigging beside them, nodded. 'He does, and Stanfield Court. He's a miserable old git, though,' she added under her breath.

'Well, he's very kindly offered me', she glanced at the piece of paper where she'd written the address, 'Number Two, Glebe Cottages.'

'That's a nice little place,' Julie said, 'but he'll want an arm and a leg.'

'Judging by the way he was looking at her,' Jan said, 'it's not her arms he's interested in.'

'Oh, he's all right like that,' the barmaid said. 'Just bloody stingy.'

'Will you come and look at it with me?' Annabel asked Jan. 'He says he'll go and get the key now if I want.'

A quarter of an hour later they were inspecting the cottage, which was freshly painted but hadn't been modernized in the previous twenty years. 'I expect I can manage without a Poggenpohl kitchen.' Annabel laughed and turned to Jan. 'Do you know, this is the first time in my life that I'll be living on my own? Apart from school, I've only been away from home for a short time when I went to London, and for a few months in a hall of residence at Bristol, before that all went wrong too,' she murmured.

'You've never told me what happened there,' Jan said quietly.

'I was on the rebound – a lecherous don. I was so gullible—.' Annabel shook her head. 'I suppose I was trying to get back at my father.' With an effort, she smiled. 'I don't want to start banging on about it now. I love this place.'

And within ten minutes she'd made up her mind to take the cottage.

As they drove down the deeply rutted track to the road, Jan spotted several pieces of broken fencing. 'They'd better start with replacing some of these knackered rails,' she said gloomily.

The Fox & Pheasant had been a pub since the seventeenth century and hadn't changed much since that time. When she saw the people in there – healthy Gloucestershire faces like her own – she guessed that most of them were descended from the men who'd used the inn for the last few hundred years.

A tall girl in her twenties with chubby cheeks, big breasts and spiky black hair was behind the bar when Jan and Annabel walked in. She gave Jan a quick, shrewd glance with her chocolate brown eyes. 'Hello, I'm Julie,' she said. 'You're the people moving into Edge Farm, aren't you?'

'She is,' Annabel disclaimed. 'I'm not, but I'll be helping out there and I'm looking for a cottage to rent in the village.'

'Oh well, you want to talk to him, then,' the barmaid nodded at a well-dressed, somewhat forbidding man sitting alone with his pewter mug on a settle in a dark corner of the pub.

'Thanks, I will.'

While Annabel walked over to talk to the unlikely looking landlord, Jan perched on a stool and told Julie that she needed a builder. A few minutes later she was being introduced to Gerry.

A local lad of twenty-five, Gerry was six foot three with a red face and hands like shovels, one of which he thrust forward shyly for Jan to shake.

'You're a builder, are you?' she asked.

'Joiner,' he mumbled. 'But I can do pretty much anything.'

'And you wouldn't try to stitch me up, just because I'm a woman?'

Gerry looked shocked at the thought. 'No – just the opposite, I should think, for someone as . . . someone like you.'

Jan smiled and wondered how he had been going to describe her. 'That's good, because once I've got my stables up, there's a whole house to build.'

conditions to the Aintree race Eddie had been so keen to win – until Bernie had jocked him off.

Eddie and Jan watched the race together, with Annabel and Roz.

'It's so sad you can't ride Eagle at Aintree,' Jan said. 'Look at this lot.' She nodded at the riders coming out onto the course to canter down to the start. Most of them looked very inexperienced compared to the professionals who rode six or more races every day.

'Good Lord!' Eddie said. 'Do *I* look that bad?'

'Not any more, you don't. You did when you first came out to ride last August, but there's not too much wrong with you now except your lack of experience.'

Eddie sighed. 'Well, I'm grateful to you for the few rides you've given me – I loved August Moon last week, but unless I get this ride back on Eagle by some bloody miracle, I don't think I'll be doing much next season.'

'Oh, Ed,' Annabel said, sounding disappointed, 'you can't give up after Jan's spent so much time on you; it wouldn't be fair to her. Anyway, maybe a miracle will turn up.'

'Yeah,' Eddie said gloomily, 'sure it will. I suppose Roger's riding him this Saturday?'

'We'll see,' Jan said. 'I haven't talked to Bernie about it yet. He hasn't even told me what he wants to do with the horse since we saw the vet last week.'

'What did the vet tell him?'

'Much the same as I had said. It might never happen again, or every so often, or it could get worse.'

'How did Bernie take it?' Eddie asked.

'He looked as if he'd just bought a car off me and found it hadn't got an engine.'

'Well,' Annabel said, 'you can ask him in a minute. I saw him earlier and invited him up to the box for a drink after this race.'

'Is he here, then? I wonder why he didn't tell me he was coming,' Jan said. 'It was nice of you to ask him up, though; you didn't have to on my account.'

'I didn't. I felt a bit sorry for him, actually; he's so pathetic, but at least he's behaved himself. I've been out twice with him now and at least he hasn't tried to pounce on me.'

'I'd knee him straight in the goolies if he tried it on me,' Jan said.

Eddie laughed. 'He's probably sussed that already.'

When he arrived, Bernie seemed subdued and somewhat overawed by Major Halstead's box.

'I asked if I could buy one of these,' he said wistfully. 'They just looked at me as if I was the poor relation and said they'd put my name on a waiting list, but they didn't foresee any coming vacant for a very long time. Someone usually has to die first, I'm told.'

'People do hang on to them,' Annabel said. 'My great-aunt took this one over from her father; it's one of the original boxes.'

Jan guessed that Eddie didn't want to talk to Bernie, given the grief Bernie's decision had caused him, so she decided to tackle Bernie head on.

'Look, Bernie, as you're here, I need to know if you definitely want Russian Eagle to run on Sunday.'

'I don't know. That vet of yours said he could easily burst another blood vessel.'

'Well, it's up to you. If you want him to run at Aintree, we need a win and we haven't got much time left. I could only get him entered for one more race after that.'

'I'll let you know tomorrow definitely.'

'And who's going to ride him?'

'It'll have to be your Billy Hanks, if I decide to run him.'

Jan looked at him. She would happily have throttled him, but she tried not to let it show. 'Make sure you ring me tomorrow then.'

Bernie went off to have a bet on the next race at the Tote counter along the corridor and Jan turned to Annabel, who was chatting to Eddie. 'Why do people have to be so bloody difficult!'

'Don't worry,' Annabel said. 'I'll talk to him about it tonight. I'm having dinner with him.'

'What?' Jan remonstrated. 'Again?'

'This'll be the very last time,' Annabel said enigmatically. 'I intend to make that clear.'

Eddie and Jan walked down to the paddock to look at the runners in the County Hurdle.

'What the hell do you think Annabel's up to? I'm sure she doesn't like Bernie, but she never wants to come out to dinner with me.'

Jan glanced at him. He looked hurt and mystified. 'I don't know,' she said truthfully, although she was forming a pretty good idea. 'Maybe she's doing it out of kindness.'

'It'd be kinder to tell him to get stuffed rather than build up his hopes. Mind you, he deserves it; he's a little shit the way he's messing around with Eagle!' Eddie shook his head in despair.

'I don't blame you for being miffed,' Jan said compassionately. 'I know you're fond of Annabel, but remember, she was quite hurt last time round even if it wasn't your fault. And she thinks you're into It-girls, whatever they are. Give her time.'

'I don't think I've got much hope there, really. I know she's not impressed by a chubby wallet like Bernie's, but I don't suppose she's interested in a total bankrupt either.'

'For a start, you're not a total bankrupt and, to be fair to her,' Jan said as they joined the crowd around the parade ring, 'I don't think she gives a damn about that sort of thing. Anyway, let's have a look at these horses if you want to win back some of the money you've lost.'

On their way back from the paddock, Jan ran almost face first into Virginia Gilbert. Unless she wanted to appear inexcusably rude in front of other people, Virginia had no choice but to say something, although the words had to be forced out between a pair of tight lips.

'Oh, hello, Jan. I gather we're going to meet at Aintree.'

'I'm looking forward to it,' Jan replied, with the most convincing smile she could muster.

Virginia glanced at Eddie, not without a gleam of interest, Jan noted. 'Are you riding?' she asked.

'If Jan thinks I'm good enough.' He gave a non-committal grin.

'I'm sure you'll be good enough for Jan,' Virginia said, lifting her beaky nose.

'Thanks,' Eddie laughed.

Virginia hurried on to catch up with the owners she was accompanying.

'Snotty cow,' Jan murmured.

'Now then, Jan. Don't sink to her level. Let's just hope Bernie doesn't screw it up.'

'He still won't let you ride, Eddie. You may as well accept it.' She glanced at him and caught him off guard. The bleakness in his eyes at the thought of losing his chance to win on Russian Eagle told her just how much it mattered to him, whatever the odds against him.

With Mr Carey's agreement, Jan asked Eddie if he would ride August Moon again at the following Sunday's point-to-point at a parkland course west of Hereford.

On the morning after Gold Cup Day, he was up at the yard early to ride out.

'Where's Annabel?' he asked, looking round as they tacked up.

'She phoned just now and asked me if she could come in late for once. After all she did for us yesterday, I couldn't say no, could I?'

'But', Eddie said, looking baffled, 'she never comes in late. What the hell has she been doing?'

'Relax, Eddie. I'm sure there's a good reason.'

'I dare say there is, but it's such a horrible thought.'

Jan smiled to herself; she guessed Eddie hated the idea that anyone, especially Bernie, might have made more progress with Annabel than he had.

When they came back with the first lot, Eddie offered to ride a second and help with the mucking out to make up for Annabel's absence. Later, after they'd all had breakfast, he still showed no signs of leaving.

'Look, Eddie,' Jan said, 'if you're going to hang around here all morning, you might as well do something useful. The bales in the hay store need restacking. You can use these.' She threw a pair of leather gloves at him.

He caught them with a grin. 'I suppose they are a bit heavy for you girls.'

Over the next hour Jan saw Eddie glance several times down the track towards the lane. She was as intrigued as Eddie to know why Annabel was late, but, unlike him, she was absolutely certain that a night of passion with Bernie Sutcliffe was not the reason.

When at last the black Golf turned off the road, Eddie was the first to look up and start walking towards the car park.

Jan enjoyed a drama and didn't want to miss anything. She followed quickly and was standing beside Eddie as Annabel pulled up. They waited while she got out and leaned back in to the car to pick up a folder. She closed the door and stood looking at them for a moment with a small, triumphant smile on her face.

'Annabel?' Jan said suspiciously. 'What have you done?'

'I've done the dirty deed with Bernie,' she said.

'What?' Eddie and Jan yelled together.

Annabel laughed, then put on a face of affronted disgust. 'God, no; not that! As if I could!'

'Well then,' Eddie asked with a tremble in his voice, 'what dirty deed have you done?'

'I've persuaded him to buy Dingle Bay!' Annabel resumed her victorious look and started walking towards the yard, while Eddie and Jan followed.

'Oh,' said Jan, feeling a little let down. 'That's great, but why did it take all night?'

'It didn't, but I arranged to meet him this morning at my solicitors in Cheltenham to get it all agreed in writing.' She patted the folder she was carrying.

Jan looked quizzically at her. 'You didn't have to do that. That's my job. Eamon only gave me the authority to deal with it.'

'Yes, of course, you'll have to sign your side of things and you'll get the money for Dingle, but it was the other half of the deal that I really wanted to tie up.'

'What other half of the deal?' Jan asked, impatient at Annabel's deliberate vagueness.

'Basically, I've bought Dingle Bay, so I'll be laying for him, and I've passed him on to Bernie in a straight swap for Russian Eagle.'

Eddie and Jan both stopped dead in their tracks. Annabel turned to see their reaction.

Eddie looked at her in puzzled astonishment, with his chest heaving. 'Jesus! That's fantastic!' he laughed.

Jan smiled and shook her head. 'But where did you get the money?'

'Do you remember, I told you, I've always had that trust my great-aunt set up for me and Charley when she left the estate to Dad? I'll have to persuade the trustees to cough up. I've made very few demands on it, though, and I don't think I'll have too much trouble but, so you don't have to wait for the money, I've organized a loan from my bank. And you can take his training fees out of my wages.'

'Are you sure you want to do this, though?'

'Of course I am. Eagle's been my favourite since he arrived at Stonewall. I know he'll win more races and I think he'll be a bloody good investment – at least, that's what I'll tell the trustees,' she added with a grin. 'So you'd better make sure he does.'

'Bel, you devious little cow! I thought you might be up to something like that,' Jan said. 'But to persuade him to swap Eagle for Dingle Bay – that was brilliant!'

'I suddenly thought of it yesterday when he came up to the box at Cheltenham, and I was pretty sure he'd go for it. He wouldn't have to part with any money and he would save face. I knew he was terrified of hanging on to Eagle, thinking he might burst another blood vessel any minute, but he didn't want to seem too wimpish about it. This way, he's got a winning horse without any question mark over it.'

'Bel,' Eddie asked carefully, 'if what you're now saying is that you own Eagle, what are your plans for him?'

'I thought, if he qualifies, I'd ask Roger Williams to ride him in the Foxhunters' for me,' she said, deadpan.

Eddie stared at her. A muscle in his jaw twitched. He looked as of he were about to say something very angry, changed his mind and walked on past Annabel, towards the tack room.

Annabel looked after him, waiting until he had almost disappeared through the door. 'Eddie,' she laughed. 'I've changed my mind. I want you to ride him.'

'For fuck's sake!' Eddie spun round. 'Don't do that to me!' He laughed. 'I didn't think you had it in you to be that nasty.'

'Of course I wouldn't have bought the horse if I hadn't known how desperate you were to ride him, though, as a matter of fact, it was your mother's idea.'

'My mother's?' Eddie said in astonishment.

'She was up here a few weeks ago,' Jan said. 'I promised not to tell you, but I didn't know she'd been to see Bel, too. Anyway, you'd better get your act together, now you've got two rides on Sunday. I just hope you're bloody well up to it.'

Jan rang Mr Carey's house next morning. Julie's mother, who cleaned for him, answered the phone and told her that Mr Carey was home from hospital. She went off for a few minutes before coming back to tell Jan that he would like to see her if she could call round early that evening.

Jan took a couple of her maidens to run at a local meeting in the afternoon. Although she came back empty-handed, both had run as well as she could have hoped and she wasn't too disappointed. When she went to Mr Carey's, she was shown up to his bedroom by an efficient but taciturn nurse. It was the first time

Jan had seen him since his heart attack and she was shocked by the change in him. He was propped up against a bank of white pillows on a large, Victorian mahogany bed. His face seemed to have collapsed into a waxy mask of pale, sagging folds. His voice was thin and breathy, but his pale blue eyes were as sharp as ever beneath their hooded brows.

He brushed aside her enquiries about his health. 'Tell me how you got on today.'

She gave him a short account of both horses' performance.

He knew which horses she was talking about and, although they weren't his, he understood exactly what she was saying. 'You're right not to be too put out,' he said. 'As a National Hunt trainer, you'd be doing very well to get one in five of your runners first past the post. Of course, you must always go out to win, but take the losers in your stride.'

'August Moon's definitely going tomorrow in the confined race, with Eddie Sullivan on board, as you agreed. He's riding Russian Eagle in the Open, too.'

'Good,' Mr Carey nodded faintly. 'I'm so pleased with the way the mare's going, I wonder if we mightn't try racing her under rules again next season?'

Jan was doubtful. 'She hasn't won an Open yet and she's getting a bit long in the tooth, though I suppose we might find a race that suits her. If she were mine, I think I'd run her between the flags for another year and then maybe send her to stud.'

'You could be right. Anyway, I'm looking forward very much to hearing how she runs tomorrow. Would you be kind enough to come in and tell me afterwards? Bring the children if you can't find a minder. The nurse will give them some tea and cake if I ask her.'

'I'll do that, Mr Carey. Would you like me to put something on August Moon for you tomorrow, if the odds aren't too bad?'

'Oh no, I never bet. For me, the sport is between the horses, not the bookmakers and the punters.'

The grey stone mansion and its ancient parkland, where the West Hereford Harriers' meeting was being held, lay under a clear, blue sky. It was a bright day, recalling the recent passing of winter with a nip in the breeze, which ruffled the budding branches of the trees around the course.

Jan responded to the change in the weather like a lark on the wing. Everything was on course with her licence application; she had recovered the debt she was owed by Eamon. Annabel was now an owner, as well as head groom, and had persuaded one of her brothers to pay for half of Russian Eagle and split the training fees. Eddie once again had the ride on him and they still had two more chances to win an open point-to-point to qualify the horse for the big race at Aintree.

Jan drove into the area roped off for lorries and managed to park beneath the broad spreading branches of a massive old oak. They had four runners on board and Billy Hanks was riding the two that Eddie wasn't.

Jan walked the course with both of them. She knew it well and it was one of her favourites. It was all on permanent pasture, but the ground could sometimes be a little boggy just before the fence on one of the bottom corners. Jan and her jockeys inspected the ground there carefully and decided the only route to take was on the inside.

Walking back to the lorry, they looked up between the parkland oaks and across the sweep of sheep-grazed turf, broken only by the white timber running rails and the big, solid birch fences, to where a large crowd was gathering below the high terraces in front of the house.

'This is such a beautiful course. I'd love to win here,' Eddie said.

Billy laughed. 'You soppy bugger! It don't matter what the bloody course looks like so long as you win.'

But Jan understood. 'I know what you mean, Eddie. So you go for it!'

Jan thought it was perfectly possible for Eddie to score a double that day. She hadn't said so and, to her surprise, Eddie hadn't mentioned it either, although everyone else in the yard had been talking about the possibility.

An hour later she legged him up on August Moon wearing Mr Carey's colours of pink and grey stripes. Watching them leave the parade ring, she thought he had just the right balance of fear and confidence to ride at his best. As the runners were going down to the start, Jan and Annabel walked across to the other side of the track, from where they could see every fence.

She was glad Annabel was with her and watched calmly as the race started. She felt very proud of Eddie and a little pleased with herself at the way he rode the mare. He was presenting her correctly at every fence and letting her travel quietly between them. He was lying comfortably within the front half of the field of twelve and cruising when they came past the post at the start of the final circuit.

The runners dropped down the slope towards the far corner, all still in contention, in a fast moving splash of colour against a backdrop of green and brown.

Jan peered through her binoculars, hoping Eddie had room to take the short way across the corner again. There were five horses abreast and Jan saw with a sudden jerk in her guts that Eddie was cutting the corner too tightly coming to the fence. As they got to it, the horse nearest him wasn't leaving him room to get a line on the obstacle. A second later, August Moon's head popped up, above the side of the wing. The mare's front legs came over, leaving her back end stranded. Eddie shot from the saddle and landed four or five yards outside the wing.

Jan gasped and trained her glasses on the pink and grey bundle until it moved and slowly stood up. She flicked her attention back to the horse, which had scrambled backwards off the wing and was trotting around aimlessly behind the fence.

The St John's ambulance was already bouncing down the far side of the track to where Eddie was limping towards them.

Jan looked at Annabel. 'What a cock up! Eh? At least they're both still standing. If I get the horse, can you check Eddie?'

'He'll be all right. They'll look after him. I'll come with you.'

The two women set of at a run diagonally across the course. As they ran, they saw a public-spirited spectator had already caught hold of the mare's reins and walked her off the course. August Moon seemed to have calmed down after the first confusion of hitting the wing and losing her jockey and had put her head down to sample some of the lush grass that grew in that part of the park.

'Get her head up!' Jan panted pointlessly into the breeze, too far away to be heard.

'At least someone's caught her,' Annabel puffed back. 'In fact, I think I'm going to walk.'

Jan slowed as well and they carried on at a brisk stride down to the corner of the track. As they reached it, the ambulance drove up and stopped. Eddie climbed out.

'How is she?' he asked, peering at August Moon.

'I haven't had a look at her yet,' Jan said. 'But she seems OK.' She turned to the man who had caught the horse. 'Thanks very much; that's saved us a lot of running about.'

'No problem,' he answered with a touch of self-importance. 'She didn't mind being caught. She's a lovely animal.' He looked at Eddie. 'You should talk to the stewards about that fella who didn't let you back in.'

Eddie shook his head wearily. 'No. It was my fault; I went too far inside to get off that patch of soft ground. He just carried on on his own line.'

Jan nodded. 'I wish he wasn't right, but I'm afraid he is. OK, Eddie, you might as well get a lift in the ambulance and get checked over. Does anything hurt?'

'Only my pride.'

'Better get checked anyway. Bel and I will walk the horse up. See you back at the lorry.'

There was one more race before the Open. Jan didn't have a runner in it and as Eddie had returned from the St John's ambulance, having been thoroughly checked over, he sat with her in the cab of the lorry, silent for the most part, chewing gum and trying to keep up his resolve.

Jan had brought some tea in a flask and poured a cup for him.

'Relax, Eddie. Just remember, though I want you to win very much, in the end it's only a horse race and, whatever happens, it isn't a matter of life and death.'

'Maybe,' he grunted, 'but it could make the difference between a comfortable life and a pretty uncertain one.'

'Eddie, the last thing I want to do is sound negative but, while I really think you could win today, the Foxhunters' is a much bigger challenge. I know it means a hell of a lot to you to win it, but you've got to be prepared for the fact that you might not.'

'I've made contingency plans in case I don't, but the last thing I want to do is to carry them out.'

'Why, what are they?'

'As I have no intention of losing today or on Thursday week, there's no point in telling you. I shouldn't even have mentioned there was another option.'

Jan sighed. It had occurred to her that she'd been trying to persuade a jockey that he might not win, when she'd always believed that going out with total self-belief was an essential tool in a jockey's armoury. 'OK. Have it your own way. Go out and win! You know you can do it.'

And she pointed out to Eddie that he had the psychological advantage: of the nine runners, three had already been beaten by Eagle that season and he hadn't met the others before.

Russian Eagle looked magnificent in the paddock and caught a lot of eyes. As a result of his performance against Melon Tree at Banbury, he was a strong favourite with the bookies.

Jan legged Eddie up into the saddle, where he sat limply, pale and nervous in Annabel's colours of blue and green hoops.

'Pull yourself together, Eddie, for God's sake,' Jan said quietly. She didn't want to show him up in front of the other jockeys.

'I'll be all right, Jan. Once we're off.'

'Just ride him like you rode Moon until you fell off. Keep in touch, watch that corner this time and start pushing him along three from home.'

Eddie nodded, squeezed Eagle's flanks and steered him towards the gate out onto the course.

Jan turned to Annabel. 'I suppose I'll have to watch this race with you too, now you're the owner.'

'I think you should,' Annabel grinned. 'Poor Eddie looks pretty ghastly, doesn't he?'

'He'll be OK.'

'But Eagle looks great!' Annabel said proudly.

'That's because his groom won't leave him alone and stop fussing over him.' Jan laughed.

They walked across the course to the same spot where they had watched August Moon's race and Darren tagged along too.

'My God,' Annabel said, 'now I own this horse, I'm beginning to realize how terrifying it is. I'm shaking like a leaf!'

Jan, too, found her heart thumping more than normal before a race, simply because it meant so much to Eddie. She gazed through her binoculars at Eagle standing quietly on one side, having his girth checked. While the others milled around, he looked as if he held their fidgeting in disdain. When the starter called them in, Eddie moved him forward and they set off from an ideal spot in the middle of the track. The nine runners went off at a good crack and took the first fence in a bunch, but by the third they'd begun to get strung out as the pace had its effect.

'What d'you think, boss?' Darren squeaked with excitement, as the field came past the winning post for the first time.

'I think there's another circuit to go, but Eagle looks happy enough.'

'Can I take him to Aintree if he wins today?'

Annabel laughed. 'Do you think he'll win, then?'

'Course I do! I've put twenty quid on.'

Jan's instincts were to give him a good rollocking there and then. Fourteen-year-old boys putting on bets like that could be habit forming, but for the moment she decided to defer the lecture. 'Then he'd bloody well better win, hadn't he?' she muttered.

Two minutes later Eagle flew over the last fence. Jan held her breath until she saw just how far he was in front of the next horse. She let it out again with a rush when she saw they had a clear five-length advantage. She had no doubts about Eagle's ability to hold on and fight off any challenge that might be launched.

Annabel grabbed her by the arm when they saw Eddie give the horse one quick slap across its quarters, just as Roger Williams had done two weeks before, and Eagle stretched a little more. By the time he reached the post he was seven lengths clear of the second and Darren, who'd shouted himself voiceless on the run in, was trembling so much Jan thought he would do himself damage.

'Darren,' she said, a little hoarse from her own vocal exertions, 'pull yourself together, lad. You've got to get down and lead that horse in for Bel.'

He looked at her, puzzled, as if he'd just come out of a dream, then his face broke into a huge smile as he turned to Annabel. 'Bloody hell, Bel! He's done it!'

'He sure has,' Annabel agreed joyfully. 'Now go and get him, you silly little monkey.'

She and Jan followed closely behind as he ran to the course, ducked under the rails and raced up the track to where Eddie had finally pulled up and was trotting back towards the paddock.

They reached him just before Darren led the horse off the course.

Jan dabbed a small tear from the corner of her eye and gave Eddie the biggest smile her face could muster. 'Eddie! I'm so proud of you! And you too, old boy,' she added, giving Eagle a hug. 'I told you you could do it!'

Eddie was breathless and beaming so broadly he could hardly speak. 'Thanks, Jan,' he managed. 'You're a star.' He turned to Annabel, who like Jan was trying to fight back the tears. 'Bel, I don't know what made you buy this horse, but thank God you did! I'm really, really grateful.'

'Don't thank me, Eddie,' she replied through her laughter. 'You were pretty bloody brilliant yourself!'

Jan persuaded everyone to postpone any celebration and merry-making until after they'd got back with the horses. She let Darren run off and find the bookie, who now owed him sixty pounds for his two-to-one bet, while she washed Eagle down, and checked for any signs of bleeding.

'He's clear,' she told Annabel, who was holding her horse's head.

'Thank God!' she said. 'You were worried he mightn't be, weren't you?'

'It was always possible that it could happen again.'

'But you thought he might, didn't you?' Eddie asked.

'I was worried,' Jan admitted. 'I've been around horses long enough to know that it doesn't take much to make them go wrong. If you've had a warning like that, you've got to take it seriously. In a way, Bernie was half-right to get so panicky – thank God he did, though,' she added with a laugh.

'And thank God for Bel. It's just too bloody fantastic. Thanks to her I got the ride back.' He shook his head. 'And there I was, thinking she'd gone off to bed with Bernie on Gold Cup Day!'

'As if I could!' Annabel protested.

'I did tell you at the time it was absolutely out of the question,' Jan reminded him. 'But don't forget I can see Bernie through a woman's eyes and I can tell you, it's not a pretty sight!'

On the way home, Jan decided that one of the first people she should see was Victor Carey. She hoped he would be well enough to appreciate the yard's success that day and as soon as she was happy that Eagle and the other horses were settled in for the night, she asked Roz to keep an eye on the children for twenty minutes while she drove down to Stanfield Court.

When she walked into his large bedroom, Mr Carey's wrinkled

features were lit by a single forty-watt bulb that shone beneath a tasselled lampshade on the far side of the room. Jan strained to see him as he listened intently to her description of the day's races.

'I can't tell you how thrilled I am you've had a win with Russian Eagle,' he said between stertorous breaths. 'And what a disappointment for Edward with Moony.'

'At least he wasn't hurt, nor was the horse. They'll have another race next week.'

'I'll look forward to that,' Mr Carey wheezed. 'And thank you so much.'

He closed his eyes and appeared to sink a little deeper into his pillows.

'Thanks, Mr Carey. Goodnight, then,' Jan said and tiptoed from the room.

The champagne was already chilled and waiting when Jan arrived back at Edge Farm. No cheap substitutes for Annabel, Jan thought with a smile. In an hour of celebration, Jan was surprised to see just how much everyone in the yard had wanted Eddie to win this race and go on to Aintree with Eagle. When Eddie suggested they go out to dinner, Jan wanted to say no, but Roz leaped in.

'You've *gotta* go, Jan. Don't worry, I'll look after the kids. You and Eddie really deserve it, and Annabel's the owner, so she's gotta go too!'

Jan would happily have stayed at home. For her, seeing the horse cross the line first was enough celebration in its own right, but she recognized that having a party with owners and jockeys was part of the job and she'd better get used to it.

News of Russian Eagle's success had already reached the Fox & Pheasant, so there was much rejoicing over Jan's win by the regulars who liked to follow local horses. Eddie had become a popular person in the pub and the pair of them were congratulated with genuine warmth.

Jan felt that, whatever difficulties she had yet to conquer to get her licence, she had the great comfort of knowing she'd been accepted here in the village. But at midnight she asked Eddie if he would drop her back at the caravan.

'It's been a great day, Eddie, but I'm absolutely cream-crackered. I started at six and I'm up again at six tomorrow.'

'Of course,' he said. 'I shouldn't have made you come.'

'I'm glad I did, though,' Jan said as they were driving up the lane back to the yard. 'And I hope it will be the first of many for you on Eagle.'

Eddie inclined his head. 'So do I and the next one's the big one! Do you know, I still find it extraordinary that all this started from my seeing a little girl about to be kicked by a mad horse at Doncaster Sales last May.'

'I sometimes think all our lives are shaped by a chain of coincidence and chance which we can't control, however much we think we're in command.'

'Do you?' Eddie said, surprised. 'So do I, as it happens, but I had the firm impression that you were very much a believer in being master of one's own destiny.'

'An individual can only do so much. Of course, you mustn't ignore the chances you're offered, but in the end you need a bit of luck, or help from God, depending on your point of view.'

'He was on our side today, eh, Jan?'

'Yeah,' she smiled. 'It looked like it.'

Eddie dropped her at the hard standing and waited there for a moment while she walked up to the caravan.

21

Three weeks after Jan had sent in her second application, the same Jockey Club inspector came to check her premises again. This time he arrived knowing that she had already sent out a flurry of winning pointers from the yard.

But, as Jan had anticipated, he first made a beeline for the gates and fences. Satisfied with these, he turned his attention to the buildings, approved the new treatment Gerry had given them and complimented Jan on the state of her grass gallop.

'We're lucky with that,' she said. 'The soil's pretty shallow here and water runs off down the hill without really soaking in, so provided we don't go on it straight after rain, it doesn't get cut up too much.'

'Good. Well, I don't think I need detain you any longer. I'm glad to be able to tell you that I will be sending in a positive report on all aspects of your establishment. I hope everything goes well for you at Portman Square next month. And I see you've got Russian Eagle entered for the Foxhunters' at Liverpool. Will he run, do you think?'

'Now he's qualified, I very much hope so,' Jan said.

'Good, and the best of luck.'

Jan didn't see Eddie all day. He'd rung in the morning to say he had to go to London early and couldn't come in to ride. He rang again on his way back and asked if she could meet him for a drink at the White Horse.

Although it was a Monday, there was a large crowd in the pub when Jan arrived just after eight, and several people had been over to Herefordshire the day before to see her horses run. Eddie had arrived before her and was on the receiving end of a lot of jokes about which part of the fence to jump. To Jan's relief, with Eagle's win under his belt, he seemed to be taking them in good part.

'Why did you want me to come for a drink, then?' she asked when she could talk to him alone.

'Just to say thanks for yesterday and sorry for mucking up on Moon, and because I thought you would bring Annabel with you.'

'Eddie, you creep! Why didn't you say so? I'd have brought her.'

'No,' Eddie retracted. 'It was you I wanted to see, I promise. I was going to ask: now I'm definitely riding in the Foxhunters', do you really think I'm up to it?'

'Hello, hello. If it isn't young Mr Sullivan,' said a voice directly behind Jan's shoulder.

She turned and saw a short, balding man in a bright green tweed suit. Standing behind him was Sharon Goldstone. *This man,* Jan thought, *is either Sharon's latest conquest or her father.*

'Hello, Cyril,' Eddie said. 'I've never seen you down here before, fraternizing with the enemy.'

'I don't consider this lot the enemy,' Cyril said, looking around him with undisguised scorn.

'That must be because you haven't got a betting shop near here. There are some formidable punters among this lot, I can assure you.'

'Hmm,' Cyril grunted cynically. 'They don't look very rich on it.'

'Shut up, Dad,' Sharon whined over his shoulder. 'They're all right. Don't be so bloody rude.'

Cyril appeared abruptly to realize that he'd been indiscreet. 'I'm sorry,' he said, looking around the room in general, though nobody seemed to have heard, or taken offence. 'But I'm glad I've seen you, Edward. I hear you had a fall yesterday.'

Eddie shrugged his shoulders as if it couldn't have mattered less. 'I'm afraid I'm a bit of a beginner.'

'But you qualified that horse for Aintree, didn't you?' Cyril's eyes hardened. 'So don't give me the old bullshit. I wasn't born yesterday, son.'

Eddie looked at him steadily. 'No I would say there was nothing of the newborn babe about you, Cyril, apart perhaps from your lack of hair.'

'You lippy young toe-rag!' Cyril's eyes blazed for a moment. 'It's no wonder you've gone bloody skint is it, chucking your money around on silly bets!'

Eddie shrugged his shoulders again. 'Oh well. I had money then. Won some, lost some. But Cyril, how rude of me! I haven't introduced you to—'

'I know who she is.'

'But she may not know who you are, Cyril.'

The little man attempted to smile through clenched teeth.

'This is Cyril Goldstone,' Eddie said to Jan. 'He owns about fifty betting shops.'

'Now you're a jockey,' Jan said with a grin, 'I'm not sure you should be talking to him, then.'

'All right. I'll stop,' Eddie answered, as if Cyril wasn't there. 'I'll just get him a drink first. What would you like, Cyril?'

'Nothing. I don't want a drink with you.'

'OK. Sharon?'

'White wine, please.'

'I'll get it, Sharon,' Cyril said. He grasped her by the upper arm and started to lead her to another part of the bar.

Sharon shook herself free. 'Piss off, Dad!'

Jan saw the back of Cyril's ears go plum red as he changed direction and headed for the door.

Sharon was looking at Eddie with bright, laughing eyes. 'God, it kills me the way you do that to him,' she tittered, covering her mouth with one hand. 'He gets so wound up 'cos he knows you don't give a shit.'

'As it happens, I do give a shit,' Eddie said. 'I just don't like him knowing.'

Eddie went up to Edge Farm two mornings later to ride out with Jan, Roz and Joe.

'I don't think you should trust Sharon Goldstone,' Jan said to him as they hacked up to the gallop under a choppy March sky.

'I don't.'

'But you admitted to her the other day at the pub, after her dad had gone, that this bet matters to you. I'm sure she'll tell him.'

'Jan, Cyril's a very wily old fox. He knows perfectly well it matters to me. Astonishingly enough, I think he just came down to find out how confident I was.' Eddie grinned. 'Even someone as rich as Cyril doesn't like to lose half a million if they can help it.'

'I don't suppose he's that worried,' Jan said. 'After all, you've only won that single race with Eagle.'

'True,' Eddie agreed. 'But he'll be thinking about it, and it might come in handy if Sharon thinks I don't know she goes back and tells him everything.'

'It made me laugh the way that tart was all over you when you gave him such a hard time. She obviously fancies you.'

'And,' Eddie said ruefully, 'as you might have noticed from what she was wearing, she hasn't got much taste.'

Jan chuckled and turned round to Roz and Joe, who were following. 'OK, let's do a bit of work!'

The four horses turned into the bottom of the grass gallop and did a half-speed in pairs. It was a steep climb for the last fifty yards, but Eagle was scarcely blowing at the top.

'Good,' Jan shouted across at Eddie. 'He's as fit as I've seen him. We mustn't overdo it if we want him spot on in eight days' time. And the fitter he is, the less chance of him bleeding again.'

When they got back to the yard, the phone in the tack room was ringing.

Jan looked at her watch. It was ten to eight; too early for most owners.

She picked up the phone. 'Hello, Edge Farm Stables.'

'Jan? It's Julie here, from the pub. My mum's just rung; she works up at Mr Carey's. She found him—'

Jan's heart missed a beat. She knew what she was going to hear.

Julie sniffed. 'She found him . . . dead.'

'Oh no! How terrible!'

'Yes, she's phoned for an ambulance and told the police; but it was probably another heart attack.'

'Oh, God!' Jan groaned. When he'd said he was on the mend, she'd believed him because she had wanted to. She suddenly realized that she cared very much, and not because she would have to find someone else to put up the bond.

Instantly she felt guilty for even allowing herself to think of this aspect of the old man's death.

'I thought you'd want to know,' Julie was saying. 'You know, him having a horse with you and everything.'

'Yes, thanks. I saw quite a bit of him recently.'

'Mum said he liked you and he was very interested in what you were doing up there.'

'Well, thanks for telling me, Julie.'

'That's all right. See you soon. 'Bye.'

Jan put down the phone and looked at it. The others had all come in, filling the tack room, and saw her face.

'Mr Carey?' Annabel asked.

Jan nodded. Annabel looked away. 'Oh. The poor old chap,' she said. 'Was it a heart attack?'

'I don't know,' Jan answered. 'Julie's mother found him and called an ambulance – a bit late really, I suppose.'

'Oh dear,' Eddie sighed. 'I was worried this might happen.'

After all the exhilarating events of the previous few weeks, with Annabel buying Eagle, Eddie getting back the ride on him, Eagle's win and the inspector's good report on Edge Farm, Jan was hit very hard by Victor Carey's death.

Now, once again, it seemed that the forces of nature were determined to block her path, just when there was light at the end of the tunnel. She cried herself to sleep, not knowing if she was crying for her own loss or for Mr Carey. Nevertheless, she prayed to God that he would give her just one more chance to make a future for her children.

Jan was awake and up early the next morning. She looked across the broad Severn Vale to see the rays of a dawn sun hit the sharp, humped back of the Malverns, as isolated clusters of fat clouds were thrust over it by a fickle March wind.

She stepped outside and faced it, wanting the cool air to cleanse her mind and blow away the doubt and fears of the night. She took several deep breaths and told herself firmly whatever mountains came her way, she would climb them.

She didn't have John, but she had a yard full of nice horses; she had almost a score of winners to her name that season and her friends were as loyal as she could have wished.

She would miss old Mr Carey, for his wisdom and for himself. She was sure, though, that somehow another backer would appear eventually from somewhere to put up the guarantee she needed.

As if to dampen her revived spirits, however, the big rain-bearing clouds decided to empty their contents over the west of England for the next two days and every Saturday point-to-point meeting in the region was abandoned.

With the familiar contrariness of the English weather, the rain stopped at midday and the sky began to clear. Philosophically Jan took the opportunity to have the afternoon off and went shopping with her children in Cheltenham.

When she got back, Annabel invited her to dinner at the cottage with Toby Waller and a few other friends interested in racing. Jan was exhausted. She couldn't get into the right mood and, feeling a little guilty at letting Annabel down, left at eleven to drive back to the caravan.

Roz, who had been babysitting again, was gathering up her things to leave as Jan walked through the door.

'Hi, Jan!' she greeted her. 'Nice evening?'

'Great, thanks, but I'm ready for bed. We've got most of the horses to take out tomorrow, I'm afraid.'

'That's OK. I'll be up at half-seven. Oh, by the way, I forgot to say, earlier this afternoon, when you were in Cheltenham, that tacky blonde girl who knows Eddie came up.'

'Which tacky blonde girl?' Jan asked.

'There's only one like this – I reckon she's called Sharon.'

Jan tensed at once and pricked her ears. 'Sharon? What did she want?'

'Well I didn't talk to her much. Joe did; he said she wanted to have a look around the yard because she was thinking of having a horse here.' Roz shrugged her shoulders. 'You've often said owners come in all shapes and sizes. Anyway, Joe spent a good hour showing her round and that, and apparently, when she went, she said she'd give you a ring about definitely sending a horse, so that's good isn't it?'

Jan didn't answer at once. 'Did she leave her number or give Joe her name?'

Roz thought for a moment. 'I don't know. I didn't ask.'

When Roz had gone, Jan told herself not to be paranoid. For a start, there wasn't much Sharon could have done, even if she'd had a good snoop. Besides, it was perfectly possible the girl did want to keep a pointer, and it was quite clear that she wouldn't mind an excuse to be hanging around Eddie a lot more. Jan smiled as she wondered what effect that might have on Annabel's attitude towards him.

She went through to look at the children, who were sleeping contentedly, and got into bed herself, where she lay awake thinking about the future.

She had no more idea than she'd had a week ago about who she could turn to for the guarantee she needed, but she was confident that if Eagle did win at Aintree in five days' time, a volunteer would appear.

22

The Martell Foxhunters' Chase took place at Aintree on the Thursday of the Grand National meeting – two days before the world-famous race was run over the same course, although it was nearly two miles shorter. The fourth race on the card, it was due to start at three forty-five.

As Jan had only a sketchy idea of the course's layout and what she was supposed to do when she got there, she decided to arrive at least four hours before the 'off'. She'd never been to Liverpool or its suburb, Aintree, but she estimated the journey time in her elderly lorry at three and a half hours and added another hour to allow for traffic jams and breakdowns.

At five-thirty she slipped out of bed, being careful not to wake the children on the other side of the flimsy partition, and walked in chilly darkness down to the yard. She let herself into Eagle's box and gave him a small feed and fresh water. Then she checked his tack, his passport and everything else she needed or might need to get him to the start of the biggest race of her career.

In the still, pre-dawn silence, with the momentous day in front of her, she felt alone and vulnerable.

In the end, she thought, if it went wrong today, whatever happened, it would be her fault: for not preparing the horse properly; for letting the wrong jockey ride it; for entering a substandard horse in the first place.

If they won, she would share the credit equally with the horse and the jockey. That was the deal. That was the way it would be perceived.

As a hint of pink seeped into the eastern sky above the Cotswold edge and the birds began their spring morning chatter, the peace was shattered by Annabel driving up the track, followed closely by Joe in his unbaffled Ford Fiesta, bringing Darren with him.

In the tack room, they drank mugs of tea and talked with subdued voices in deference to the day ahead of them.

At six-fifteen Roz arrived and went with Jan up to the caravan. They checked that everything Megan and Matty would need for the day was ready. When the children woke, Roz was going to give them breakfast then drive them over to Jan's mother. It was Reg's idea that they should spend the day there, so Mary wouldn't get lonely while he was up at Aintree watching the race. He thought the children might take her mind off all the tension of the day.

When Jan was satisfied that she'd thought of everything they would need, she left Roz and went back down to the yard, where she switched on all the lights. Annabel came out of the tack room and they went to Eagle's stable. Annabel held the horse while Jan bandaged his legs and buckled on his travel rug.

She led him up the lowered ramp of the lorry, carefully secured his head-collar rope and shot down the bolts of the partitions. Everything that she had done before a thousand times she checked and double-checked today. Finally, she made sure the horse was settled and they closed the ramp.

On a list she'd made, she ticked off everything they had to take. Once she was completely satisfied, Joe and Darren clambered into the box, while she got up into the cab with Annabel and started the engine. She didn't speak for the first twenty minutes, as they trundled towards the motorway junction at Tewkesbury, but once they were on the M5, which was comparatively uncongested at that time of the morning, she relaxed.

She glanced at Annabel. 'Nervous?' she asked.

'Not yet. But this is about the most exciting thing I've ever done in my life. I think it's incredible, really – there I was riding out over the Welsh hills to get away from the crowds and hassle of

London and, though I've always loved horses, I had absolutely no interest in racing and all the bull that goes with it.' Annabel laughed. 'But now here I am, an owner for heaven's sake, taking a horse to Aintree to race over the Grand National course!'

Jan smiled because she understood what Annabel was saying. It had pleased her to see how her friend had blossomed and opened up since she'd moved to Stanfield and Edge Farm.

'I think it was fantastic, what you did for Eddie,' Jan said.

'I didn't do it for him; I did it for me.'

'In which case, lucky Eddie.'

'He's one of life's lucky men,' Annabel said enigmatically.

'Not if his business career is anything to go by,' Jan said realistically.

'There's a lot more to life than business. And I really, deeply hope he's lucky today.'

'Don't we all!' Jan agreed with a laugh.

At seven-thirty they hit a traffic jam on the motorway, where it ran through the Black Country. Jan looked out across the sprawl of factories, tower blocks and nineteenth-century industrial housing and thought of Bernie.

'I wonder if Eagle's former owner will come today,' she said.

'I don't know,' Annabel shrugged. 'Now my negotiations with Bernie are over, I haven't seen anything of him.'

'He hasn't phoned me for over a week,' Jan said. 'I wonder if he's fed up with racing.'

'He's still got two good horses, Dingle Bay and Arctic Hay,' Annabel said, 'but maybe he is. I don't think his heart was ever really in it. By the way, didn't your mother-in-law want to come with us too?'

'No way!' Jan raised her eyebrows. 'But she would have been the first to ring and moan if I hadn't asked her. My mum's not coming either; she's looking after the kids and, anyway, she felt she couldn't take the excitement. Mind you, I'm not sure *I* can, the way my gut's feeling. But at least Eddie's bringing Dad and Gerry.'

The two friends chatted sporadically as the lorry rumbled north past the Potteries, over the flat lands of Cheshire and was buffeted by wind on the high-backed bridge across the Manchester ship canal. At ten o'clock there was already a lot of traffic converging on Aintree racecourse, but there were no serious hold-ups and Jan was soon steering her old lorry into the parking area.

Russian Eagle had travelled well, although he had sweated a little under his rug. They lowered the ramp and Joe unbolted the partition. He swung it to one side to let Jan lead the horse off. Once in the stable yard, they washed the sticky sweat off his neck and shoulders with warm water and tidied up his mane and tail. When they'd finished, Darren walked him round for twenty minutes in a paddock by the stables to give his legs a stretch, while Annabel and Jan went off to find the loos and a cup of tea.

On this first morning of the National meeting, there was already a buzz about Aintree, though, Jan guessed, not as much as there would be on Saturday, when the world's greatest steeplechase would be run. She made her way to the stables, three blocks of brick-built boxes that had clearly seen better days and many generations of runners in the Grand National, some with the names of famous winners over the top door. She found which stable had been allocated to Russian Eagle and Darren led him in.

Afterwards she and Annabel went back to the lorry and sat in the cab. Annabel was reading the racing papers and trying to keep calm. She was thrilled to see her green and blue colours with her name printed alongside Eagle's on the day's card.

There were twenty-two runners declared and, below the list, a brief summary of their form and projected odds.

'Who's favourite?' Jan asked.

'The Irish horse – Supreme General. He belongs to A.D. O'Hagan with Mickey Flanagan on board. He's the Irish amateur champion, isn't he?'

'Yes,' Jan said. 'Though why A.D. O'Hagan's bothering with hunter chases when he owns the favourite for the Grand National, God only knows.'

'They've got Eagle at twenty to one!' Annabel said. 'And Rear Gunner at sixteens!'

There were seven horses listed at shorter odds. They were all animals with more experience than Russian Eagle or Gunner and, she had to admit, ridden by far more experienced jockeys than Eddie.

'But you saw Eagle and Eddie going round last time they raced,' Jan said, 'so you shouldn't be feeling too nervous. The fences are much bigger, of course, but that won't be a problem for Eagle. If Gunner's fit, I'd say he'd be as much of a danger to us as Supreme General. In the end it's going to be a matter of stamina and finishing speed. And I think we might have enough of both.'

'Do you really believe we can do it?' Annabel asked doubtfully. 'I assumed you entered him for a bit of fun and because Eddie wanted it so badly.'

'I promise you, I wouldn't have entered him if I thought he had absolutely no chance. I've said all along, with luck in running, it's possible.'

'Don't worry,' Annabel laughed nervously. 'I'm not holding my breath.' She looked at her watch. 'Shall we wander up and see if we can find Eddie and your dad?'

Jan had arranged to meet Eddie, Reg and Gerry outside the weighing room at twelve o'clock, to make their final declarations before they walked the course.

Trying to keep a lid on their excitement, they walked up a little early to find the three men already waiting outside the old cream-painted timber building.

'Oh dear,' Annabel said into Jan's ear before they'd reached them, 'Eddie looks like a ghost.'

'Don't tell him,' Jan warned. 'Hello, Dad,' she said more loudly. 'Morning, Eddie. Hi, Gerry! You didn't get lost then?'

'No,' said Eddie in a croaky voice.

'Great. Eagle's fine. He's had a bit of a walk and now he's in a tatty old stable having a good look at what's going on.'

'I think I'll go and have a look at him,' Eddie said.

'He's fine, Eddie. They won't allow you in anyway because you haven't got a stable pass. I'll just declare him and then we'll walk the course.'

Jan went inside and tried to keep herself from trembling as she filled in the declaration form, confirming to the clerk of the scales that her horse was there and would be running. It was a very different procedure from the point-to-points she was used to and the officials, who seemed to understand her nervousness, smiled and reassured her with a few words of encouragement.

As she went back out, she thought that, now they were utterly committed, she just wished they could get on with it.

'Right,' she said. 'Who's coming?'

The lads stayed with the horse while Jan set off towards the world-famous course with Eddie, Annabel, Reg and Gerry.

A light wind ruffled the dark green turf, blowing out the moisture from a slight fall of rain the night before. The sky above them was patchily blue, with high, mackerel clouds crossing slowly from the west.

'He'll like this ground,' Jan observed as they walked towards the first fence.

Eddie nodded, stopping to hack his heel into the earth. 'Just as long as there's a bit of a cut.'

'This'll be the fourth,' Jan said as they reached the plain fence. 'You start back over there,' she pointed across the angle of the course to a point on the far side of the stands, 'and before you turn for this one you'll already have jumped a plain fence, the Chair and the water, but we'll have a look at how to take them on the way back.'

Jan couldn't ignore a profound sense of history, walking the famous course she'd seen so many times on the television. She and Eddie had played dozens of videos of previous runnings of the Foxhunters' and of the Grand National itself. But nothing could have prepared them for actually being on the course and standing in front of the massive spruce-topped fences; they looked so much bigger in real life.

They walked in a line between each of the obstacles down the long straight, judging the best place to take them. 'I reckon there's always less traffic up the inside,' Jan said to Eddie. 'The fences are a little higher here, but that won't bother Eagle.'

Eddie nodded, but as they gazed at Becher's Brook she knew he was still very unsure of himself.

'He won't have any problems with this,' she said as lightly as she could. 'Try to take it on the inner; there'll be less chance of any fallers as you land.'

As they walked on to the Canal Turn and Valentine's, Jan didn't let Eddie see just how daunted she was by the reality of the notoriously demanding course. She also had to control her irritation at her father and Gerry, who didn't help by gasping at every fence and looking sorrowfully at Eddie.

They crossed the Melling Road and turned left-handed into the home straight, heading for the stands, which would soon start filling up, until they reached the point from which the Foxhunters' Chase would start.

'OK, Eddie.' Jan tried to sound businesslike. 'There are going to be twenty-two of you galloping up to the first plain fence, all on top of each other, and anyone at the back just isn't going to see it, so for God's sake, try to jump off quickly, go up the inside and give your horse a bit of light for the first few fences. Most of these hunters will be able to jump; but there'll be plenty of pilot errors to cause problems.'

As they carried on to the Chair and the Water, Jan looked at Eddie again. Where he had been pale before, he was now eau de Nil. She took a deep breath, relieved that she hadn't eaten any breakfast.

Bloody hell! What am I doing here? she thought. *There's no way this can work, not with Eddie. He's bound to bottle out – he just doesn't know enough!*

She stood beside him in front of the water jump. 'Whatever you do, Eddie, you've got to stay committed; you *mustn't* lose heart going into these fences. Eagle can jump them all, big and tidily. You know that, so just don't forget it!'

They had a couple of hours to kill before they needed to think about getting ready, but nobody wanted to go to the public areas, where their nervousness would be seen. They went instead to the marquee that served as the lads' canteen, where they had endless cups of tea while they watched the racing on television. Jan noticed that, although Rear Gunner had been declared, there was no sign of Virginia or any of her staff.

Jan could see that Eddie was making a supreme effort to keep himself together. Although there was still a nervous tremble in his voice, he was trying to make a few jokes and talk about the race in a calm, workmanlike way. But she wasn't surprised that he didn't want anything to eat or drink. She insisted, though, that he swallow a small glass of water before he made his way back to the changing room.

Jan and Annabel began to prepare Eagle for his big day as soon as they arrived back in the stable yard. They gave the tack a final polish and sent him out with a plaited mane, gleaming oiled hooves and diamonds on his quarters. Eagle seemed to know something special was happening and bounced around the pre-parade ring while Jan went to collect his saddle from the weighing room.

She tacked him up carefully, running a surcingle over the tiny racing saddle and lifting each of his front legs in turn to make sure that no skin was being pinched under the girth.

Darren and Joe led him back to the parade ring, while Gerry and Reg leaned over the rails outside. Jan and Annabel followed Eagle.

'Well,' Jan said. 'This is it.'

'Don't worry,' Annabel said with a smile. 'You've got him here in wonderful shape; I know they'll do their best. All I care about is that they both come back safe and sound – and I mean that.'

'Thanks, Bel. D'you know, if I'd had any idea that it was going to be as stressful as this, I just don't think I'd have come.'

'You're going to have to get used to it, Jan, when you get your licence.'

'*If* I get my licence.'

'Of course you will. Now, you've done all you can for this race, so relax and try to enjoy it.'

As Eddie and the other twenty-one jockeys were walking into the ring, Jan caught sight of Harold Powell's colours as his jockey, Jimmy Marlow, marched up to his owner, who was standing with Virginia Gilbert. Virginia looked studiedly calm and a little aloof from the mostly amateur trainers who filled the arena.

Among the jockeys, Eddie was by no means the only one showing signs of nerves. She guessed it must be much tougher for these amateurs than for the pros who would be riding the same course – but twice round – in two days' time.

'You'll be OK, Eddie,' she said as he reached them. 'Usual instructions – keep in touch with the leaders all the way round and start pushing on when you turn for home with two left to jump. And don't forget what I said about the run in – the Chair will be fenced off and you have to cut across towards the elbow to pick up the running rail, so don't lose your way. Try to get there first and stay alongside it to help keep him balanced up to the line.'

They had rehearsed this on their walk round. Eddie nodded. 'Sure,' he managed to croak. 'Eagle looks great.'

'Thanks.' Jan forced a faint smile. 'He's fine and raring to go. He'll give you a great ride.'

As Jan legged him up onto the horse a few minutes later, she felt his knee quiver and gave it a quick squeeze. 'You can do it, Ed,' she smiled, and stood back to watch him rejoin the other runners circling the ring.

When the horse had left the paddock, Jan left Annabel to

watch in the members' stand with Gerry and Reg, while she made her way up to the owners' and trainers' stand.

On her way to Aintree that morning, Jan had made up her mind that she didn't want anyone with her while she watched the race.

On the trainers' stand she was unknown and anonymous, alone but surrounded by an almost tangible buzz and the nervous fretting of people who didn't often run horses at meetings as big as this. She made her way to the front and took her binoculars from their case to watch Eddie and Russian Eagle canter down to the start.

For those few brief moments of limbo before the 'Off', Jan felt terribly exposed and vulnerable. She'd chosen to put herself in this position, but now she was finding it hard to cope on her own and once again she longed for John's quiet presence.

She closed her eyes and took several deep breaths. When she was ready she resumed her scrutiny of the field and tried to concentrate on the green and blue hoops as they circled round behind the starting tape. She couldn't help keeping half an eye on Jimmy Marlow on Rear Gunner. She had to admit that Jimmy gave his horse a useful advantage. He'd had a good season riding under rules for Virginia and must have been one of the most experienced amateurs on the circuit. She could only pray that Eagle's strong finish would make up for Eddie's greenness.

When they were finally called into line, Jan was glad to see that Eddie had managed to find a gap towards the inside. As the tape flew up, he was in the front line of runners, galloping in a ragged charge towards the first fence.

Eagle held his position and took it abreast of another five, gained a little ground and galloped on towards the Chair. Jan swallowed and closed her eyes for a few seconds. She opened them, to see her horse fly over the formidable obstacle behind three others and touch down fluidly.

She felt herself relax a little now they were running and the first major obstacle was out of the way. As far she could see, Eddie had a good hold of the horse and they cleared the Water comfortably.

The runners headed for the tight left-hand bend before the long straight, swung well wide and curved back to line themselves up for the first of the six fences down the back. Sensibly Eddie eased up a little before he reached it, lying sixth and still on the inside rail.

Jan glanced back quickly over the rest of the field to identify the horses that had fallen at the first two fences, reducing the field to nineteen. One fancied horse had gone, but Supreme General in A.D. O'Hagan's famous colours was still in the race, going easily near the front. Just behind Eagle, Rear Gunner was still cruising with his long easy stride.

They took one, then two plain fences on the straight with no fallers. The open ditch halfway down claimed two victims and the next two fences removed one more. As they approached Becher's, Jan prayed quietly. 'God, please let him jump this!' He did it with ease, but three other runners weren't so lucky.

At each fence Jan wasn't sure what to expect. Every time Eagle's head and Eddie's blue and green colours bobbed back into view she felt a surge of relief as he picked up and galloped on to the next fence.

Jan knew Eddie was dreading the sharp bend on the inside of the Canal Turn and she felt her body tense vicariously as he headed straight for the corner. She gasped with relief when he took off and cleared it as well as any of his rivals.

There were six fences and eleven horses left in the race, with the leaders still going strongly. Jan studied her horse for signs of fatigue, but Eddie seemed to have him on the bit as easily as he would have done at this distance in any of the point-to-points in which they'd run.

At Valentine's Brook before the Melling Road, Eagle passed a horse in the air on his inside and a loose horse on his outer. With a deft twist as he landed, he avoided a collision with the riderless animal and was in fourth place with only five lengths separating him from the leader, and Eddie still wasn't kicking.

'Well done, Eddie!' Jan whispered to herself, hardly able to believe what she was seeing, but when they'd turned the bend towards the stands, Eddie started to move on the horse, his hands and heels in unison, working like pistons. Eagle began to progress up the field towards the leaders. Jan dared not even think there'd be a problem with the last two fences: just to be in the first four would be triumph enough for her!

But her excitement almost boiled over when Russian Eagle put in a huge jump over the open ditch. Within two strides of landing he'd passed all bar one of his rivals. Only Supreme General was in front, urged on by howls of support from all the Irishmen in the stands.

Halfway between the last two fences Eddie lifted his stick and brought it down just once. Eagle knew what he had to do. He stood right off at the last plain fence and projected himself into a leap that drew an audible gasp from the crowd, and a groan from the Irish as he landed half a length ahead.

Jan gasped too, but with sudden shock.

When Eddie landed his right stirrup lifted a little as his saddle slipped to the left. He managed to jerk it straight again by stepping down hard on his offside iron. Jan felt a stab of guilt for sending the horse out in such a way that this could have happened. She thanked God there were no more fences to jump. She was sure, just as long as Eddie could keep balanced on the run in, he would get there.

Gripping her binoculars, her knuckles white, Jan watched as Eddie resolutely gathered Eagle up and tracked slightly right to cut across the elbow and pick up the rail at the far end. The Chair was now railed off, leaving a small gap on the left to encourage riderless horses to leave the course before the run in.

Jan saw the disaster that was about to happen seconds before Eddie.

The loose horse, ranging up on his outside, had made up his mind to head for the gap between the Chair and the inner rail. He veered sharply left, cannoning into Russian Eagle. The two animals hit each other with a thud that could be heard in the stands and the momentum of the crash seemed to tip Eddie's saddle halfway round the horse's side. There was a long, anguished 'Oooooh!' from the crowd as he crashed to the ground, leaving his left foot still in the stirrup. He was dragged, bouncing like a doll, for several strides before his boot slipped from the iron and he fell away.

Eagle galloped on in confusion, carried to the left by the loose horse who had caused all the mayhem, forcing him on the wrong side of the running rail, past the Water Jump and on towards the winning post.

Jan froze for a moment, rigid with disbelief. She trained her binoculars on Eddie's green and blue colours as she had a few weeks before, willing him to move.

This time he didn't.

Jan didn't know how long she waited, oblivious to all the sounds of jubilation around her as the Irish horse came home to tumultuous applause, followed by a hard-finishing Rear Gunner, who must have passed three horses since clearing the second from home.

At last, as if by a small miracle, she saw Eddie stir. Slowly he raised his head, then propped himself up on his elbow. By the time the ambulance reached him, he was sitting up and rubbing his shoulder.

'Thank God!' Jan gasped. 'He's alive! He can move!'

And it was only now that she started to think about what could have led to his crashing fall.

A loose horse had hit Russian Eagle, but for some inexplicable reason Eddie's girth had got loose and the collision had sent the saddle slithering round Eagle's belly and tipped his rider over the side.

She couldn't begin to think how, but for some reason she hadn't tacked the horse up properly. In the nervous excitement of the build-up to the race, she must have forgotten something.

Eddie and Eagle had been on their way to win! They had been pulling away from the Irish horse with no sign of weakening.

She had to get to them.

She turned and was confronted by a sea of people heading for the narrow spiral staircase that was the only way down from the trainers' stand.

She pushed between the backs that blocked her way. 'Sorry!' she gasped, thrusting wildly towards the vortex at the top of the stairs. She could think of nothing but getting out of this place, out onto the course, and everywhere there were people stopping her. It seemed like hours before she got to the stairs and plunged down them, banging her wrists against the rails as she went, and shoved on through the crowds on the lower levels until she reached the ground. She burst out into the open with an impenetrable mass of people still cheering home the heavily backed winner. She dived headlong into the melee and pushed her way through blindly until she reached the rails and clambered over them, not giving a damn what anyone thought. She ran wildly down the course until she met the ambulance creeping gingerly towards her.

She stood in front of it, waving until the driver realized she wanted him to stop.

'I'm the trainer!' she gasped between searing breaths. 'How's Eddie?'

'He's your jockey, is he?' the driver asked.

'Yes. Yes. I need to know how he is.'

The driver opened his door and let Jan lean in to see Eddie sitting on a bench in the back of the vehicle with another paramedic beside him.

'Eddie! Are you all right?'

To her intense relief, he managed a weak grin. 'I'm alive; I think I've bust my collarbone.'

'Oh, thank God!'

Jan almost collapsed onto the driver's lap. She pulled herself up. She didn't care if her eyes were streaming with tears. 'I've got to see about Eagle. I'm so sorry, Eddie. I just don't know what happened – why it slipped!'

'It's OK, Jan. Go and see the horse. I'll see you later.'

Darren had reached Russian Eagle before Jan. He was still on the course, holding the horse's reins, up by the far end of the stands in front of a large, watching crowd. He and Eagle were walking quietly back to a gate at the corner of the track. The horse seemed no more than a little indignant about what had happened and perfectly sound.

'Thank God!' Jan heard herself say again.

Darren looked over to see her running towards them. There were tears in his eyes too.

'He's all right, Jan. He's fine,' he stuttered. 'How's Eddie?'

'Broken collarbone.'

Darren looked relieved. 'It was a hell of crash. And the bugger was going to win!' He winced.

Jan didn't dare think how much money he had put on Eagle.

Then, with savage abruptness, she was reminded how much Eddie had been going to win from Cyril Goldstone.

'Oh my God,' she groaned. Everything, the whole disaster, Eagle losing the race, Eddie losing his money and nearly being killed – it was all her fault because she'd insisted on doing everything herself and she'd got it wrong!

Somehow, somewhere, she'd totally screwed the whole thing up.

'Didn't his saddle slip?' she asked.

'Yes, I just slid it back over again, so I could lead him in.'

'Just stop a moment, for God's sake!'

In a few short strides, she was beside the horse on his near side, unbuckling the surcingle, which she pulled off, and she watched as the girth, unrestrained now, flopped off and dangled beneath the horse's belly.

'What the hell—?'

She reached down and lifted the end, to find there was no buckle. A few ends of thread where it had been attached, projected randomly from the heavy nylon web.

She lifted the saddle flap and found the metal buckle in its leather sleeve still fixed to the girth straps. There was nothing random about the threads on the inner side – they had all been neatly cut.

The relief of knowing that she wasn't to blame, intense as it was, didn't sustain her for long. It didn't change the fact that her dream of winning this premier race, when it had come so close to reality, had collapsed, and all the hopes she'd pinned on it, however unreasonable they might have seemed, had been justified as Eagle jumped the last in front.

Somehow, to reorient her mind, she concentrated on the immediate problem. 'I'll take the horse,' she said to Darren. 'Thanks.'

Darren handed her the reins.

'You take the saddle back to the weighing room,' she told him, 'but give me that girth and buckle.'

Gingerly, clearly aware of the significance of the severed stitching, the boy unbuckled both ends and passed them to Jan, who shoved them into a pocket of her sheepskin.

With Darren trailing unhappily behind, she led Eagle through the gate and around the back of the stands to the stables. Her father, Annabel and Gerry were waiting at the entrance, looking like the chief mourners at a funeral.

Jan clenched her teeth and resolved not to break down again. She led the horse into his stable and took his bridle off while the others watched in silence. She threw a sweat rug over him and let herself out.

She looked around at all the other trainers and lads getting their horses ready to race, or washing down others who had just run. 'We'll leave him there for a minute. Darren, you stop with him. Give him a wash and then a small drink – and make sure it's lukewarm.' She turned to the others. 'Let's go to the lorry.'

When they were all crammed into the cab, Jan looked at them. She pulled the girth and the severed buckle from her pocket and put them on Annabel's lap. 'We were sabotaged,' she said simply.

Annabel picked up the buckle and webbing strap and examined the uniformly, cleanly severed threads.

'But who, who on earth would do it?' she asked, in a state of shock.

'Did any of you know, except Bel, that Eddie had five grand at a hundred to one for Eagle to win with him on board?'

'Jesus,' Gerry said. 'He was going to win half a million?' he whispered.

'You told me he'd had a big bet, but you didn't say how much or who with,' Annabel corrected her.

'Cyril Goldstone.'

The three of them gazed at Jan in stunned silence.

'My God, Jan,' Reg said at last. 'What have you let yourself in for?'

'I haven't let myself in for anything, Dad. Eddie had a bet. I told him at the time I thought he was crazy, but he had every right to try and win.' Jan had been watching Annabel. 'You knew about the bet, didn't you?' she said to her.

'Yes. Mrs Sullivan told me.'

'Because I told her,' Jan sighed. 'Was that why you bought Eagle from Bernie?'

'Partly. I knew no one else was going to help Eddie; and, besides, I thought it was a good deal. I loved seeing him run today, and, as far as I'm concerned, he was the winner.'

'Too right,' Gerry agreed. 'He ran an absolute blinder and never put a foot wrong. I just couldn't believe it when he took off for home after the last. He was never going to get caught.'

'OK, OK,' Jan said impatiently. 'What am I going to do about it?'

'You'll never prove a thing,' Reg said.

'That depends on who actually cut the stitching,' Gerry said.

'Hold on! Has anyone seen Joe?' Jan asked.

'Not since before the race and he was already half-cut by then.'

'If it was him,' Annabel said, 'the only way you'll get anywhere is not to let him think you remotely suspect him – perhaps not even to mention that you know it was done at all. If he thinks he's in the clear, sooner or later he's bound to do or say something that'll incriminate him.'

Jan thought for a moment. No action was always better than a knee jerk. 'OK. We're just going to pretend the saddle slipped without any outside help – agreed. I'd better get straight back and tell Darren not to say anything to Joe. I just hope he hasn't seen him already.'

'OK,' Annabel nodded calmly.

'We'll go and find Eddie and tell him what happened and what we're going to do about it. We'll aim to get back here in half an hour. Just make damn sure no one else hears a word about this,' Jan warned.

Jan hurried back to the stables and found Darren sitting morosely on a straw bale in front of Eagle's box.

'Darren, come in the box with me,' she said.

He looked at her, puzzled, but followed her.

Inside Jan closed the door and beckoned him into the far corner, beyond Eagle. 'Have you seen Joe?'

'Nope. He was getting well pissed before the race and I didn't want to go round with him.'

'If you see him, I don't want you to say a word about the broken girth. Do you understand?'

Comprehension flickered slowly in the boy's eyes. 'Yeah, I think I do.'

'Just tell him we think the saddle slipped with all the sweat and stretching the horse had to do over those jumps, and that I couldn't have tightened the girth properly.'

'I get you.' Darren nodded with a complicit grin. 'The bastard!'

'Darren.' Jan gave him her steeliest look. 'You promise me you'll say and do nothing to let him or anyone else know we suspect him. Just treat him absolutely as normal, otherwise I'll skin you alive.'

'Don't you worry, Jan, I won't tell him nothing!'

'Good. Now, put all the tack in the bag as normal in case he comes back and let Eagle have a bit of hay. I'm just going for a pee, then we'll put him in the lorry.'

Jan stayed in the ladies' for a few minutes, needing the chance to sit down on her own. She stared at the back of the door and wondered if there was anything she could have done to stop this happening.

She could honestly say it had never occurred to her that Cyril Goldstone would try to save his money with blatant skulduggery, and yet it had been so easy for him!

From where she looked at the moment, there was very little to prove he'd been responsible, other than purely circumstantial evidence, and anyway, in the end, in full view of twenty thousand spectators, Eddie had still been on his way to win the race until the loose horse had collided with him, which even Cyril couldn't have organized.

There was no way they could ever pin it on him, or even point the finger at him, unless Joe Paley confessed.

Jan made her way back through the stands, hoping that she might see Joe. Most people were preoccupied with the next race and were either heading outside, jostling to get money on at the Tote or gazing up at the television view of the horses going down to the start of the Mildmay course.

Outside there was a rush of people coming from the paddock and the Tote windows. Jan, standing indecisive for a moment, felt herself jostled and then, distinctly, a hand on the small of her back. She spun round, eyes blazing, ready to rebuke the groper and found herself staring into Harold Powell's opaque blue eyes.

'What bad luck!' he said, so insincerely that the thought flashed through her mind that he might have been responsible for what had been done to Eagle's girth. But she did everything she could to disguise her suspicion.

'Yes, wasn't it? Comes of using an amateur, I suppose,' she said, keeping up the charade by half-blaming herself. 'But he did insist.'

'It's not his horse, though.'

'No, but he has a lot of influence with the owner. Listen, Harold, he's hurt now and I've got to go and see how he is.'

'Well, I can't say I was sorry to see him fall. There's a nice lot of money for the runner-up.' Harold gave her a freezing smile before pushing his way past her back into the stands.

She gazed at him for a moment, enraged by all he'd put her through. By God, she thought, if there was any justice in the world, she'd see him pay dearly.

As she turned to carry on back to the stables, she saw Eamon Fallon a little apart from the main flow of people and just about to head up the stairs to the private boxes. She hadn't seen him for weeks, not since the day he'd told her she would have to sell Dingle Bay to settle his account with her.

Since then, and Annabel buying the horse to swap it for Russian Eagle, Jan had rung him to say that she had the cash he wanted and he'd sent a tall, taciturn Irishman to collect it. She had made the courier sign for the money, but she'd had no further acknowledgement from Eamon, and felt a little resentful, in view of all the trouble she'd taken. She was considering whether she really wanted to talk to him right then, when he happened to turn and see her.

He smiled broadly and beckoned her over with a friendly wave.

A little guardedly, she walked to the bottom of the steps. 'Hello Eamon. Did you get that money?'

His eyes slid to one side for a minute and he frowned. 'I did,' he said. 'Thanks. But Jan, what terrible bad luck with your horse! It was a really fine run and I'd have backed it myself but I'm here with the man who owns the winner.' He nodded over his shoulder to where, a few steps above him, another man stood. Although in the periphery of her vision Jan had been conscious of a compelling presence, only when she raised her eyes did she realize it was none other than A.D. O'Hagan. 'He'd like to congratulate you,' Eamon said and stepped aside deferentially.

O'Hagan nodded and a quick uplift at the corner of his mouth registered her existence while his intense blue eyes seemed to burn into her. Jan felt almost mesmerized by the legendary man, whom she'd met just once before at the Doncaster Sales, the day Eddie had bought Russian Eagle.

'Well done,' he said. 'you had my fella beat and that other one you used to train. It was an impressive performance.' His mouth widened a little and his eyes glittered in appreciation. 'We'll meet again for sure when you have another crack at us. Even before that, maybe.' He turned and his immaculate brown brogues clicked up the concrete steps.

Eamon winked at her. 'Take care now,' he said and turned to follow O'Hagan.

She stared after them, her speculation over the connection between these two enigmatic Irishmen replacing for a moment the horrible aftermath of Eagle's race. But her preoccupation was disturbed by another familiar voice behind her shoulder.

''Ello, Jan,' a deep voice said, which despite its strong cockney vowels, had more than a little in common with Eddie's. 'You're keepin' illustrious company.'

Jan turned round to find Ron Sullivan standing languidly in the loudest check suit of pink and green tweed she'd ever seen. There was a smile on his face as he looked at her and A.D. O'Hagan's disappearing back.

'Hello, Ron,' she smiled. 'I didn't know you were here. Have you seen your son?' she went on quickly, suddenly reminded of Eddie's condition.

'I have now,' Ron said. 'I found him in the hospital they've got here having his collarbone strapped.'

'I haven't even seen him since he was carted off in the ambulance,' Jan said. 'I've been rushing around trying to sort Eagle and find out . . .'

'What the hell happened?' Ron finished for her.

She nodded, biting her lip with a fresh rush of frustration.

'But how's Eddie?' she asked.

'He's fine,' Ron smiled. 'He'll be a little sore and, as you can imagine, he's more than a bit pissed off at losing the race.'

He still doesn't know about the bet, Jan thought. 'He did well,' she said, thinking how lame that sounded.

'Well?' Ron guffawed. 'He was absolutely effing fantastic! I couldn't believe the way he rode round that course, and you, my girl, are a little genius. Because if he can keep clear of them loose horses, he'll beat Superior General next time!'

'That's what O'Hagan just said.'

'Anyway,' Ron said. 'I'd get you a drink, darlin', but I've got to make tracks a bit sharpish. I shouldn't have come today, but I didn't want to miss my boy,' he chuckled. 'And I'm bloody glad I didn't!'

'Are you seeing Eddie again?'

'Not just now,' Ron answered.

'See you soon, then, I hope,' Jan said.

He leaned down and kissed her on both cheeks.

'Maybe,' he said before he spun round and marched off, straight into the oncoming flow of people surging out to watch the race that was about to start.

Jan stood for a moment, trying to fathom out what it was about their brief meeting that she found disturbing. She was sorry he'd gone so quickly, too, because she thought he could have given her some useful advice about how to deal with what had happened to Eagle's tack.

But by now Annabel and the others would be wondering where she'd got to. They'd be waiting to get Eagle into the lorry and go home. She turned and walked briskly towards the stables.

Darren was still outside Eagle's box.

'Any sign of Joe?'

'Yeh,' Darren nodded. 'He comes back looking dead rough, like he's been in a fight. He goes, "Where's the boss?" and I go, "I don't know," and he says, "Tell her not to wait for me. I'll be getting a lift back."'

'What!' Jan exploded.

'It's not my fault, Jan,' Darren said, alarmed by her outburst.

'I know,' she said quickly. 'I'm not blaming you, but I'm bloody angry at Joe. But if he's gone, he's gone,' she said more calmly. 'Let's get Eagle out of here and take him home.'

The long journey back to Gloucestershire from Aintree was one of the most miserable Jan had ever made.

Darren was in the back with Eagle and Annabel was in the cab beside her, trying hard to cheer her up, but nothing could shift the black cloud of depression that enveloped Jan.

Having come so close to winning, watching Eddie do exactly what they had set out to achieve when he'd bought Russian Eagle, then seeing it all crumble, whether through accident or malicious intent, was devastating and had left her almost choking with rage.

Jan couldn't bear the inane music and chatter on the radio, and the journey passed in almost total silence. It persisted back at the yard, four hours after leaving Aintree racecourse when, in the gusty drizzle falling on the Cotswold edge, they unloaded Eagle and bedded him down for the night.

Roz was waiting for them and had done all the other horses with Emma. She had already picked up the children from Riscombe and put them to bed. She was almost as gloomy as the others, having watched the race on television. She told Jan that Gerry had phoned an hour before to say that Eddie had been taken to the Fazakerley Hospital, which he'd been allowed to leave once his shoulder had been rebandaged. Gerry was now driving him home with Reg in the Land Rover.

At half-past nine Darren and Roz finally went home. Jan asked Annabel if she would stay with her for a while and they made their way back up to the caravan.

'Do you think we'll ever see Joe Paley again?' Annabel asked.

Jan shrugged. 'It must have been him who did it – there's no one else. I don't see how he could come back here and face us.'

'He hasn't really got any roots in the village, has he?'

'None at all – his family are travellers. I think they happened to be in the area last year when I was looking for more lads; he probably heard from Roz and just showed up. I always felt he was a bit dodgy, but I put up with him because he's a bloody good work rider.'

'So he could go anywhere now and find a job in a yard, just on the strength of his riding?'

'Well, I certainly won't be giving him a reference,' Jan said wryly.

Annabel smiled at this sign that Jan was starting to see beyond the immediate catastrophe.

Jan was also beginning to accept that what had happened would have happened anyway, even if someone hadn't nicked the stitching on the girth. The loose horse had hit Eagle so hard that if the saddle hadn't slipped and dumped Eddie on terra firma, he would certainly never have recovered and got straight again in time to challenge Supreme General. It was just possible that a really experienced professional jockey might have seen the loose horse ranging up on him and managed to take avoiding action, but professional jockeys didn't ride in hunter chases.

They talked for a while longer, until Jan yawned. 'I expect you want to go to bed, Bel,' she said. 'It's a long time since five o'clock this morning.'

Annabel yawned too and stood up. 'Yes, I'll have to go or I'll end up on the floor in here. I wonder how the others are getting on.'

'No doubt they'll be up here in the morning like larks. We'll start a bit later, at eight, OK?'

'Sure,' Annabel nodded. 'I'm sorry you've had such a hell of a day. I'm sure it won't look so bad in the morning and at least we know Eagle's a winner.'

'There's no doubt about that. Thanks, Bel.' Jan managed another weary smile. 'Goodnight.'

At midnight, when Jan had already fallen into a deep sleep, she was woken by a furious shrieking.

She came to in a panic, wondering what all the commotion was, when she realized it was only the phone beside her bed.

She picked it up.

'Hello,' she murmured.

'Hi, Jan! I've woken you, I'm sorry. It's Eddie.'

Jan shrugged and tried to focus. 'What do you want, Eddie?'

'Just to let you know that the bloody Land Rover's broken down; none of us know what the hell's wrong with it, but it won't start again and we've booked into a little motel somewhere near Stoke-on-Trent. Your dad says he doesn't want to wake your mother now, but could you ring her first thing in the morning and tell her?'

'Sure. The poor old thing will be worried as hell when she wakes without him.'

'Thanks. Sorry to have woken you.'

'That's OK. How are you, by the way? I'm sorry I never got back to see you again.'

'Not too bad,' Eddie said, with a hint of understatement. 'At least I didn't get kicked in the head or anything.'

'Did the others tell you what happened?'

'Yes, it's OK, Jan. I know it wasn't your fault.'

'I don't know who I'm bloody angrier with, Joe or that loose horse.'

'It may not have been Joe,' Eddie said.

'We won't talk about it now,' Jan said. 'Are you coming here tomorrow?'

'That depends how long they take to repair the Land Rover. But I'll be in Saturday morning, for sure.'

'See you then, and if I forgot to tell you before – you rode brilliantly!'

She could hear Eddie's pleased laugh. 'Thanks Jan; it was all down to you.'

'No it wasn't, but I'll see you tomorrow. G'night.'

'Night Jan.'

23

By Friday evening Eddie hadn't appeared, but Reg had phoned to say he was home. Edge Farm had more or less settled back into its usual routine. Although the Grand National was being held the next day, Jan had four runners to send out to point-to-points.

She was up at six-thirty on Saturday morning and was joined by Emma, Roz and Darren, who had taken a day to recover from the Aintree trip. As Jan had predicted, they hadn't seen or heard anything from Joe Paley; she guessed they never would and there seemed to be a tacit understanding that his name would not even be mentioned in the yard from now on, in the faint hope that it would help erase the awful memory of the race.

Around ten o'clock Eddie, pasty-faced and with his arm in a sling, limped quietly into the yard to see Eagle. Jan noticed how his status had altered as a result of his heroic ride. She found herself regarding him in a new light, too, as someone who, having identified an impossible target, had gone out and all but achieved it.

He hadn't stayed long, though, and she hadn't had a chance – if she was honest she had avoided it – to talk to him about Ron's Italian bankers. However, he said he'd be up again that evening to watch a replay of the Grand National on her video.

Even a successful day at the races, with a win and two seconds, didn't do a lot to improve Jan's frame of mind. She couldn't shift the dark cloud that still hung over her. She was pleased to see

Eddie, though, when he arrived with a bottle of wine just as she'd finished putting the children to bed.

Eddie poured the wine and Jan turned on her video. During the preamble that led up to the Grand National, when they'd just settled themselves down on the bench, there was a knock at the door. Jan got up and opened it and was astonished to see Joe Paley standing outside.

She looked at him in amazement.

His thin, bony white face was bruised and haggard, and his eyes looked as if all the fluid his body contained had drained through them.

'Joe? What the hell do you want?' Jan asked.

'Can I come in?'

Jan nodded, and stepped back to allow the skinny young man in grimy black jeans and leather jacket into the caravan.

Eddie switched off the video and leaned back on the bench, while Jan stared at the prodigal lad, waiting for an explanation.

'Can I have a drink?' he said in a small voice.

'Tea?' Jan asked.

He nodded, and Jan put a kettle on the top of the wood-burner.

'Joe, you'd better sit down.'

The lad perched on a small wooden chair at the end of the table, put his hands down and stared at his filthy fingernails in silence. Finally, he mumbled, 'I'm sorry, Jan.'

'It's Eddie you nearly killed. It's him you'd better say sorry to.'

Joe raised his eyes and allowed them to rest for a few moments on Eddie's, before he looked down again with his lower jaw working quietly on a piece of gum. 'It was that Sharon's fault,' he said. 'When she come here, she said after I was to meet her up by the big wood at the Manor – you know, where she lives. And when I gets there, she's not there, but her dad's waiting. He's done it deliberate, like, to get me where no one's going to see us.' Joe took a deep, sobbing breath and shook his head.

Jan poured some boiling water over the tea bag in a mug, topped it with milk, heaped in the three spoonsful of sugar, which she knew he liked, and put it on the table in front of him. No one spoke while he picked it up and took a long gulp.

'Shit, I'm sorry!' he muttered jerkily. 'But that fuckin' Goldstone – he pulls a wedge of twenties from his pocket and waves it under my nose. He goes, "I hear you like a bit of a bet." "So?" I says, and he goes, "You can have plenty of bets with this; this is a grand, and it's all yours if you do me a very small favour. It won't take you more than ten seconds." And he pulls a girth like one of ours from his pocket and shows me how it's been nicked only on the back side of the buckle, so's you'd never see it unless you was looking for it. He goes, "You do that on Thursday with Russian Eagle's girth, and this grand is yours, all right?" And he puts it away. "Is that all?" I says.'

Joe lifted his head and looked at them both, the lids of his small brown eyes twitching. 'Well, it was a grand, like. I didn't want to do you no harm, Eddie, but I never seen so much dosh!' His shoulders shook.

Jan looked at Eddie. His eyebrows lifted. 'Poor little sod. Did you get the money?' he asked Joe directly.

'Nah! The fat bastard! I was watching him during the race. He was on the rail and when he saw you jump the last in front, he goes effing mad, all red and screaming until that loose horse come out of nowhere and knocked you off. After the race, when he's calmed down a bit, I goes up to him and says, "Can I have my grand?" like, and he just says to fuck off 'cos I never done what he said, and Eddie's fallen off 'cos of the other horse, which were nothing to do with me.'

Joe took another breath and leaned back in his chair. 'I was already a bit pissed and I felt real bad about what had happened to Eddie, so I went mad, telling him what a bloody crook he was, and two of his geezers got hold of me, carted me round the back of the stables and gave me a right duffing.' Joe's nasal voice was working up to a crescendo. 'They says if I ever say anything like that again, or tell anyone Mr Goldstone said he'd give me some money to do what I done, he'd fucking have me topped!' Joe's shoulders began to heave again and he flopped forward on to the table, shaking his head and sobbing.

Jan and Eddie looked at him and at each other. Eddie stretched out a hand and put it on the lad's quivering shoulder. 'Joe, it's OK. Just tell me why you came back and told us all this.'

Slowly the heaving subsided. Joe raised his thin torso in his scuffed leather jacket and looked warily at Eddie. 'I come back because I never should have done it, not to you, not to Eagle, not to her.' He indicated Jan with a backward nod of his head. 'She's been good to me here, bailed me out when I've needed it; treated me with a bit of respect.'

'And what do you expect us to do about it?'

'Please, Eddie, don't do nuffin'! You'll never prove Goldstone done it, even if I stands up and points the finger. He never gave me no money, no one saw us talking. He'll just say it's a load of bollocks and then he'll fuckin' do me!' Joe's voice cracked again.

'Jesus!' Jan said, looking at Eddie. 'What do we do?'

Eddie leaned his back against the wall of the caravan. He winced as he twisted his shoulder, then smiled ruefully. 'Nothing, for the moment. There's no point. But at least we know for sure who did it and who ordered it. But I swear to you one day, when the dust has settled and he's least expecting it, I'll get Cyril Goldstone. I'm in no hurry, but when I do I'll make him sweat and I'll get every penny out of him I should have won.'

Jan looked at him in a way she wouldn't have done a few days before. Now that she knew what he was capable of once he was resolved, with a guilty tingle of excitement, she believed him.

'OK, Joe,' she said. 'Sit up and pull yourself together.'

The lad shuffled himself upright in the chair.

'Have you got somewhere to go tonight?' Jan asked.

'Yeh,' he nodded. 'I still got my room at Mrs Stoddard's.'

'And you've got your bike outside?'

Joe nodded. 'Yeh.'

'Well, get off home, then, and I'm very glad you came back and told me what happened. It must have taken a lot of guts. But there's one more thing I've got to ask you.'

Joe cocked an eyebrow, unused to telling people any more than was absolutely necessary. 'What's that?' he grunted.

'That cousin of yours, Amos Smith – did he ever come back?'

'Maybe – I dunno.'

'But it's possible he's back, or might still come back?'

'Yeh. He's been gone all winter. He'll want to get back to see his family for the summer.'

'We really want to talk to him still,' Eddie said. 'If you see him, could you tell him that if I come and look for him again and he can answer a couple of questions, we won't do anything that'll get him into trouble.'

Joe shrugged his skinny shoulders. 'I can tell him, I s'pose, if I see him.'

'Would you do that, Joe – try and convince him that it'll be OK?' Jan said gently. 'Please, for me?'

'Maybe,' said Joe, 'but I ain't promising.'

'All right.' Jan thought it better not to press him. 'In the meantime, take the day off tomorrow and get some sleep. Then come in sharp Monday morning. All right?'

Joe nodded, pushed back his chair and got to his feet. There was the ghost of a smile on his face, hurriedly banished, in case Jan thought he'd got off too lightly.

'It's OK, Joe, you can smile. But if you ever do anything like this again, you've had it; there'll be no second chance. Understood?'

He bit his lip and wriggled his feet. 'Yeh. Thanks, Jan. Thanks, Eddie.'

He turned abruptly and let himself out of the caravan.

Eddie looked at Jan. 'Do you feel better now?'

She nodded with a smile. 'Much.'

'Good. I'm pleased about that.'

Eddie switched the video back on and they settled down to watch the Grand National. When they'd seen it all, they played the race over twice, gazing at the running rail and the elbow, where, in their race, Eagle had been forced off the track.

'So, what a week, eh?' Eddie said when Jan had turned off the television. 'How do you feel about it all now?'

'Horrible. Knowing that someone deliberately tried to sabotage us, without giving a damn who got hurt!' Jan shook her head, as if she still couldn't believe it. 'And I haven't cancelled my appointment with the Jockey Club yet.'

'When is it?'

'Monday week, nine days' time.'

'You'll have to,' Eddie grimaced. 'You can't just turn up and tell them your backer's dead.'

'No,' Jan said, resigned. 'I'll ring them first thing this Monday and tell them.'

They talked a little more before Eddie yawned unstoppably and announced that he would have to go home.

'Eddie, is it really safe for you to drive with your arm in a sling?'

'It's OK; I can use my elbow to steer when I'm changing gear,' he grinned.

'Don't get caught and take care, all right?' Jan said gently. 'You're lucky to be alive as it is.'

After he'd gone, Jan tidied up and went in to settle Megan, who had woken up and called for her. She was still reading her a story when there was another burst of knocking on the door.

She put the book down and went warily to see who was there. She found Eddie standing outside again.

Just for a moment it crossed her mind that he had come back to spend more time with her, and she wasn't sure if she was pleased or not about this.

'Sorry, Jan,' he said. 'I know this sound crazy, but could I doss down in your hay barn?'

'Why on earth do you want to do that? Has your Land Rover broken down again?'

'No. When I got home, I found the gates open and I'm pretty sure I left them closed. Being just a little cautious at the moment,

I drove on past and parked up the lane. I walked back and let myself into the garden at the far end. I crept back round the side of the house and saw a great silver Cadillac parked behind the gate so I wouldn't have seen it until I'd driven in. There was a couple of blokes sitting in it, smoking and talking – too quietly for me to hear anything. Then one of them got out; he was absolutely massive. I know one thing: whatever they were doing, they weren't there for the good of my health, so I didn't hang about.'

'But why would they be after you?'

'I don't know, but I bet they've somehow clocked the connection between me and my old man, perhaps after that race was on telly. It's possible they knew Dad was up at Aintree. Anyway, right now', Eddie said ruefully, patting his bandaged arm, 'I'm not in a position to help them and, call me a coward if you like, but I'm in no condition to deal with a pair of professional heavies.'

'But, Eddie, if they saw you racing, it wouldn't be hard for them to connect you with this place, either,' Jan said nervously.

'I know, I know. I'll go tomorrow, but just for tonight they're not going to come here. If anyone does turn up out of the blue, I'll lie low. Tell them you haven't seen me since Thursday and you think I've gone to Italy to buy pictures or something – yes, that'll do, Italy.'

Jan sighed. She thought she had enough on her plate without trying to fob off a pair of oversized debt collectors, but, on the other hand, she felt she owed Eddie and he had a right to ask a favour, at least, just for a night.

'OK, if you think you'll be all right in the barn.'

'I'll be fine. It won't be the first time I've crashed out among the hay bales.'

'But I bet you weren't on your own last time.'

Eddie grinned. 'I can't remember.' He gave her a wave and headed back down the hill into the darkness.

'We're not starting till late tomorrow, with everyone so knackered and it being Sunday,' she called after him. 'So nobody'll be in to wake you too early.'

'OK, thanks. Goodnight.'

She stood in the doorway, wondering if she was being a little cruel by making him sleep in the barn. Still, she thought, it was his idea, not hers.

Jan enjoyed the luxury of a lie-in once in a while. And after a busy but successful day at the point-to-point the day before and Eddie's late visit, she didn't stir until after nine.

She had to wake the children, too, and walked through into the living area of the caravan and drew back the skimpy curtains to reveal a pleasing view across the broad river valley to the Malverns, with Bredon Hill on the right, basking in the morning glow.

A flash of reflected sunlight from a car windscreen on the lane below caught her eye and she saw a large, black Mercedes cruising along the narrow road. She was wondering idly who was driving around in such a flashy car at this time of the morning, when it slowed and turned in at the bottom of her drive.

Jan gasped. Maybe this was something to do with the heavies in the Cadillac who'd called on Eddie the night before. The men he'd seen must have tracked him down after all and called up their boss to deal with him.

By now the Mercedes was progressing slowly but smoothly up the rough track. She thought about running down to the barn to warn Eddie, but there was no way she could get there before the car reached the top. Determined not to show any fear, Jan hurriedly pulled on some jeans, a T-shirt and a fleece, poked her feet into a pair of boots and dragged a brush through her hair before she went out and walked down to greet her visitors. As she walked she glanced nervously at the yard and the open door of the hay barn, and prayed that Eddie had heard the car and checked it out before he showed himself.

The black limousine pulled up and a chauffeur in a cap got out to open the rear door. It occurred to Jan briefly that this was a very extravagant way to collect debts, but she guessed if these people had lent Ron half a million there must be substantial resources behind the organization. Then, with a sudden, horrified spasm, Jan realized that the Mercedes was parked right next to Eddie's battered old Land Rover. These people must surely know the number of his car!

On legs like rubber, she watched as a man in a light tan cashmere coat stepped from the car, putting on dark glasses as he did so.

There was, extraordinarily, something familiar about him and Jan struggled through her memory banks to pinpoint it.

'Good morning.' His voice floated up through the still air and Jan recognized it instantly. She had heard it just three days before at Aintree. Even with his piercing blue eyes obscured, there was an unmistakable aura about A.D. O'Hagan.

Jan tried to smile. She couldn't believe it. How on earth could Ron be in hock to someone like O'Hagan? The crazy coincidence was just too horrible.

'Hello,' she murmured, hearing the words come out thin and croaky. 'What can I do for you?'

'Plenty, I hope,' O'Hagan said with one of his disappearing smiles. 'I apologize for coming like this, so early and unannounced, but Eamon Fallon convinced me a trainer of your skill wouldn't be far from her horses at this time of day.'

Jan wondered why he was being so affable if he'd come looking for Eddie, but she saw no point in not playing along for the moment.

'I'd business in Cheltenham after the National yesterday,' he went on. 'I won't fly, so now we're on our way to catch the Fishguard ferry back to Waterford, so I felt it was too good an opportunity to miss.'

Jan was daring to believe, just faintly, that maybe A.D. O'Hagan wasn't here on a debt-collecting mission, and she was beginning to think that, whatever his business was, he was far too big a wheel to be doing that kind of thing himself.

'That's fine, Mr O'Hagan,' Jan said. 'How can I help you?'

'Is there anywhere we could sit and have a cup of coffee for a moment?'

'Yes, of course, if you don't mind my caravan. It's a bit of a mess because I was up late with a friend watching a replay of the National. I expect you were too,' she added, remembering that O'Hagan's horse had come third.

'I did watch it a couple of times,' he agreed lightly. 'And don't worry about the mess.'

In fact the caravan was as spick and span as Jan always liked to keep it, and a good glow was coming from the wood-burner. O'Hagan stepped up and looked around appreciatively. 'This caravan's a bit more upmarket than the one my dad was born in,' he said with a smile.

Jan waved him to one of the benches and he slid in while she spooned some coffee into a cafetière. When it was made, she filled two cups and put them on the table between herself and her visitor.

'Now, Jan – if I may call you that? – you remember what I said to you when we first met at Doncaster?'

Jan gulped and nodded. Did she remember! She could have repeated it word for word.

'As I recall, I told you that if you could train that yoke to win a good hunter chase, I'd send you half a dozen horses of my own.'

Jan felt herself trembling. The abrupt switch from rank fear five minutes earlier to the unspeakable joy she was now experiencing was almost too much to bear.

'I remember very well,' she said. 'I thought you were joking.'

'I was, but I still meant it. And what you've achieved in ten months with that animal is little short of a miracle. I hear you'd not an easy task with the pilot, either.'

Jan was grinning so widely now she could hardly speak. 'When I saw the horse, I thought he might be easy to train and I was lucky.'

'T'wasn't luck. You just have a very good eye and there's no doubt that you're an exceptional trainer. But Eamon tells me you've set your heart on taking out a professional licence.'

Jan nodded and smiled painfully. 'I've got my interview a week tomorrow.'

'I also hear you can't put up the funds the Jockey Club need and the fella who was going to do it for you has just rather inconsiderately gone to meet his maker.'

'You could say that,' Jan admitted.

'Well, no problem. If you write down all your details for me now, one of my people will be up to look through your books – that is, if you don't mind?'

'No, that's fine,' Jan said faintly.

'We'll get that all sorted and the paperwork done by the end of the week. I'll also tell the Jockey Club that I'll be sending you six good horses. You could come over to Ireland next month and pick some you like. Now, how would that suit you, Mrs Hardy?'

Jan tried to control her delight. She managed a cheeky grin. 'How do you think it would suit me, Mr O'Hagan? I can't thank you enough.'

A.D. O'Hagan was already on his way, with the Mercedes crunching quietly down Jan's drive, when she went into the barn.

'Eddie? Where are you?'

A moment later, a dishevelled figure appeared at the top of the stack of hay bales, and Eddie slithered down. He arrived at the bottom, blinking in the sun and trying to get rid of some of the hay clinging to his clothing.

'Who just drove off?'

'You're not going to believe this!' Jan said and spent the next ten minutes convincing him.

'Bloody hell!' Eddie laughed. 'What a story! That makes up for everything that's gone wrong and a whole lot more besides. Are you sure he means it?'

'Oh, he means it all right. A man as rich as him doesn't bother to go around bullshitting. After all, when you think about it, everything he said about what I've done with Eagle is perfectly true.'

'Now then, I don't want you getting all big-headed, especially if I'm not going to be around to keep you in your place.'

'Well, why wouldn't you be around?' Jan asked.

'I'm afraid I'm going to have to disappear for a bit. I won't be much of a loss, though, will I, if I've only got one useful arm.'

'How long are you going for?' Jan frowned.

'I'm not sure. Not long, I shouldn't think. You know, there's quite a mess to sort out, then we'll see.'

Jan knew Eddie well enough to know that when he didn't want to be pressed, he wouldn't be. 'Don't go for too long,' she said, a little plaintively. 'You're part of the furniture round here now.'

Eddie brushed the last bits of hay off his jersey. 'I'll be back, I promise.' He leaned down and kissed her on each cheek, perhaps a little longer than a goodbye required. ''Bye Jan,' he said. He turned and walked briskly across the yard to his Land Rover.

Jan felt a few tears fall as he had to turn over the engine of the old vehicle several times before it would fire, and then he was off, bouncing wildly down the track.

I'll have to get that drive seen to if A.D. O'Hagan's going to be coming here, she thought, trying to displace what she was thinking about Eddie.

Joe Paley drove his motorbike up the track in the early gloom of Monday morning before anyone else had arrived. Jan was delighted but surprised to see a passenger hunched on the small pillion seat. She wondered if Joe had brought a new recruit; she hoped not, because, just now, she had no plans to take on any more staff.

Joe stopped his bike and they both jumped off. While he wheeled it into an old shed where he liked to keep it out of the weather, his passenger walked up to meet Jan as she was on her way down to the yard.

'Hello?' Jan said, not recognizing the young man, though he looked as if he came from a similar mould to Joe.

He nodded back curtly. He was small, in his late teens with dark, unwashed hair and a row of rings down the edge of one ear.

'I'm Amos,' he announced in a thin, throaty voice. 'A bloke called Gerry says you been looking for me.'

Jan was stunned. She'd given up any hope of ever seeing Amos Smith, but here he was, offering himself up.

'Good Lord,' she said before she could stop herself. 'Yes, I did want to see you for a chat. I'll just tell Joe what to do. Go on up to the caravan. It's a bit warmer in there.'

'A'right,' he grunted.

She almost ran down to the yard, suddenly reluctant to leave such a dodgy character in her home without supervision. But when she got back he was sitting at the table, looking at the pictures in a TV magazine.

'Thanks for coming,' Jan said, thinking this sounded a bit lame. 'Would you like some tea?'

'A'right.'

Jan put a kettle on the wood-burner, which was still roasting hot. 'Did Gerry tell you why we wanted to see you?'

'Nope, but Joe reckoned he knew why.'

'What did Joe say?'

'Said you wanted to know if a bloke in a black Range Rover talked to me at the Star, in the car park, back in the autumn.'

'Yes,' Jan said. 'That's right. Did you talk to him?'

The boy nodded.

Jan waited, but he didn't offer any more.

'Well,' she prompted impatiently. 'What did he want?'

Amos Smith lifted one shoulder, as if his answer was utterly inconsequential. 'He said if I loosed open a gate to one of your fields, he'd drop me a hundred quid.'

Jan stared at him, hardly able to believe his admission, and the confirmation at last of Harold Powell's guilt.

'So, you did it,' she added, unnecessarily, she thought.

'Nope.' He shook his head.

'But you must have done,' Jan said sharply. 'After the horses got out we went and found that someone had pulled out the staple that holds the gate bolt.'

'Maybe they did, but it weren't me. When I got there, at half-past six in the morning, like he told me, the gate was open like, swinging into the lane down there.'

Jan shuddered. She didn't want him to be telling the truth, but her every instinct said he was. She didn't want him to see her dilemma, though, and walked through to the other end of the caravan, wishing Eddie was around to give his advice.

She screwed up her eyes. 'Bloody hell!' she hissed.

'Mumma?' Megan asked.

'Oh sorry, Meg. Go back to sleep for a bit, will you?'

Then Jan thought of Toby. He sometimes stayed at the Fox & Pheasant at weekends, not returning to London until midday on Monday.

She went back into the living room and smiled at Amos. 'I never made your tea,' she said, quickly pouring boiling water onto a tea bag in a mug and shoving a bowl of sugar across the table. 'Would you mind hanging on for a friend of mine to come up and hear what you've told me?'

'Not the police, or nuffink?'

'No, of course not. No one wants to incriminate you when you haven't done anything.'

Amos lifted one eyebrow. 'A'right,' he shrugged. 'I'll want something for my time.'

Jan looked away and picked up her phone. She punched Toby's mobile number, praying that he was still down in the village.

He answered in a thick, sleepy voice. Jan had obviously woken him. She glanced guiltily at her watch; it was still only five to seven.

'Toby, I'm really sorry to ring you so early, but it's important. There's a chap up here I need you to come and see. Where are you now?'

Toby was still in the Fox and wanted to know who was with Jan.

'I can't tell you, not over the phone. But please, will you come?'

A few moments later, when she put the phone down, Toby was on his way.

Jan and Amos had a stilted conversation while they waited until Toby arrived, freshly shaved, in a little over fifteen minutes.

'Thanks for coming,' Jan said as she opened the door of the

caravan. She waved a hand at the surly boy, still sucking tea from his mug. 'This is Amos Smith.'

Toby raised his eyebrows, impressed, while Jan told him what the boy had said. He nodded as he listened and, when Jan had stopped, sat down at the table opposite Amos.

'Now, Amos, if you can give me good straight, clear answers to what I'm going to ask you, I'll give you a hundred quid. And if you come back later and say the same to a gentleman from my solicitors', I'll give you another. OK?'

Amos nodded. It was clear he understood. Jan, uncomfortable about paying for the information, stifled her reservations. Toby was a practical man; he knew what he was doing.

'You told Jan that the man in the Range Rover offered you a hundred pounds to open the gate at the bottom of her lane, right?'

'Yeh.'

'Do you know what the man was called?'

'Harold Powell.'

'How do you know?'

''Cos he give me his address to come and get the money when I done the job.'

'And did you go and get the money?'

'Yeh,' Amos said. 'He heard the horses got out. I never told him the gate was already open.'

Toby smiled. 'Good. That's very helpful and, as far as I can tell, you haven't committed a crime apart from fraudulently extracting a hundred quid from Harold Powell and I don't suppose he'll be reporting you for that. And now you've earned another hundred,' Toby said smoothly, taking a wallet from his jacket and pulling five twenty-pound notes from it. 'Come here tomorrow, at the same time, and say exactly what you've just said to me, and there'll be five more twenties.'

'I'll want two hundred,' Amos said quickly. 'If it's another bloke.'

After that, the rest of the week was one of wary optimism for Jan. She didn't tell any of the staff about O'Hagan until, on Wednesday, an accountant from his organization phoned and asked if he could come up the following day to go over Jan's records.

Then, she felt, it was safe to announce that A.D. O'Hagan was putting up the guarantee she needed and would be sending six top-class horses to Edge Farm.

Roz, Emma, Joe and even Annabel were stunned, then ecstatic that their loyalty and effort had been so impressively recognized. They immediately went about their work in the warming spring sunshine with smiles to match and a lightness that had been noticeably missing since Eddie's fall.

24

Five days later Jan walked out of the main door of a plain, post-war office building in a big, leafy London square. She looked with distaste at the constant stream of traffic that swirled around it – noisy, smelly, mechanical and a hundred miles from the scent of spring grass, the tang of horse sweat and the soft creak of leather that characterized her world.

She turned left and walked along a wide pavement, thronged with strangers who couldn't give a damn whether she lived or died before she reached the end of the square.

I agree with Annabel, Jan thought, *I don't like London. I don't ever want to come up here again.*

She paused at the side of the road, waited for a green flashing pedestrian and crossed over. She turned right and carried on walking, bemused by the vast diversity of people milling around the entrance of the big modern hotel which filled one side of the square.

She stopped outside, beneath the hotel's oriental-looking canopy. She took a tentative step towards the entrance and changed her mind. She wasn't ready yet. She wanted more time on her own to allow the Jockey Club's decision to sink in.

She carried on; she would walk right round the square first before she went back into the hotel. As she walked, she thought back to the beginning of the previous year, when she'd seen John dead and she'd finally had to accept that she was on her own.

She thought about her decision to move from Stonewall, to start a new life and to make a living by doing the only thing she knew. As she crossed the road and remembered Harold Powell's deceit, she grimaced.

With a smile, she acknowledged the advice and wisdom of her father. She also understood her mother's timid reaction to her plans, all the sewing and support with the children that Mary had given freely despite her misgivings. She wondered, too, how far she could have got without Annabel's quiet loyalty.

Loyalty, she thought, was an underrated virtue. Mr Carey, once he had made up his mind, had shown her great loyalty. At his funeral the week before, she'd seen how many people he had shown generosity to under the cloak of his shyness. Most of the owners at Edge Farm, appreciating what he had done for Jan, had been there: Penny Price, solidly respectful; Gwillam Evans, all the way from Brecon, and Colonel Gilbert, standing rigidly to attention at the graveside in Stanfield churchyard as a mark of his regard.

That morning, before Annabel had come to collect Jan, a letter had arrived from Mr Carey's solicitors to say in dry, legal terms that he had left a mare, August Moon, to Mrs Janine Hardy. Whatever else happened to her that day, she felt, Mr Carey's kind legacy would at least make it bearable.

She'd had another letter, too, from Toby's solicitors in Lincoln's Inn.

They were pleased to inform her that Harold Powell, having taken into consideration all the facts as presented by them, had agreed that he would reimburse to Mrs Hardy the full difference between the original sales price achieved by his firm at auction and the subsequent private treaty sale price of Stonewall Farm, less, of course, their normal agent's commission on that difference, plus expenses.

Jan had thought the agent's fee was a bit of a nerve, but, in the end, the eighty thousand pounds she would be left with after paying the solicitors' bill would go a long way to paying for the improvements she needed at Edge Farm, without going cap in hand to A.D. O'Hagan.

She crossed another broad street, clogged with panting cars and stinking diesel taxis, and wished Eddie could have been with her today.

She thought how much he would have enjoyed seeing her in action, inside the hallowed doors of the Jockey Club. She smiled and even laughed a little to herself at the memory.

She'd been shaking as she walked through the grand, forbidding doors. Inside, her throat had dried up as she asked where to go.

In the soundless stuffiness of the lift she'd been alone, staring at the doors when it stopped. She waited for them to open and panicked when she thought they never would – until she saw that another pair of doors had silently slid back behind her to reveal a reception area. Some people were there grinning at her as she reddened, and stepped out feeling a complete fool.

What a way to start the most important interview of my life, she'd thought. *I can't even find my way out of the lift.*

It was worse, much worse, than going to see the bank manager.

The receptionist greeted her with no more than a faint raising of the eyebrows.

I bet she did more than raise her eyebrows to Virginia High and Mighty Gilbert, Jan thought, while she sat for what seemed like an age in reception, bursting to go to the loo, but not daring to ask in case her moment came and she wasn't there.

Eventually a minion, a dapper, tight-lipped young man, appeared and ushered her into the stark committee room.

God, Jan panicked, *what the hell am I doing here? They'll never accept me.*

She felt as if she was up on a charge of murder.

But at least she was invited to sit down at one end of a highly polished, antique mahogany table, which looked the length of a cricket pitch. At the far end sat three Jockey Club stewards, traditional, old-school representatives of the governing body of British horse racing, talking in whispers so that she wouldn't hear what they were saying, and passing little notes to each other as she answered their queries.

How rude, she thought.

Now, less than half an hour later, she could barely remember any of the questions they'd asked.

Some, she recalled, seemed quite irrelevant, and a darned cheek: like how much money had her husband left her in his will.

She'd become indignant. 'What's that got to do with anything?'

They hadn't liked that and, for a while, she wondered if she'd blown it.

Finally, they released her and told her to wait in reception.

She'd sat there in a trance, hardly daring to move, in case it jeopardized her chances of being granted her licence.

The same minion had reappeared, still po-faced, and asked her to come back in front of the committee to hear their verdict.

Jan saw three sombre faces at the distant end of the table.

Oh shit! she thought. *This is it.*

As she walked round the square, her self-confidence grew. By the time she'd done a complete circuit and arrived back once more beneath the hotel's deep canopy, she knew she was ready and she could handle anything the future could throw at her.

She took a deep breath, straightened the skirt of the suit which Annabel had chosen with her and walked through the wide doors into the lobby where she'd left her parents an hour earlier.

Annabel was with them. She had said she would take Mary and Reg through to the coffee shop and keep them calm until Jan returned. But evidently they hadn't made it that far; they were still in the lobby, sitting in deep, slightly awkward tub chairs around a coffee table. Reg had a pint of bitter in front of him, half full, Mary had a sweet sherry, hardly touched, and Annabel a glass of sparkling Perrier water.

Jan saw them first.

'Hi,' she said, more loudly than she meant to, and they turned together to look at her.

At first, mischievously, she didn't allow any expression on her face and the few seconds of uncertainty seemed to linger on theirs for several moments, until she clenched her fist, raised her arm and punched the air above her head. She didn't care who saw or who heard.

'Mum, Dad, Bel!' she shouted triumphantly as the tears began to flow. 'Guess what? I got it! I've got my licence. At last . . .' She tried to stifle her sobs. '. . . It's real! I'm a proper racehorse trainer!'

Epilogue

Two days later, when Annabel was on her way up to have breakfast with Jan, the postman arrived and handed her the mail. As she stepped into the caravan, she was idly flipping through it, out of habit, when she stopped and extracted a postcard. She turned it over. 'It's not really rude to read other people's postcards, is it?' she grinned naughtily. 'After all, the postman could, if he felt like it.'

'Where's it from?' Jan asked.

'Australia.'

'Oh, great!' Jan said. 'It'll be from Ben! I wonder when he's coming home?'

'It's not from Ben,' Annabel said, passing the card to Jan. 'And I feel there's something you haven't been telling me.'

Jan looked at the photo on the card briefly, as part of a guessing game she liked to play – trying to think who would have chosen a particular card. This one was a slightly dull, inactive shot of the empty stands at Melbourne race course, which looked as if it had been given away for nothing. But that was enough of a hint and she was ready for the surprisingly arty, italic hand on the other side.

> *Hi Jan,*
> *Up to my knees in horse shit still, but in another world.*
> *See you, and thanks for everything.*
> *Love, E.*

Jan sniffed and didn't look at her friend for a moment. When she did, she gave her a sheepish grin. 'Sorry, Bel. I don't think I really wanted to believe it.'

'You and Eddie?' Annabel put her head on one side and shook it. 'I don't think so.'

'No, I know, but I miss him, Bel. I wish he'd told me why he was going.'

'I think they've all gone,' Annabel said thoughtfully. 'I mean Ron, Eddie and Susan. I saw an advert for her house in *Country Life* last month. I think they just decided to sell up, back together and go away. Susan hinted at it when she came to see me, though she would have liked Eddie to win his bet as well.'

'It's ridiculous, isn't it,' Jan mused. 'When you think how much was hanging on that one race and what the outcome of it has been.'

'Maybe you're right when you say life's just a game of chance and a chain of coincidence which we can't control.'

'God knows, but right now I don't care!'